THE STORIES
THAT SHOULD HAVE WON!

In 1952, "Firewater": After the Half-Wars, the aliens invaded earth. Their mission? Not to bury man, nor to conquer or enslave him. They wanted to ignore him!

In 1954, "The Golden Helix": Handpicked to populate Terra Prime, they were trained to adapt to thin atmosphere, to life in pressure domes, to flash-mutants of strange impulses. But when they opened the door of their Pods, they found something they weren't meant to adapt to at all . . . and their ship was gone.

In 1955, "One Ordinary Day, with Peanuts": A man who radiated well-being and good-will and who spent his days in the service of man, found a peculiar kind of balance to his virtue.

These Outstanding Stories Represent the Best in the Extensive Field of Science Fiction. Handpicked by Richard A. Lupoff, They Will Astound, Delight and Amaze You!

WHAT IF?

Volume 1

Stories That Should Have Won the Hugo

Edited by

Richard A. Lupoff

PUBLISHED BY POCKET BOOKS NEW YORK

Distributed in Canada by PaperJacks Ltd., a Licensee
of the trademarks of Simon & Schuster, a division of
Gulf + Western Corporation.

Another *Original* publication of POCKET BOOKS

 POCKET BOOKS, a Simon & Schuster division of
GULF & WESTERN CORPORATION
1230 Avenue of the Americas, New York, N.Y. 10020
In Canada distributed by PaperJacks Ltd.,
330 Steelcase Road, Markham, Ontario.

ISBN: 0-671-83189-5

First Pocket Books printing September, 1980

10 9 8 7 6 5 4 3 2 1

Acknowledgments

"Firewater!" by William Tenn copyright © 1952 by Street & Smith
Publications, Inc. Originally published in *Astounding Science Fiction*
for February 1952. Reprinted by permission of the author.

"Four in One" by Damon Knight copyright © 1953 by Galaxy Publishing Corporation. Originally appeared in *Galaxy Science Fiction*
for February 1953. Reprinted by permission of the author.

"The Golden Helix" by Theodore Sturgeon copyright © 1954 by
Standard Magazines, Inc. Originally published in *Thrilling Wonder
Stories* for Summer 1954. Reprinted by permission of the author and
his agent, Kirby McCauley, Ltd.

"One Ordinary Day, with Peanuts" by Shirley Jackson copyright ©
1955 by Shirley Jackson. Originally published in *The Magazine of
Fantasy and Science Fiction*. Reprinted by permission of Brandt &
Brandt Literary Agency, Inc.

"The Man Who Came Early" by Poul Anderson. Reprinted by permission of the author and the author's agents, Scott Meredith Literary Agency, Inc., 845 Third Avenue, New York, New York 10022.
10022.

"The Mile-Long Spaceship" by Kate Wilhelm copyright © 1957 by
Street & Smith Publications, Inc. Originally published in *Astounding
Science Fiction* for April 1957. Reprinted by permission of the
author.

"Two Dooms" by Cyril M. Kornbluth copyright © 1958 by Mercury
Press, Inc. Originally published in *Venture Science Fiction* for July
1958. Reprinted by permission of the author's agent, Robert P. Mills,
Ltd.

Contents

Earned Glory

AN INTRODUCTION BY
RICHARD A. LUPOFF

HERE IN THE science fiction community we've always liked to give out awards. Not that that's anything unusual. The movies have their Oscars, Broadway has its Tonys, the National Hockey League has the Stanley Cup, and politics has the Presidency of the United States. Each is a prize, the symbol of success in a tough, competitive arena.

The Hugos—the Science Fiction Achievement Awards —were instituted in 1953, a perfect time for that event. Science fiction was enjoying a major boom, the third such in modern times. Science fiction was almost exclusively a magazine field in those days: few science fiction novels appeared as either hardbound or paperbound books, and volumes of science fiction short stories were scarcer still.

But those magazines!

The first science fiction magazine boom was essentially a phenomenon of the 1920s. The very first attempt at a science fiction magazine was the unsuccessful hybrid *Thrill Book* that appeared (and disappeared) in 1919. *Weird Tales,* another and more successful hybrid, came along in 1923. The first all-out science fiction magazine, *Amazing Stories,* was started in 1926; the *Wonder* group, in '29; the long-lived *Astounding,* in 1930; and *Miracle Science and Fantasy Stories,* in '31.

By 1931 there were about a dozen magazines of science fiction or associated fantasy stories being published, but most of them were toppled by the Depression. Within a few years there were a mere handful left, several of those barely surviving on slim budgets and irregular schedules.

A second boom started as the Depression eased in the late 1930s. New titles appeared, older magazines regained vitality, established publications added subsidiary titles. New authors and editors entered the field.

But then the Second World War came along, and wartime paper shortages, materials allocation programs, and military priorities laid the science fiction magazines low for the second time.

With the end of the war in 1945, the nation entered a period of reconversion to civilian ways, civilian institutions, and civilian-oriented consumer products, including science fiction magazines. For the third time, the field enjoyed a boom. Magazines that had barely limped through the war regained their stride. Suspended titles were revived and new ones were added.

An important aspect of this situation was the dominance of one magazine (and, naturally, its editor) in the life of the science fiction community. The magazine was *Astounding*. Its editor was John W. Campbell, Jr.

With the mighty Street & Smith publishing company behind it and the brilliant, dynamic, and idiosyncratic Campbell at its helm, *Astounding* had been in a class by itself since the 1930s. Street & Smith paid the highest rates in the field; consequently, the magazine got the best material. Not that *every* story in *Astounding* was automatically better than everything in *Super Science* or *Startling* or *Planet* or *Worlds Beyond* or any of the other competitors.

Naturally not.

But issue by issue, year by year, *Astounding* showed itself *consistently* to be the best in the marketplace.

And in addition to paying its writers the highest rates, Street & Smith had the financial strength and stability and the field organization to turn out by far the largest pressrun in the field, to distribute its copies the most effectively, and ultimately to sell the greatest number of copies.

All of this fed back into the magazine. It led to a strong cash position, supported the continuing payment of high rates to authors, drew the best stories being produced, and brought the process full circle.

This sounds like an ideal situation, but it contained a hidden flaw. For John Campbell, for all his virtues, was also a man of peculiar limitations and rigid attitudes. What

2

he wanted, he wanted in his stories. And what he wanted in his stories, he got—whether it was psionics, neo-feudalism, or a universe in which *no* alien race could be portrayed as more intelligent than good old *homo sap.*

If you didn't toe Campbell's line, you didn't sell to *Astounding.** And if you couldn't land *Astounding,* where were you going to peddle your stories? Maybe *Cosmic Stories,* which paid nothing now, promised something later (maybe), and went out of business after precisely three issues.

But this third boom, this postwar boom, changed that.

It seems to me that the new period of growth reached its finest flowering (if not the greatest raw number of titles or issues) in 1950. In fact, I'm inclined to nominate 1950 as the most important year in the history of science fiction.

For sure, there are other strong candidates: 1818 (first publication of *Frankenstein*); 1863 (first appearance of Jules Verne's first science fiction story, "Five Weeks in a Balloon"); 1895 (first edition of Wells's *The Time Machine*); 1896 (Frank A. Munsey converts children's paper *The Golden Argosy* to *Argosy* magazine, the first pulp); 1923 (J. C. Henneberger establishes *Weird Tales*); 1926 (Hugo Gernsback establishes *Amazing Stories*). . . .

But my candidate is still 1950.

That year appeared the first issues of both *The Magazine of Fantasy and Science Fiction** and *Galaxy Science Fic-*

---

* Frederik Pohl, who was a literary agent in those days and sold his clients' stories to Campbell, and consequently ought to know what is talking about, offers a slightly different angle on this matter. Campbell did *not* insist that stories conform to his personal line-of-the-moment, Pohl insists. If anything, he encouraged writers to challenge his ideas—or tried to. The problem was, Campbell argued so aggressively and persistently for his views that many writers psyched themselves into thinking he would brook no disagreement.

It should be noted that not everyone offers testimony in agreement with Pohl's. Philip Klass and Isaac Asimov, to mention only two, take a line more to the effect that Campbell *did* enforce his personal views upon his writers. It would be fascinating to ask Campbell himself, but he is no longer alive to be asked, alas.

* A single issue of *The Magazine of Fantasy,* a forerunner of the familiar *F&SF,* appeared in 1949. It was distinctly experimental, with an emphasis on creepy-crawlies well exemplified by the cover illustration, a low-cut photographer's model being menaced by something that looks like an aerosol spray of lime Jell-O.

To find suitable material for the magazine, the editors dredged up fifty-year-old chestnuts by Victorian writers like Oliver Onions and Fitz-James O'Brien. They also found some worthwhile new stories, the most notable in that single issue of *The Magazine of Fantasy* being "The Hurkle is a Happy Beast," by Theodore Sturgeon.

3

Suddenly, the science fiction field no longer had a single undisputed leader followed by a pack of erratic, occasionally brilliant, but usually inferior hangers-on.

Suddenly, the writers had not one quality market followed by a rag-tag squad of salvage markets. Instead, there were *three* leading markets, each with its distinct editorial character and requirements, each with a staff and a personality all its own.

Suddenly, the readers faced a new situation. For a decade and more, *Astounding* had been the class of the field. Any self-respecting *aficionado* found it *de rigeur* to praise Campbell and Campbell's magazine while disdaining all the others and expressing surprise when one of them published an outstanding story.

Now there were *three* quality magazines, demanding material of the highest quality, competing for first look at the works of the best authors, bidding in at the highest rates (as high as 3¢ a word!), and offering fiction and "package" —physical design and production—at a fully competitive level. There was a real choice, and reader loyalties were divided between Campbell traditionalists and radicals willing to switch their loyalties to the new magazines.

As a fanatical science fiction reader in those days—and as a writer of science fiction in these—I can testify to the benefits of multiple, top-quality markets. Benefits that accrue to writers and readers equally.

With a single editor controlling the "class" outlet of the field, writers were impelled to slant their work in accord with his desires. It is debatable whether Campbell *meant* to impose his own thinking upon his writers (and consequently upon his readers). But whether this was his intention or not, it was the effect.

The new magazines in effect smashed the fetters from the writers' wrists. Campbell's "party line" had been a sort of technocratic, elitist quasi-fascism. In contrast to this, Boucher and McComas offered in *F&SF* a basically apolitical, ultra-humane, and at times even mystical vision. And

---

When sales figures and reader responses came in, editors Anthony Boucher and J. Francis McComas reassessed their product, revamped *The Magazine of Fantasy* into *The Magazine of Fantasy and Science Fiction*, and gave it another try. The first issue of the new *Magazine of Fantasy and Science Fiction* was dated Winter-Spring 1950. But it bore the indicia of Volume I, Number 2, counting the experimental *Magazine of Fantasy* of the previous year. Thus there never was a Volume I, Number 1 of *F&SF*, to speak quite strictly.
tion.

Horace L. Gold, the editor of *Galaxy*, opted for an often acerbic, frequently satirical, social criticism.

Established writers within the field flocked to write for the new magazines, and others who had avoided science fiction were attracted by the new literary and political freedom.

The new *F&SF* and *Galaxy* swiftly gained circulation and challenged *Astounding*'s traditional lead. Nor did their success seriously harm the older, existing periodicals; in fact, the opposite occurred. Clearly, Campbell felt the competition and *Astounding* got better, not worse. Magazines like *Startling Stories* and even the despised *Planet* perked up with fine contributions by Philip Jose Farmer, Leigh Brackett, John D. MacDonald, Ray Bradbury, and others.

Still more publishers entered the field. Some of them did so opportunistically, ignorantly, with under-budgeted, tawdry, obviously non-viable magazines. But others created distinctly worthwhile products edited by knowledgeable and talented men like Lester del Rey, Harry Harrison, Larry T. Shaw, and the veteran Robert W. Lowndes. Even the venerable Hugo Gernsback, founder of *Amazing Stories* in 1926 and of *Science Wonder Stories* in 1929, returned to publish *Science Fiction Plus*, a physically elaborate, if editorially regressive, monthly.

The statistically minded fan and critic Ed Wood recorded the growth of the field in this manner:

At the end of the war in 1945 there were only eight science fiction (and/or fantasy) magazines published in the U.S. and Britain. By the end of 1949 this had grown to a dozen. By the end of 1950 the number was over 20. Within two more years it approached 30. And in 1953, the all-time peak year for science fiction magazine publishing, a grand total of 43 different titles appeared in the English language!

Those were salad days, indeed!

Such was the state of science fiction publishing as of 1953. The idea of a literary award for science fiction was in the air.

In fact, there had been a number of earlier attempts to create such an award. As early as the most primitive days of fan magazine publishing, in the early 1930s, there had been polls for the favorite books, stories, comic strips, and motion pictures of the day.

These had evolved into a short-lived Jules Verne Prize Club under the tutelage of Raymond Palmer, as early as 1933. The Jules Verne Prize Club made little headway, but polls continued throughout the 1930s and '40s. For some years *Startling Stories* ran its own "Science Fiction Hall of Fame" department—but this was chiefly a device for reprinting popular stories of earlier years without having to pay the authors a second time.

In 1951 a group of four British *aficionados* established the International Fantasy Award, which survived for several years and gained a certain distinction. The four founders were Leslie Flood (later a literary agent), John Beynon Harris (who himself wrote excellent science fiction as John Beynon, John Beynon Harris, John Wyndham, and Lucas Parkes), G. Ken Chapman, and Frank A. Cooper.

International Fantasy Awards were given between 1951 and 1957. Only books were eligible, no magazines or individual stories, although collections of short stories might win. The list of recipients for fiction (there were also awards for non-fiction) shines brightly to this day: George R. Stewart *(Earth Abides);* John Collier *(Fancies and Goodnights);* Clifford D. Simak *(City);* Theodore Sturgeon *(More than Human);* Edgar Pangborn *(A Mirror for Observers);* and J. R. R. Tolkien *(The Lord of the Rings).*

Winners were selected by jury, the members of which included Anthony Boucher, P. Schuyler Miller, Judith Merril, Groff Conklin, Basil Davenport, and John Carnell.

The International Fantasy Award was prestigious, and considerable regret was expressed when the series ended. But the award suffered from a fatal weakness in that it had no real constituency. The four men who created it were a self-appointed committee operating under a charter from no one. The winners were selected by a jury selected by the committee. It was a distinguished jury, and one that did its duty conscientiously and well. But it was a jury appointed by a self-appointed committee. It had a "constituency" of just four men!

The International Fantasy Awards were given from 1951 to 1955, lapsed in 1956, were revived in 1957, and then were permanently suspended. They had been, in a sense, rendered superfluous by the Hugos. The Hugos had their faults; they have them to this day. But lack of a constituency is not one of them!

In 1953 an attempt was made to revive the Jules Verne Prize. A distinguished committee consisting of Donald A. Wollheim, Forrest J. Ackerman, and Otto v. St. Whitelock was formed, a trophy was struck—a plaque, actually, bearing a miniature of Jules Verne's tombstone—and twelve winning stories were selected.

These were published in a volume titled *Prize Science Fiction,* and an excellent volume it was, readable to this day. The honored authors were Charles Beaumont, Leigh Brackett, Arthur C. Clarke, Mark Clifton, Alfred Coppel, Gordon R. Dickson, C. M. Kornbluth, Robert Donald Locke, Walter M. Miller, Jr., Eric Frank Russell, and the team of "Martin Pearson" and "Cecil Corwin." ("Pearson" was Wollheim and "Corwin" was Kornbluth.)

But the Jules Verne Prize was stillborn in this incarnation, too, and for a familiar reason: no constituency. Besides, another event took place in 1953, the year that the first and only edition of *Prize Science Fiction* was published. . . .

The Hugo was created by the World Science Fiction Convention.

Conventions drawing together science fiction fans, writers, editors, and publishers had been established in the late 1930s. Suspended during the Second World War, they had resumed in 1946 and by 1953 were a well-established institution. From an attendance of a few score hardcore fanatics at the earliest conventions, they had grown to a regular participation of many hundreds. (They have continued to grow, and by the late 1970s attendance in the range of 5,000 to 6,000 persons had become common.)

The 1953 convention was scheduled for Philadelphia's Bellevue-Stratford Hotel, later famous as the home of Legionnaire's Disease. Convention committee members mulled over ideas for new features to add a sense of excitement to the impending event.

One of the committee's members was Harold V. Lynch, himself a sometime science fiction writer with short story credits in both Campbell's *Astounding* and Boucher and McComas's *Fantasy and Science Fiction.* Lynch proposed a set of awards for the year's outstanding achievements in science fiction, suggesting further that the award be named for the founder of *Amazing Stories,* the world's first science fiction magazine: Hugo Gernsback.

The physical trophy was rather obvious in the context of 1950s science fiction: a shiny rocketship. The design was not very different from that of the International Fantasy Awards trophy—the Hugo was a little more streamlined, with a more gracefully tapered fuselage and with only a modest set of tail fins. The International Fantasy Award trophy had sported a pair of stubby wings halfway up the body, as if the designers weren't quite certain that they *meant* a spaceship: their rocket might have doubled as a high-speed, super rocket-driven airplane.

In all the years since 1953 the basic design of the Hugo rocket has remained the same. The trophies have been fabricated of gold, silver (or at least made to look like gold or silver), clear plastic, anodized aluminum; they have been mounted on square pedestals and flat bases of wood and of plastic; but the basic design of the rocket remains unaltered. A much-belated credit for so durable a design must be given to fans Jack McKnight and Ben Jason—with more than a slight assist from the late Werner von Braun.

The early rules of the Hugo awards were very sketchy. It seems in retrospect that nobody realized that the Hugos were going to be a permanent series, or that they would ever be taken very seriously beyond the narrowest circle of deeply dedicated fans. The whole scheme was just a fillip to the World Convention program. That's what they thought in 1953!

But one result of this offhand attitude was longtime confusion over what was *meant* by the phrase "the year." Were the Hugos awarded in 1953 designed to recognize the achievements of the previous year—that is, of 1952? Or were they for a "Hugo year" comparable to a "fiscal year," which ran for twelve months immediately preceding the convention? In the latter case, since World Science Fiction Conventions are traditionally held each Labor Day weekend, the "Hugo year" might run from September 1 through August 31.

This question was not soon resolved. In fact, in a sense, there are still disputes over it, and a whole body of "case law" has evolved. Consider the following thorny problem:

Hypothetical author Jules Wollstonecraft Wells writes a novel. It is purchased for serialization in *Fabulous Galactic Tales* magazine, and appears in the issues dated November 1980, December 1980, January 1981, and February 1981, under the title *Starbug Come Home*.

A general hardcover edition of the novel, retitled *Tomorrow's Proust,* is published in the fall of 1981, and is duplicated by a book club edition early in 1982. The general and book club editions do so well that second or even third printings are made, and a mass-paperback edition is issued. This edition is officially published in January 1983, although advance copies are in circulation late in '82. (For the mass market, by the way, the book is retitled *Monster Alert!*)

Question: When is Wells's novel eligible for a Hugo? In 1980? 1981? 1982? Or 1983?

Does author Wells have any say in which version of the book is eligible? In the matter of which year it is eligible in? Even in the matter of which *title* the book will compete under?

Or are all of these matters to be decided by the fans' own convention committee?

Another problem is that of categories of awards. The original Hugos were presented in seven categories; a total of nine awards were given.

And only *one* of these Science Fiction Achievement Awards was actually given for a work of science fiction! This was best novel of the year, awarded to Alfred Bester for *The Demolished Man*, serialized in *Galaxy Science Fiction* for January, February, and March of 1952, and published as a hardcover book by Shasta in 1953. So if you think my example of the hypothetical J. W. Wells's book was farfetched, consider this: the January 1952 *Galaxy* appeared in December 1951. The February '52 *Galaxy* went on sale in January of that year, but there were advance copies around in December '51. And following the Shasta edition of *The Demolished Man* there were both book club and paperback editions.

Was *The Demolished Man* really a novel of 1951, 1952, 1953, or 1954?

The Philadelphia World Convention committee decided to give it an award in 1953, for "the previous year," and that will have to do.

For purposes of the present anthology, *What If?*, I have cut through this Gordian knot with the assistance of my Pocket Books editor, David G. Hartwell. I have arbitrarily (although I think not unfairly) declared 1952 to be "the previous year" of 1953, and presented a story from 1952. In like fashion I have chosen a story from 1953, one from 1954, and so on. Anyone who considers this approach incorrect is entitled to hold that opinion, of course.

The other winners in that first year of the Hugo were as follows:

- Best Professional Magazine: *Astounding Science Fiction, Galaxy Science Fiction* (tie)
- Best Interior Illustrator: Virgil Finlay
- Best Cover Artist: Ed Emshwiller, Hannes Bok (tie)
- Excellence in Fact Articles: Willy Ley
- Best New Author: Philip Jose Farmer
- Number One Fan Personality: Forrest J. Ackerman

Ackerman, it is reported, accepted his toy rocket ship and returned with it to his seat. He then turned toward his neighbor, the British fan Ken Slater, and gave the award to him. That shows how seriously those first Hugos were taken!

You'll also notice that there were no awards for fiction of less than novel length, so any story published in "the previous year," which might otherwise have been eligible for a Hugo, was simply ruled out! The several hundred short stories, novelettes, and novellas published that year didn't lose—they were never even permitted to compete!

The following year the World Science Fiction Convention was held in San Francisco. There were no Hugos. Why should there have been? The stunt had been used, it had succeeded, the fans had had a good time, and for 1954 something else could be tried to liven up the convention. Maybe an all-night beer bust, a good hot political fight at the official business meeting, or a game of "throw the pro in the pool."

So if you happened to write a story of *any* length that would have been eligible for a Hugo at the 1954 convention—forget it. A lapse in the Hugos in 1954 was somehow appropriate, anyway. There had been an upheaval in the magazine distribution business late in '53, and most of the science fiction magazines (along with hundreds of other periodicals) were dragged under in the process.

Some of the magazines had started dying off in 1952, more disappeared in '53, and others continued to drop away in the years that followed. From a peak of some 43 titles, the magazine field stabilized at half a dozen or so, and in all the years since then, despite mini-booms and mini-collapses, the number has stayed about the same.

But science fiction book publishing was on the upswing.

10

Both Ballantine Books and Ace Books had recently been founded, each with a heavy commitment to science fiction. The gloom that pervaded science fiction at the collapse of the pulps gave way to renewed optimism, and science fiction has grown in terms of volume of works published, popular, critical, and academic acceptance, and media penetration ever since. In a strange way, the end of the pulp-publishing era—that looked like disaster at the time—proved to be the beginning of science fiction's major growth.

The San Francisco convention committee in 1954 had dropped the Hugos, considering them a one-time stunt on the part of the 1953 convention. But the fans howled their dismay. The 1955 convention was held in Cleveland, and the committee chairperson, Noreen Kane Falasca, saw to the reintroduction of the awards.

The categories were shuffled, and the single writer's award, that for best novel of the year, was extended to include awards also for best novelette and best short story.

In later years these categories were shuffled again and again. It was not until the Science Fiction Writers of America established their own annual series of Nebula awards (1965), with four categories by length, that the fans followed suit and a sensible degree of stability was achieved.

For some years now there have been annual awards for novel, novella, novelette, and short story. The distinctions are arbitrary; SFWA took its definitions from the older Mystery Writers of America; the fans took their definitions from SFWA. In *What If?* we will of necessity concern ourselves with the three shorter categories. Most or all Hugo-winning novels are in print, anyway, and to include them here would have been superfluous as well as physically impractical.

It had been my original hope to include in this anthology "what if" stories for all three non-novel categories, for all the years since 1952. Unfortunately, that totaled out to something on the order of a million words of fiction, and my publisher was not prepared to handle the project. So I will offer *one* story for each year, along with appropriate commentary telling which stories were honored that year.

A wealth of outstanding stories have been passed over for Hugos, and for a variety of reasons. Sometimes a given category was simply not recognized in a particular year.

Sometimes two or more positively superb stories appeared in the same year in the same category. Sometimes an outstanding story would appear in a secondary periodical, in an original anthology that did not enjoy a large sale, in a magazine whose circulation was primarily outside the science fiction field, or in a British publication. (The rules don't require publication in the United States, but most of the voters are Americans and simply don't get to see many periodicals of overseas origin.)

Voters have stampeded to give awards for sentimental reasons. Authors get hot; particular groups or styles or individuals are temporarily trendy; sometimes there's an "old boy" vote; sometimes there's a Young Turk vote; sometimes there's a feminist vote.

Sometimes there's shameless politicking. Many fans (and in more recent years, since the institution of the Nebula Awards, many professionals) can testify to having been asked to vote for this story or that. Fan clubs and convention committees have been known to caucus and cast ballots *en bloc*.

Promotional advertisements have appeared in the science fiction trade press shortly before voting deadlines. The similarity to Hollywood practices at Oscar-time is obvious.

Nor are paranoid fantasies unknown. Not long ago I was told a heartrending tale by one very prominent writer. He detailed the dastardly fashion in which a rival electioneered an award away from him (the first writer) and to himself (the second writer). The anecdote was distressingly plausible. But—upon checking award records—I found that the incident could not possibly have happened. The "victim" had twice been nominated for awards. On the first occasion the "villain" was not even on the list. On the second, while both authors were nominated, a third party altogether won!

What If? may not remedy all such injustices of the past three decades, but it will give recognition to a lot of stories that deserve better treatment than they got.

There have been many series of awards in the science fiction field, but except for the Hugo and the Nebula, none have ever achieved very much recognition or acceptance, either by the reading public or by the publishing industry. Even today, awards are given annually by academics specializing in science fiction (the Jupiter award), by at least one newsletter of science fiction (the Locus Poll), and by at least one self-appointed and self-sustaining committee operating rather in the fashion of the old International Fan-

12

tasy Awards committee (the John Campbell award). Further, because the winners of the Hugo and Nebula are almost always American or British writers, fans in other parts of the world have initiated national or regional competitions.

Still, none of these have attained much stature. I suspect that none of them will.

Why not?

Well, most of them suffer from the same problem as the International Fantasy Awards: no constituency. You or I or anyone else could set ourselves up as donors of an annual trophy for whatever kind of achievement we chose to recognize. Our choices might be exemplary. Doubtless the winners would be pleased to accept any trophy, certificate, publicity, or cash award we could offer them. (Especially a cash award!) But, still—what would it mean?

Some years ago *Spectrum*—one of the pioneering science fiction book review magazines and basically an excellent publication that happened to arrive before its time—offered an array of annual Spectrum Awards. The categories included best science fiction novel of the year, best fantasy novel of the year, best science fiction anthology or collection of the year. . . . The selections were excellent, but they were merely the personal choices of the editor of *Spectrum*. Neither the award series nor the magazine itself survived very long.

Of present-day award series, only the Locus Poll claims a constituency comparable to the Hugo and Nebula. In some years, in fact, the publisher of *Locus* claims a body of voters *larger* than the other awards. But it seems that such a poll, affiliated as it is with a specific publication, cannot claim the objectivity of one sponsored by the fans themselves, or by a professional association like SFWA. For comparison, one may compare the annual *Photoplay* awards in the film industry with the Oscar.

I think that the Hugo and Nebula are here to stay, and of the two I think that the Hugo is more popularly and more firmly entrenched, and likely to survive for many years, with considerable prestige. In fact, a general array of past Hugo (and Nebula) winners indicates that *most* of the choices have been pretty good ones. For all of the tinkering that has been done over the years, with actual or proposed modifications in nominating and voting procedures, changes in categories and eligibility rules, suggestions of jury systems in place of or in addition to popular balloting, charges (sometimes quite credible ones) of electioneering, bloc-voting, and ballot-box stuffing . . .

. . . for all of these, the system has worked pretty well. But there is *still* an array of truly splendid stories that have been denied their earned glory. *What If?* will provide at least some degree of that glory which those unrecognized works deserve.

—RICHARD A. LUPOFF

1952

To REITERATE, THERE were no 1952 Hugos, as such. The first set of awards was made in 1953 for the works of a rather ambiguously understood "previous year." There was only one fiction award, to Alfred Bester for his novel *The Demolished Man,* and since this had first appeared in *Galaxy* starting in January 1952, one infers that "previous year" *means* 1952, not just the twelve months preceding Labor Day weekend, 1953.

There were no awards for shorter science fiction. *Galaxy* and *The Magazine of Fantasy and Science Fiction* had hit their strides. Campbell, at *Astounding,* clearly stung by the competition, was turning out one splendid issue after another. And literally dozens of second- and third-line magazines, ranging from the oldest of old-timers *(Weird Tales, Amazing, Thrilling Wonder Stories)* to the newest of the new *(Dynamic, Imagination, If, Marvel, Other Worlds, Science Fiction Adventures, Space Science Fiction)* could also turn up an occasional gem.

Consider this sampling of the science fiction of 1952. The novels that Bester had to beat included *Gunner Cade* by "Cyril Judd" (Cyril Kornbluth and Judith Merril) and *The Currents of Space* by Isaac Asimov, both serialized in *Astounding; Gravy Planet* (also known as *The Space Merchants*) by Kornbluth and Frederik Pohl, serialized in *Galaxy; Ring Around the Sun* by Clifford Simak, overlapping 1952 and 1953 in *Galaxy;* and *Journey to Barkut* by Murray Leinster and *The Lovers* by Philip Jose Farmer, both in *Startling Stories.*

Short fiction included "That Share of Glory" by Kornbluth, "Fast Falls the Eventide" by Eric Frank Russell, and "The Impacted Man" by Robert Sheckley, all in *Astounding.* Ziff-Davis Publications revamped the old pulp *Fantastic Adventures* into a slick new package and shortened the name to *Fantastic.* In fact, they started the new

15

magazine with a fresh volume-and-issue series and let both versions overlap for a short time, before merging the old pulp magazine into the new smaller version—thus causing unmeasured woe for later indexers and bibliographers.

The new *Fantastic,* in 1952, ran "The Smile" by Ray Bradbury, "Three to Get Ready" by Horace Gold, "I'm Looking for Jeff" by Fritz Leiber, and one of the more bizarre exploitation pieces on record, "The Veiled Woman," supposedly by Mickey Spillane. (The story is generally believed to have been ghosted for Spillane by the magazine's editor, Howard Browne.)

Galaxy was a wealth of fine stories, including "The Year of the Jackpot" by Robert A. Heinlein, "Lover When You're Near Me" by Richard Matheson, "Surface Tension" by James Blish, "Game for Blondes" by John D. MacDonald, "Baby is Three" by Theodore Sturgeon, and "The Martian Way" by Isaac Asimov.

Fantasy and Science Fiction ran "SRL Ad" by Matheson, "The Anomaly of the Empty Man" by Anthony Boucher himself, and "The Third Level" by Jack Finney.

Startling Stories and *Thrilling Wonder Stories* (essentially interchangeable in those days) featured "The Well of the Worlds" by Henry Kuttner, "Sail On, Sail On" by Farmer, "The Foodlegger" by Matheson, and "What's It Like Out There?" possibly the finest single story in the career of veteran Edmond Hamilton.

Even the lowly *Planet Stories* could boast a wealth of Leigh Brackett, Poul Anderson, and Philip K. Dick's "Beyond Lies the Wub."

Pick one story from the output of 1952? Some task! I think that few readers will cavil, however, at "Firewater!" by William Tenn. Tenn (a pseudonym of Philip Klass) had been one of the crop of new writers to appear just after World War II. A few of his earliest stories were somewhat clumsy efforts at space opera and similar conventional forms, but he quickly found his true voice.

Throughout the 1950s he produced a stream of memorable stories, combining a keen insight into the psychological and sociological foibles of humanity. All of his better stories contain heavy doses of satire; many of them are filled with black humor. He gave us "Flat-Eyed Monster," "Betelgeuse Bridge," "Project Hush," "Will You Walk a Little Faster," "Venus and the Seven Sexes," and dozens of others. One of his earliest stories, "Brooklyn Project," is utterly unforgettable, and one of his last, "The Masculinist Revolt," is equally so.

In the 1960s, to the pleasure of a long series of students and the dismay of the science fiction reading public, Klass began an academic career at Penn State. He rose to the rank of professor, which he still holds. One can hardly fault him for preferring the respected role of an academic (along with its regular paychecks!) to the somewhat harried and frenetic life of the freelance writer (and its proverbial fiscal chanciness). Happily, Klass does still set trousers to typing chair and fingertips to keyboard on occasion, and produces a short story or critical piece as trenchant and polished as ever. And he has, of late, spoken encouragingly of settling down to write a novel—his first in too many years!

As for "Firewater!," Klass had trouble sliding it past John W. Campbell's *mankind uber alles* test, but somehow he did, and the result was, at least in my judgment, the best science fiction story of 1952.

Firewater!

WILLIAM TENN

THE HAIRIEST, DIRTIEST and oldest of the three visitors from Arizona scratched his back against the plastic of the webfoam chair. "Insinuations are lavender nearly," he remarked by way of opening the conversation.

His two companions—the thin young man with dripping eyes, and the woman whose good looks were marred chiefly by incredibly decayed teeth—giggled and relaxed. The thin young man said "Gabble, gabble, honk!" under his breath, and the other two nodded emphatically.

Greta Seidenheim looked up from her tiny stenographic machine. "That too, Mr. Hebster?"

The president of Hebster Securities, Inc., nodded and said resonantly, "That too, Miss Seidenheim. Close phonetic approximations of the gabble-honk and remember to indicate when it sounds like a question and when like an exclamation."

He rubbed his recently manicured fingernails across the desk drawer containing his fully loaded Parabellum. Check. The communication buttons with which he could summon any quantity of Hebster Securities personnel up to the nine hundred working at present in the Hebster Building lay some eight inches from the other hand. Check. And there were the doors here, the doors there, behind which his uniformed bodyguard stood poised to burst in at a signal

18

which would blaze before them the moment his right foot came off the tiny spring set in the floor. *And* check.

Algernon Hebster could talk business—even with Primeys.

Courteously, he nodded at each one of his visitors from Arizona; he smiled ruefully at what the dirty shapeless masses they wore on their feet were doing to the calf-deep rug that had been woven specially for his private office. He had greeted them when Miss Seidenheim had escorted them in. They had laughed in his face.

"Suppose we rattle off some introductions. You know me. I'm Hebster, Algernon Hebster—you asked for me specifically at the desk in the lobby. If it's important to the conversation, my secretary's name is Greta Seidenheim. And you, sir?"

He had addressed the old fellow, but the thin young man leaned forward in his seat and held out a taut, almost transparent hand. "Names?" he inquired. "Names are round if not revealed. Consider names. How many names? Consider names, *reconsider* names!"

The woman leaned forward too, and the smell from her diseased mouth reached Hebster even across the enormous space of his office. "Rabble and reaching and all the upward clash," she intoned, spreading her hands as if in agreement with an obvious point. "Emptiness derogating itself into infinity—"

"Into duration," the older man corrected.

"Into infinity," the woman insisted.

"Gabble, gabble, honk?" the young man queried bitterly.

"Listen!" Hebster roared. "When I asked for—"

The communicator buzzed and he drew a deep breath and pressed a button. His receptionist's voice boiled out rapidly, fearfully:

"I remember your orders, Mr. Hebster, but those two men from the UM Special Investigating Commission are here again and they look as if they mean business. I mean they look as if they'll make trouble."

"Yost and Funatti?"

"Yes, sir. From what they said to each other, I think they know you have three Primeys in there. They asked me what are you trying to do—deliberately inflame the Firsters? They said they're going to invoke full supranational powers and force an entry if you don't—"

"Stall them."

"But, Mr. Hebster, the *UM Special Investigating—*"

19

"Stall them, I said. Are you a receptionist or a swinging door? Use your imagination, Ruth. You have a nine-hundred-man organization and a ten-million-dollar corporation at your disposal. You can stage any kind of farce in that outer office you want—up to and including the deal where some actor made up to look like me walks in and drops dead at their feet. Stall them and I'll nod a bonus at you. *Stall them.*" He clicked off, looked up.

His visitors, at least, were having a fine time. They had turned to face each other in a reeking triangle of gibberish. Their voices rose and fell argumentatively, pleadingly, decisively; but all Algernon Hebster's ears could register of what they said were very many sounds similar to *gabble* and an occasional, indisputable *honk!*

His lips curled contempt inward. Humanity prime! *These* messes? Then he lit a cigarette and shrugged. Oh, well. Humanity prime. And business is business.

Just remember they're not supermen, he told himself. *They may be dangerous, but they're not supermen. Not by a long shot. Remember that epidemic of influenza that almost wiped them out, and how you diddled those two other Primeys last month. They're not supermen, but they're not humanity either. They're just different.*

He glanced at his secretary and approved. Greta Seidenheim clacked away on her machine as if she were recording the curtest, the tritest of business letters. He wondered what system she was using to catch the intonations. Trust Greta, though, she'd do it.

"Gabble, honk! Gabble, gabble, gabble, honk, honk. Gabble, honk, gabble, gabble, honk? Honk."

What had precipitated all this conversation? He'd only asked for their names. Didn't they use names in Arizona? Surely, they knew that it was customary here. They claimed to know at least as much as he about such matters.

Maybe it was something else that had brought them to New York this time—maybe something about the Aliens? He felt the short hairs rise on the back of his neck and he smoothed them down self-consciously.

Trouble was it was so *easy* to learn their language. It was such a very simple matter to be able to understand them in these talkative moments. Almost as easy as falling off a log—or jumping off a cliff.

Well, his time was limited. He didn't know how long Ruth could hold the UM investigators in his outer office. Somehow he had to get a grip on the meeting again without offending them in any of the innumerable, highly dangerous ways in which Primeys could be offended.

He rapped the desk top—gently. The gabble-honk stopped short at the hyphen. The woman rose slowly.

"On this question of names," Hebster began doggedly, keeping his eyes on the woman, "since you people claim—"

The woman writhed agonizingly for a moment and sat down on the floor. She smiled at Hebster. With her rotted teeth, the smile had all the brilliance of a dead star.

Hebster cleared his throat and prepared to try again.

"If you want names," the older man said suddenly, "you can call me Larry."

The president of Hebster Securities shook himself and managed to say "Thanks" in a somewhat weak but not too surprised voice. He looked at the thin young man.

"You can call me Theseus." The young man looked sad as he said it.

"Theseus? Fine!" One thing about Primeys when you started clicking with them, you really moved along. But *Theseus!* Wasn't that just like a Primey? Now the woman, and they could begin.

They were all looking at the woman, even Greta with a curiosity which had sneaked up past her beauty-parlor glaze.

"Name," the woman whispered to herself. "Name a name."

Oh, no, Hebster groaned. *Let's not stall here.*

Larry evidently had decided that enough time had been wasted. He made a suggestion to the woman. "Why not call yourself Moe?"

The young man—Theseus, it was now—also seemed to get interested in the problem. "Rover's a good name," he announced helpfully.

"How about Gloria?" Hebster asked desperately.

The woman considered. "Moe, Rover, Gloria," she mused. "Larry, Theseus, Seidenheim, Hebster, me." She seemed to be running a total.

Anything might come out, Hebster knew. But at least they were not acting snobbish any more: they were talking down on his level now. Not only no gabble-honk, but none of this sneering double-talk which was almost worse. At least they were making sense—of a sort.

"For the purposes of this discussion," the woman said at last, "my name will be . . . will be— My name *is* S.S. Lusitania."

21

"Fine!" Hebster roared, letting the word he'd kept bubbling on his lips burst out. "That's a *fine* name. Larry, Theseus and . . . er, S.S. Lusitania. Fine bunch of people. Sound. Let's get down to business. You came here on business, I take it?"

"Right," Larry said. "We heard about you from two others who left home a month ago to come to New York. They talked about you when they got back to Arizona."

"They did, eh? I hoped they would."

Theseus slid off his chair and squatted next to the woman who was making plucking motions at the air. "They talked about you," he repeated. "They said you treated them very well, that you showed them as much respect as a thing like you could generate. They also said you cheated them."

"Oh, well, Theseus," Hebster spread his manicured hands. "I'm a businessman."

"You're a businessman," S.S. Lusitania agreed, getting to her feet stealthily and taking a great swipe with both hands at something invisible in front of her face. "And here, in this spot, at this moment, so are we. You can have what we've brought, but you'll pay for it. And don't think you can cheat *us*."

Her hands, cupped over each other, came down to her waist. She pulled them apart suddenly and a tiny eagle fluttered out. It flapped toward the fluorescent panels glowing in the ceiling. Its flight was hampered by the heavy, striped shield upon its breast, by the bunch of arrows it held in one claw, by the olive branch it grasped with the other. It turned its miniature bald head and gasped at Algernon Hebster, then began to drift rapidly down to the rug. Just before it hit the floor, it disappeared.

Hebster shut his eyes, remembering the strip of bunting that had fallen from the eagle's beak when it had turned to gasp. There had been words printed on the bunting, words too small to see at the distance, but he was sure the words would have read *"E Pluribus Unum."* He was as certain of that as he was of the necessity of acting unconcerned over the whole incident, as unconcerned as the Primeys. Professor Kleimbocher said Primeys were mental drunkards. But why did they give everyone else the D.T.'s?

He opened his eyes. "Well," he said, "what have you to sell?"

Silence for a moment. Theseus seemed to forget the point he was trying to make; S.S. Lusitania stared at Larry.

Larry scratched his right side through heavy, stinking cloth.

"Oh, an infallible method for defeating anyone who attempts to apply the *reductio ad absurdum* to a reasonable proposition you advance." He yawned smugly and began scratching his left side.

Hebster grinned because he was feeling so good. "No. Can't use it."

"Can't use it?" The old man was trying hard to look amazed. He shook his head. He stole a sideways glance at S.S. Lusitania.

She smiled again and wriggled to the floor. "Larry still isn't talking a language you can understand, Mr. Hebster," she cooed, very much like a fertilizer factory being friendly. "We came here with something we know you need badly. Very badly."

"Yes?" *They're like those two Primeys last month,* Hebster exulted: *they don't know what's good and what isn't. Wonder if their masters would know. Well, and if they did—who does business with Aliens?*

"We . . . have," she spaced the words carefully, trying pathetically for a dramatic effect, "a new shade of red, but not merely that. Oh, *no!* A new shade of red, and a full set of color values derived from it! A complete set of color values derived from this one shade of red, Mr. Hebster! Think what a non-objectivist painter can do with such a—"

"Don't sell me, lady. Theseus, do you want to have a go now?"

Theseus had been frowning at the green foundation of the desk. He leaned back, looking satisfied. Hebster realized abruptly that the tension under his right foot had disappeared. Somehow, Theseus had become cognizant of the signal-spring set in the floor; and, somehow, he had removed it.

He had disintegrated it without setting off the alarm to which it was wired.

Giggles from three Primey throats and a rapid exchange of "gabble-honk." Then they all knew what Theseus had done and how Hebster had tried to protect himself. They weren't angry, though—and they didn't sound triumphant. Try to understand Primey behavior!

No need to get unduly alarmed—the price of dealing with these characters was a nervous stomach. The rewards, on the other hand—

23

Abruptly, they were businesslike again.

Theseus snapped out his suggestion with all the finality of a bazaar merchant making his last, absolutely the last offer. "A set of population indices which can be correlated with—"

"No, Theseus," Hebster told him gently.

Then, while Hebster sat back and enjoyed, temporarily forgetting the missing coil under his foot, they poured out more, desperately, feverishly, weaving in and out of each other's sentences.

"A portable neutron stabilizer for high altit—"

"More than fifty ways of saying 'however' without—"

". . . So that every housewife can do an *entrechat* while cook—"

". . . Synthetic fabric with the drape of silk and manu-factura—"

". . . Decorative pattern for bald heads using the follicles as—"

". . . Complete and utter refutation of all pyramidologists from—"

"All right!" Hebster roared, *"All right!* That's enough!"

Greta Seidenheim almost forgot herself and sighed with relief. Her stenographic machine had been sounding like a centrifuge.

"Now," said the executive. "What do you want in exchange?"

"One of those we said is the one you want, eh?" Larry muttered. "Which one—the pyramidology refutation? That's it, I betcha."

S.S. Lusitania waved her hands contemptuously. "Bishop's miters, you fool! The new red color values excited him. The new—"

Ruth's voice came over the communicator. "Mr. Hebster, Yost and Funatti are back. I stalled them, but I just received word from the lobby receptionist that they're back and on their way upstairs. You have two minutes, maybe three. And they're so mad they almost look like Firsters themselves!"

"Thanks. When they climb out of the elevator, do what you can without getting too illegal." He turned to his guests. "Listen—"

They had gone off again.

"Gabble, gabble, honk, honk, honk? Gabble, honk, *gabble,* gabble! Gabble, honk, gabble, honk, gabble, honk, honk."

24

Could they honestly make sense out of these throat-clearings and half-sneezes? Was it really a language as superior to all previous languages of man as . . . as the Aliens were supposed to be to man himself? Well, at least they could communicate with the Aliens by means of it. And the Aliens, the Aliens—

He recollected abruptly the two angry representatives of the world state who were hurtling toward his office.

"Listen, friends. You came here to sell. You've shown me your stock, and I've seen something I'd like to buy. *What* exactly is immaterial. The only question now is what you want for it. And let's make it fast. I have some other business to transact."

The woman with the dental nightmare stamped her foot. A cloud no larger than a man's hand formed near the ceiling, burst and deposited a pailful of water on Hebster's fine custom-made rug.

He ran a manicured forefinger around the inside of his collar so that his bulging neck veins would not burst. Not right now, anyway. He looked at Greta and regained confidence from the serenity with which she waited for more conversation to transcribe. There was a model of business precision for you. The Primeys might pull what one of them had in London two years ago, before they were barred from all metropolitan areas—increased a housefly's size to that of an elephant—and Greta Seidenheim would go on separating fragments of conversation into the appropriate shorthand symbols.

With all their power, why didn't they *take* what they wanted? Why trudge wearisome miles to cities and attempt to smuggle themselves into illegal audiences with operators like Hebster, when most of them were caught easily and sent back to the reservation and those that weren't were cheated unmercifully by the "straight" humans they encountered? Why didn't they just blast their way in, take their weird and pathetic prizes and toddle back to their masters? For that matter, why didn't their masters— But Primey psych was Primey psych—not for this world, nor of it.

"We'll tell you what we want in exchange," Larry began in the middle of a honk. He held up a hand on which the length of the fingernails was indicated graphically by the grime beneath them and began to tot up the items, bending a digit for each item. "First, a hundred paper-bound copies of Melville's 'Moby Dick.' Then, twenty-five crystal radio

25

sets, with earphones; two earphones for each set. Then, two Empire State Buildings or three Radio Cities, whichever is more convenient. We want those with foundations intact. A reasonably good copy of the 'Hermes' statue by Praxiteles. And an electric toaster, *circa* 1941. That's about all, isn't it, Theseus?"

Theseus bent over until his nose rested against his knees.

Hebster groaned. The list wasn't as bad as he'd expected —remarkable the way their masters always yearned for the electric gadgets and artistic achievements of Earth—but he had so little time to bargain with them. *Two* Empire State Buildings!

"Mr. Hebster," his receptionist chattered over the communicator. "Those SIC men—I managed to get a crowd out in the corridor to push toward their elevator when it came to this floor, and I've locked the . . . I mean I'm trying to . . . but I don't think— Can you—"

"Good girl! You're doing fine!"

"Is that all we want, Theseus?" Larry asked again. "Gabble?"

Hebster heard a crash in the outer office and footsteps running across the floor.

"See here, Mr. Hebster," Theseus said at last, "if you don't want to buy Larry's *reductio ad absurdum* exploder, and you don't like my method of decorating bald heads for all its innate artistry, how about a system of musical notation—"

Somebody tried Hebster's door, found it locked. There was a knock on the door, repeated most immediately with more urgency.

"He's *already* found something he wants," S.S. Lusitania snapped. "Yes, Larry, that was the complete list."

Hebster plucked a handful of hair from his already receding forehead. "Good! Now, look, I can give you everything but the two Empire State Buildings and the three Radio Cities."

"*Or* the three Radio Cities," Larry corrected. "Don't try to cheat us! Two Empire State Buildings *or* three Radio Cities. Whichever is more convenient. Why . . . isn't it worth that to you?"

"Open this door!" a bull-mad voice yelled. "Open this door in the name of United Mankind!"

"Miss Seidenheim, open the door," Hebster said loudly and winked at his secretary who rose, stretched and began a thoughtful, slow-motion study in the direction of the

26

locked panel. There was a crash as of a pair of shoulders being thrown against it. Hebster knew that his office door could withstand a medium-sized tank. But there was a limit even to delay when it came to fooling around with the UM Special Investigating Commission. Those boys knew their Primeys and their Primey-dealers; they were empowered to shoot first and ask questions afterwards—as the questions occurred to them.

"It's not a matter of whether it's worth my while," Hebster told them rapidly as he shepherded them to the exit behind his desk. "For reasons I'm sure you aren't interested in, I just can't give away two Empire State Buildings and-or three Radio Cities with foundations intact—not at the moment. I'll give you the rest of it, and—"

"Open this door or we start blasting it down!"

"Please, gentlemen, please," Greta Seidenheim told them sweetly. "You'll kill a poor working girl who's trying awfully hard to let you in. The lock's stuck." She fiddled with the door knob, watching Hebster with a trace of anxiety in her fine eyes.

"And to replace those items," Hebster was going on, "I will—"

"What I mean," Theseus broke in, "is this. You know the greatest single difficulty composers face in the twelve-tone technique?"

"I can offer you," the executive continued doggedly, sweat bursting out of his skin like spring freshets, "complete architectural blueprints of the Empire State Building and Radio City, plus five . . . no, I'll make it ten . . . scale models of each. And you get the rest of the stuff you asked for. That's it. Take it or leave it. Fast!"

They glanced at each other, as Hebster threw the exit door open and gestured to the five liveried bodyguards waiting near his private elevator. *"Done,"* they said in unison.

"Good!" Hebster almost squeaked. He pushed them through the doorway and said to the tallest of the five men: "Nineteenth floor!"

He slammed the exit shut just as Miss Seidenheim opened the outer office door. Yost and Funatti, in the bottle-green uniform of the UM, charged through. Without pausing, they ran to where Hebster stood and plucked the exit open. They could all hear the elevator descending.

Funatti, a little, olive-skinned man, sniffed. "Primeys,"

27

he muttered. "He had Primeys here, all right. Smell that unwash, Yost?"

"Yeah," said the bigger man. "Come on. The emergency stairway. We can track that elevator!"

They holstered their service weapons and clattered down the metal-tipped stairs. Below, the elevator stopped.

Hebster's secretary was at the communicator. "Maintenance!" She waited. "Maintenance, automobile locks on the nineteenth floor exit until the party Mr. Hebster just sent down gets to a lab somewhere else. And keep apologizing to those cops until then. Remember, they're SIC."

"Thanks, Greta," Hebster said, switching to the personal now that they were alone. He plumped into his desk chair and blew out gustily: "There must be easier ways of making a million."

She raised two perfect 'blond eyebrows. "Or of being an absolute monarch right inside the parliament of man?"

"If they wait long enough," he told her lazily, "I'll *be* the UM, modern global government and all. Another year or two might do it."

"Aren't you forgetting one Vandermeer Dempsey? His huskies also want to replace the UM. Not to mention their colorful plans for you. And there are an awful, awful lot of them."

"They don't worry me, Greta. *Humanity First* will dissolve overnight once that decrepit old demagogue gives up the ghost." He stabbed at the communicator button. "Maintenance! Maintenance, that party I sent down arrived at a safe lab yet?"

"No, Mr. Hebster. But everything's going all right. We sent them up to the twenty-fourth floor and got the SIC men rerouted downstairs to the personnel levels. Uh, Mr. Hebster—about the SIC. We take your orders and all that, but none of us wants to get in trouble with the Special Investigating Commission. According to the latest laws, it's practically a capital offense to obstruct 'em."

"Don't worry," Hebster told him. "I've never let one of my employees down yet. The boss fixes everything is the motto here. Call me when you've got those Primeys safely hidden and ready for questioning."

He turned back to Greta. "Get that stuff typed before you leave and into Professor Kleimbocher's hands. He thinks he may have a new angle on their gabble-honk."

She nodded. "I wish you could use recording apparatus instead of making me sit over an old-fashioned click-box."

"So do I. But Primeys enjoy reaching out and putting a hex on electrical apparatus—when they aren't collecting it for the Aliens. I had a raft of wire and tape recorders busted in the middle of Primey interviews before I decided that human stenos were the only answer. And a Primey may get around to bollixing them some day."

"Cheerful thought. I must remember to dream about the possibility some cold night. Well, I should complain," she muttered as she went into her own little office, "Primey hexes built this business and pay my salary as well as supply me with the sparkling little knicknacks I love so well."

That was not quite true, Hebster remembered as he sat waiting for the communicator to buzz the news of his recent guests' arrival in a safe lab. Something like ninety-five per cent of Hebster Securities had been built out of Primey gadgetry extracted from them in various fancy deals, but the base of it all had been the small investment bank he had inherited from his father, back in the days of the Half-War—the days when the Aliens had first appeared on Earth.

The fearfully intelligent dots swirling in their variously shaped multicolored bottles were completely outside the pale of human understanding. There had been no way at all to communicate with them for a time.

A humorist had remarked back in those early days that the Aliens came not to bury man, not to conquer or enslave him. They had a truly dreadful mission—to ignore him!

No one knew, even today, what part of the galaxy the Aliens came from. Or why. No one knew what the total of their small visiting population came to. Or how they operated their wide-open and completely silent spaceships. The few things that had been discovered about them on the occasions when they deigned to swoop down and examine some human enterprise, with the aloof amusement of the highly civilized tourist, had served to confirm a technological superiority over Man that strained and tore the capacity of his richest imagination. A sociological treatise Hebster had read recently suggested that they operated from concepts as far in advance of modern science as a meteorologist sowing a drought-struck area with dry ice was beyond the primitive agriculturist blowing a ram's horn at the

29

heavens in a frantic attempt to wake the slumbering gods of rain.

Prolonged, infinitely dangerous observation had revealed, for example, that the dots-in-bottles seemed to have developed past the need for prepared tools of any sort. They worked directly on the material itself, shaping it to need, evidently creating and destroying matter at will!

Some humans had communicated with them—

They didn't stay human.

Men with superb brains had looked into the whirring, flickering settlements established by the outsiders. A few had returned with tales of wonders they had realized dimly and not quite seen. Their descriptions always sounded as if their eyes had been turned off at the most crucial moments or a mental fuse had blown just this side of understanding.

Others—such celebrities as a President of Earth, a three-time winner of the Nobel Prize, famous poets—had evidently broken through the fence somehow. These, however, were the ones who didn't return. They stayed in the Alien settlements of the Gobi, the Sahara, the American Southwest. Barely able to fend for themselves, despite newly-acquired and almost unbelievable powers, they shambled worshipfully around the outsiders speaking, with weird writhings of larynx and nasal passage, what was evidently a human approximation of their masters' language—a kind of pidgin Alien. Talking with a Primey, someone had said, was like a blind man trying to read a page of Braille originally written for an octopus.

And that these bearded, bug-ridden, stinking derelicts, these chattering wrecks drunk and sodden on the logic of an entirely different life-form, were the heavy yellow cream of the human race didn't help people's egos any.

Humans and Primeys despised each other almost from the first; humans for Primey subservience and helplessness in human terms, Primeys for human ignorance and ineptness in Alien terms. And, except when operating under Alien orders and through barely legal operators like Hebster, Primeys didn't communicate with humans any more than their masters did.

When institutionalized, they either gabble-honked themselves into an early grave or, losing patience suddenly, they might dissolve a path to freedom right through the walls of the asylum and any attendants who chanced to be in the way. Therefore the enthusiasm of sheriff and deputy, nurse and orderly, had waned considerably and the forcible incarceration of Primeys had almost ceased.

Since the two groups were so far apart psychologically as to make mating between them impossible, the ragged miracle-workers had been honored with the status of a separate classification:

Humanity Prime. Not better than humanity, not necessarily worse—but different, and dangerous.

What made them that way? Hebster rolled his chair back and examined the hole in the floor from which the alarm spring had spiraled. Theseus had disintegrated it—*how?* With a thought? Telekinesis, say, applied to all the molecules of the metal simultaneously, making them move rapidly and at random. Or possibly he had merely moved the spring somewhere else. Where? In space? In hyperspace? In time? Hebster shook his head and pulled himself back to the efficiently smooth and sanely useful desk surface.

"Mr. Hebster?" the communicator inquired abruptly, and he jumped a bit, "this is Margritt of General Lab 23B. Your Primeys just arrived. Regular check?"

Regular check meant drawing them out on every conceivable technical subject by the nine specialists in the general laboratory. This involved firing questions at them with the rapidity of a police interrogation, getting them off balance and keeping them there in the hope that a useful and unexpected bit of scientific knowledge would drop.

"Yes," Hebster told him. "Regular check. But first let a textile man have a whack at them. In fact let him take charge of the check."

A pause. "The only textile man in this section is Charlie Verus."

"Well?" Hebster asked in mild irritation. "Why put it like that? He's competent I hope. What does personnel say about him?"

"Personnel says he's competent."

"Then there you are. Look, Margritt, I have the SIC running around my building with blood in its enormous eye. I don't have time to muse over your departmental feuds. Put Verus on."

"Yes, Mr. Hebster. Hey Bert! Get Charlie Verus. Him."

Hebster shook his head and chuckled. These technicians! Verus was probably brilliant and nasty.

The box crackled again: "Mr. Hebster? Mr. Verus." The voice expressed boredom to the point of obvious affectation. But the man was probably good despite his neurosis. Hebster Securities, Inc., had a first-rate personnel department.

"Verus? Those Primeys, I want you to take charge of the check. One of them knows how to make a synthetic fabric with the drape of silk. Get that first and then go after anything else they have."

"Primeys, Mr. Hebster?"

"I said Primeys, Mr. Verus. You are a textile technician, please to remember, and not the straight or Ping-Pong half of a comedy routine. Get humping. I want a report on that synthetic fabric by tomorrow. Work all night if you have to."

"Before we do, Mr. Hebster, you might be interested in a small piece of information. There is *already* in existence a synthetic which falls better than silk—"

"I know," his employer told him shortly. "Cellulose acetate. Unfortunately, it has a few disadvantages: low melting point, tends to crack; separate and somewhat inferior dyestuffs have to be used for it; poor chemical resistance. Am I right?"

There was no immediate answer, but Hebster could feel the dazed nod. He went on. "Now, we also have protein fibers. They dye well and fall well, have the thermoconductivity control necessary for wearing apparel, but don't have the tensile strength of synthetic fabrics. An *artificial* protein fiber might be the answer: it would drape as well as silk, might be we could use the acid dyestuffs we use on silk which result in shades that dazzle female customers and cause them to fling wide their pocketbooks. There are a lot of *ifs* in that, I know, but one of those Primeys said something about a synthetic with the drape of silk, and I don't think he'd be sane enough to be referring to cellulose acetate. Nor nylon, Orlon, vinyl chloride, or anything else we already have and use."

"You've looked into textile problems, Mr. Hebster."

"I have. I've looked into everything to which there are big gobs of money attached. And now suppose you go look into those Primeys. Several million women are waiting breathlessly for the secrets concealed in their beards. Do you think, Verus, that with the personal and scientific background I've just given you it's possible you might get around to doing the job you are paid to do?"

"Um-m-m. Yes."

Hebster walked to the office closet and got his hat and

32

coat. He liked working under pressure; he liked to see people jump up straight whenever he barked. And now, he liked the prospect of relaxing.

He grimaced at the webfoam chair that Larry had used. No point in having it resquirted. Have a new one made.

"I'll be at the University," he told Ruth on his way out. "You can reach me through Professor Kleimbocher. But don't, unless it's very important. He gets unpleasantly annoyed when he's interrupted."

She nodded. Then, very hesitantly: "Those two men—Yost and Funatti—from the Special Investigating Commission? They said no one would be allowed to leave the building."

"Did they now?" he chuckled. "I think they were angry. They've been that way before. But unless and until they can hang something on me—And Ruth, tell my bodyguard to go home, except for the man with the Primeys. He's to check with me, wherever I am, every two hours."

He ambled out, being careful to smile benevolently at every third executive and fifth typist in the large office. A private elevator and entrance was all very well for an occasional crisis, but Hebster liked to taste his successes in as much public as possible.

It would be good to see Kleimbocher again. He had a good deal of faith in the linguistic approach; grants from his corporation had tripled the size of the university's philology department. After all, the basic problem between man and Primey as well as man and Alien was one of communication. Any attempt to learn their science, to adjust their mental processes and logic into safer human channels, would have to be preceded by understanding.

It was up to Kleimbocher to find that understanding, not him. "I'm Hebster," he thought. "I *employ* the people who solve problems. And then I make money off them."

Somebody got in front of him. Somebody else took his arm. "I'm Hebster," he repeated automatically, but out loud. "*Algernon* Hebster."

"Exactly the Hebster we want," Funatti said holding tightly on to his arm. "You don't mind coming along with us?"

"Is this an arrest?" Hebster asked the larger Yost who now moved aside to let him pass. Yost was touching his holstered weapon with dancing fingertips.

The SIC man shrugged. "Why ask such questions?" he

33

countered. "Just come along and be sociable, kind of. People want to talk to you."

He allowed himself to be dragged through the lobby ornate with murals by radical painters and nodded appreciation at the doorman who, staring right through his captors, said enthusiastically, "Good *afternoon*, Mr. Hebster." He made himself fairly comfortable on the back seat of the dark-green SIC car, a late model Hebster Monowheel.

"Surprised to see you minus your bodyguard," Yost, who was driving, remarked over his shoulder.

"Oh, I gave them the day off."

"As soon as you were through with the Primeys? No," Funatti admitted, "we never did find out where you cached them. That's one big building you own, mister. And the UM Special Investigating Commission is notoriously understaffed."

"Not forgetting it's also notoriously underpaid," Yost broke in.

"I couldn't forget that if I tried," Funatti assured him. "You know, Mr. Hebster, I wouldn't have sent my bodyguard off if I'd been in your shoes. Right now there's something about five times as dangerous as Primeys after you. I mean Humanity Firsters."

"Vandermeer Dempsey's crackpots? Thanks, but I think I'll survive."

"That's all right. Just don't give any long odds on the proposition. Those people have been expanding fast and furious. *The Evening Humanitarian* alone has a tremendous circulation. And when you figure their weekly newspapers, their penny booklets and throwaway handbills, it adds up to an impressive amount of propaganda. Day after day they bang away editorially at the people who're making money off the Aliens and Primeys. Of course, they're really hitting at the UM, like always, but if an ordinary Firster met you on the street, he'd be as likely to cut your heart out as not. Not interested? Sorry. Well, maybe you'll like this. *The Evening Humanitarian* has a cute name for you."

Yost guffawed. "Tell him, Funatti."

The corporation president looked at the little man inquiringly.

"They call you," Funatti said with great deliberation, "they call you an interplanetary pimp!"

Emerging at last from the crosstown underpass, they sped up the very latest addition to the strangling city's facilities—the East Side Air-Floating Super-Duper High-

34

way, known familiarly as Dive-Bomber Drive. At the Forty-second Street offway, the busiest road exit in Manhattan, Yost failed to make a traffic signal. He cursed absent-mindedly and Hebster found himself nodding the involuntary passenger's agreement. They watched the elevator section dwindling downward as the cars that were to mount the highway spiraled up from the right. Between the two, there rose and fell the steady platforms of harbor traffic while, stacked like so many decks of cards, the pedestrian stages awaited their turn below.

"Look! Up there, straight ahead! See it?"

Hebster and Funatti followed Yost's long, waggling forefinger with their eyes. Two hundred feet north of the offway and almost a quarter of a mile straight up, a brown object hung in obvious fascination. Every once in a while a brilliant blue dot would enliven the heavy murk imprisoned in its bell-jar shape only to twirl around the side and be replaced by another.

"Eyes? You think they're eyes?" Funatti asked, rubbing his small dark fists against each other futilely. "I know what the scientists say—that every dot is equivalent to one person and the whole bottle is like a family or a city, maybe. But how do they know? It's a theory, a guess. *I* say they're eyes."

Yost hunched his great body half out of the open window and shaded his vision with his uniform cap against the sun. "Look at it," they heard him say, over his shoulder. A nasal twang, long-buried, came back into his voice as heaving emotion shook out its cultivated accents. "A-setting up there, a-staring and a-staring. So all-fired interested in how we get on and off a busy highway! Won't pay us no never mind when we try to talk to it, when we try to find out what it wants, where it comes from, who it is. Oh, no! It's too superior to talk to the likes of us! But it can watch us, hours on end, days without end, light and dark, winter and summer; it can watch us going about our business; and every time we dumb two-legged animals try to do something *we* find complicated, along comes a blasted 'dots-in-bottle' to watch and sneer and—"

"Hey there, man," Funatti leaned forward and tugged at his partner's green jerkin. "Easy! We're SIC, on business."

"All the same," Yost grunted wistfully, as he plopped back into his seat and pressed the power button, "I wish I had Daddy's little old M-1 Garand right now." They

35

bowled forward, smoothed into the next long elevator section and started to descend. "It would be worth the risk of getting *pinged*."

And this was a UM man, Hebster reflected with acute discomfort. Not only UM, at that, but member of a special group carefully screened for their lack of anti-Primey prejudice, sworn to enforce the reservation laws without discrimination and dedicated to the proposition that Man could somehow achieve equality with Alien.

Well, how much dirt-eating could people do? People without a business sense, that is. His father had hauled himself out of the pick-and-shovel brigade hand over hand and raised his only son to maneuver always for greater control, to search always for that extra percentage of profit.

But others seemed to have no such abiding interest, Algernon Hebster knew regretfully.

They found it impossible to live with achievements so abruptly made inconsequential by the Aliens. To know with certainty that the most brilliant strokes of which they were capable, the most intricate designs and clever careful workmanship, could be duplicated—and surpassed—in an instant's creation by the outsiders and was of interest to them only as a collector's item. The feeling of inferiority is horrible enough when imagined; but when it isn't feeling but *knowledge*, when it is inescapable and thoroughly demonstrable, covering every aspect of constructive activity, it becomes unbearable and maddening.

No wonder men went berserk under hours of unwinking Alien scrutiny—watching them as they marched in a colorfully uniformed lodge parade, or fished through a hole in the ice, as they painfully maneuvered a giant transcontinental jet to a noiseless landing or sat in sweating, serried rows chanting to a single, sweating man to "knock it out of the park and sew the whole thing up!" No wonder they seized rusty shotgun or gleaming rifle and sped shot after vindictive shot into a sky poisoned by the contemptuous curiosity of a brown, yellow or vermillion "bottle."

Not that it made very much difference. It did give a certain release to nerves backed into horrible psychic corners. But the Aliens didn't notice, and that was most important. The Aliens went right on watching, as if all this shooting and uproar, all these imprecations and weapon-wavings, were all part of the self-same absorbing show they had paid to witness and were determined to see

36

through if for nothing else than the occasional amusing fluff some member of the inexperienced cast might commit.

The Aliens weren't injured, and the Aliens didn't feel attacked. Bullets, shells, buckshot, arrows, pebbles from a slingshot—all Man's miscellany of anger passed through them like the patient and eternal rain coming in the opposite direction. Yet the Aliens had solidity somewhere in their strange bodies. One could judge that by the way they intercepted light and heat. And also—

Also by the occasional *ping*.

Every once in a while, someone would evidently have hurt an Alien slightly. Or more probably just annoyed it by some unknown concomitant of rifle-firing or javelin-throwing.

There would be the barest suspicion of a sound—as if a guitarist had lunged at a string with his fingertip and decided against it one motor impulse too late. And, after this delicate and hardly heard *ping*, quite unspectacularly, the rifleman would be weaponless. He would be standing there sighting stupidly up along his empty curled fingers, elbow cocked out and shoulder hunched in, like a large oafish child who had forgotten when to end the game. Neither his rifle nor a fragment of it would ever be found. And—gravely, curiously, intently—the Alien would go on watching.

The *ping* seemed to be aimed chiefly at weapons. Thus, occasionally, a 155 mm. howitzer was *pinged,* and also, occasionally, unexpectedly, it might be a muscular arm, curving back with another stone, that would disappear to the accompaniment of a tiny elfin note. And yet sometimes—could it be that the Alien, losing interest, had become careless in its irritation?—the entire man, murderously violent and shrieking, would *ping* and be no more.

It was not as if a counter-weapon were being used, but a thoroughly higher order of reply, such as a slap to an insect bite. Hebster, shivering, recalled the time he had seen a black tubular Alien swirl its amber dots over a new substreet excavation, seemingly entranced by the spectacle of men scrabbling at the earth beneath them.

A red-headed Sequoia of Irish labor had looked up from Manhattan's stubborn granite just long enough to shake the sweat from his eyelids. So doing, he had caught sight of the dot-pulsing observer and paused to snarl and lift his pneumatic drill, rattling it in noisy, if functionless, bravado at the sky. He had hardly been noticed by his mates, when the long, dark, speckled representative of a race beyond the stars turned end over end once and *pinged*.

The heavy drill remained upright for a moment, then dropped as if it had abruptly realized its master was gone. Gone? Almost, he had never been. So thorough had his disappearance been, so rapid, with so little flicker had he been snuffed out—harming and taking with him nothing else—that it had amounted to an act of gigantic and positive noncreation.

No, Hebster decided, making threatening gestures at the Aliens was suicidal. Worse, like everything else that had been tried to date, it was useless. On the other hand, wasn't the *Humanity First* approach a complete neurosis? What *could* you do?

He reached into his soul for an article of fundamental faith, found it. "I can make money," he quoted to himself. "That's what I'm good for. That's what I can always do."

As they spun to a stop before the dumpy, brown-brick armory that the SIC had appropriated for its own use, he had a shock. Across the street was a small cigar store, the only one on the block. Brand names which had decorated the plate-glass window in all the colors of the copyright had been supplanted recently by great gilt slogans. Familiar slogans they were by now—but this close to a UM office, the Special Investigating Commission itself?

At the top of the window, the proprietor announced his affiliation in two huge words that almost screamed their hatred across the street:

HUMANITY FIRST!

Underneath these, in the exact center of the window, was the large golden initial of the organization, the wedded letters HF arising out of the huge, symbolic safety razor.

And under that, in straggling script, the theme repeated, reworded and sloganized:

"Humanity first, last and all the time!"

The upper part of the door began to get nasty:

"Deport the Aliens! Send them back to wherever they came from!"

And the bottom of the door made the store-front's only concession to business:

"Shop here! Shop Humanitarian!"

"Humanitarian!" Funatti nodded bitterly beside Hebster.

38

"Ever see what's left of a Primey if a bunch of Firsters catch him without SIC protection? Just about enough to pick up with a blotter. I don't imagine you're too happy about boycott-shops like that?"

Hebster managed a chuckle as they walked past the saluting, green-uniformed guards. "There aren't very many Primey-inspired gadgets having to do with tobacco. And if there were, one *Shop Humanitarian* outfit isn't going to break me."

But it is, he told himself disconsolately. It is going to break me—if it means what it seems to. Organization membership is one thing and so is planetary patriotism, but business is something else.

Hebster's lips moved slowly, in half-remembered catechism: Whatever the proprietor believes in or does not believe in, he has to make a certain amount of money out of that place if he's going to keep the door free of bailiff stickers. He can't do it if he offends the greater part of his possible clientele.

Therefore, since he's still in business and, from all outward signs, doing quite well, it's obvious that he doesn't have to depend on across-the-street UM personnel. Therefore, there must be a fairly substantial trade to offset this among entirely transient customers who not only don't object to his Firstism but are willing to forego the interesting new gimmicks and lower prices in standard items that Primey technology is giving us.

Therefore, it is entirely possible—from this one extremely random but highly significant sample—that the newspapers I read have been lying and the socioeconomists I employ are incompetent. It is entirely possible that the buying public, the only aspect of the public in which I have the slightest interest, is beginning a shift in general viewpoint which will profoundly affect its purchasing orientation.

It is possible that the entire UM economy is now at the top of a long slide into Humanity First domination, the secure zone of fanatic blindness demarcated by men like Vandermeer Dempsey. The highly usurious, commercially speculative economy of Imperial Rome made a similar transition in the much slower historical pace of two millennia ago and became, in three brief centuries, a static unbusinesslike world in which banking was a sin and wealth which had not been inherited was gross and dishonorable.

Meanwhile, people may already have begun to judge

manufactured items on the basis of morality instead of usability, Hebster realized, as dim mental notes took their stolid place beside forming conclusions. He remembered a folderful of brilliant explanation Market Research had sent up last week dealing with unexpected consumer resistance to the new Evvakleen dishware. He had dismissed the pages of carefully developed thesis—to the effect that women were unconsciously associating the product's name with a certain Katherine Evvakios who had recently made the front page of every tabloid in the world by dint of some fast work with a breadknife on the throats of her five children and two lovers—with a yawning smile after examining its first brightly colored chart.

"Probably nothing more than normal housewifely suspicion of a radically new idea," he had muttered, "after washing dishes for years, to be told it's no longer necessary! She can't believe her Evvakleen dish is still the same after stripping the outermost film of molecules after a meal. Have to hit that educational angle a bit harder—maybe tie it in with the expendable molecules lost by the skin during a shower."

He'd penciled a few notes on the margin and flipped the whole problem onto the restless lap of Advertising and Promotion.

But then there had been the seasonal slump in furniture—about a month ahead of schedule. The surprising lack of interest in the Hebster Chubbichair, an item which should have revolutionized men's sitting habits.

Abruptly, he could remember almost a dozen unaccountable disturbances in the market recently, and all in consumer goods. That fits, he decided; any change in buying habits wouldn't be reflected in heavy industry for at least a year. The machine tools plants would feel it before the steel mills; the mills before the smelting and refining combines; and the banks and big investment houses would be the last of the dominoes to topple.

With its capital so thoroughly tied up in research and new production, his business wouldn't survive even a temporary shift of this type. Hebster Securities, Inc. could go like a speck of lint being blown off a coat collar.

Which is a long way to travel from a simple little cigar store. Funatti's jitters about growing Firstist sentiment are contagious! he thought.

If only Kleimbocher could crack the communication problem! If we could talk to the Aliens, find some sort of

40

*place for ourselves in their universe. The Firsters would
be left without a single political leg!*

Hebster realized they were in a large, untidy, map-
spattered office and that his escort was saluting a huge,
even more untidy man who waved their hands down impatiently and nodded them out of the door. He motioned
Hebster to a choice of seats. This consisted of several
long walnut-stained benches scattered about the room.

P. Braganza, said the desk nameplate with ornate Gothic
flow. P. Braganza had a long, twirlable and tremendously
thick mustache. Also, P. Braganza needed a haircut badly.
It was as if he and everything in the room had been carefully designed to give the maximum affront to Humanity
Firsters. Which, considering their crew-cut, closely-shaven,
"Cleanliness is next to Manliness" philosophy, meant that
there was a lot of gratuitous unpleasantness in this office
when a raid on a street demonstration filled it with jostling
fanatics, antiseptically clean and dressed with bare-bone
simplicity and neatness.

"So you're worrying about Firster effect on business?"
Hebster looked up, startled.

"No, I don't read your mind," Braganza laughed through
tobacco-stained teeth. He gestured at the window behind
his desk. "I saw you jump just the littlest bit when you
noticed that cigar store. And then you stared at it for two
full minutes. I knew what you were thinking about."

"Extremely perceptive of you," Hebster remarked dryly.

The SIC official shook his head in a violent negative.
"No, it wasn't. It wasn't a bit perceptive. I knew what you
were thinking about because I sit up here day after day staring at that cigar store and thinking exactly the same thing.
Braganza, I tell myself, that's the end of your job. That's
the end of scientific world government. Right there on that
cigar-store window."

He glowered at his completely littered desk top for a
moment. Hebster's instincts woke up—there was a sales
talk in the wind. He realized the man was engaged in the
unaccustomed exercise of looking for a conversational gam-
bit. He felt an itch of fear crawl up his intestines. Why
should the SIC, whose power was almost above law and
certainly above governments, be trying to dicker with him?

Considering his reputation for asking questions with
the snarling end of a rubber hose, Braganza was being
entirely too gentle, too talkative, too friendly. Hebster felt

41

like a trapped mouse into whose disconcerted ear a cat was beginning to pour complaints about the dog upstairs.

"Hebster, tell me something. What are your goals?"

"I beg your pardon?"

"What do you want out of life? What do you spend your days planning for, your nights dreaming about? Yost likes the girls and wants more of them. Funatti's a family man, five kids. He's happy in his work because his job's fairly secure, and there are all kinds of pensions and insurance policies to back up his life."

Braganza lowered his powerful head and began a slow, reluctant pacing in front of the desk.

"Now, I'm a little different. Not that I mind being a glorified cop. I appreciate the regularity with which the finance office pays my salary, of course; and there are very few women in this town who can say that I have received an offer of affection from them with outright scorn. But the one thing for which I would lay down my life is United Mankind. *Would* lay down my life? In terms of blood pressure and heart strain you might say I've already done it! Braganza, I tell myself, you're a lucky dope. You're working for the first world government in human history. Make it count."

He stopped and spread his arms in front of Hebster. His unbuttoned green jerkin came apart awkwardly and exposed the black slab of hair on his chest. "That's me. That's basically all there is to Braganza. Now if we're to talk sensibly I have to know as much about you. I ask— what are your goals?"

The President of Hebster Securities, Inc., wet his lips. "I am afraid I'm even less complicated."

"That's all right," the other man encouraged. "Put it any way you like."

"You might say that before everything else I am a businessman. I am interested chiefly in becoming a better businessman, which is to say a bigger one. In other words, I want to be richer than I am."

Braganza peered at him intently. "And that's all?"

"All? Haven't you ever heard it said that money isn't everything, but that what it isn't it can buy?"

"It can't buy me."

Hebster examined him coolly. "I don't know if you're a sufficiently desirable commodity. I buy what I need, only occasionally making an exception to please myself."

"I don't like you." Braganza's voice had become thick

42

and ugly. "I never liked your kind and there's no sense being polite. I might as well stop trying. I tell you straight out—I think your guts stink."

Hebster rose. "In that case, I believe I should thank you for—"

"Sit *down!* You were asked here for a reason. I don't see any point to it, but we'll go through the motions. Sit down."

Hebster sat. He wondered idly if Braganza received half the salary he paid Greta Seidenheim. Of course, Greta was talented in many different ways and performed several distinct and separately useful services. No, after tax and pension deductions, Braganza was probably fortunate to receive one third of Greta's salary.

He noticed that a newspaper was being proffered him. He took it. Braganza grunted, clumped back behind his desk and swung his swivel chair around to face the window.

It was a week-old copy of *The Evening Humanitarian*. The paper had lost the "voice-of-a-small-but-highly-articulate-minority" look, Hebster remembered from his last reading of it, and acquired the feel of publishing big business. Even if you cut in half the circulation claimed by the box in the upper left-hand corner, that still gave them three million paying readers.

In the upper right-hand corner, a red-bordered box exhorted the faithful to *"Read Humanitarian!"* A green streamer across the top of the first page announced that *"Making sense is human—to gibber, Prime!"*

But the important item was in the middle of the page. A cartoon.

Half-a-dozen Primeys wearing long, curved beards and insane, tongue-lolling grins, sat in a rickety wagon. They held reins attached to a group of straining and portly gentlemen dressed—somewhat simply—in high silk hats. The fattest and ugliest of these, the one in the lead, had a bit between his teeth. The bit was labeled *"crazy-money"* and the man, "Algernon Hebster."

Crushed and splintering under the wheels of the wagon were such varied items as a "Home Sweet Home" framed motto with a piece of wall attached, a clean-cut youngster in a Boy Scout uniform, a streamlined locomotive and a gorgeous young woman with a squalling infant under each arm.

The caption inquired starkly: "Lords of Creation—*Or Serfs?*"

43

"This paper seems to have developed into a fairly filthy scandal sheet," Hebster mused out loud. "I shouldn't be surprised if it makes money."

"I take it then," Braganza asked without turning around from his contemplation of the street, "that you haven't read it very regularly in recent months?"

"I am happy to say I have not."

"That was a mistake."

Hebster stared at the clumped locks of black hair. "Why?" he asked carefully.

"Because it *has* developed into a thoroughly filthy and extremely successful scandal sheet. You're its chief scandal." Braganza laughed. "You see these people look upon Primey dealing as more of a sin than a crime. And, according to that morality, you're close to Old Nick himself!"

Shutting his eyes for a moment, Hebster tried to understand people who imagined such a soul-satisfying and beautiful concept as profit to be a thing of dirt and crawling maggots. He sighed. "I've thought of Firstism as a religion myself."

That seemed to get the SIC man. He swung around excitedly and pointed with both forefingers. "I tell you that you are right! It crosses all boundaries—incompatible and warring creeds are absorbed into it. It is willful, witless denial of a highly painful fact—that there are intellects abroad in the universe which are superior to our own. And the denial grows in strength every day that we are unable to contact the Aliens. If, as seems obvious, there is no respectable place for humanity in this galactic civilization, why, say men like Vandermeer Dempsey, then let us preserve our self-conceit at the least. Let's stay close to and revel in the things that are undeniably human. In a few decades, the entire human race will have been sucked into this blinkered vacuum."

He rose and walked around the desk again. His voice had assumed a terribly earnest, tragically pleading quality. His eyes roved Hebster's face as if searching for a pinpoint of weakness, an especially thin spot in the frozen calm.

"Think of it," he asked Hebster. "Periodic slaughters of scientists and artists who, in the judgment of Dempsey, have pushed out too far from the conventional center of so-called humanness. An occasional *auto-da-fe* in honor of a merchant caught selling Primey goods—"

"I shouldn't like that," Hebster admitted, smiling. He

44

thought a moment. "I see the connection you're trying to establish with the cartoon in *The Evening Humanitarian*."

"Mister, I shouldn't have to. They want your head on the top of a long stick. They want it because you've become a symbol of dealing successfully for your own ends, with these stellar foreigners, or at least their human errand-boys and chambermaids. They figure that maybe they can put a stop to Primey-dealing generally if they put a bloody stop to you. And I tell you this—maybe they are right."

"What exactly do you propose?" Hebster asked in a low voice.

"That you come in with us. We'll make an honest man of you—officially. We want you directing our investigation; except that the goal will not be an extra buck but all-important interracial communication and eventual inter-stellar negotiation."

The president of Hebster Securities, Inc., gave himself a few minutes on that one. He wanted to work out a careful reply. And he wanted time—above all, he wanted time!

He was so close to a well-integrated and worldwide commercial empire! For ten years, he had been carefully fitting the component industrial kingdoms into place, establishing suzerainty in this production network and squeezing a little more control out of that economic satrapy. He had found delectable tidbits of power in the dissolution of his civilization, endless opportunities for wealth in the shards of his race's self-esteem. He required a bare twelve months now to consolidate and coordinate. And suddenly—with the open-mouthed shock of a Jim Fiske who had cornered gold on the Exchange only to have the United States Treasury defeat him by releasing enormous quantities from the Government's own hoard—suddenly, Hebster realized he wasn't going to have the time. He was too experienced a player not to sense that a new factor was coming into the game, something outside his tables of actuarial figures, his market graphs and cargo loading indices.

His mouth was clogged with the heavy nausea of unexpected defeat. He forced himself to answer:

"I'm flattered. Braganza, I *really* am flattered. I see that Dempsey has linked us—we stand or fall together. But—I've always been a loner. With whatever help I can buy, I take care of myself. I'm not interested in any goal but that extra buck. First and last, I'm a businessman."

"Oh, stop it!" The dark man took a turn up and down

45

the office angrily. "This a planet-wide emergency. There are times when you can't be a businessman."

"I deny that. I can't conceive of such a time."

Braganza snorted. "You can't be a businessman if you're strapped to a huge pile of blazing faggots. You can't be a businessman if people's minds are so thoroughly controlled that they'll stop eating at their leader's command. You can't be a businessman, my slavering, acquisitive friend, if demand is so well in hand that it ceases to exist."

"That's impossible!" Hebster had leaped to his feet. To his amazement, he heard his voice climb up the scale to hysteria. "There's *always* demand. Always! The trick is to find what new form it's taken and then fill it!"

"Sorry! I didn't mean to make fun of your religion."

Hebster drew a deep breath and sat down with infinite care. He could almost feel his red corpuscles simmering.

Take it easy, he warned himself, take it easy! This is a man who must be won, not antagonized. They're changing the rules of the market, Hebster, and you'll need every friend you can buy.

Money won't work with this fellow. But, there are *other* values—

"Listen to me, Braganza. We're up against the psycho-social consequences of an extremely advanced civilization hitting a comparatively barbarous one. Are you familiar with Professor Kleimbocher's Firewater Theory?"

"That the Alien's logic hits us mentally in the same way as whisky hit the North American Indian? And the Primeys, representing our finest minds, are the equivalent of those Indians who had the most sympathy with the white man's civilization? Yes. It's a strong analogy. Even carried to the Indians who, lying sodden with liquor in the streets of frontier towns, helped create the illusion of the treacherous, lazy, kill-you-for-a-drink aborigines while being so thoroughly despised by their tribesmen that they didn't dare go home for fear of having their throats cut. I've always felt—"

"The only part of that I want to talk about," Hebster interrupted, "is the firewater concept. Back in the Indian villages, an ever-increasing majority became convinced that firewater and gluttonous paleface civilization were synonymous, that they must rise and retake their land forcibly, killing in the process as many drunken renegades as they came across. This group can be equated with the Humanity Firsters. Then there was a minority who recog-

46

nized the white men's superiority in numbers and weapons, and desperately tried to find a way of coming to terms with his civilization—terms that would not include his booze. For them read the UM. Finally, there was my kind of Indian."

Braganza knitted voluminous eyebrows and hitched himself up to a corner of the desk. "Hah?" he inquired. "What kind of Indian were *you*, Hebster?"

"The kind who had enough sense to know that the paleface had not the slightest interest in saving him from slow and painful cultural anemia. The kind of Indian, also, whose instincts were sufficiently sound so that he was scared to death of innovations like firewater and wouldn't touch the stuff to save himself from snake bite. But the kind of Indian—"

"Yes? Go on!"

"The kind who was fascinated by the strange transparent container in which the firewater came! Think how covetous an Indian potter might be of the whisky bottle, something which was completely outside the capacity of his painfully acquired technology. Can't you see him hating, despising and terribly afraid of the smelly amber fluid, which toppled the most stalwart warriors, yet wistful to possess a bottle minus contents? That's about where I see myself, Braganza—the Indian whose greedy curiosity shines through the murk of hysterical clan politics and outsiders' contempt like a lambent flame. I want the new kind of container somehow separated from the firewater."

Unblinkingly, the great dark eyes stared at his face. A hand came up and smoothed each side of the arched mustachio with long, unknowing twirls. Minutes passed.

"Well. Hebster as our civilization's noble savage," the SIC man chuckled at last, "it almost feels right. But what does it mean in terms of the overall problem?"

"I've told you," Hebster said wearily, hitting the arm of the bench with his open hand, "that I haven't the slightest interest in the overall problem."

"And you only want the bottle. I heard you. But you're not a potter, Hebster—you haven't an elementary particle of craftsman's curiosity. All of that historical romance you spout—you don't care if your world drowns in its own agonized juice. You just want a profit."

"I never claimed an altruistic reason. I leave the general solution to men whose minds are good enough to juggle its complexities—like Kleimbocher."

"Think somebody like Kleimbocher could do it?"

"I'm almost certain he will. That was our mistake from the beginning—trying to break through with historians and psychologists. Either they've become limited by the study of human societies or—well, this is personal, but I've always felt that the science of the mind attracts chiefly those who've already experienced grave psychological difficulty. While they might achieve such an understanding of themselves in the course of their work as to become better adjusted eventually than individuals who had less problems to begin with, I'd still consider them too essentially unstable for such an intrinsically shocking experience as establishing *rapport* with an Alien. Their internal dynamics inevitably make Primeys of them."

Braganza sucked at a tooth and considered the wall behind Hebster. "And all this, you feel, wouldn't apply to Kleimbocher?"

"No, not a philology professor. He has no interest, no intellectual roots in personal and group instability. Kleimbocher's a comparative linguist—a technican, really—a specialist in basic communication. I've been out to the university and watched him work. His approach to the problem is entirely in terms of his subject—communicating with the Aliens instead of trying to understand them. There's been entirely too much intricate speculation about Alien consciousness, sexual attitudes and social organization, about stuff from which we will derive no tangible and immediate good. Kleimbocher's completely pragmatic."

"All right. I follow you. Only he went Prime this morning."

Hebster paused, a sentence dangling from his dropped jaw. "Professor Kleimbocher? *Rudolf* Kleimbocher?" he asked idiotically. "But he was so close . . . he almost had it . . . an elementary signal dictionary . . . he was about to—"

"He *did*. About nine forty-five. He'd been up all night with a Primey one of the psych professors had managed to hypnotize and gone home unusually optimistic. In the middle of his first class this morning, he interrupted himself in a lecture on medieval Cyrillic to . . . to gabble-honk. He sneezed and wheezed at the students for about ten minutes in the usual Primey pattern of initial irritation, then, abruptly giving them up as hopeless, worthless idiots, he levitated himself in that eerie way they almost always do at first. Banged his head against the ceiling and knocked

48

himself out. I don't know what it was, fright, excitement, respect for the old boy perhaps, but the students neglected to tie him up before going for help. By the time they'd come back with the campus SIC man, Kleimbocher had revived and dissolved one wall of the Graduate School to get out. Here's a snapshot of him about five hundred feet in the air, lying on his back with his arms crossed behind his head, skimming west at twenty miles an hour."

The executive studied the little paper rectangle with blinking eyes. "You radioed the air force to chase him, of course."

"What's the use? We've been through *that* enough times. He'd either increase his speed and generate a tornado, drop like a stone and get himself smeared all over the countryside or materialize stuff like wet coffee grounds and gold ingots inside the jets of the pursuing plane. Nobody's caught a Primey yet in the first flush of . . . whatever they do feel at first. And we might stand to lose anything from a fairly expensive hunk of aircraft, including pilot, to a couple of hundred acres of New Jersey topsoil."

Hebster groaned. "But the eighteen years of research that he represented!"

"Yeah. That's where we stand. Blind Alley umpteen hundred thousand or thereabouts. Whatever the figure is, it's awfully close to the end. If you can't crack the Alien on a straight linguistic basis, you can't crack the Alien at all, period, end of paragraph. Our most powerful weapons affect them like bubble pipes, and our finest minds are good for nothing better than to serve them in low, fawning idiocy. But the Primeys are all that's left. We might be able to talk sense to the Man if not the Master."

"Except that Primeys, by definition, don't talk sense."

Braganza nodded. "But since they were human—*ordinary* human—to start with, they represent a hope. We always knew we might some day have to fall back on our only real contact. That's why the Primey protective laws are so rigid; why the Primey reservation compounds surrounding Alien settlements are guarded by our military detachments. The lynch spirit has been evolving into the pogrom spirit as human resentment and discomfort have been growing. Humanity First is beginning to feel strong enough to challenge United Mankind. And honestly, Hebster, at this point neither of us know which would survive a real fight. But you're one of the few who have talked to Primeys, worked with them—"

"Just on business."

"Frankly, that much of a start is a thousand times further along than the best that we've been able to manage. It's so blasted ironical that the only people who've had any conversation at all with the Primeys aren't even slightly interested in the imminent collapse of civilization! Oh, well. The point is that in the present political picture, you sink with us. Recognizing this, my people are prepared to forget a great deal and document you back into respectability. How about it?"

"Funny," Hebster said thoughtfully. "It can't be knowledge that makes miracle-workers out of fairly sober scientists. They all start shooting lightnings at their families and water out of rocks far too early in Primacy to have had time to learn new techniques. It's as if by merely coming close enough to the Aliens to grovel, they immediately move into position to tap a series of cosmic laws more basic than cause and effect."

The SIC man's face slowly deepened into purple. "Well, are you coming in, or aren't you? Remember, Hebster, in these times, a man who insists on business as usual is a traitor to history."

"I think Kleimbocher *is* the end," Hebster nodded to himself. "Not much point in chasing Alien mentality if you're going to lose your best men on the way. I say let's forget all this nonsense of trying to live as equals in the same universe with Aliens. Let's concentrate on human problems and be grateful that they don't come into our major population centers and tell us to shove over."

The telephone rang. Braganza had dropped back into his swivel chair. He let the instrument squeeze out several piercing sonic bubbles while he clicked his strong square teeth and maintained a carefully-focused glare at his visitor. Finally, he picked it up, and gave it the verbal minima:

"Speaking. He is here. I'll tell him. 'Bye."

He brought his lips together, kept them pursed for a moment and then, abruptly, swung around to face the window.

"Your office, Hebster. Seems your wife and son are in town and have to see you on business. She the one you divorced ten years ago?"

Hebster nodded at his back and rose once more. "Probably wants her semiannual alimony dividend bonus. I'll have to go. Sonia never does office morale any good."

This meant trouble, he knew. "Wife-and-son" was ex-

50

ecutive code for something seriously wrong with Hebster Securities, Inc. He had not seen his wife since she had been satisfactorily maneuvered into giving him control of his son's education. As far as he was concerned, she had earned a substantial income for life by providing him with a well-mothered heir.

"Listen!" Braganza said sharply as Hebster reached the door. He still kept his eyes studiously on the street. "I tell you this: You don't want to come in with us. All right! You're a businessman first and a world citizen second. All right! But keep your nose clean, Hebster. If we catch you the slightest bit off base from now on, you'll get hit with everything. We'll not only pull the most spectacular trial this corrupt old planet has ever seen, but somewhere along the line, we'll throw you and your entire organization to the wolves. We'll see to it that *Humanity First* pulls the Hebster Tower down around your ears."

Hebster shook his head, licked his lips. *"Why?* What would that accomplish?"

"Hah! It would give a lot of us here the craziest kind of pleasure. But it would also relieve us temporarily of some of the mass pressure we've been feeling. There's always the chance that Dempsey would lose control of his hotter heads, that they'd go on a real gory rampage, make with the sound and the fury sufficiently to justify full deployment of troops. We could knock off Dempsey and all of the big-shot Firsters then, because John Q. United Mankind would have seen to his own vivid satisfaction and injury what a dangerous mob they are."

"This," Hebster commented bitterly, "is the idealistic, legalistic world government!"

Braganza's chair spun around to face Hebster and his fist came down on the desk top with all the crushing finality of a magisterial gavel. "No, it is not! It is the SIC, a plenipotentiary and highly practical bureau of the UM, especially created to organize a relationship between Alien and human. Furthermore, it's the SIC in a state of the greatest emergency when the reign of law and world government may topple at a demagogue's belch. Do you think" —his head snaked forward belligerently, his eyes slitted to thin lines of purest contempt—"that the career and fortune, even the life, let us say, of as openly selfish a slug as you, Hebster, would be placed above that of the representative body of two billion *socially* operating human beings?"

51

The SIC official thumped his sloppily buttoned chest. "Braganza, I tell myself now, you're lucky he's too hungry for his blasted profit to take you up on that offer. Think how much fun it's going to be to sink a hook into him when he makes a mistake at last! To drop him onto the back of *Humanity First* so that they'll run amuck and destroy themselves! Oh, get out, Hebster. I'm through with you."

He had made a mistake, Hebster reflected as he walked out of the armory and snapped his fingers at a gyrocab. The SIC was the most powerful single government agency in a Primey-infested world; offending them for a man in his position was equivalent to a cab driver delving into the more uncertain aspects of a traffic cop's ancestry in the policeman's popeyed presence.

But what could he do? Working with the SIC would mean working under Braganza—and since maturity, Algernon Hebster had been quietly careful to take orders from no man. It would mean giving up a business which, with a little more work and a little more time, might somehow still become the dominant combine on the planet. And worst of all, it would mean acquiring a social orientation to replace the calculating businessman's viewpoint which was the closest thing to a soul he had ever known.

The doorman of his building preceded him at a rapid pace down the side corridor that led to his private elevator and flourished aside for him to enter. The car stopped on the twenty-third floor. With a heart that had sunk so deep as to have practically foundered, Hebster picked his way along the wide-eyed clerical stares that lined the corridor. At the entrance to General Laboratory 23B, two tall men in the gray livery of his personal bodyguard moved apart to let him enter. If they had been recalled after having been told to take the day off, it meant that a full-dress emergency was being observed. He hoped that it had been declared in time to prevent any publicity leakage.

It had, Greta Seidenheim assured him. "I was down here applying the clamps five minutes after the fuss began. Floors twenty-one through twenty-five are closed off and all outside lines are being monitored. You can keep your employees an hour at most past five o'clock—which gives you a maximum of two hours and fourteen minutes."

He followed her green-tipped fingernail to the far corner of the lab where a body lay wrapped in murky rags. Theseus. Protruding from his back was the yellowed ivory handle of quite an old German S.S. dagger, 1942 edition. The silver swastika on the hilt had been replaced by an ornate symbol—an HF. Blood had soaked Theseus' long matted hair into an ugly red rug.

A dead Primey, Hebster thought, staring down hopelessly. In *his* building, in the laboratory to which the Primey had been spirited two or three jumps ahead of Yost and Funatti. This was capital offense material—if the courts ever got a chance to weigh it.

"Look at the dirty Primey-lover!" a slightly familiar voice jeered on his right. "He's scared! Make money out of *that,* Hebster!"

The corporation president strolled over to the thin man with the knobby, completely shaven head who was tied to an unused steampipe. The man's tie, which hung outside his laboratory smock, sported an unusual ornament about halfway down. It took Hebster several seconds to identify it. A miniature gold safety razor upon a black "3."

"He's a third echelon official of *Humanity First!*"

"He's also Charlie Verus of Hebster Laboratories," an extremely short man with a corrugated forehead told him. "My name is Margritt, Mr. Hebster, Dr. J. H. Margritt. I spoke to you on the communicator when the Primeys arrived."

Hebster shook his head determinedly. He waved back the other scientists who were milling around him self-consciously. "How long have third echelon officials, let alone ordinary members of *Humanity First,* been receiving salary checks in my laboratories?"

"I don't know." Margritt shrugged up at him. "Theoretically no Firsters can be Hebster employees. Personnel is supposed to be twice as efficient as the SIC when it comes to sifting background. They probably are. But what can they do when an employee joins *Humanity First* after he passed his probationary period? These proselytizing times you'd need a complete force of secret police to keep tabs on all the new converts!"

"When I spoke to you earlier in the day, Margritt, you indicated disapproval of Verus. Don't you think it was your duty to let me know I had a Firster official about to mix it up with Primeys?"

The little man beat a violent negative back and forth with his chin. "I'm paid to supervise research, Mr. Hebster, not to coordinate your labor relations nor vote your political ticket!"

53

Contempt—the contempt of the creative researcher for the businessman-entrepreneur who paid his salary and was now in serious trouble—flickered behind every word he spoke. Why, Hebster wondered irritably, did people so despise a man who made money? Even the Primeys back in his office, Yost and Funatti, Braganza, Margritt—who had worked in his laboratories for years. It was his only talent. Surely, as such, it was as valid as a pianist's?

"I've never liked Charles Verus," the lab chief went on, "but we never had reason to suspect him of Firstism! He must have hit the third echelon rank about a week ago, eh, Bert?"

"Yeah," Bert agreed from across the room. "The day he came in an hour late, broke every Florence flask in the place and told us all dreamily that one day we might be very proud to tell our grandchildren that we'd worked in the same lab with Charles Bolop Verus."

"Personally," Margritt commented, "I thought he might have just finished writing a book which proved that the Great Pyramid was nothing more than a prophecy in stone of our modern textile designs. Verus was that kind. But it probably was his little safety razor that tossed him up so high. I'd say he got the promotion as a sort of payment in advance for the job he finally did today."

Hebster ground his teeth at the carefully hairless captive who tried, unsuccessfully, to spit in his face; he hurried back to the door where his private secretary was talking to the bodyguard who had been on duty in the lab.

Beyond them, against the wall, stood Larry and S.S. Lusitania conversing in a low-voiced and anxious gabble-honk. They were evidently profoundly disturbed. S.S. Lusitania kept plucking tiny little elephants out of her rags which, kicking and trumpeting tinnily, burst like malformed bubbles as she dropped them on the floor. Larry scratched his tangled beard nervously as he talked, periodically waving a hand at the ceiling which was already studded with fifty or sixty replicas of the dagger buried in Theseus. Hebster couldn't help thinking anxiously of what could have happened to his building if the Primeys had been able to act human enough to defend themselves.

"Listen, Mr. Hebster," the bodyguard began, "I was told not to—"

"Save it," Hebster rapped out. "This wasn't your fault. Even Personnel isn't to blame. Me and my experts deserve to have our necks chopped for falling so far behind the

54

times. We can analyze any trend but the one which will make us superfluous. Greta! I want my roof helicopter ready to fly and my personal stratojet at LaGuardia alerted. Move, girl. And *you* . . . Williams is it?" he queried, leaning forward to read the bodyguard's name on his badge, "Williams, pack these two Primeys into my helicopter upstairs and stand by for a fast take-off."

He turned. "Everyone else!" he called. "You will be allowed to go home at six. You will be paid one hour's overtime. Thank you."

Charlie Verus started to sing as Hebster left the lab. By the time he reached the elevator, several of the clerks in the hallway had defiantly picked up the hymn. Hebster paused outside the elevator as he realized that fully one-fourth of the clerical personnel, male and female, were following Verus' cracked and mournful but terribly earnest tenor.

> *Mine eyes have seen the coming of*
> *the glory of the shorn:*
> *We will overturn the cesspool*
> *where the Primey slime is born,*
> *We'll be wearing cleanly garments*
> *as we face a human morn—*
> *The First are on the march!*
> *Glory, glory, hallelujah,*
> *Glory, glory, halleujah . . .*

If it was like this in Hebster Securities, he thought wryly as he came into his private office, how fast was *Humanity First* growing among the broad masses of people? Of course, many of those singing could be put down as sympathizers rather than converts, people who were suckers for choral groups and vigilante posses—but how much more momentum did an organization have to generate to acquire the name of political juggernaut?

The only encouraging aspect was the SIC's evident awareness of the danger and the unprecedented steps they were prepared to take as countermeasure.

Unfortunately, the unprecedented steps would take place upon Hebster.

He now had a little less than two hours, he reflected, to squirm out of the most serious single crime on the books of present World Law.

He lifted one of his telephones. "Ruth," he said. "I want

55

to speak to Vandermeer Dempsey. Get me through to him personally."

She did. A few moments later he heard the famous voice, as rich and slow and thick as molten gold. "Hello Hebster, Vandermeer Dempsey speaking." He paused as if to draw breath, then went on sonorously: *"Humanity—may it always be ahead, but, ahead or behind, Humanity!"* He chuckled. "Our newest. What we call our telephone toast. Like it?"

"Very much," Hebster told him respectfully, remembering that his former video quizmaster might shortly be church and state combined. "Er . . . Mr. Dempsey, I notice you have a new book out, and I was wondering—"

"Which one? 'Anthropolitics'?"

"That's it. A fine study! You have some very quotable lines in the chapter headed, 'Neither More Nor Less Human.' "

A raucous laugh that still managed to bubble heavily. "Young man, I have quotable lines in every chapter of every book! I maintain a writer's assembly line here at headquarters that is capable of producing up to fifty-five memorable epigrams on any subject upon ten minutes' notice. Not to mention their capacity for political metaphors and two-line jokes with sexy implications! But you wouldn't be calling me to discuss literature, however good a job of emotional engineering I have done in my little text. What is it about, Hebster? Go into your pitch."

"Well," the executive began, vaguely comforted by the Firster chieftain's cynical approach and slightly annoyed at the openness of his contempt, "I had a chat today with your friend and my friend, P. Braganza."

"I know."

"You do? How?"

Vandermeer Dempsey laughed again, the slow, good-natured chortle of a fat man squeezing the curves out of a rocking chair. "Spies, Hebster, *spies*. I have them everywhere practically. This kind of politics is twenty per cent espionage, twenty per cent organization and sixty per cent waiting for the right moment. My spies tell me everything you do."

"They didn't by any chance tell you what Braganza and I discussed?"

"Oh, they did, young man, they did!" Dempsey chuckled a carefree scale exercise. Hebster remembered his pictures: the head like a soft and enormous orange, gouged by

56

a brilliant smile. There was no hair anywhere on the head —all of it, down to the last eyelash and follicled wart was removed regularly through electrolysis. "According to my agents, Braganza made several strong representations on behalf of the Special Investigating Commission which you rightly spurned. Then, somewhat out of sorts, he announced that if you were henceforth detected in the nefarious enterprises which everyone knows have made you one of the wealthiest men on the face of the Earth, he would use you as bait for our anger. I must say I admire the whole ingenious scheme immensely."

"And you're not going to bite," Hebster suggested. Greta Seidenheim entered the office and made a circular gesture at the ceiling. He nodded.

"On the contrary, Hebster, we *are* going to bite. We're going to bite with just a shade more vehemence than we're expected to. We're going to swallow this provocation that the SIC is devising for us and go on to make a worldwide revolution out of it. We *will*, my boy."

Hebster rubbed his left hand back and forth across his lips. "Over my dead body!" He tried to chuckle himself and managed only to clear his throat. "You're right about the conversation with Braganza, and you may be right about how you'll do when it gets down to paving stones and baseball bats. But, if you'd like to have the whole thing a lot easier, there is a little deal I have in mind—"

"Sorry, Hebster my boy. No deals. Not on this. Don't you see we really *don't* want to have it easier? For the same reason, we pay our spies nothing despite the risks they run and the great growing wealth of *Humanity First*. We found that the spies we acquired through conviction worked harder and took many more chances than those forced into our arms by economic pressure. No, we desperately need *L'affaire Hebster* to inflame the populace. We need enough excitement running loose so that it transmits to the gendarmerie and the soldiery, so that conservative citizens who normally shake their heads at a parade will drop their bundles and join the rape and robbery. Enough such citizens and Terra goes *Humanity First*."

"Heads you win, tails I lose."

The liquid gold of Dempsey's laughter poured. "I see what you mean, Hebster. Either way, UM or HF, you wind up a smear-mark on the sands of time. You had your chance when we asked for contributions from public-spirited businessmen four years ago. Quite a few of your competitors were able to see the valid relationship between economics and politics. Woodran of the Underwood Investment Trust is a first echelon official today. Not a single one of *your* top executives wears a razor. But, even so, whatever happens to you will be mild compared to the Primeys."

"The Aliens may object to their body-servants being mauled."

"There are no Aliens!" Dempsey replied in a completely altered voice. He sounded as if he had stiffened too much to be able to move his lips.

"No Aliens? Is that your latest line? You don't mean that!"

"There are only Primeys—creatures who have resigned from human responsibility and are therefore able to do many seemingly miraculous things, which real humanity refuses to do because of the lack of dignity involved. But there are no Aliens. Aliens are a Primey myth."

Hebster grunted. "That is the ideal way of facing an unpleasant fact. Stare right through it."

"If you insist on talking about such illusions as Aliens," the rustling and angry voice cut in, "I'm afraid we can't continue the conversation. You're evidently going Prime, Hebster."

The line went dead.

Hebster scraped a finger inside the mouthpiece rim. "He believes his own stuff!" he said in an awed voice. "For all of the decadent urbanity, he has to have the same reassurance he gives his followers—the horrible, superior thing just isn't there!"

Greta Seidenheim was waiting at the door with his briefcase and both their coats. As he came away from the desk, he said, "I won't tell you not to come along, Greta, but—"

"Good," she said, swinging along behind him. "Think we'll make it to—wherever we're going?"

"Arizona. The first and largest Alien settlement. The place our friends with the funny names come from."

"What can you do there that you can't do here?"

"Frankly, Greta, I don't know. But it's a good idea to lose myself for a while. Then again, I want to get in the area where all this agony originates and take a close look; I'm an off-the-cuff businessman; I've done all of my important figuring on the spot."

There was bad news waiting for them outside the helicopter. "Mr. Hebster," the pilot told him tonelessly while cracking a dry stick of gum," the stratojet's been seized by the SIC. Are we still going? If we do it in this thing, it won't be very far or very fast."

"We're still going," Hebster said after a moment's hesitation.

They climbed in. The two Primeys sat on the floor in the rear, sneezing conversationally at each other. Williams waved respectfully at his boss. "Gentle as lambs," he said. "In fact, they made one. I had to throw it out."

The large pot-bellied craft climbed up its rope of air and started forward from the Hebster Building.

"There must have been a leak," Greta muttered angrily. "They heard about the dead Primey. Somewhere in the organization there's a leak that I haven't been able to find. The SIC heard about the dead Primey and now they're hunting us down. Real efficient, I am!"

Hebster smiled at her grimly. She *was* very efficient. So was Personnel and a dozen other subdivisions of the organization. So was Hebster himself. But these were functioning members of a normal business designed for stable times. *Political* spies! If Dempsey could have spies and saboteurs all over Hebster Securities, why couldn't Braganza? They'd catch him before he had even started running; they'd bring him back before he could find a loophole.

They'd bring him back for trial, perhaps, for what in all probability would be known to history as the Bloody Hebster Incident. The incident that had precipitated a world revolution.

"Mr. Hebster, they're getting restless," Williams called out. "Should I relax 'em out, kind of?"

Hebster sat up sharply, hopefully. "No," he said. "Leave them alone!" He watched the suddenly agitated Primeys very closely. This was the odd chance for which he'd brought them along! Years of haggling with Primeys had taught him a lot about them. They were good for other things than sheer gimmick-craft.

Two specks appeared on the windows. They enlarged sleekly into jets with SIC insignia.

"Pilot!" Hebster called, his eyes on Larry who was pulling painfully at his beard. "Get away from the controls! Fast! Did you hear me? That was an *order! Get away from those controls!*"

The man moved off reluctantly. He was barely in time. The control board dissolved into rattling purple shards behind him. The vanes of the gyro seemed to flower into indigo saxophones. Their ears rang with supersonic frequencies as they rose above the jets on a spout of unimaginable force.

Five seconds later they were in Arizona.

They piled out of their weird craft into a sage-cluttered desert.

"I don't ever want to know what my windmill was turned into," the pilot commented, "or what was used to push it along—but how did the Primey come to understand the cops were after us?"

"I don't think he knew that," Hebster explained, "but he was sensitive enough to know he was going home, and that somehow those jets were there to prevent it. And so he functioned, in terms of his interests in what was almost a human fashion. He protected himself!"

"Going home," Larry said. He'd been listening very closely to Hebster, dribbling from the righthand corner of his mouth as he listened. "Haemostat, hammersdarts, hump. Home is where the hate is. Hit is where the hump is. Home and locks the door."

S.S. Lusitania had started on one leg and favored them with her peculiar fleshy smile. "Hindsight," she suggested archly, "is no more than home site. Gabble, honk?"

Larry started after her, some three feet off the ground. He walked the air slowly and painfully as if the road he traveled were covered with numerous small boulders, all of them pitilessly sharp.

"Good-bye, people," Hebster said. "I'm off to see the wizard with my friends in greasy gray here. Remember, when the SIC catches up to your unusual vessel—stay close to it for that purpose, by the way—it might be wise to refer to me as someone who forced you into this. You can tell them I've gone into the wilderness looking for a solution, figuring that if I went Prime I'd still be better off than as a punching bag whose ownership is being hotly disputed by such characters as P. Braganza and Vandermeer Dempsey. I'll be back with my mind or on it."

He patted Greta's cheek on the wet spot; then he walked deftly away in pursuit of S.S. Lusitania and Larry. He glanced back once and smiled as he saw them looking curiously forlorn, especially Williams, the chunky young man who earned his living by guarding other people's bodies.

The Primeys followed a route of sorts, but it seemed to have been designed by someone bemused by the motions of an accordion. Again and again it doubled back upon itself,

60

folded across itself, went back a hundred yards and started all over again.

This was Primey country—Arizona, where the first and largest Alien settlement had been made. There were mighty few humans in this corner of the southwest any more—just the Aliens and their coolies.

"Larry," Hebster called as an uncomfortable thought struck him. "Larry! Do . . . do your masters know I'm coming?"

Missing his step as he looked up at Hebster's peremptory question, the Primey tripped and plunged to the ground. He rose, grimaced at Hebster and shook his head. "You are not a businessman," he said. "Here there can be no business. Here there can be only humorous what-you-might-call-worship. The movement to the universal, the inner nature— The realization, complete and eternal, of the partial and evanescent that alone enables . . . that alone enables—" His clawed fingers writhed into each other, as if he were desperately trying to pull a communicable meaning out of the palms. He shook his head with a slow rolling motion from side to side.

Hebster saw with a shock that the old man was crying. Then going Prime had yet another similarity to madness! It gave the human an understanding of something thoroughly beyond himself, a mental summit he was constitutionally incapable of mounting. It gave him a glimpse of some psychological promised land, then buried him, still yearning, in his own inadequacies. And it left him at last bereft of pride in his realizable accomplishments with a kind of myopic half-knowledge of where he wanted to go but with no means of getting there.

"When I first came," Larry was saying haltingly, his eyes squinting into Hebster's face, as if he knew what the businessman was thinking, "when first I tried to know . . . I mean the charts and textbooks I carried here, my statistics, my plotted curves were so useless. All playthings I found, disorganized, based on shadow-thought. And then, Hebster, to watch real-thought, real-control! You'll see the joy— You'll serve beside us, you will! Oh, the enormous lifting—"

His voice died into angry incoherencies as he bit into his fist. S.S. Lusitania came up, still hopping on one foot. "Larry," she suggested in a very soft voice, "gabble-honk Hebster away?"

He looked surprised, then nodded. The two Primeys

linked arms and clambered laboriously back up to the invisible road from which Larry had fallen. They stood facing him for a moment, looking like a weird, ragged, surrealistic version of Tweedledee and Tweedledum.

Then they disappeared and darkness fell around Hebster as if it had been knocked out of the jar. He felt under himself cautiously and sat down on the sand which retained all the heat of daytime Arizona.

Now!

Suppose an Alien came. Suppose an Alien asked him point-blank what it was that he wanted. That would be bad. Algernon Hebster, businessman extraordinary—slightly on the run, at the moment, of course—didn't know what he wanted; not with reference to Aliens.

He didn't want them to leave, because the Primey technology he had used in over a dozen industries was essentially an interpretation and adaptation of Alien methods. He didn't want them to stay because whatever was orderly in his world was dissolving under the acids of their omnipresent superiority.

He also knew that he personally did not want to go Prime.

What was left then? Business? Well, there was Braganza's question. What does a businessman do when demand is so well controlled that it can be said to have ceased to exist?

Or what does he do in a case like the present, when demand might be said to be nonexistent, since there was nothing the Aliens seemed to want of Man's puny hoard?

"He *finds* something they want," Hebster said out loud.

How? *How?* Well, the Indian still sold his decorative blankets to the paleface as a way of life, as a source of income. And he insisted on being paid in cash—not firewater. If *only,* Hebster thought, he could somehow contrive to meet an Alien—he'd find out soon enough what its needs were, what was basically desired.

And then as the retort-shaped, the tube-shaped, the bell-shaped bottles materialized all around him, he understood! They had been forming the insistent questions in his mind. And they weren't satisfied with the answers he had found thus far. They liked answers. They liked answers very much indeed. If he was interested, there was always a way—

A great dots-in-bottle brushed his cortex and he screamed. "No! I don't *want* to!" he explained desperately.

Ping! went the dots-in-bottle and Hebster grabbed at his

body. His continuing flesh reassured him. He felt very much like the girl in Greek mythology who had begged Zeus for the privilege of seeing him in the full regalia of his godhood. A few moments after her request had been granted, there had been nothing left of the inquisitive female but a fine feathery ash.

The bottles were swirling in and out of each other in a strange and intricate dance from which there radiated emotions vaguely akin to curiosity, yet partaking of amusement and rapture.

Why rapture? Hebster was positive he had caught that note, even allowing for the lack of similarity between mental patterns. He ran a hurried dragnet through his memory, caught a few corresponding items and dropped them after a brief, intensive examination. What was he trying to remember—what was his supremely efficient businessman's instinct trying to remind him of?

The dance became more complex, more rapid. A few bottles had passed under his feet and Hebster could see them, undulating and spinning some ten feet below the surface of the ground as if their presence had made the Earth a transparent as well as permeable medium. Completely unfamiliar with all matters Alien as he was, not knowing—not caring!—whether they danced as an expression of the counsel they were taking together, or as a matter of necessary social ritual, Hebster was able none the less to sense an approaching climax. Little crooked lines of green lightning began to erupt between the huge bottles. Something exploded near his left ear. He rubbed his face fearfully and moved away. The bottles followed, maintaining him in the imprisoning sphere of their frenzied movements.

Why *rapture?* Back in the city, the Aliens had had a terribly studious air about them as they hovered, almost motionless, above the works and lives of mankind. They were cold and careful scientists and showed not the slightest capacity for . . . for—

So he had something. At last he had something. But what do you do with an idea when you can't communicate it and can't act upon it yourself?

Ping!

The previous invitation was being repeated, more urgently. *Ping! Ping! Ping!*

"No!" he yelled and tried to stand. He found he couldn't. "I'm not . . . I don't want to go Prime!"

63

There was detached, almost divine laughter.

He felt that awful scrabbling inside his brain as if two or three entities were jostling each other within it. He shut his eyes hard and thought. He was close, he was very close. He had an idea, but he needed time to formulate it—a little while to figure out just exactly what the idea was and just exactly what to do with it!

Ping, ping, ping! Ping, ping, ping!

He had a headache. He felt as if his mind were being sucked out of his head. He tried to hold on to it. He couldn't.

All right, then. He relaxed abruptly, stopped trying to protect himself. But with his mind and his mouth, he yelled. For the first time in his life and with only a partially formed conception of whom he was addressing the desperate call to, Algernon Hebster screamed for help.

"I can do it!" he alternately screamed and thought. "Save money, save time, save whatever it is you want to save, whoever you are and whatever you call yourself—I can help you save! Help me, *help me*— *We* can do it— but *hurry*. Your problem can be solved— Economize. The balance-sheet— *Help*—"

The words and frantic thoughts spun in and out of each other like the contracting rings of Aliens all around him. He kept screaming, kept the focus on his mental images, while, unbearably, somewhere inside him, a gay and jocular force began to close a valve on his sanity.

Suddenly, he had absolutely no sensation. Suddenly, he knew dozens of things he had never dreamed he could know and had forgotten a thousand times as many. Suddenly, he felt that every nerve in his body was under control of his forefinger. Suddenly, he—

Ping, ping, ping! Ping! Ping! PING! PING! PING! PING!

". . . Like that," someone said.

"What, for example?" someone else asked.

"Well, they don't even lie normally. He's been sleeping like a human being. They twist and moan in their sleep, the Primeys do, for all the world like habitual old drunks. Speaking of moans, here comes our boy."

Hebster sat up on the army cot, rattling his head. The fears were leaving him, and, with the fears gone, he would no longer be hurt. Braganza, highly concerned and unhappy, was standing next to his bed with a man who was obviously a doctor. Hebster smiled at both of them, manfully resisting the temptation to drool out a string of nonsense syllables.

"Hi, fellas," he said. "Here I come, ungathering nuts in May."

"You don't mean to tell me you communicated" Braganza yelled. "You communicated and didn't go Prime!"

Hebster raised himself on an elbow and glanced out past the tent flap to where Greta Seidenheim stood on the other side of a port-armed guard. He waved his fist at her, and she nodded a wide-open smile back.

"Found me lying in the desert like a waif, did you?"

"*Found* you!" Braganza spat. "You were brought in by Primeys, man. First time in history they ever did that. We've been waiting for you to come to in the serene faith that once you did, everything would be all right."

The corporation president rubbed his forehead. "It will be, Braganza, it will be. Just Primeys, eh? No Aliens helping them?"

"*Aliens?*" Braganza swallowed. "What led you to believe— What gave you reason to hope that . . . that *Aliens* would help the Primeys bring you in?"

"Well, perhaps I shouldn't have used the word 'help.' But I did think there would be a few Aliens in the group that escorted my unconscious body back to you. Sort of an honor guard, Braganza. It would have been a real nice gesture, don't you think?"

The SIC man looked at the doctor who had been following the conversation with interest. "Mind stepping out for a minute?" he suggested.

He walked behind the man and dropped the tent flap into place. Then he came around to the foot of the army cot and pulled on his mustache vigorously. "Now, see here, Hebster, if you keep up this clowning, so help me I will slit your belly open and snap your intestines back in your face! *What happened!*"

"What happened?" Hebster laughed and stretched slowly, carefully, as if he were afraid of breaking the bones of his arm. "I don't think I'll ever be able to answer that question completely. And there's a section of my mind that's very glad that I won't. This much I remember clearly: I had an idea. I communicated it to the proper and interested party. We concluded—this party and I—a tentative agreement as agents, the exact terms of the agreement to be decided by our principals and its complete ratification to be contingent upon their acceptance. Fur-

65

thermore, we— All right, Braganza, all right! I'll tell it straight. Put down that folding chair. Remember, I've just been through a pretty unsettling experience!"

"Not any worse than the world is about to go through," the official growled. "While you've been out on your three-day vacation, Dempsey's been organizing a full-dress revolution every place at once. He's been very careful to limit it to parades and verbal fireworks so that we haven't been able to make with the riot squads, but it's pretty evident that he's ready to start using muscle. Tomorrow might be it; he's spouting on a world-wide video hookup and it's the opinion of the best experts we have available that his tag line will be the signal for action. Know what their slogan is? It concerns Verus who's been indicted for murder; they claim he'll be a martyr."

"And you were caught with your suspicions down. How many SIC men turned out to be Firsters?"

Braganza nodded. "Not too many, but more than we expected. More than we could afford. He'll do it, Dempsey will, unless you've hit the real thing. Look, Hebster," his heavy voice took on a pleading quality, "don't play with me any more. Don't hold my threats against me; there was no personal animosity in them, just a terrible, fearful worry over the world and its people and the government I was supposed to protect. If you still have a gripe against me, I, Braganza, give you leave to take it out of my hide as soon as we clear this mess up. But let me know where we stand first. A lot of lives and a lot of history depend on what you did out there in that patch of desert."

Hebster told him. He began with the extraterrestrial *Walpurgis Nacht.* "Watching the Aliens slipping in and out of each other in that cock-eyed and complicated rhythm, it struck me how different they were from the thoughtful dots-in-bottles hovering over our busy places, how different all creatures are in their home environments—and how hard it is to get to know them on the basis of their company manners. And then I realized that this place wasn't their home."

"Of course. Did you find out which part of the galaxy they come from?"

"That's not what I mean. Simply because we have marked this area off—and others like it in the Gobi, in the Sahara, in Central Australia—as a reservation for those of our kind whose minds have crumbled under the

66

clear, conscious and certain knowledge of inferiority, we cannot assume that the Aliens around whose settlements they have congregated have necessarily settled themselves."

"Huh?" Braganza shook his head rapidly and batted his eyes.

"In other words we had made an assumption on the basis of the Aliens' very evident superiority to ourselves. But that assumption—and therefore that superiority—was in our own terms of what is superior and inferior, and not the Aliens'. And it especially might not apply to those Aliens on . . . the reservation."

The SIC man took a rapid walk around the tent. He beat a great fist into an open sweaty palm. "I'm beginning to, just beginning to—"

"That's what I was doing at that point, just beginning to. Assumptions that don't stand up under the structure they're supposed to support have caused the ruin of more close-thinking businessmen than I would like to face across any conference table. The four brokers, for example, who, after the market crash of 1929—"

"All right," Braganza broke in hurriedly, taking a chair near the cot. "Where did you go from there?"

"I still couldn't be certain of anything; all I had to go on were a few random thoughts inspired by extra-substantial adrenaline secretions and, of course, the strong feeling that these particular Aliens weren't acting the way I had become accustomed to expect Aliens to act. They reminded me of something, of somebody. I was positive that once I got that memory tagged, I'd have most of the problem solved. And I was right."

"How were you right? What was the memory?"

"Well, I hit it backwards, kind of. I went back to Professor Kleimbocher's analogy about the paleface inflicting firewater on the Indian. I've always felt that somewhere in that analogy was the solution. And suddenly, thinking of Professor Kleimbocher and watching those powerful creatures writhing their way in and around each other, suddenly I knew what was wrong. Not the analogy, but our way of using it. We'd picked it up by the hammer head instead of the handle. The paleface gave firewater to the Indian, all right—but he got something in return."

"What?"

"Tobacco. Now there's nothing very much wrong with tobacco if it isn't misused, but the first white men to smoke probably went as far overboard as the first Indians to drink. And both booze and tobacco have this in common—they make your awfully sick if you use too much for your initial experiment. See, Braganza? These Aliens out here in the desert reservation are *sick*. They have hit something in our culture that is as psychologically indigestible to them as . . . well, whatever they have that sticks in our mental gullet and causes ulcers among us. They've been put into a kind of isolation in our desert areas until the problem can be licked."

"Something that's as indigestible psychologically— What could it be, Hebster?"

The businessman shrugged irritably. "I don't know. And I don't want to know. Perhaps it's just that they can't let go of a problem until they've solved it—and they can't solve the problems of mankind's activity because of mankind's inherent and basic differences. Simply because we can't understand them, we had no right to assume that they could and did understand us."

"That wasn't all, Hebster. As the comedians put it—everything we can do, they can do better."

"Then why did they keep sending Primeys in to ask for those weird gadgets and impossible gimcracks?"

"They could duplicate anything we made."

"Well, maybe that is it," Hebster suggested. "They could duplicate it, but could they design it? They show every sign of being a race of creatures who never had to make very much for themselves; perhaps they evolved fairly early into animals with direct control over matter, thus never having had to go through the various stages of artifact design. This, in our terms, is a tremendous advantage; but it inevitably would have concurrent disadvantages. Among other things, it would mean a minimum of art forms and a lack of basic engineering knowledge of the artifact itself if not of the directly activated and altered material. The fact is I was right, as I found out later.

"For example. Music is not a function of theoretical harmonics, of complete scores in the head of a conductor or composer—these come later, much later. Music is first and foremost a function of the particular instrument, the reed pipe, the skin drum, the human throat—it is a function of tangibles which a race operating upon electrons, positrons and mesons would never encounter in the course of its construction. As soon as I had that, I had the other flaw in the analogy—the assumption itself."

"You mean the assumption that we are necessarily inferior to the Aliens?"

"Right, Braganza. They can do a lot that we can't do, but vice very much indeed versa. How many special racial talents we possess that they don't is a matter of pure conjecture—and may continue to be for a good long time. Let the theoretical boys worry that one a century from now, just so they stay away from it at present."

Braganza fingered a button on his green jerkin and stared over Hebster's head. "No more scientific investigation of them, eh?"

"Well, we can't right now and we have to face that mildly unpleasant situation. The consolation is that they have to do the same. Don't you see? It's not a basic inadequacy. We don't have enough facts and can't get enough at the moment through normal channels of scientific observation because of the implicit psychological dangers to both races. Science, my forward-looking friend, is a complex of interlocking theories, *all derived from observation.*

"Remember, long before you had any science of navigation you had coast-hugging and river-hopping traders who knew how the various currents affected their leaky little vessels, who had learned things about the relative dependability of the moon and the stars—without any interest at all in integrating these scraps of knowledge into broader theories. Not until you have a sufficiently large body of these scraps, and are able to distinguish the preconceptions from the actual observations, can you proceed to organize a science of navigation without running the grave risk of drowning while you conduct your definitive experiments.

"A trader isn't interested in theories. He's interested only in selling something that glitters for something that glitters even more. In the process, painlessly and imperceptibly, he picks up bits of knowledge which gradually reduce the area of unfamiliarity. Until one day there are enough bits of knowledge on which to base a sort of preliminary understanding, a working hypothesis. And then, some Kleimbocher of the future, operating in an area no longer subject to the sudden and unexplainable mental disaster, can construct meticulous and exact laws out of the more obviously valid hypotheses."

"I might have known it would be something like this, if you came back with it, Hebster! So their theorists and our theorists had better move out and the traders move in. Only how do we contact their traders—if they have any such animals?"

The corporation president sprang out of bed and began dressing. "They have them. Not a Board of Director type perhaps—but a business-minded Alien. As soon as I realized that the dots-in-bottles were acting, relative to their balanced scientific colleagues, very like our own high IQ Primeys, I knew I needed help. I needed someone I could tell about it, someone on their side who had as great a stake in an operating solution as I did. There had to be an Alien in the picture somewhere who was concerned with profit and loss statements, with how much of a return you get out of a given investment of time, personnel, material and energy. I figured with him I could talk—*business*. The simple approach: What have you got that we want and how little of what we have will you take for it. No attempts to understand completely incompatible philosophies. There had to be that kind of character somewhere in the expedition. So I shut my eyes and let out what I fondly hoped was a telepathic *yip* channeled to him. I was successful.

"Of course, I might not have been successful if he hadn't been searching desperately for just that sort of *yip*. He came buzzing up in a rousing United States Cavalry-routs-the-redskins type of rescue, stuffed my dripping psyche back into my subconscious and hauled me up into some sort of never-never-ship. I've been in this interstellar version of Mohammed's coffin, suspended between Heaven and Earth, for three days, while he alternately bargained with me and consulted the home office about developments.

"We dickered the way I do with Primeys—by running down a list of what each of us could offer and comparing it with what we wanted; each of us trying to get a little more than we gave to the other guy, in our own terms, of course. Buying and selling are intrinsically simple processes; I don't imagine our discussions were very much different from those between a couple of Phoenician sailors and the blue-painted Celtic inhabitants of early Britain."

"And this . . . this business-Alien never suggested the possibility of taking what they wanted—"

"By force? No, Braganza, not once. Might be they're too civilized for such shenanigans. Personally, I think the big reason is that they don't have any idea of what it is they do want from us. We represent a fantastic enigma to them—a species which uses matter to alter matter, pro-

70

ducing objects which, while intended for similar functions, differ enormously from each other. You might say that we ask the question *'how?'* about their activities; and they want to know the *'why?'* about ours. Their investigators have compulsions even greater than ours. As I understand it, the intelligent races they've encountered up to this point are all comprehensible to them since they derive from parallel evolutionary paths. Every time one of their researchers gets close to the answer of why we wear various colored clothes even in climates where clothing is unnecessary, he slips over the edges and splashes.

"Of course, that's why this opposite number of mine was so worried. I don't know his exact status—he may be anything from the bookkeeper to the business-manager of the expedition—but it's his bottle-neck if the outfit continues to be uneconomic. And I gathered that not only has his occupation kind of barred him from doing the investigation his unstable pals were limping back from into the asylums he's constructed here in the deserts, but those of them who've managed to retain their sanity constantly exhibit a healthy contempt for him. They feel, you see, that their function is that of the expedition. He's strictly supercargo. Do you think it bothers them one bit," Hebster snorted, "that he has a report to prepare, to show how his expedition stood up in terms of a balance sheet—"

"Well, you did manage to communicate on that point, at least," Braganza grinned. "Maybe traders using the simple, earnestly chiseling approach will be the answer. You've certainly supplied us with more basic data already than years of heavily subsidized research. Hebster, I want you to go on the air with this story you told me and show a couple of Primey Aliens to the video public."

"Uh-uh. You tell 'em. You can use the prestige. I'll think a message to my Alien buddy along the private channel he's keeping open for me, and he'll send you a couple of human-happy dots-in-bottles for the telecast. I've got to whip back to New York and get my entire outfit to work on a really encyclopedic job."

"Encyclopedic?"

The executive pulled his belt tight and reached for a tie. "Well, what else would you call the first edition of the Hebster Interstellar Catalogue of all Human Activity and Available Artifacts, prices available upon request with the understanding that they are subject to change without notice?"

71

1953

THE 1954 WORLD Science Fiction Convention was held in San Francisco. The 600 members of the convention would have voted on recipients of Hugos for 1953, but nobody bothered to set up a second batch of the awards. It's a pity, for 1953 was another fine year for science fiction.

Further, it was a pivotal year in the history of science fiction. The specialized magazines reached their all-time peak, with over 43 different titles appearing. Avon, which had been issuing two series of reprint magazines, one of science fiction and one of fantasy, dropped them in favor of a single, excellent *Science Fiction and Fantasy Reader* comprising new stories by authors of the caliber of Arthur C. Clarke, John Christopher, Milton Lesser, and Jack Vance.

Galaxy, under the tutelage of Horace Gold, added a companion magazine of fantasy, *Beyond*. This duplicated the former *Astounding/Unknown* pairing of a decade earlier, and the quality of material in *Beyond* was exemplary. Early issues featured stories by something very close to an all-star roster of authors: Sturgeon, Knight, the veteran T. L. Sherred, Frank M. Robinson, Jerome Bixby, Richard Matheson, Robert Bloch, Philip K. Dick, John Wyndham, Margaret St. Clair, Zenna Henderson, Algis Budrys, and Isaac Asimov.

A new magazine called *Fantastic Universe* appeared at the then-appalling price of 50¢ per copy—in return for which the customer received a huge 196-page package. The magazine specialized in short to very short stories, so a single issue might contain as many as 14 stories (at an average price of just over 3½¢ each). And the authors! The first issue alone had Chandler, Long, Price, Derleth, Clarke, Dick, Bradbury, Lesser, and Russell!

That's just a sampling, and that's the way it was in 1953. Even Hugo Gernsback, the Founding Father himself, returned from the wilds of *Radio News* and *Sexology* to publish *Science Fiction Plus* and feature an astonishing mélange of old-timers and new talents: Farmer, Eando Binder, Raymond Z. Gallun, Clifford Simak, Murray Leinster, Jack Williamson, James H. Schmitz, and—the very first story ever sold by a young woman named Anne McCaffrey.

But the pulp field crashed in '53, and from the wreckage there emerged the fast-growing book specialists, Ballantine and Ace. Science fiction would never be the same.

Outstanding novels of 1953 included Hal Clement's classic *Mission of Gravity*, serialized in *Astounding;* Asimov's *The Caves of Steel*, serialized in *Galaxy;* the first segment of James Blish's *A Case of Conscience* in one issue of *If;* Geoff St. Reynard's *The Fist of Shiva* in the humble *Imagination;* Poul Anderson's *Three Hearts and Three Lions*, serialized in *Fantasy and Science Fiction;* and Lester del Rey's *Police Your Planet* (published under the byline Erik van Lhin), serialized in *Science Fiction Adventures.* Ballantine issued Clarke's powerful *Childhood's End* and Bradbury's *Fahrenheit 451*, the latter expanded from "The Fireman" in *Galaxy*.

Some year!

The shorter lengths were just as wealthy. The slimmest sampling included "The Old Die Rich" by Gold, "Tangle Hold" by F. L. Wallace, "The Big Jump" by Leigh Brackett, "Earthman Come Home" by Blish, "Death of a Sensitive" by Harry Bates, "Home is the Hunter" by Kuttner and Moore, "Saucer of Loneliness" and "The Silken-Swift" both by Sturgeon, "Time Bum" by Kornbluth, "Hall of Mirrors" by Fredric Brown, and "The Big Holiday" by Fritz Leiber.

My candidate for the best (and most overlooked) story of 1953 is "Four in One" by Damon Knight, from the February issue of *Galaxy*. Philip K. Dick has praised this story as one of the most important and original to appear in the past 30 years. It has not been ignored entirely by anthologists, but as far as I can find, it has been out of print for almost ten years, and it ought not to be out of print.

(Of course, the exigencies of publishing being what they are, it will appear in four anthologies, a single-author collection, and a new magazine version, all next week. Well, all the better if it does!)

Damon Knight himself was, and is, a science fiction phenomenon. He first came to light as a fanzine publisher, circa 1940. A fan group of the era was making loud noises in New York. Not that there's anything unusual in that, except that *this* fan group, styled the Futurians, consisted of Fred Pohl, Cyril Kornbluth, Judith Merril, Isaac Asimov, Donald Wollheim, Richard Wilson, and others of similar talent.

Knight traveled from his home in the Pacific Northwest to join the others and become the Littlest Futurian. He broke into the magazines as both an illustrator and author, later becoming one of the field's *première* editors, critics, translators, and teachers, as well. His half-dozen or so novels have met with rather lukewarm receptions, but his many short stories—just about 100 of them the last time I looked—are marked by a trenchancy, a power, and a wit achieved by few other writers in the science fiction field—or out of it.

Four in One

DAMON KNIGHT

I

GEORGE MEISTER HAD once seen the nervous system of a man—a display specimen achieved by coating the smaller fibers until they were coarse enough to be seen, then dissolving all the unwanted tissue and replacing it by clear plastic. A marvelous job; that fellow on Torkas III had done it. What was his name . . . ? At any rate, having seen the specimen, Meister knew what he himself must look like at the present moment.

Of course, there were distortions. For example, he was almost certain that the distance between his visual center and his eyes was now at least thirty centimeters. Also, no doubt, the system as a whole was curled up and spread out rather oddly, since the musculature it had originally controlled was gone; and he had noticed certain other changes which might or might not be reflected by gross structural differences. The fact remained that he—all that he could still call *himself*—was nothing more than a brain, a pair of eyes, a spinal cord, and a spray of neurons.

George closed his eyes for a second. It was a feat he had learned to do only recently and he was proud of it. That first long period, when he had had no control whatever, had been very bad. He had decided later that the paralysis had been due to the lingering effects of some anesthetic—the agent, whatever it was, that had kept him unconscious while his body was—

Well.

Either that or the neuron branches had simply not yet knitted firmly in their new positions. Perhaps he could verify one or the other supposition at some future time. But at first, when he had only been able to see and not to move, knowing nothing beyond the moment when he had fallen face-first into that mottled green and brown puddle of gelatin . . . that had been upsetting.

He wondered how the others were taking it. There were others, he knew, because occasionally he would feel a sudden acute pain down where his legs used to be, and at the same instant the motion of the landscape would stop with a jerk. That could only be some other brain, trapped like his, trying to move their common body in another direction.

Usually the pain stopped immediately, and George could go on sending messages down to the nerve-endings which had formerly belonged to his fingers and toes, and the gelatinous body would go on creeping slowly forward. When the pains continued, there was nothing to do but stop moving until the other brain quit—in which case George would feel like an unwilling passenger in a very slow vehicle—or try to alter his own movements to coincide, or at least produce a vector with the other brain's.

He wondered who else had fallen in. Vivian Bellis? Major Gumbs? Miss McCarty? All three of them? There ought to be some way of finding out.

He tried looking down once more and was rewarded with a blurry view of a long, narrow strip of mottled green and brown, moving sluggishly along the dry stream bed they had been crossing for the last hour or more. Twigs and shreds of dry vegetable matter were stuck to the dusty, translucent surface.

He was improving; the last time, he had only been able to see the thinnest possible edge of his new body.

When he looked up again, the far side of the stream bed was perceptibly closer. There was a cluster of stiff-looking, dark-brown vegetable shoots just beyond, on the rocky shoulder; George was aiming slightly to the left of it. It had been a plant very much like that one that he'd been reaching for when he lost his balance and got himself into this situation.

76

He might as well have a good look at it, anyhow.

The plant would probably turn out to be of little interest. It would be out of all reason to expect every new lifeform to be a startling novelty; and George Meister was convinced that he had already stumbled into the most interesting organism on this planet. Something-or-other *meisterii,* he thought, named after him, of course. He had not settled on a generic term—he would have to learn more about it before he decided—but *meisterii* certainly. It was his discovery and nobody could take it away from him. Or, unhappily, him away from it. Ah, well!

It was a really lovely organism, though. Primitive—less structure of its own than a jellyfish, and only on a planet with light surface gravity like this one could it ever have hauled itself up out of the sea. No brain, no nervous system at all, apparently. But it had the perfect survival mechanism. It simply let its rivals develop highly organized nervous tissue, sat in one place (looking exactly like a deposit of leaves and other clutter) until one of them fell into it, and then took all the benefit.

It wasn't parasitism, either. It was a true symbiosis, on a higher level than any other planet, so far as George knew, had ever developed. The captive brain was nourished by the captor; wherefore it served the captive's interest to move the captor toward food and away from danger. *You steer me, I feed you.* It was fair.

They were close to the plant, almost touching it. George inspected it. As he had thought, it was a common grass type.

Now his body was tilting itself up a ridge he knew to be low, although from his eye-level it looked tremendous. He climbed it laboriously and found himself looking down into still another gully. This could probably go on indefinitely. The question was—did he have any choice?

He looked at the shadows cast by the low-hanging sun. He was heading approximately northwest, directly away from the encampment. He was only a few hundred meters away; even at a crawl, he could make the distance easily enough . . . if he turned back.

He felt uneasy at the thought and didn't know why. Then it struck him that his appearance was not obviously that of a human being in distress. The chances were that he looked like a monster which had eaten and partially digested one or more people.

77

If he crawled into camp in his present condition, it was a certainty that he would be shot at before any questions were asked, and only a minor possibility that narcotic gas would be used instead of a machine rifle.

No, he decided, he was on the right course. The idea was to get away from camp, so that he wouldn't be found by the relief party which was probably searching for him now. Get away, bury himself in the forest, and study his new body: find out how it worked and what he could do with it, whether there actually were others in it with him, and if so, whether there was any way of communicating with them.

It would take a long time, he realized, but he could do it.

Limply, like a puddle of mush oozing over the edge of a tablecloth, George started down into the gully.

Briefly, the circumstances leading up to George's fall into the Something-or-other *meisterii* were as follows:

Until as late as the mid-twenty-first century, a game invented by the ancient Japanese was still played by millions in the eastern hemisphere of earth. The game was called *go*. Although its rules were almost childishly simple, its strategy included more permutations and was more difficult to master than chess.

Go was played at the height of development—just before the geological catastrophe that wiped out most of its devotees—on a board with nine hundred shallow holes, using small pill-shaped counters. At each turn, one of the two players placed a counter on the board, wherever he chose, the object being to capture as much territory as possible by surrounding it completely.

There were no other rules; and yet it had taken the Japanese almost a thousand years to work up to that thirty-by-thirty board, adding perhaps one rank and file per century. A hundred years was not too long to explore all the possibilities of that additional rank and file.

At the time George Meister fell into the gelatinous green-and-brown monster, toward the end of the twenty-third century A.D., a kind of *go* was being played in a three-dimensional field which contained more than ten billion positions. The Galaxy was the board, the positions were star-systems, men were the counters. The loser's penalty was annihilation.

The Galaxy was in the process of being colonized by

two opposing federations, both with the highest aims and principles. In the early stages of this conflict, planets had been raided, bombs dropped, and a few battles had even been fought by fleets of spaceships. Later, that haphazard sort of warfare became impossible. Robot fighters, carrying enough armament to blow each other into dust, were produced by the trillion. In the space around the outer stars of a cluster belonging to one side or the other, they swarmed like minnows.

Within such a screen, planets were safe from attack and from any interference with their commerce . . . unless the enemy succeeded in colonizing enough of the surrounding star-systems to set up and maintain a second screen outside the first. It was *go,* played for desperate stakes and under impossible conditions.

Everyone was in a hurry; everyone's ancestors for seven generations had been in a hurry. You got your education in a speeded-up, capsulized form. You mated early and bred frantically. And if you were assigned to an advance ecological team, as George was, you had to work without proper preparation.

The sensible, the obvious thing to do in opening up a new planet with unknown life-forms would have been to begin with at least ten years of immunological study conducted from the inside of a sealed station. After the worst bacteria and viruses had been conquered, you might proceed to a little cautious field work and exploration. Finally —total elapsed time fifty years, say—the colonists would be shipped in.

There simply wasn't that much time.

Five hours after the landing, Meister's team had unloaded fabricators and set up barracks enough to house its 2,628 members.

An hour after that, Meister, Gumbs, Bellis and McCarty had started out across the level cinder and ash left by the transport's tail jets to the nearest living vegetation, six hundred meters away. They were to trace a spiral path outward from the camp site to a distance of a thousand meters, and then return with their specimens—providing nothing too large and hungry to be stopped by machine rifle had previously eaten them.

Meister, the biologist, was so hung down with collecting boxes that his slender torso was totally invisible. Major Gumbs had a survival kit, binoculars and a machine rifle.

Vivian Bellis, who knew exactly as much mineralogy as had been contained in the three-month course prescribed for her rating, and no more, carried a light rifle, a hammer and a specimen sack. Miss McCarty—no one knew her first name—had no scientific function. She was the group's Loyalty Monitor. She wore two squat pistols and a bandolier bristling with cartridges. Her only job was to blow the cranium off any team member caught using an unauthorized communicator, or in any other way behaving oddly.

All of them were heavily gloved and booted, and their heads were covered by globular helmets, sealed to their tunic collars. They breathed through filtered respirators, so finely meshed that—in theory—nothing larger than an oxygen molecule could get through.

On their second circuit of the camp, they had struck a low ridge and a series of short, steep gullies, most of them choked with the dusty-brown stalks of dead vegetation. As they started down into one of these, George, who was third in line—Gumbs leading, then Bellis, and McCarty behind George—stepped out onto a protruding slab of stone to examine a cluster of plant stalks rooted on its far side.

His weight was only a little more than twenty kilograms on this planet, and the slab looked as if it were firmly cemented into the wall of the gully. Just the same, he felt it shift under him as soon as his weight was fully on it. He found himself falling, shouted, and caught a flashing glimpse of Gumbs and Bellis, standing as if caught by a high-speed camera. He heard a rattling of stones as he went by. Then he saw what looked like a shabby blanket of leaves and dirt floating toward him, and he remembered thinking, *It looks like a soft landing, anyhow. . . .*

That was all, until he woke up feeling as if he had been prematurely buried, with no part of him alive but his eyes.

Much later, his frantic efforts to move had resulted in the first fractional success. From then on, his field of vision had advanced fairly steadily, perhaps a meter every fifty minutes, not counting the times when someone else's efforts had interfered with his own.

His conviction that nothing remained of the old George Meister except a nervous system was not supported by observation, but the evidence was regrettably strong. To begin with, the anesthesia of the first hours had worn off, but his body was not reporting the position of the torso, head and four limbs he had formerly owned. He had, instead, a vague impression of being flattened and spread out over an enormous area. When he tried to move his fingers and toes, the response he got was so multiplied that he felt like a centipede.

He had no sense of cramped muscles, such as would normally be expected after a long period of paralysis—*and he was not breathing.* Yet his brain was evidently being well supplied with food and oxygen; he felt clearheaded, at ease and healthy.

He wasn't hungry, either, although he had been using energy steadily for a long time. There were, he thought, two possible reasons for that, depending on how you looked at it. One, that he wasn't hungry because he no longer had any stomach lining to contract; two, that he wasn't hungry because the organism he was riding in had been well nourished by the superfluous tissues George had contributed.

Two hours later, when the sun was setting, it began to rain. George saw the big, slow falling drops and felt their dull impacts on his "skin." He didn't know whether rain would do him any damage or not, but crawled under a bush with large, fringed leaves just to be on the safe side. When the rain stopped, it was night and he decided he might as well stay where he was until morning. He did not feel tired, and it occurred to him to wonder whether he still needed to sleep. He composed himself as well as he could to wait for the answer.

He was still wakeful after a long time had passed, but had made no progress toward deciding whether this answered the question or prevented it from being answered, when he saw a pair of dim lights coming slowly and erratically toward him.

George watched them with an attentiveness compounded of professional interest and apprehension. Gradually, as they came closer, he made out that the lights were attached to long, thin stalks which grew from an ambiguous shape below—either light organs, like those of some deepsea fish, or simply luminescent eyes.

George noted a feeling of tension in himself which seemed to suggest that adrenaline or an equivalent was being released somewhere in his system. He promised himself to follow this lead at the first possible moment; mean-

81

while, he had a more urgent problem to consider. Was this approaching organism the kind which the Something *meisterii* ate, or the kind which devoured the Something *meisterii*? If the latter, what could he do about it?

For the present, at any rate, sitting where he was seemed to be indicated. The body he inhabited made use of camouflage in its normal, or untenanted state, and was not equipped for speed. So George held still and watched, keeping his eyes half-closed, while he considered the possible nature of the approaching animal.

The fact that it was nocturnal, he told himself, meant nothing. Moths were nocturnal; so were bats—no, the devil with bats, they were carnivores.

The light-bearing creature came nearer, and George saw the faint gleam of a pair of long, narrow eyes below the two stalks.

Then the creature opened its mouth.

It had a great many teeth.

George found himself crammed into some kind of crevice in a wall of rock, without any clear recollection of how he had got there. He remembered a flurry of branches as the creature sprang at him, and a moment's furious pain, and nothing but vague, starlit glimpses of leaves and soil.

How had he got away?

He puzzled over it until dawn came, and then, looking down at himself, he saw something that had not been there before. Under the smooth edge of gelatinous flesh, three or four projections of some kind were visible. It struck George that his sensation of contact with the stone underneath him had changed, too. He seemed to be standing on a number of tiny points instead of lying flat.

He flexed one of the projections experimentally, then thrust it out straight ahead of him. It was a lumpy, single-jointed caricature of a finger or a leg.

II

Lying still for a long time, George Meister thought about it with as much coherence as he could muster. Then he waggled the limb again. It was there, and so were all the others, as solid and real as the rest of him.

He moved forward experimentally, sending the same messages down to his finger-and-toe nerve-ends as before.

82

His body lurched out of the cranny with a swiftness that very nearly tumbled him down over the edge of a minor precipice.

Where he had crawled like a snail before, he now scuttled like an insect.

But how? No doubt, in his terror when the thing with the teeth attacked, he had unconsciously tried to run as if he still had legs. Was that all there was to it?

George thought of the carnivore again, and of the stalks supporting the organs which he had thought might be eyes. That would do as an experiment. He closed his eyes and imagined them rising outward, imagined the mobile stalks growing, growing . . . He tried to convince himself that he had eyes like that, had always had them, that everyone who was anyone had eyes on stalks.

Surely, something was happening.

George opened his eyes again and found himself looking straight down at the ground, getting a view so close that it was blurred, out of focus. Impatiently, he tried to look up. All that happened was that his field of vision moved forward a matter of ten or twelve centimeters.

It was at this point that a voice shattered the stillness. It sounded like someone trying to shout through half a meter of lard. "Urghh! Lluhh! *Eeraghh!*"

George leaped convulsively, executed a neat turn and swept his eyes around a good two hundred and forty degrees of arc. He saw nothing but rocks and lichens. On a closer inspection, it appeared that a small green and orange larva or grub of some kind was moving past him. George regarded it with suspicion for a long moment, until the voice broke out again:

"Ellfff! Elffneee!"

The voice, somewhat higher this time, came from behind. George whirled again, swept his eyes around—

Around an impossibly wide circuit. His eyes *were* on stalks, and they were mobile whereas a moment ago he had been staring at the ground, unable to look up. George's brain clattered into high gear. He had grown stalks for his eyes, all right, but they'd been limp, just extensions of the jellylike mass of his body, without a stiffening cell-structure or muscular tissue to move them. Then, when the voice had startled him, he'd got the stiffening and the muscles in a hurry.

That must have been what had happened the previous night. Probably the process would have been completed,

83

but much more slowly, if he hadn't been frightened. A protective mechanism, obviously. As for the voice—

George rotated once more, slowly, looking all around him. There was no question about it; he was alone. The voice, which had seemed to come from someone or something standing just behind him, must in fact have issued from his own body.

The voice started again, at a less frantic volume. It burbled a few times, then said quite clearly in a high tenor, "Whass happen'? Wheh am I?"

George was floundering in enough bewilderment. He was in no condition to adapt quickly to more new circumstances, and when a large, dessicated lump fell from a nearby bush and bounced soundlessly to within a meter of him, he simply stared at it.

He looked at the hard-shelled object and then at the laden bush from which it had dropped. Slowly, painfully, he worked his way through to a logical conclusion. The dried fruit had fallen without a sound. This was natural, because he had been totally deaf ever since his metamorphosis. But he had heard a voice!

Ergo, hallucination or telepathy.

The voice began again. "Help! Oh, dear, I wish someone would answer!"

Vivian Bellis. Gumbs, even if he affected that tenor voice, wouldn't say, "Oh, dear." Neither would Miss McCarty.

George's shaken nerves were returning to normal. He thought intently, *I get scared, grow legs. Bellis gets scared, grows a telepathic voice. That's reasonable, I guess—her first and only impulse would be to yell.*

George tried to put himself into a yelling mood. He shut his eyes and imagined himself cooped up in a terrifyingly alien medium, without any control or knowledge of his predicament. He tried to shout: "Vivian!"

He went on trying, while the girl's voice continued at intervals. Finally she stopped abruptly in the middle of a sentence.

George said, "Can you hear me?"

"Who's that? What do you want?"

"This is George Meister, Vivian. Can you understand what I'm saying?"

"What—"

George kept at it. His pseudo-voice, he judged, was a

little garbled, just as Bellis's had been at first. At last the girl said, "Oh, George—I mean Mr. Meister! Oh, I've been so frightened. Where are you?"

George explained, apparently not very tactfully, because Bellis shrieked when he was through and then went back to burbling.

George sighed, and said, "Is there anyone else on the premises? Major Gumbs? Miss McCarty? Can you hear me?"

A few minutes later two sets of weird sounds began almost simultaneously. When they became coherent, it was no trouble to identify the voices.

Gumbs, the big, red-faced professional soldier, shouted, "Why the hell don't you watch where you're going, Meister? If you hadn't started that rock-slide, we wouldn't be in this mess!"

Miss McCarty, who had a grim white face, a jutting jaw, and eyes the color of mud, said coldly, "Meister, all of this will be reported. *All* of it."

It appeared that only Meister and Gumbs had kept the use of their eyes. All four of them had some muscular control, though Gumbs was the only one who had made any serious attempt to interfere with George's locomotion. Miss McCarty, not to George's surprise, had managed to retain a pair of functioning ears.

But Bellis had been blind, deaf and dumb all through the afternoon and night. The only terminal sense organs she had been able to use had been those of the skin—the perceptors of touch, heat and cold, and pain. She had heard nothing, seen nothing, but she had felt every leaf and stalk they had brushed against, the cold impact of every rain drop, and the pain of the toothy monster's bite. George's opinion of her went up several notches when he learned this. She had been terrified, but she hadn't been driven into hysteria or insanity.

It further appeared that nobody was doing any breathing and nobody was aware of a heartbeat.

George would have liked nothing better than to continue this discussion, but the other three were united in believing that what had happened to them after they got in was of less importance than how they were going to get out.

"We can't get *out*," said George. "At least, I don't see

85

any possibility of it in the present state of our knowledge. If we—"

"But we've got to get out!" Vivian cried.

"We'll go back to camp," said McCarty coldly. "Immediately. And you'll explain to the Loyalty Committee why you didn't return as soon as you regained consciousness."

"That's right," Gumbs put in self-consciously. "If you can't do anything, Meister, maybe the other technical fellows can."

George patiently explained his theory of their probable reception by the guards at the camp. McCarty's keen mind detected a flaw. "You grew legs, and stalks for your eyes, according to your own testimony. If you aren't lying, you can also grow a mouth. We'll announce ourselves as we approach."

"That may not be easy," George told her. "We couldn't get along with just a mouth. We'd need teeth, tongue, hard and soft palates, lungs or the equivalent, vocal cords, and some kind of substitute for a diaphragm to power the whole business. I'm wondering if it's possible at all because when Miss Bellis finally succeeded in making herself heard, it was by the method we're using now. She didn't—"

"You talk too much," McCarty interrupted. "Major Gumbs, Miss Bellis, you and I will try to form a speak-apparatus. The first to succeed will receive a credit mark on his record. Commence."

George, being left out of the contest by implication, used his time trying to restore his hearing. It seemed to him likely that the Whatever-it-was *meisterii* had some sort of division of labor built into it, since Gumbs and he—the first two to fall in—had kept their sight without making any special effort, while matters like hearing and touch had been left for the latecomers. This was fine in principle, and George approved of it, but he didn't like the idea of Miss McCarty's being the sole custodian of any part of the apparatus whatever.

Even if he were able to persuade the other two to follow his lead—and at the moment this prospect seemed dim—McCarty was certain to be a holdout. And it might easily be vital to all of them, at some time in the near future, to have their hearing hooked into the circuit.

He was distracted at first by muttered comments between Gumbs and Vivian—"Getting anywhere?" "I don't think so. Are you?"—interpersed between yawps, humming sounds and other irritating noises as they tried unsuccessfully to switch over from mental to vocal communication. Finally McCarty snapped, "Concentrate on forming the necessary organs instead of braying like jackasses."

George settled down to work, using the same technique he had found effective before. With his eyes shut, he imagined that the thing with all the teeth was approaching in darkness—*tap; slither; tap; click.* He wished valiantly for ears to catch those faint approaching sounds. After a long time he thought he was beginning to succeed—or were those mental sounds, unconsciously emitted by one of the other three? *Click. Slither. Swish. Scrape.*

George opened his eyes, genuinely alarmed. A hundred meters away, facing him across the shallow slope of rocky ground, was a uniformed man just emerging from a stand of black vegetation spears. As George raised his eye-stalks, the man paused, stared back at him, then shouted and raised his rifle.

George ran. Instantly there was a babble of voices inside him, and the muscles of his "legs" went into wild spasms.

"Run, dammit!" he said frantically. "There's a trooper with—"

The rifle went off with a deafening roar and George felt a sudden hideous pain aft of his spine. Vivian Bellis screamed. The struggle for possession of their common legs stopped and they scuttled full speed ahead for the cover of a nearby boulder.

The rifle roared again. George heard rock splinters screeching through the foliage overhead. Then they were plunging down the side of a gully, up the other slope, over a low hummock and into a forest of tall, bare-limbed trees.

George spotted a leaf-filled hollow and headed for it, fighting somebody else's desire to keep on running in a straight line. They plopped into the hollow and crouched there while three running men went past them.

Vivian was moaning steadily. Raising his eye-stalks cautiously, George was able to see that several jagged splinters of stone had penetrated the monster's gelatinous flesh near the far rim. They had been very lucky. The shot had apparently been a near miss—accountable only on the grounds that the trooper had been shooting downhill at a moving target—and had shattered the boulder behind them.

Looking more closely, George observed something which excited his professional interest. The whole surface of the monster appeared to be in constant slow ferment, tiny pits opening and closing as if the flesh were boiling . . . except that here the bubbles of air were not forcing their way outward, but were being engulfed at the surface and pressed down into the interior.

He could also see, deep under the mottled surface of the huge lens-shaped body, four vague clots of darkness which must be the living brains of Gumbs, Bellis, McCarty—and Meister.

Yes, there was one which was radially opposite his own eye-stalks. It was an odd thing, George reflected, to be looking at your own brain. He hoped he could get used to it in time.

The four dark spots were arranged close together in an almost perfect square at the center of the lens. The spinal cords, barely visible, crossed between them and rayed outward from the center.

Pattern, George thought. The thing was designed to make use of more than one nervous system. It arranged them in an orderly fashion, with the brains inward for greater protection—and perhaps for another reason. Maybe there was even a provision for conscious cooperation among the passengers: a matrix that somehow promoted the growth of communication cells between the separate brains. If that were so, it would account for their ready success with telepathy. George wished acutely that he could get inside and find out.

Vivian's pain was diminishing. Hers was the brain opposite George's and she had taken most of the effect of the rock splinters. But the fragments were sinking now, slowly, through the gelid substance of the monster's tissues. Watching carefully, George could see them move. When they got to the bottom, they would be excreted, no doubt, just as the indigestible parts of their clothing and equipment had been.

George wondered idly which of the remaining two brains was McCarty's and which was Gumbs's. The answer proved easy to find. To George's left, as he looked back toward the center of the mound, was a pair of blue eyes set flush with the surface. They had lids apparently grown from the monster's substance, but thickened and opaque.

To his right, George could make out two tiny openings, extending a few centimeters into the body, which could only be Miss McCarty's ears. George had an impulse to see if he could devise a method of dropping dirt into them.

Anyhow, the question of returning to camp had been settled, at least for the moment. McCarty said nothing more about growing a set of speech organs, although George was sure she was determined to keep on trying.

He didn't think she would succeed. Whatever the mechanism was by which these changes in bodily structure were accomplished, amateurs like themselves probably could succeed only under the pressure of considerable emotional strain, and then just with comparatively simple tasks which involved one new structure at a time. And as he had already told McCarty, the speech organs in Man were extraordinarily diverse and complicated.

It occurred to George that speech might be achieved by creating a thin membrane to serve as a diaphragm, and an air chamber behind it, with a set of muscles to produce the necessary vibrations and modulate them. He kept the notion to himself, though, because he didn't want to go back.

George was a rare bird: a scientist who was actually fitted for his work and loved it for its own sake. And right now he was sitting squarely in the middle of the most powerful research tool that had ever existed in his field: a protean organism, with the observer *inside* it, able to order its structure and watch the results; able to devise theories of function and test them on the tissues of what was effectively his own body—able to construct new organs, new adaptations to environment!

George saw himself at the point of an enormous cone of new knowledge and some of the possibilities he glimpsed humbled and awed him.

He *couldn't* go back, even if it were possible to do it without getting killed. If only he alone had fallen in— No, then the others would have pulled him out and killed the monster.

There were, he felt, too many problems demanding solutions all at once. It was hard to concentrate; his mind kept slipping maddeningly out of focus.

Vivian, whose pain had stopped some time ago, began to wail again. Gumbs snapped at her. McCarty cursed both of them. George himself felt that he had had very nearly all he could take, cooped up with three idiots who had no more sense than to squabble among themselves.

89

"Wait a minute," he said. "Do you all feel the same way? Irritable? Jumpy? As if you'd been working for sixty hours straight and were too tired to sleep?"

"Stop talking like a video ad," Vivian said angrily. "Haven't we got enough trouble without—"

"We're hungry," George interrupted. "We didn't realize it, because we haven't got the organs that usually signal hunger. But the last thing this body ate was *us*, and that was a whole day ago. We've got to find something to ingest. And soon, I'd say."

"Good Lord, you're right," said Gumbs. "But if this thing only eats people—I mean to say—"

"It never met people until we landed," George replied curtly. "Any protein should do."

He started off in what he hoped was the direction they had been following all along—directly away from camp. At least, he thought, if they put enough distance behind them, they might get thoroughly lost.

III

They moved out of the trees and down the long slope of a valley, over a wiry carpet of dead grasses, until they reached a watercourse in which a thin trickle was still flowing. Far down the bank, partly screened by clumps of skeletal shrubbery, George saw a group of animals that looked vaguely like miniature pigs. He told the others about it, and started cautiously in that direction.

"Which way is the wind blowing, Vivian?" he asked. "Can you feel it?"

She said, "No, I could before, when we were going downhill, but now I think we're facing into it."

"Good. We may be able to sneak up on them."

"But we're not going to eat *animals*, are we?"

"Yes, how about it, Meister?" Gumbs put in. "I don't say I'm a squeamish fellow, but after all—"

George, who felt a little squeamish himself—like all the others, he had been brought up on a diet of yeasts and synthetic protein—said testily, "What else can we do? You've got eyes; you can see that it's autumn here. Autumn after a hot summer, at that. Trees bare, streams dried up. We eat meat or go without—or would you rather hunt for insects?"

Gumbs, shocked to the core, muttered for a while and then gave up.

Seen at closer range, the animals looked less porcine and even more unappetizing than before. They had lean, segmented, pinkish-gray bodies, four short legs, flaring ears, and blunt scimitar-like snouts with which they were rooting in the ground, occasionally turning up something which they gulped, ears flapping.

George counted thirty of them, grouped fairly closely in a little space of clear ground between the bushes and the river. They moved slowly, but their short legs looked powerful; he guessed that they could run fast enough when they had to.

He inched forward, keeping his eye-stalks low, stopping instantly whenever one of the beasts looked up. Moving with increasing caution, he had approached to within ten meters of the nearest when McCarty said abruptly:

"Meister, has it occurred to you to wonder just *how* we are going to eat these animals?"

"Don't be foolish," he said irritably. "We'll just—" He stopped, baffled.

Did the thing's normal method of assimiliation stop as soon as it got a tenant? Were they supposed to grow fangs and a gullet and all the rest of the apparatus? Impossible; they'd starve to death first. But on the other hand—*damn* this fuzzy-headed feeling—wouldn't it have to stop, to prevent the tenant from being digested with his first meal?

"Well?" McCarty demanded.

That guess was wrong, George knew, but he couldn't say why; and it was a distinctly unpleasant thought. Or, even worse, suppose the meal became the tenant, and the tenant the meal?

The nearest animal's head went up, and four tiny red eyes stared directly at George. The floppy ears snapped to attention. It was no time for speculation.

"He's seen us!" George shouted mentally. *"Run!"*

One instant they were lying still in the prickly dry grass; the next they were skimming across the ground, with the herd galloping away straight ahead of them. The hams of the nearest beast loomed up closer and closer, bounding furiously; then they had run it down and vaulted over it.

Casting an eye backward, George saw that it was lying motionless in the grass—unconscious or dead.

They ran down another one. *The anesthetic,* George

thought lucidly. *One touch does it.* And another, and another. *Of course we can digest them,* he thought, with relief. *It has to be selective to begin with or it couldn't have separated out our nervous tissue.*

Four down. Six down. Three more together as the herd bunched between the last arm of the thicket and the steep river bank; then two that tried to double back; then four stragglers, one after the other.

The rest of the herd disappeared into the tall grass up the slope, but fifteen bodies were strewn behind them.

Taking no chances, George went back to the beginning of the line and edged the monster's body under the first carcass.

"Crouch down, Gumbs," he said. "We have to slide under it . . . that's far enough. Leave the head hanging over."

"What for?" barked the soldier.

"You don't want his brain in here with us, do you? We don't know how many this thing is equipped to take. It might even like this one better than any of ours. But I can't see it bothering to keep the rest of the nervous system, if we make sure not to eat the head."

"Oh!" said Vivian.

"I beg your pardon, Miss Bellis," George said contritely. "It shouldn't be too unpleasant, though, if we don't let it bother us. It isn't as if we had taste buds or—"

"It's all right," she said. "Just please let's not talk about it."

"I should think not," Gumbs put in. "A little more tact, don't you think, Meister?"

Accepting this reproof, George turned his attention to the corpse that lay on the monster's glabrous surface, between his section and Gumbs's. It was sinking, just visibly, into the flesh. A cloud of opacity was spreading around it.

When it was almost gone and the neck had been severed, they moved on to the next. This time, at George's suggestion, they took aboard two at once. Gradually their irritable mood faded; they began to feel at ease and cheerful, and George found it possible to think consecutively without having vital points slip out of his reach.

They were on their eighth and ninth courses, and George was happily engaged in an intricate chain of speculation as to the monster's circulatory system, when Miss McCarty broke a long silence to announce:

"I have now perfected a method by which we can return to camp safely. We will begin at once."

Startled and dismayed, George turned his eyes toward McCarty's quadrant of the monster. Protruding from the rim was a stringy, jointed something that looked like—yes, it was!—a grotesque but recognizable arm and hand. As he watched, the lumpy fingers fumbled with a blade of grass, tugged, uprooted it.

"Major Gumbs!" said McCarty. "It will be your task to locate the following articles as quickly as possible. One, a surface suitable for writing. I suggest a large leaf, light in color, dry but not brittle, or a tree from which a large section of bark can be easily peeled. Two, a pigment. No doubt you will be able to discover berries yielding suitable juice. If not, mud will do. Three, a twig or reed for use as a pen. When you have directed me to all these essential items, I will employ them to write a message outlining our predicament. You will read the result and point out any errors, which I will then correct. When the message is completed, we will return with it to the camp, approaching at night, and deposit it in a conspicuous place. We will retire until daybreak, and when the message has been read, we will approach again. Begin, Major."

"Well, yes," said Gumbs, "that ought to work, except— I suppose you've figured out some system for holding the pen, Miss McCarty?"

"Fool!" she replied. "I have made a hand, of course."

"Well, in that case, by all means. Let's see, I believe we might try this thicket first—" Their common body gave a lurch in that direction.

George held back. "Wait a minute," he said desperately. "Let's at least have the common sense to finish this meal before we go. There's no telling when we'll get another."

McCarty demanded, "How large are these creatures, Major?"

"About sixty centimeters long, I should say."

"And we have consumed nine of them, is that correct?"

"Nearer eight," George corrected. "These two are only half gone."

"In other words," McCarty said, "we have had two apiece. That should be ample. Don't you agree, Major?"

George said earnestly, "Miss McCarty, you're thinking in terms of human food requirements, whereas this organism has a different metabolic rate and at least three times

93

the mass of four human beings. Look at it this way—the four of us together had a mass of about three hundred kilos, and yet twenty hours after this thing absorbed us, it was hungry again. Well, these animals wouldn't weigh much more than twenty kilos apiece at one G—and according to your scheme, we've got to hold out until after daybreak tomorrow."

"Something in that," Gumbs agreed. "Yes, on the whole, Miss McCarty, I think we had better forage while we can. It won't take us more than half an hour longer, at this rate."

"Very well. Be as quick as you can, though."

They moved on to the next pair of victims. George's brain was working furiously. It was no good arguing with McCarty. If he could only convince Gumbs, then Bellis would fall in with the majority—maybe. It was the only hope he had.

"Gumbs," he said, "have you given any thought to what's going to happen to us when we get back?"

"Not my line, you know. I leave that to the technical fellows like yourself."

"No, that isn't what I mean. Suppose you were the C. O. of this team, and four other people had fallen into this organism instead of us—"

"What? What? I don't follow."

George patiently repeated it.

"Yes, I see what you mean. So?"

"What orders would you give?"

Gumbs thought a moment. "Turn the thing over to the bio section, I suppose."

"You don't think you might order it destroyed as a possible menace?"

"Good Lord, I suppose I might. No, but you see, we'll be careful what we say in the note. We'll point out that we're a valuable specimen and so on. Handle with care."

"All right," George said, "suppose that works, then what? Since it's out of your line, I'll tell you. Nine chances out of ten, bio section will classify us as a possible biological enemy weapon. That means, first of all, that we'll go through a full-dress interrogation and I don't have to tell you what that can be like—"

"Major Gumbs," said McCarty stridently, "Meister will be executed for disloyalty at the first opportunity. You are forbidden to talk to him, under the same penalty."

"But she can't stop you from listening to me," George said tensely. "In the second place, Gumbs, they'll take samples. Without anesthesia. Finally, they'll either destroy us just the same, or they'll send us back to the nearest strong point for more study. We will then be Federation property, Gumbs, in a top-secret category, and since nobody in Intelligence will ever dare to take the responsibility of clearing us, we'll *stay* there.

"Gumbs, this *is* a valuable specimen, but it will never do anybody any good if we go back to camp. Whatever we discover about it, even if it's knowledge that could save billions of lives, that will be top-secret, too, and it'll never get past the walls of Intelligence. . . . If you're still hoping that they can get you out of this, you're wrong. This isn't like limb grafts. *Your whole body has been destroyed,* Gumbs, everything but your nervous system and your eyes. The only new body we'll get is the one we make ourselves. We've got to stay here and—and work this out ourselves."

"Major Gumbs," said McCarty, "I think we have wasted quite enough time. Begin your search for the materials I need."

For a moment, Gumbs was silent and their collective body did not move.

Then he said: "Miss McCarty—unofficially, of course—there's one point I'd like your opinion on. Before we begin. That is to say, they'll be able to patch together some sort of bodies for us, don't you think? I mean one technical fellow says one thing, another says the opposite. Do you see what I'm driving at?"

George had been watching McCarty's new limb uneasily. It was flexing rhythmically and, he was almost certain, gradually growing larger. The fingers groped in the dry grass, plucking first a single blade, then two together, finally a whole tuft. Now she said: "I have no opinion, Major. The question is irrelevant. Our duty is to return to camp. That is all we need to know."

"Oh, I quite agree with you there," said Gumbs. "And besides," he added, "there really isn't any alternative, is there?"

George, staring down at one of the fingerlike projections visible below the rim of the monster, was passionately willing it to turn into an arm. He had, he suspected, started much too late.

"The alternative," he said, "is simply to keep on going as we are. Even if the Federation holds this planet for a century, there'll be places on it that will never be explored. We'll be safe."

"I mean to say," Gumbs went on as if he had only paused for thought, "a fellow can't very well cut himself off from civilization, can he?" There was a thoughtful tone to his voice.

Again George felt a movement toward the thicket; again he resisted it. Then he found himself overpowered as another set of muscles joined themselves to Gumbs's. Quivering, crabwise, the Something-or-other *meisterii* moved half a meter. Then it stopped, straining.

"I believe you, Mr. Meister—George," Vivian Bellis said. "I don't want to go back. Tell me what you want me to do."

"You're doing beautifully right now," George assured her after a speechless instant. "Except if you can grow an arm, I imagine that will be useful."

"Now we know where we stand," said McCarty to Gumbs.

"Yes. Quite right."

"Major Gumbs," she said crisply, "you are opposite me, I believe?"

"Am I?" asked Gumbs doubtfully.

"Never mind. I believe you are. Now is Meister to your right or left?"

"Left. I know that, anyhow. Can see his eye-stalks out of the corner of my eye."

"Very well." McCarty's arm rose, with a sharp-pointed fragment of rock clutched in the blobby fingers.

Horrified, George watched it bend backward across the curve of the monster's body. The long, knife-sharp point probed tentatively at the surface three centimeters short of the area over his brain. Then the fist made an abrupt up-and-down movement and a fierce stab of pain shot through him.

"Not quite long enough, I think," McCarty said. She flexed the arm, then brought it back. "Major Gumbs, after my next attempt, you will tell me if you notice any reaction in Meister's eye-stalks."

The pain was still throbbing along George's nerves. With one half-blinded eye, he watched the embryonic arm that was growing, too slowly, under the rim; with the other, fascinated, he watched McCarty's arm lengthen slowly toward him.

It was growing visibly, he suddenly realized, but it wasn't getting any nearer. In fact, incredibly enough it seemed to be losing ground.

The monster's flesh was flowing away under it, expanding in both directions.

McCarty stabbed again, with vicious strength. This time the pain was less acute.

"Major?" she asked. "Any result?"

"No," said Gumbs, "no, I think not. We seem to be moving forward a bit, though, Miss McCarty."

"A ridiculous error," she replied. "We are being forced *back*. Pay attention, Major."

"No, really," he protested. "That is to say, we're moving toward the thicket. Forward to me, backward to you."

"Major Gumbs, *I* am moving forward, *you* are moving back."

They were both right, George discovered. The monster's body was no longer circular; it was extending itself along the axis. A suggestion of concavity was becoming visible in the center. Below the surface, too, there was motion.

The four brains now formed an oblong, not a square.

The positions of the spinal cords had shifted. His own and Vivian's seemed to be about where they were, but Gumbs's now passed under McCarty's brain, and vice versa.

Having increased its mass by some two hundred kilos, the Something-or-other *meisterii* was fissioning into two individuals—and tidily separating its tenants, two to each. Gumbs and Meister in one, McCarty and Bellis in the other.

Next time it happened, he realized, each product of the fission would be reduced to one brain—and the time after that, one of the new individuals out of each pair would be a monster in the primary state, quiescent, camouflaged, waiting to be stumbled over.

But that meant that, like the common amoeba, this fascinating organism was immortal, barring accidents. It simply grew and divided.

Not the tenants, though, unfortunately. Their tissues would wear out and die.

Or would they? Human nervous tissue didn't regenerate,

97

but neither did it proliferate as George's and Miss Mc-Carty's had done; neither did *any* human tissue build new cells fast enough to account for George's eye-stalks or Miss McCarty's arm.

There was no question about it: none of that new tissue could possibly be human; it was all counterfeit, produced by the monster from its own substance according to the structural "blueprints" in the nearest genuine cells. And it was a perfect counterfeit: the new tissues knit with the old, axones coupled with dendrites, muscles contracted or expanded on command.

And therefore, when nerve cells wore out, they could be replaced. Eventually the last human cell would go, the human tenant would have become totally monster—but "a difference that makes no difference is no difference." Effectively, the tenant would still be human and he would be immortal.

Barring accidents.

Or murder.

Miss McCarty was saying, "Major Gumbs, you are being ridiculous. The explanation is quite obvious. Unless you are deliberately deceiving me, for what reason I cannot imagine, then our efforts to move in opposing directions must be pulling this creature apart."

McCarty was evidently confused in her geometry. Let her stay that way—it would keep her off balance until the fission was complete. No, that was no good. George himself was out of her reach already and getting farther away, but how about Bellis? Her brain and McCarty's were, if anything, closer together. . . .

What was he to do? If he warned the girl, that would only draw McCarty's attention to her sooner.

There wasn't much time left, he realized abruptly. If some physical linkage between the brains actually had occurred to make communication possible, those cells couldn't hold out much longer; the gap between the two pairs of brains was widening steadily. He had to keep McCarty from discovering how the four of them would be paired.

"Vivian!" he said.

"Yes, George?"

"Listen, we're not pulling this body apart. It's splitting. That's the way it reproduces. You and I will be in one half, Gumbs and McCarty in the other," he lied convincingly.

"If they don't give us any trouble, we can all go where we please."

"Oh, I'm so glad!" What a warm voice she had. . . .

"Yes," said George nervously, "but we may have to fight them; it's up to them. So *grow an arm,* Vivian."

"I'll try," she said uncertainly.

McCarty's voice cut across hers. "Major Gumbs, since you have eyes, it will be your task to see to it that those two do not escape. Meanwhile, I suggest that you also grow an arm."

"Doing my best," said Gumbs.

Puzzled, George glanced downward, past his own half-formed arm. There, almost out of sight, a fleshy bulge appeared under Gumbs's section of the rim! The Major had been working on it in secret, keeping it hidden . . . and it was already better-developed than George's.

"Oh-oh," said Gumbs abruptly. "Look here, Miss Mc-Carty, Meister's been leading you up the garden path. Deceiving you, you understand. Clever, I must say. I mean you and I aren't going to be in the same half. How could we be? We're on *opposite sides* of the blasted thing. It's going to be you and Miss Bellis, me and Meister."

The monster was developing a definite waistline. The spinal cords had rotated now, so that there was clear space between them in the center.

"Yes," said McCarty faintly. "*Thank* you, Major Gumbs."

"George!" came Vivian's frightened voice, distant and weak. "What shall I do?"

"Grow an arm!" he shouted.

There was no reply.

IV

Frozen, George watched McCarty's arm, the rock-fragment still clutched at the end of it, rise into view and swing leftward at full stretch over the bubbling surface of the monster. He had time to see it bob up and viciously down again; time to think. *Still short, thank God—that's McCarty's right arm, it's farther from Vivian's brain than it was from mine;* time, finally, to realize that he could not possibly help Vivian before McCarty lengthened the arm the few centimeters more that were necessary. The fission was only half complete, yet he could no more move to

99

where he wanted to be than a Siamese twin could walk around his brother.

Then his time was up. A flicker of motion warned him, and he looked back to see a lumpy, distorted pseudo-hand clutching for his eye-stalks.

Instinctively he brought his own up, grasped the other's wrist and hung on desperately. It was half again the size of his, and so strongly muscled that although his leverage was better, he couldn't force it back or hold it away. He could only keep the system oscillating up and down, adding his strength to Gumbs's so that the mark was overshot.

Gumbs began to vary the force and rhythm of his movements, trying to catch him off guard. A thick finger brushed the base of one eye-stalk.

"Sorry about this, Meister," said Gumbs. "No hard feelings, you understand. Between us [oof] I don't fancy that McCarty woman much—but [ugh! almost had you that time] way I see it, I've got to look after myself. Mean to say [ugh] if I don't, who will? See what I mean?"

George did not reply. Astonishingly enough, he was no longer afraid, either for himself or for Vivian; he was simply overpoweringly, ecstatically, monomaniacally angry. Power from somewhere was surging into his arm. Fiercely concentrating, he thought *Bigger! Stronger! Longer! More arm!*

The arm grew. Visibly, it added substance to itself, it lengthened, thickened, bulked with muscle. So did Gumbs's, however.

He began another arm. So did Gumbs.

All around him the surface of the monster was bubbling violently. And, George realized, the lenticular bulk of it was perceptibly shrinking. Its curious breathing system was inadequate; the thing was cannibalizing itself, destroying its own tissues to make up the difference.

How small could it get and still support two human tenants?

And which brain would it dispense with first?

He had no leisure to think about it. Scrabbling in the grass with his second hand, Gumbs had failed to find anything that would serve as a weapon. Now, with a sudden lurch, he swung their entire body around.

The fission was complete.

That thought reminded George of Vivian and McCarty. He risked a split-second's glance behind him, saw nothing but a featureless ovoid mound, and looked back in time to

100

see Gumbs's half-grown right fist pluck up a long, sharp-pointed dead branch and drive it murderously at his eyes.

The lip of the river-bank was a meter away to the left. George made it in one abrupt surge. Their common body slipped, tottered, hesitated, hands clutching wildly—and toppled, end over end, hurtling in a cloud of dust and pebbles down the breakneck slope to a meaty smash at the bottom.

The universe made one more giant turn around them and came to rest. Half-blinded, George groped for the hold he had lost, found the wrist and seized it.

"Oh, Lord!" said Gumbs. "I'm hurt, Meister. Go on, man, finish it, will you? Don't waste time."

George stared at him suspiciously, without relaxing his grip. "What's the matter with you?"

"Paralyzed. I can't move."

They had fallen onto a small boulder, George saw, one of many with which the riverbed was strewn. This one was roughly conical; they were draped over it, and the blunt point was directly under Gumbs's spinal cord, a few centimeters from the brain.

"Gumbs, that may not be as bad as you think. If I can show you it isn't, will you give up and put yourself under my orders?"

"How do you mean? My spine's crushed."

"Never mind that now. Will you or won't you?"

"Why, yes," agreed Gumbs. "That's very decent of you, Meister, matter of fact. You have my word, for what it's worth."

"All right," said George. Straining hard, he managed to get their body off the boulder. Then he stared up at the slope down which they had tumbled. Too steep; he'd have to find an easier way back. He turned and started off to eastward, paralleling the thin stream that flowed in the center of the watercourse.

"What's up now?" Gumbs asked after a moment.

"We've got to find a way up to the top," George said impatiently. "I may still be able to help Vivian."

"Ah, yes. Afraid I was thinking about myself, Meister. If you don't mind telling me, what's the damage?"

She couldn't still be alive, George was thinking despondently, but if there were any small chance—

101

"You'll be all right," he said. "If you were still in your old body, that would be a fatal injury, or permanently disabling, anyhow, but not in this thing. You can repair yourself as easily as you can grow a new limb."

"Stupid of me not to think of that," said Gumbs. "But does that mean we were simply wasting our time trying to kill one another?"

"No. If you'd crushed my brain, I think the organism would have digested it and that would be the end of me. But short of anything that drastic, I believe we're immortal."

"Immortal? That does rather put another face on it, doesn't it?"

The bank was becoming a little lower, and at one point, where the raw ground was thickly seeded with boulders, there was a talus slope that looked as if it could be climbed. George started up it.

"Meister," said Gumbs after a moment.

"What do you want?"

"You're right, you know—I'm getting some feeling back already. Look here, is there anything this beast *can't* do? I mean, for instance, do you suppose we could put ourselves back together the way we were, with all the—appendages, and so on?"

"It's possible," George said curtly. It was a thought that had been in the back of his mind, but he didn't feel like discussing it with Gumbs just now.

They were halfway up the slope.

"Well, in that case," said Gumbs meditatively, "the thing has *military* possibilities, you know. Man who brought a thing like that direct to the War Department could write his own ticket, more or less."

"After we split up," George offered, "you can do whatever you please."

"But dammit," said Gumbs in an irritated tone, "that won't do."

"Why not?"

"Because," said Gumbs, "they might find you." His hands reached up abruptly, pried out a small boulder before George could stop him.

The large boulder above it trembled, dipped and leaned ponderously outward. George, directly underneath, found that he could move neither forward nor back.

"Sorry again," he heard Gumbs saying, with what

102

sounded like genuine regret. "But you know the Loyalty Committee. I simply can't take the chance."

The boulder seemed to take forever to fall. George tried twice more, with all his strength, to move out of its path. Then, instinctively, he put his arms up straight under it.

It struck.

George felt his arms breaking like twigs, and saw a looming grayness that blotted out the sky; he felt a sledge impact that made the ground shudder beneath him.

He heard a splattering sound.

And he was still alive. That astonishing fact kept him fully occupied for a long time after the boulder had clattered its way down the slope into silence. Then, at last, he looked down to his right.

The resistance of his stiffened arms, even while they broke, had been enough to lever the falling boulder over, a distance of some thirty centimeters. The right half of the monster was a flattened, shattered ruin. He could see a few flecks of pasty gray matter, melting now into green-brown translucence as the mass flowed slowly together again.

In twenty minutes, the last remnants of a superfluous spinal cord had been absorbed, the monster had collected itself back into its normal lens shape, and George's pain was diminishing. In five minutes more, his mended arms were strong enough to use.

They were also more convincingly shaped and colored than before—the tendons, the fingernails, even the wrinkles of the skin were in good order. In ordinary circumstances this discovery would have left George happily bemused for hours. Now, in his impatience, he barely noticed it. He climbed to the top of the bank.

Thirty meters away, a humped green-brown body like his own lay motionless on the dry grass.

It contained, of course, only one brain. Whose?

McCarty's, almost certainly; Vivian hadn't had a chance. But then how did it happen that there was no visible trace of McCarty's arm?

Unnerved, George walked around the creature for a closer inspection.

On the far side, he encountered two dark-brown eyes, with an oddly unfinished appearance. They focused on him after an instant and the whole body quivered slightly, moving toward him.

Vivian's eyes had been brown; George remembered them distinctly. Brown eyes with heavy dark lashes in a tapering slender face. But did that prove anything? What color had McCarty's eyes been? He couldn't remember.

George moved closer, hoping fervently that the Something-or-other *meisterii* was at least advanced enough to conjugate, instead of trying to devour members of its own species. . . .

The two bodies touched, clung and began to flow together. Watching, George saw the fissioning process reverse itself. From paired lenses, the alien flesh melted into a slipper-shape, to an ovoid, to a lens-shape again. His brain and the other drifted closer together, the spinal cords crossing at right angles.

And it was only then that he noticed an oddity about the other brain. It seemed to be more solid and compact than his, the outline sharper.

"Vivian?" he said worriedly. "Is that you?"

No answer. He tried again; and again.

Finally:

"George! Oh, dear—I want to cry, but I don't seem able to do it."

"No lachrymal glands," George said automatically. "Uh, Vivian?"

"Yes, George?" That warm voice again . . .

"What happened to Miss McCarty? How did you—"

"I don't know. She's gone, isn't she? I haven't heard her for a long time."

"Yes," said George, "she's gone. You mean you don't *know?* Tell me what you did."

"Well, I wanted to make an arm, because you told me to, but I didn't think I had time enough. So I made a skull instead. And those things to cover my spine—"

"Vertebrae." *Now why,* he thought discontentedly, *didn't I think of that?* "And then?"

"I think I'm crying now," she said. "Yes, I am. It's such a relief— And then, after that, nothing. She was still hurting me, and I just lay still and thought how wonderful it would be if she weren't in here with me. After a while, she wasn't. And then I grew eyes to look for you."

The explanation, it seemed to George, was more perplexing than the enigma. Staring around in a vague search for enlightenment, he caught sight of something he hadn't noticed before. Two meters to his left, just visible in the grass, was a damp-looking grayish lump, with a suggestion of a stringy extension trailing off from it.

There must, he decided suddenly, be some mechanism in the Something-or-other *meisterii* for disposing of tenants who failed to adapt themselves—brains that went into catatonia, or hysteria, or suicidal frenzy. An eviction clause in the lease.

Somehow, Vivian had managed to stimulate that mechanism—to convince the organism that McCarty's brain was not only superfluous but dangerous—"Toxic" was the word.

It was the ultimate ignominy. Miss McCarty had not been digested. She'd been excreted.

By sunset, twelve hours later, they had made a good deal of progress. They had reached an understanding very agreeable to them both. They had hunted down another herd of the pseudo-pigs for their noon meal. They had not once quarreled or even irritated each other. And for divergent reasons—on George's side because the monster's normal metabolism was unsatisfactory when it had to move quickly, and on Vivian's because she refused to believe that any man could be attracted to her in her present condition—they had begun a serious attempt to reshape themselves.

The first trials were extraordinarily difficult, the rest surprisingly easy. Again and again, they had to let themselves collapse back into an ameboid shape, victims of some omitted or malfunctioning organ, but each failure smoothed the road. They were at last able to stand breathless but breathing, swaying but stable, face to face—two preliminary sketches of self-made Man.

They had also put thirty kilometers between themselves and the Federation camp. Standing on the crest of a rise and looking southward across the shallow valley, George could see a faint funereal glow: the mining machines, chewing out metals to feed the fabricators that would spawn lethal spaceships.

"We'll never go back there, will we?" begged Vivian.

"No," said George confidently. "We'll let them find us. When they do, they'll be a lot more disconcerted than we will. We can make ourselves anything we want to be, remember."

"I want you to want me, so I'm going to be beautiful."

"More beautiful than any woman ever was," he agreed, "and both of us will have super-intelligence. I don't see why not. We can direct our growth in any way we choose. We'll be more than human."

"I'd like that," said Vivian.

"They won't. The McCartys and the Gumbses and all the rest would never have a chance against us. We're the future."

There was one thing more, a small matter, but important to George, because it marked his sense of accomplishment, of one phase ended and a new one begun. He had finally completed the name of his discovery.

It wasn't Something-or-other *meisterii* at all.

It was *Spes hominis*—Man's hope.

1954

THE HUGO CAME back in 1955—recognizing achievements of 1954, just to keep that confusing business straight—and it's been back ever since. The annual convention moved to Cleveland. Noreen Kane Falasca, who shared the chairmanship with her husband, read the mood of the fans and saw to it that the previous committee's mistake was not repeated.

Furthermore, the structure of categories, although it was to be subjected to endless tinkering in later years, took recognizable shape with the awards presented in Cleveland. In addition to the trophy for best novel of 1954, the convention added categories for best novelette and best short story, recognizing for the first time competition in the shorter lengths.

The winner for best novel of 1954 was *They'd Rather Be Right*, by Mark Clifton and Frank Riley. *They'd Rather Be Right* had been serialized in *Astounding;* it was later published by the fan-owned Gnome Press, and had a third incarnation as a Galaxy novel—a sort of half-book/half-magazine series that had limped along in the shadow of *Galaxy* magazine between 1950 and 1961.

It's generally agreed that *They'd Rather Be Right* is the weakest novel ever to win a Hugo; it's the only one that's been out of print for years. And it certainly wasn't for lack of stronger competition that it won. The year 1954 had seen any number of memorable novels either serialized in the surviving science fiction magazines or published as hardbound books or paperback originals. The serials included Asimov's *Sucker Bait* in *Astounding*, Poul Anderson's *Question and Answer* in the same magazine, Pohl and Kornbluth's *Gladiator-at-Law* in *Galaxy*, and Heinlein's *Star Lummox* in *Fantasy and Science Fiction*.

Three novels that had appeared in partial or fragmented

form in the magazines had their first complete publication as books: Poul Anderson's *Brain Wave* (Ballantine); Murray Leinster's *The Forgotten Planet* (Gnome); and J. T. McIntosh's *One in 300* (Doubleday). There might have been legalistic hair-splitting over those three. But there should have been none over Richard Matheson's *I Am Legend* (Fawcett), Chad Oliver's *Shadows in the Sun* (Ballantine), Edgar Pangborn's *A Mirror for Observers* (Doubleday), or Wilson Tucker's *Wild Talent* (Rinehart).

But a quarter-century has passed; one expects to see more clearly. Put it down to some passing aberration.

The winners in the shorter categories were "The Darfsteller" by Walter M. Miller (novelette), and "Allamagoosa" by Eric Frank Russell. All three winners had appeared in *Astounding*. *Astounding* itself won the Hugo for best magazine, and Frank Kelly Freas, an illustrator closely identified with *Astounding*, was named best artist. The sweep of awards was complete.

I'm not comfortable with this, in retrospect. I do *not* suggest dishonesty, falsification of results, stuffing of ballot boxes, or any other skullduggery. I *do* suspect that the *Astounding* loyalists were rallying against the depredations of the new magazines. *Astounding* still had the largest circulation and the strongest grip upon the kind of activist fan likely to vote for Hugo awards.

Certainly there were plenty of noteworthy stories published in 1954. In the length that would today be called "novella" there were Simak's "Immigrant," Brown's hilarious "Martians Go Home," and Anderson's "The Big Rain," all in *Astounding;* Jerome Bixby's "The Murder-Con" in *Fantastic;* Pohl's "The Midas Plague" in *Galaxy;* and Jack Vance's "The Houses of Iszm" and Wilson Tucker's "The Time Masters," both in *Startling*.

Noteworthy novelettes included Blish's "At Death's End" and Budrys's "The End of Summer" in *Astounding;* T. L. Sherred's "Cure, Guaranteed" in *Future;* William Tenn's "Down Among the Dead Men," Pangborn's "The Music Master of Babylon," and Sheckley's "Skulking Permit," all in *Galaxy;* Zenna Henderson's "Gilead" in *Fantasy and Science Fiction;* and Leigh Brackett's "Mars Minus Bisha" in *Planet*.

Short stories included Frederic Brown's "Keep Out" in *Amazing;* Clifford Simak's "Immigrant" and Tom Godwin's instant classic "The Cold Equations" in *Astounding;* Sturgeon's "Beware the Fury" in *Fantastic;* and William Tenn's

"Project Hush" in *Galaxy*. Ballantine Books had found a way around the decline of the magazines with the *Star Science Fiction* volumes, edited by Frederik Pohl. Two volumes had appeared in 1953, and a third followed in 1954. The idea of a continuing series of original anthologies is, of course, commonplace today, but in the early 1950s it was revolutionary. Pohl worked wonders in these books. The 1954 volume had fine stories by Asimov, Bradbury, Clarke, del Rey, Dick, Gerald Kersh, Matheson, Oliver, and Jack Williamson—not a "non-name" author in the book, and a number of truly splendid stories.

But I think the dubious honor of most unsung achievement of 1954 goes to Theodore Sturgeon's "The Golden Helix." This novella appeared in the summer issue of *Thrilling Wonder Stories*. That was the magazine's official Golden Anniversary Edition, based on a lineage traced back to Hugo Gernsback's *Science Wonder Stories* of 1929. Sturgeon says that editor Sam Mines was striving desperately to upgrade his magazine's image and its contents, and "The Golden Helix" should have done plenty to help.

But—alas—it was too little, too late. *Thrilling Wonder* lasted only one more issue. Its companion, *Startling Stories*, staggered through another year and then, also, expired.

There were a number of attempts to revive the old titles in one form or another, in later years. *Wonder Stories* came back with a single edition, reprinting material from back files, in 1957. There was another edition with much the same contents in 1963. Then the title was changed to *Treasury of Great Science Fiction Stories* for two editions, and then changed again to *Science Fiction Yearbook*.

Finally, the body was permitted to lie at rest.

But *Thrilling Wonder Stories* produced many memorable yarns in its long and troubled career, and few, if any, of them are more memorable than "The Golden Helix."

The Golden Helix

THEODORE STURGEON

TOD

I

(TED) AWOKE FIRST, probably because he was so curious, so deeply alive; perhaps because he was (or had been) seventeen. He fought back, but the manipulators would not be denied. They bent and flexed his arms and legs, squeezed his chest, patted and rasped and abraded him. His joints creaked, his sluggish blood clung sleepily to the walls of his veins, reluctant to move after so long.

He gasped and shouted as needles of cold played over his body, gasped again and screamed when his skin sensitized and the tingling intensified to a scald. Then he fainted, and probably slept, for he easily reawoke when someone else started screaming.

He felt weak and ravenous, but extraordinarily well rested. His first conscious realization was that the manipulators had withdrawn from his body, as had the needles from the back of his neck. He put a shaky hand back there and felt the traces of spot-tape, already half fused with his healing flesh.

He listened comfortably to this new screaming, satisfied that it was not his own. He let his eyes open, and a great wonder came over him when he saw that the lid of his Coffin stood open.

He clawed upward, sat a moment to fight a vicious swirl

of vertigo, vanquished it, and hung his chin on the edge of the Coffin.

The screaming came from April's Coffin. It was open too. Since the two massive boxes touched and their hinges were on opposite sides, he could look down at her. The manipulators were at work on the girl's body, working with competent violence. She seemed to be caught up in some frightful nightmare, lying on her back, dreaming of riding a runaway bicycle with an off-center pedal sprocket and epicyclic hubs. And all the while her arms seemed to be flailing at a cloud of dream-hornets round her tossing head. The needle-cluster rode with her head, fanning out behind the nape like the mechanical extrapolation of an Elizabethan collar.

Tod crawled to the end of his Coffin, stood up shakily, and grasped the horizontal bar set at chest level. He got an arm over it and snugged it close under his armpit. Half-suspended, he could then manage one of his feet over the edge, then the other, to the top step. He lowered himself until he sat on it, outside the Coffin at last, and slumped back to rest. When his furious lungs and battering heart calmed themselves, he went down the four steps one at a time, like an infant, on his buttocks.

April's screams stopped.

Tod sat on the bottom step, jackknifed by fatigue, his feet on the metal floor, his knees in the hollows between his pectorals and his shoulders. Before him, on a low pedestal, was a cube with a round switch-disc on it. When he could, he inched a hand forward and let it fall on the disc. There was an explosive tinkle and the front panel of the cube disappeared, drifting slowly away as a fine glittering dust. He lifted his heavy hand and reached inside. He got one capsule, two, carried them to his lips. He rested, then took a beaker from the cube. It was three-quarters full of purple crystals. He bumped it on the steel floor. The beaker's cover powdered and fell in, and the crystals were suddenly a liquid, effervescing violently. When it subsided, he drank it down. He belched explosively, and then his head cleared, his personal horizons expanded to include the other Coffins, the compartment walls, the ship itself and its mission.

Out there somewhere—somewhere close, now—was Sirius and its captive planet, Terra Prime. Earth's first major colony, Prime would one day flourish as Earth never had,

111

for it would be a planned and tailored planet. Eight and a half light-years from Earth, Prime's population was composed chiefly of Earth immigrants, living in pressure domes and slaving to alter the atmosphere of the planet to Earth normal. Periodically there must be an infusion of Earth blood to keep the strain as close as possible on both planets, for unless a faster-than-light drive could be developed, there could be no frequent interchange between the worlds. What took light eight years took humans half a lifetime. The solution was the Coffins—the marvellous machine in which a man could slip into a sleep which was more than sleep while still on Earth, and awake years later in space, near his destination, subjectively only a month or so older. Without the Coffins there could be only divergence, possibly mutation. Humanity wanted to populate the stars— but with humanity.

Tod and his five shipmates were hand-picked. They had superiorities—mechanical, mathematical, and artistic aptitudes. But they were not all completely superior. One does not populate a colony with leaders alone and expect it to live. They, like the rest of their cargo (machine designs, microfilms of music and art, technical and medical writings, novels and entertainment) were neither advanced nor extraordinary. Except for Teague, they were the tested median, the competent; they were basic blood for a mass, rather than an elite.

Tod glanced around the blank walls and into the corner where a thin line delineated the sealed door. He ached to fling it open and skid across the corridor, punch the control which would slide away the armor which masked the port, and soak himself in his first glimpse of outer space. He had heard so much about it, but he had never seen it— they had all been deep in their timeless sleep before the ship blasted off.

But he sighed and went instead to the Coffins.

Alma's was still closed, but there was sound and motion, in varying degrees, from all the others.

He glanced first into April's Coffin. She seemed to be asleep now. The needle-cluster and manipulators had withdrawn. Her skin glowed; it was alive and as unlike its former monochrome waxiness as it could be. He smiled briefly and went to look at Teague.

Teague, too, was in real slumber. The fierce vertical line between his brows was shallow now, and the hard, deft hands lax and uncharacteristically purposeless. Tod had

112

never seen him before without a focus for those narrow, blazing green eyes, without decisive spring and balance in his pose. It was good, somehow, to feel that for all his responsibilities, Teague could be as helpless as anyone.

Tod smiled as he passed Alma's closed Coffin. He always smiled at Alma when he saw her, when he heard her voice, when she crossed his thoughts. It was possible to be very brave around Alma, for gentleness and comfort were so ready that it was almost not necessary to call upon them. One could bear anything, knowing she was there.

Tod crossed the chamber and looked at the last pair. Carl was a furious blur of motion, his needle-cluster swinging free, his manipulators in the final phase. He grunted instead of screaming, a series of implosive, startled gasps. His eyes were open but only the whites showed.

Moira was quite relaxed, turned on her side, poured out on the floor of the Coffin like a long golden cat. She seemed in a contented abandonment of untroubled sleep.

He heard a new sound and went back to April. She was sitting up, cross-legged, her head bowed apparently in deep concentration. Tod understood; he knew that sense of achievement and the dedication of an entire psyche to the proposition that these weak and trembling arms which hold one up shall *not* bend.

He reached in and gently lifted the soft white hair away from her face. She raised the albino's fathomless ruby eyes to him and whimpered.

"Come on," he said quietly. "We're here." When she did not move, he balanced on his stomach on the edge of the Coffin and put one hand between her shoulder blades. "Come on."

She pitched forward but he caught her so that she stayed kneeling. He drew her up and forward and put her hands on the bar. "Hold tight, Ape," he said. She did, while he lifted her thin body out of the Coffin and stood her on the top step. "Let go now. Lean on me."

Mechanically she obeyed, and he brought her down until she sat, as he had, on the bottom step. He punched the switch at her feet and put the capsules in her mouth while she looked up at him numbly, as if hypnotized. He got her beaker, thumped it, held it until its foaming subsided, and then put an arm around her shoulders while she drank. She closed her eyes and slumped against him, breathing deeply

113

at first, and later, for a moment that frightened him, not at all. Then she sighed. "Tod. . . ."

"I'm here, Ape."

She straightened up, turned and looked at him. She seemed to be trying to smile, but she shivered instead. "I'm cold."

He rose, keeping one hand on her shoulder until he was sure she could sit up unassisted, and then brought her a cloak from the clips outside the Coffin. He helped her with it, knelt and put on her slippers for her. She sat quite still, hugging the garment tight to her. At last she looked around and back; up, around, and back again. "We're—there!" she breathed.

"We're *here*," he corrected.

"Yes, here. Here. How long do you suppose we . . ."

"We won't know exactly until we can take some readings. Twenty-five, twenty-seven years—maybe more."

She said, "I could be old, old—" She touched her face, brought her fingertips down to the sides of her neck. "I could be forty, even!"

He laughed at her, and then a movement caught the corner of his eye. "Carl!"

Carl was sitting sidewise on the edge of his Coffin, his feet still inside. Weak or no, bemused as could be expected, Carl should have grinned at Tod, should have made some healthy, swaggering gesture. Instead he sat still, staring about him in utter puzzlement. Tod went to him. "Carl! Carl, we're here!"

Carl looked at him dully. Tod was unaccountably disturbed. Carl always shouted, always bounced; Carl had always seemed to be just a bit larger inside than he was outside, ready to burst through, always thinking faster, laughing more quickly than anyone else.

He allowed Tod to help him down the steps, and sat heavily while Tod got his capsules and beaker for him. Waiting for the liquid to subside, he looked around numbly. Then drank, and almost toppled. April and Tod held him up. When he straightened again, it was abruptly. "Hey!" he roared. "We're here!" He looked up at them. "April! Tod-o! Well what do you know—how are you, kids?"

"Carl?" The voice was the voice of a flute, if a flute could whisper. They looked up. There was a small golden surf of hair tumbled on and over the edge of Moira's Coffin.

Weakly, eagerly, they clambered up to Moira and helped

114

her out. Carl breathed such a sigh of relief that Tod and April stopped to smile at him, at each other.

Carl shrugged out of his weakness as if it were an uncomfortable garment and went to be close to Moira, to care about Moira and nothing else.

A deep labored voice called, "Who's up?"

"Teague! It's Teague . . . all of us, Teague," called Tod. "Carl and Moira and April and me. All except Alma."

Slowly Teague's great head rose out of the Coffin. He looked around with the controlled motion of a radar sweep. When his head stopped its one turning, the motion seemed relayed to his body, which began to move steadily upward. The four who watched him knew intimately what this cost him in sheer will-power, yet no one made any effort to help. Unasked, one did not help Teague.

One leg over, the second. He ignored the bar and stepped down to seat himself on the bottom step as if it were a throne. His hands moved very slowly but without faltering as he helped himself to the capsules, then the beaker. He permitted himself a moment of stillness, eyes closed, nostrils pinched; then life coursed strongly into him. It was as if his muscles visibly filled out a little. He seemed heavier and taller, and when he opened his eyes, they were the deeply vital, commanding light-sources which had drawn them, linked them, led them all during their training.

He looked toward the door in the corner. "Has anyone—"

"We were waiting for you," said Tod. "Shall we . . . can we go look now? I want to see the stars."

"We'll see to Alma first." Teague rose, ignoring the lip of his Coffin and the handhold it offered. He went to Alma's. With his height, he was the only one among them who could see through the top plate without mounting the steps.

Then, without turning, he said, "Wait."

The others, half across the room from him, stopped. Teague turned to them. There was no expression on his face at all. He stood quite motionless for perhaps ten seconds, and then quietly released a breath. He mounted the steps of Alma's Coffin, reached, and the side nearest his own machine sank silently into the floor. He stepped down, and spent a long moment bent over the body inside. From where they stood, tense and frightened, the others could not see inside. They made no effort to move closer.

115

"Tod," said Teague, "get the kit. Surgery *Lambda*. Moira, I'll need you."

The shock of it went to Tod's bones, regenerated, struck him again; yet so conditioned was he to Teague's commands that he was on his feet and moving before Teague had stopped speaking. He went to the after bulkhead and swung open a panel, pressed a stud. There was a metallic whisper, and the heavy case slid out at his feet. He lugged it over to Teague, and helped him rack it on the side of the Coffin. Teague immediately plunged his hands through the membrane at one end of the kit, nodding to Moira to do likewise at the other. Tod stepped back, studiously avoiding a glance in at Alma, and returned to April. She put both her hands tight around his left biceps and leaned close. *"Lambda . . ."* she whispered. "That's . . . parturition, isn't it?"

He shook his head. "Parturition is Surgery *Kappa*," he said painfully. He swallowed. *"Lambda's* Caesarian."

Her crimson eyes widened. "Caesarian? *Alma?* She'd never need a Caesarian!"

He turned to look at her, but he could not see, his eyes stung so. "Not while she lived, she wouldn't," he whispered. He felt the small white hands tighten painfully on his arm. Across the room, Carl sat quietly. Tod squashed the water out of his eyes with the heel of his hand. Carl began pounding knuckles, very slowly, against his own temple.

Teague and Moira were busy for a long time.

II

Tod pulled in his legs and lowered his head until the kneecaps pressed cruelly against his eyebrow ridges. He hugged his shins, ground his back into the wall-panels, and in this red-spangled blackness he let himself live back and back to Alma and joy, Alma and comfort, Alma and courage.

He had sat once, just this way, twisted by misery and anger, blind and helpless, in a dark corner of an equipment shed at the spaceport. The rumor had circulated that April would not come after all, because albinism and the Sirius Rock would not mix. It turned out to be untrue, but that did not matter at the time. He had punched her, punched *Alma!* because in all the world he had been given nothing else to strike out at, and she had found him and had sat

116

down to be with him. She had not even touched her face, where the blood ran; she simply waited until at last he flung himself on her lap and wept like an infant. And no one but he and Alma ever knew of it. . . .

He remembered Alma with the spaceport children, rolling and tumbling on the lawn with them, and in the pool; and he remembered Alma, her face still, looking up at the stars with her soft and gentle eyes, and in those eyes he had seen a challenge as implacable and pervasive as space itself. The tumbling on the lawn, the towering dignity—these co-existed in Alma without friction. He remembered things she had said to him; for each of the things he could recall the kind of light, the way he stood, the very smell of the air at the time. "Never be afraid, Tod. Just think of the worst possible thing that might happen. What you're afraid of will probably not be *that* bad—and anything else just has to be better." And she said once, "Don't confuse logic and truth, however good the logic. You can stick one end of logic in solid ground and throw the other end clear out of the cosmos without breaking it. Truth's a little less flexible." And, "Of *course* you need to be loved, Tod! Don't be ashamed of that, or try to change it. It's not a thing you have to worry about, ever. You are loved. April loves you. And I love you. Maybe I love you even more than April, because she loves everything you are, but I love everything you were and ever will be."

And some of the memories were deeper and more important even than these, but were memories of small things —the meeting of eyes, the touch of a hand, the sound of laughter or a snatch of song, distantly.

Tod descended from memory into a blackness that was only loss and despair, and then a numbness, followed by a reluctant awareness. He became conscious of what, in itself, seemed the merest of trifles: that there was a significance in his pose there against the bulkhead. Unmoving, he considered it. It was comfortable, to be so turned in upon oneself, and so protected, unaware . . . and Alma would have hated to see him this way.

He threw up his head, and self-consciously straightened from his foetal posture. *That's over now,* he told himself furiously, and then, dazed, wondered what he had meant.

He turned to look at April. She was huddled miserably against him, her face and body lax, stopped, disinterested. He thumped his elbow into her ribs, hard enough to make

117

her remember she had ribs. She looked up into his eyes and said, "How? How could . . ."

Tod understood. Of the three couples standard for each ship of the Sirian project, one traditionally would beget children on the planet; one, earlier, as soon as possible after awakening; and one still earlier, for conception would take place within the Coffin. But—not *before* awakening, and surely not long enough before to permit of gestation. It was an impossibility; the vital processes were so retarded within the Coffin that, effectively, there would be no stirring of life at all. So—"How?" April pleaded. "How could . . ."

Tod gazed upon his own misery, then April's, and wondered what it must be that Teague was going through.

Teague, without looking up, said, "Tod."

Tod patted April's shoulder, rose and went to Teague. He did not look into the Coffin. Teague, still working steadily, tilted his head to one side to point. "I need a little more room here."

Tod lifted the transparent cube Teague had indicated and looked at the squirming pink bundle inside. He almost smiled. It was a nice baby. He took one step away and Teague said, "Take 'em all, Tod."

He stacked them and carried them to where April sat. Carl rose and came over, and knelt. The boxes hummed— a vibration which could be felt, not heard—as nutrient-bearing air circulated inside and back to the power-packs. "A nice normal deliv— I mean, a nice normal batch o' brats," Carl said. "Four girls, one boy. Just right."

Tod looked up at him. "There's one more, I think."

There was—another girl. Moira brought it over in the sixth box. "Sweet," April breathed, watching them. "They're sweet."

Moira said, wearily, "That's all."

Tod looked up at her.

"Alma . . . ?"

Moira waved laxly toward the neat stack of incubators. "That's all," she whispered tiredly, and went to Carl.

That's all there is of Alma, Tod thought bitterly. He glanced across at Teague. The tall figure raised a steady hand, wiped his face with his upper arm. His raised hand touched the high end of the Coffin, and for an instant held a grip. Teague's face lay against his arm, pillowed, hidden and still. Then he completed the wiping motion and began stripping the sterile plastic skin from his hands. Tod's heart went out to him, but he bit the insides of his cheeks and kept silent. *A strange tradition,* thought Tod, *that makes it impolite to grieve. . . .*

Teague dropped the shreds of plastic into the disposal slot and turned to face them. He looked at each in turn, and each in turn found some measure of control. He turned then, and pulled a lever, and the side of Alma's Coffin slid silently up.

Good-bye. . . .

Tod put his back against the bulkhead and slid down beside April. He put an arm over her shoulders. Carl and Moira sat close, holding hands. Moira's eyes were shadowed but very much awake. Carl bore an expression almost of sullenness. Tod glanced, then glared at the boxes. Three of the babies were crying, though of course they could not be heard through the plastic incubators. Tod was suddenly conscious of Teague's eyes upon him. He flushed, and then let his anger drain to the capacious inner reservoir which must hold it and all his grief as well.

When he had their attention, Teague sat cross-legged before them and placed a small object on the floor.

Tod looked at the object. At first glance it seemed to be a metal spring about as long as his thumb, mounted vertically on a black base. Then he realized that it was an art object of some kind, made of a golden substance which shimmered and all but flowed. It was an interlocked double spiral; the turns went round and up, round and down, round and up again, with the texture of the gold clearly indicating, in a strange and alive way, which symbolized a rising and falling flux. Shaped as if it had been wound on a cylinder and the cylinder removed, the thing was formed of a continuous wire or rod which had no beginning and no end, but which turned and rose and turned and descended again in an exquisite continuity. . . . Its base was formless, an almost-smoke just as the gold showed an almost-flux; and it was as lightless as ylem.

Teague said, "This was in Alma's Coffin. It was not there when we left Earth."

"It must have been," said Carl flatly.

Teague silently shook his head. April opened her lips, closed them again. Teague said, "Yes, April?"

April shook her head. "Nothing, Teague. Really nothing." But because Teague kept looking at her, waiting, she

119

said, "I was going to say . . . it's beautiful." She hung her head.

Teague's lips twitched. Tod could sense the sympathy there. He stroked April's silver hair. She responded, moving her shoulder slightly under his hand. "What is it, Teague?"

When Teague would not answer, Moira asked, "Did it . . . have anything to do with Alma?"

Teague picked it up thoughtfully. Tod could see the yellow loom it cast against his throat and cheek, the golden points it built in his eyes. "Something did." He paused. "You know she was supposed to conceive on awakening. But to give birth—"

Carl cracked a closed hand against his forehead. "She must have been awake for anyway two hundred and eighty days!"

"Maybe she made it," said Moira.

Tod watched Teague's hand half-close on the object as if it might be precious now. Moira's was a welcome thought, and the welcome could be read on Teague's face. Watching it, Tod saw the complicated spoor of a series of efforts—a gathering of emotions, a determination; the closing of certain doors, the opening of others.

Teague rose. "We have a ship to inspect, sights to take, calculations . . . we've got to tune in Terra Prime, send them a message if we can. Tod, check the corridor air."

"The stars—we'll see the stars!" Tod whispered to April, the heady thought all but eclipsing everything else. He bounded to the corner where the door controls waited. He punched the test button, and a spot of green appeared over the door, indicating that with their awakening, the evacuated chambers, the living and control compartments, had been flooded with air and warmed. "Air okay."

"Go on, then."

They crowded around Tod as he grasped the lever and pushed. *I won't wait for orders,* Tod thought. *I'll slide right across the corridor and open the guard plate and there it'll be—space, and the stars!*

The door opened.

There was no corridor, no bulkhead, no armored porthole, no—

No *ship!*

There was a night out there, dank, warm. It was wet. In it were hooked, fleshy leaves and a tangle of roots; a thing with legs which hopped up on the sill and shimmered its

120

wings for them; a thing like a flying hammer which crashed in and smote the shimmering one and was gone with it, leaving a stain on the deck-plates. There was a sky aglow with a ghastly green. There was a thrashing and a scream out there, a pressure of growth, and a wrongness.

Blood ran down Tod's chin. His teeth met through his lower lip. He turned and looked past three sets of terrified eyes to Teague, who said, "Shut it!"

Tod snatched at the control. It broke off in his hand. . . .

How long does a thought, a long thought, take?

Tod stood with the fractured metal in his hand and thought:

We were told that above all things we must adapt. We were told that perhaps there would be a thin atmosphere by now, on Terra Prime, but that in all likelihood we must live a new kind of life in pressure-domes. We were warned that what we might find would be flash-mutation, where the people could be more or less than human. We were warned, even, that there might be no life on Prime at all. But look at me now—look at all of us. We weren't meant to adapt to this! And we can't. . . .

Somebody shouted while somebody shrieked, each sound a word, each destroying the other. Something thick as a thumb, long as a hand, with a voice like a distant airhorn, hurtled through the door and circled the room. Teague snatched a folded cloak from the clothing-rack and, poising just a moment, batted it out of the air. It skittered, squirming, across the metal floor. He threw the cloak on it to capture it. "Get that door closed."

Carl snatched the broken control lever out of Tod's hand and tried to fit it back into the switch mounting. It crumbled as if it were dried bread. Tod stepped outside, hooked his hands on the edge of the door, and pulled. It would not budge. A lizard as long as his arm scuttled out of the twisted grass and stopped to stare at him. He shouted at it, and with forelegs much too long for such a creature, it pressed itself upward until its body was forty-five degrees from the horizontal. It flicked the end of its long tail upward, and something flew over its head toward Tod, buzzing angrily. Tod turned to see what it was, and as he did the lizard struck from one side and April from the other.

April succeeded and the lizard failed, for its fangs clashed and it fell forward, but April's shoulder had taken

121

Tod on the chest and, off balance as he was, he went flat on his back. The cold, dry, pulsing tail swatted his hand. He gripped it convulsively, held on tight. Part of the tail broke off and buzzed, flipping about on the ground like a click-beetle. But the rest held. Tod scuttled backward to pull the lizard straight as it began to turn on him, got his knees under him, then his feet. He swung the lizard twice around his head and smashed it against the inside of the open door. The part of the tail he was holding then broke off, and the scaly thing thumped inside and slid, causing Moira to leap so wildly to get out of its way that she nearly knocked the stocky Carl off his feet.

Teague swept away the lid of the Surgery *Lambda* kit, inverted it, kicked the clutter of instruments and medicaments aside and clapped the inverted box over the twitching, scaly body.

"April!" Tod shouted. He ran around in a blind semicircle, saw her struggling to her feet in the grass, snatched her up and bounded inside with her. "Carl!" he gasped, "Get the door. . . ."

But Carl was already moving forward with a needle torch. With two deft motions he sliced out a section of the power-arm which was holding the door open. He swung the door to, yelling, "Parametal!"

Tod, gasping, ran to the lockers and brought a length of the synthetic. Carl took the wide ribbon and with a snap of the wrists broke it in two. Each half he bent (for it was very flexible when moved slowly) into a U. He placed one against the door and held out his hand without looking. Tod dropped the hammer into it. Carl tapped the parametal gently and it adhered to the door. He turned his face away and struck it sharply. There was a blue-white flash and the U was rigid and firmly welded to the door. He did the same thing with the other U, welding it to the nearby wall plates. Into the two gudgeons thus formed, Moira dropped a luxalloy bar, and the door was secured.

"Shall I sterilize the floor?" Moira asked.

"No," said Teague shortly.

"But—bacteria . . . spores . . ."

"Forget it," said Teague.

April was crying. Tod held her close, but made no effort to stop her. Something in him, deeper than panic, more essential than wonderment, understood that she could use this circumstance to spend her tears for Alma, and that

122

these tears must be shed now or swell and burst her heart. *So cry,* he pled silently, *cry for both of us, all of us.*

With the end of action, belated shock spread visibly over Carl's face. "The ship's gone," he said stupidly. "We're on a planet." He looked at his hands, turned abruptly to the door, stared at it and began to shiver. Moira went to him and stood quietly, not touching him—just being near, in case she should be needed. April grew gradually silent. Carl said, "I—" and then shook his head.

Click. Shh. Clack, click. Methodically Teague was stacking the scattered contents of the medical kit. Tod patted April's shoulder and went to help. Moira glanced at them, peered closely into Carl's face, then left him and came to lend a hand. April joined them, and at last Carl. They swept up, and racked and stored the clutter, and when Teague lowered a table, they helped get the dead lizard on it and pegged out for dissection. Moira cautiously disentangled the huge insect from the folds of the cloak and clapped a box over it, slid the lid underneath to bring the feebly squirming thing to Teague. He studied it for a long moment, then set it down and peered at the lizard. With forceps he opened the jaws and bent close. He grunted. "April . . ."

She came to look. Teague touched the fangs with the tip of a scalpel. "Look there."

"Grooves," she said. "Like a snake."

Teague reversed the scalpel and with the handle he gingerly pressed upward, at the root of one of the fangs. A cloudy yellow liquid beaded, ran down the groove. He dropped the scalpel and slipped a watch-glass under the tooth to catch the droplet. "Analyze that later," he murmured. "But I'd say you saved Tod from something pretty nasty."

"I didn't even think," said April. "I didn't . . . I never knew there was any animal life on Prime. I wonder what they call this monster."

"The honors are yours, April. You name it."

"They'll have a classification for it already!"

"Who?"

Everyone started to talk, and abruptly stopped. In the awkward silence Carl's sudden laugh boomed. It was a wondrous sound in the frightened chamber. There was comprehension in it, and challenge, and above all, Carl himself—boisterous and impulsive, quick, sure. The laugh was triggered by the gush of talk and its sudden cessation,

123

a small thing in itself. But its substance was understanding, and with that an emotional surge, and with that, the choice of the one emotional expression Carl would always choose.

"Tell them, Carl," Teague said.

Carl's teeth flashed. He waved a thick arm at the door. "That isn't Sirius Prime. Nor Earth. Go ahead, April—name your pet."

April, staring at the lizard, said, *"Crotalidus,* then, because it has a rattle and fangs like a diamondback." Then she paled and turned to Carl, as the full weight of his statement came on her. "Not—*not Prime?"*

Quietly, Teague said, "Nothing like these ever grew on Earth. And Prime is a cold planet. It could never have a climate like that," he nodded toward the door, "no matter how much time has passed."

"But what . . . where . . ." It was Moira.

"We'll find out when we can. But the instruments aren't here—they were in the ship."

"But if it's a new . . . another planet, why didn't you let me sterilize? What about airborne spores? Suppose it had been methane out there or—"

"We've obviously been conditioned to anything in the atmosphere. As to its composition—well, it isn't poisonous, or we wouldn't be standing here talking about it. Wait!" He held up a hand and quelled the babble of questions before it could fully start. "Wondering is a luxury like worrying. We can't afford either. We'll get our answers when we get more evidence."

"What shall we do?" asked April faintly.

"Eat," said Teague. "Sleep." They waited. Teague said, "Then we go outside."

III

There were stars like daisies in a field, like dust in a sunbeam, and like flying, flaming mountains; near ones, far ones, stars of every color and every degree of brilliance. And there were bands of light which must be stars too distant to see. And something was stealing the stars, not taking them away, but swallowing them up, coming closer, eating as it came. And at last there was only one left. Its name was Alma, and it was gone, and there was nothing left but an absorbent blackness and an aching loss.

In this blackness Tod's eyes snapped open, and he gasped, frightened and lost.

"You awake, Tod?" April's small hand touched his face. He took it and drew it to his lips, drinking comfort from it.

From the blackness came Carl's resonant whisper, "We're awake, Teague . . . ?"

The lights flashed on, dim first, brightening swiftly, but not so fast as to dazzle unsuspecting eyes. Tod sat up and saw Teague at the table. On it was the lizard, dissected and laid out as neatly as an exploded view in a machine manual. Over the table, on a gooseneck, was a floodlamp with its lens masked by an infrared filter. Teague turned away from the table, pushing up his "black-light" goggles, and nodded to Tod. There were shadows under his eyes, but otherwise he seemed the same as ever. Tod wondered how many lonely hours he had worked while the two couples slept, doing that meticulous work under the irritating glow so that they would be undisturbed.

Tod went to him. "Has my playmate been talking much?" He pointed at the remains of the lizard.

"Yes and no," said Teague. "Oxygen-breather, all right, and a true lizard. He had a secret weapon—that tail-segment he flips over his head toward his victims. It has primitive ganglia like an Earth salamander's, so that the tail-segment trembles and squirms, sounding the rattles, after he throws it. He also has a skeleton that—but all this doesn't matter. Most important is that he's the analog of our early Permian life, which means [unless he's an evolutionary dead-end like a cockroach] that this planet is a billion years old at the least. And the little fellow here"—he touched the flying thing—"bears this out. It's not an insect, you know. It's an arachnid."

"With *wings?*"

Teague lifted the slender, scorpion-like pincers of the creature and let them fall. "Flat chitinous wings are no more remarkable a leg adaptation than those things. Anyway, in spite of the ingenuity of his engineering, internally he's pretty primitive. All of which lets us hypothesize that we'll find fairly close analogs of what we're used to on Earth."

"Teague," Tod interrupted, his voice lowered, his eyes narrowed to contain the worry that threatened to spill over, "Teague, what's happened?"

"The temperature and humidity here seems to be ex-

125

actly the same as that outside," Teague went on, in precisely the same tone as before. "This would indicate either a warm planet, or a warm season on a temperate planet. In either case it is obvious that—"

"But, *Teague*—"

"—that a good deal of theorizing is possible with a very little evidence, and we need not occupy ourselves with anything else but that evidence."

"Oh," said Tod. He backed off a step. "Oh," he said again, "sorry, Teague." He joined the others at the food dispensers, feeling like a cuffed puppy. *But he's right,* he thought. *As Alma said . . . of the many things which might have happened, only one actually has. Let's wait then, and worry about that one thing when we can name it.*

There was a pressure on his arm. He looked up from his thoughts and into April's searching eyes. He knew that she had heard, and he was unreasonably angry at her. "Damn it, he's so cold-blooded," he blurted defensively, but in a whisper.

April said, "He has to stay with things he can understand, every minute." She glanced swiftly at the closed Coffin. "Wouldn't you?"

There was a sharp pain and a bitterness in Tod's throat as he thought about it. He dropped his eyes and mumbled, "No, I wouldn't. I don't think I could." There was a difference in his eyes as he glanced back at Teague. *But it's so easy, after all, for strong people to be strong,* he thought.

"Teague, what'll we wear?" Carl called.

"Skinflex."

"Oh, no!" cried Moira. "It's so clingy and hot!"

Carl laughed at her. He swept up the lizard's head and opened its jaws. "Smile at the lady. She wouldn't put any tough old skinflex in the way of your pretty teeth!"

"Put it down," said Teague sharply, though there was a flicker of amusement in his eyes. "It's still loaded with God-knows-what alkaloid. Moira, he's right. Skinflex just doesn't puncture."

Moira looked respectfully at the yellow fangs and went obediently to storage, where she pulled out the suits.

"We'll keep close together, back to back," said Teague as they helped each other into the suits. "All the weapons are . . . were . . . in the forward storage compartment, so we'll improvise. Tod, you and the girls each take a globe

126

of anesthene. It's the fastest anesthetic we have and it ought to take care of anything that breathes oxygen. I'll take scalpels. Carl—"

"The hammer," Carl grinned. His voice was fairly thrumming with excitement.

"We won't attempt to fasten the door from outside. I don't mean to go farther than ten meters out, this first time. Just—you, Carl—lift off the bar as we go out, get the door shut as quickly as possible, and prop it there. Whatever happens, do not attack anything out there unless you are attacked first, or unless I say so."

Hollow-eyed, steady, Teague moved to the door with the others close around him. Carl shifted the hammer to his left hand, lifted the bar and stood back a little, holding it like a javelin. Teague, holding a glittering lancet lightly in each hand, pushed the door open with his foot. They boiled through, stepped aside for Carl as he butted the rod deep into the soil and against the closed door. "All set."

They moved as a unit for perhaps three meters, and stopped.

It was daytime now, but such a day as none of them had dreamed of. The light was green, very nearly a lime-green, and the shadows were purple. The sky was more lavender than blue. The air was warm and wet.

They stood at the top of a low hill. Before them a tangle of jungle tumbled up at them. So vital, so completely alive, it seemed to move by its own power of growth. Stirring, murmuring, it was too big, too much, too wide and deep and intertwined to assimilate at a glance, the thought, *this is a jungle,* was a pitiable understatement.

To the left, savannah-like grassland rolled gently down to the choked margins of a river—calm-faced, muddy and secretive. It too seemed astir with inner growings. To the right, more jungle. Behind them, the bland and comforting wall of their compartment.

Above—

It may have been April who saw it first; in any case, Tod always associated the vision with April's scream.

They moved as she screamed, five humans jerked back then like five dolls on a single string, pressed together and to the compartment wall by an overwhelming claustrophobia. They were ants under a descending heel, flies on an anvil . . . together their backs struck the wall and they cowered there, looking up.

And it was not descending. It was only—big. It was just

127

that it was there, over them.

April said, later, that it was like a cloud. Carl would argue that it was cylindrical, with flared ends and a narrow waist. Teague never attempted to describe it, because he disliked inaccuracies, and Moira was too awed to try. To Tod, the object had no shape. It was a luminous opacity between him and the sky, solid, massive as mountains. There was only one thing they agreed on, and that was that it was a ship.

And out of the ship came the golden ones.

They appeared under the ship as speckles of light, and grew in size as they descended, so that the five humans must withstand a second shock: they had known the ship was huge, but had not known until now how very high above them it hung.

Down they came, dozens, hundreds. They filled the sky over the jungle and around the five, moving to make a spherical quadrant from the horizontal to the zenith, a full hundred and eighty degrees from side to side—a radiant floating shell with its concave surface toward, around, above them. They blocked out the sky and the jungle-tops, cut off most of the strange green light, replacing it with their own—for each glowed coolly.

Each individual was distinct and separate. Later, they would argue about the form and shape of the vessel, but the exact shape of these golden things was never even mentioned. Nor did they ever agree on a name for them. To Carl they were an army, to April, angels. Moira called them (secretly) "the seraphim," and to Tod they were masters. Teague never named them.

For measureless time they hung there, with the humans gaping up at them. There was no flutter of wings, no hum of machinery to indicate how they stayed aloft, and if each individual had a device to keep him afloat, it was of a kind the humans could not recognize. They were beautiful, awesome, uncountable.

And nobody was afraid.

Tod looked from side to side, from top to bottom of this incredible formation, and became aware that it did not touch the ground. Its lower edge was exactly horizontal, at his eye level. Since the hill fell away on all sides, he could see under this lower edge, here the jungle, there down across the savannah to the river. In a new amazement he saw eyes, and protruding heads.

In the tall grass at the jungle margin was a scurry and cease, scurry and cease, as newtlike animals scrambled not quite into the open and froze, watching. Up in the lower branches of the fleshy, hook-leaved trees, the heavy scaly heads of leaf-eaters showed, and here and there was the armed head of a lizard with catlike tearing tusks.

Leather-winged fliers flapped clumsily to rest in the branches, hung for a moment for all the world like broken umbrellas, then achieved balance and folded their pinions. Something slid through the air, almost caught a branch, missed it and tumbled end-over-end to the ground, resolving itself into a broad-headed, scaly thing with wide membranes between fore and hind legs. And Tod saw his acquaintance of the night before, with its serrated tail and needle fangs.

And though there must have been eater and eaten here, hunter and hunted, they all watched silently, turned like living compass-needles to the airborne mystery surrounding the humans. They crowded together like a nightmare parody of the Lion and the Lamb, making a constellation, a galaxy of bright and wondering eyes; their distance from each other being, in its way, cosmic.

Tod turned his face into the strange light, and saw one of the golden beings separate from the mass and drift down and forward and stop. Had this living shell been a segment of curving mirror, this one creature would have been at its focal point. For a moment there was complete stillness, a silent waiting. Then the creature made a deep . . . *gesture.* Behind it, all the others did the same.

If ten thousand people stand ten thousand meters away, and if, all at once, they kneel, it is hardly possible to see just what it is they have done; yet the aspect of their mass undergoes a definite change. So it was with the radiant shell—it changed, all of it, without moving. There was no mistaking the nature of the change, though its meaning was beyond knowing. It was an obeisance. It was an expression of profound respect, first to the humans themselves, next, and hugely, to something the humans represented. It was unquestionably an act of worship.

And what, thought Tod, *could we symbolize to these shining ones?* He was a scarab beetle or an Egyptian cat, a Hindu cow or a Teuton tree, told suddenly that it was sacred.

All the while there flooded down the thing which Carl

129

had tried so ineptly to express: *"We're sorry. But it will be all right. You will be glad. You can be glad now."*

At last there was a change in the mighty formation. The center rose and the wings came in, the left one rising and curling to tighten the curve, the right one bending inward without rising. In a moment the formation was a column, a hollow cylinder. It began to rotate slowly, divided into a series of close-set horizontal rings. Alternate rings slowed and stopped and began a counter-rotation, and with a sudden shift, became two interlocked spirals. Still the over-all formation was a hollow cylinder, but now it was composed of an upward and a downward helix.

The individuals spun and swirled down and down, up and up, and kept this motion within the cylinder, and the cylinder quite discrete, as it began to rise. Up and up it lifted, brilliantly, silently, the living original of that which they had found by Alma's body . . . up and up, filling the eye and the mind with its complex and controlled ascent, its perfect continuity; for here was a thing with no beginning and no end, all flux and balance where each rising was matched by a fall and each turn by its counterpart.

High, and higher, and at last it was a glowing spot against the hovering shadow of the ship, which swallowed it up. The ship left then, not moving, but fading away like the streamers of an aurora, but faster. In three heartbeats it was there, perhaps it was there, it was gone.

Tod closed his eyes, seeing that dynamic double helix. The tip of his mind was upon it; he trembled on the edge of revelation. He *knew* what that form symbolized. He knew it contained the simple answer to his life and their lives, to this planet and its life and the lives which were brought to it. If a cross is more than an instrument of torture, more than the memento of an event; if the *crux ansata*, the Yin-and-Yang, David's star and all such crystallizations were but symbols of great systems of philosophy, then this dynamic intertwined spiral, this free-flowing, rigidly choreographed symbol was . . . was—

Something grunted, something screamed, and the wondrous answer turned and rose spiraling away from him to be gone in three heartbeats. Yet in that moment he knew it was there for him when he had the time, the phasing, the bringing-together of whatever elements were needed. He could not use it yet but he had it. He had it.

Another scream, an immense thrashing all about. The spell was broken and the armistice over. There were chargings and fleeings, cries of death-agony and roaring challenges in and over the jungle, through the grasses to the suddenly boiling river. Life goes on, and death with it, but there must be more than life when too much life is thrown together.

IV

It may be that their five human lives were saved, in that turbulent reawakening, only by their alienness, for the life around them was cheek-and-jowl with its familiar enemy, its familiar quarry, its familiar food, and there need be no experimenting with the five soft containers of new rich juices standing awestruck with their backs to their intrusive shelter.

Then slowly they met one another's eyes. They cared enough for each other so that there was a gladness of sharing. They cared enough for themselves so that there was also a sheepishness, a troubled self-analysis: *What did I do while I was out of my mind?*

They drew together before the door and watched the chase and slaughter around them as it subsided toward its usual balance of hunting and killing, eating and dying. Their hands began to remember the weapons they held, their minds began to reach for reality.

"They were angels," April said, so softly that no one but Tod heard her. Tod watched her lips tremble and part, and knew that she was about to speak the thing he had almost grasped, but then Teague spoke again, and Tod could see the comprehension fade from her and be gone. "Look! Look there!" said Teague, and moved down the wall to the corner.

What had been an inner compartment of their ship was now an isolated cube, and from its back corner, out of sight until now, stretched another long wall. At regular intervals were doors, each fastened by a simple outside latch of parametal.

Teague stepped to the first door, the others crowding close. Teague listened intently, then stepped back and threw the door open.

Inside was a windowless room, blazing with light. Around the sides, machines were set. Tod instantly recog-

131

nized their air-cracker, the water-purifiers, the protein-converter and one of the auxiliary power-plants. In the center was a generator coupled to a light-metal fusion motor. The output buses were neatly insulated, coupled through fuseboxes and resistance controls to a "Christmas tree" multiple outlet. Cables ran through the wall to the Coffin compartment and to the line of unexplored rooms to their left.

"They've left us power, at any rate," said Teague. "Let's look down the line."

Fish, Tod snarled silently. *Dead man! After what you've just seen you should be on your knees with the weight of it, you should put out your eyes to remember better. But all you can do is take inventory of your nuts and bolts.*

Tod looked at the others, at their strained faces and their continual upward glances, as if the bright memory had magnetism for them. He could see the dream fading under Teague's untimely urgency. *You couldn't let us live with it quietly, even for a moment.* Then another inward voice explained to him, *But you see, they killed Alma.*

Resentfully he followed Teague.

Their ship had been dismantled, strung out along the hilltop like a row of shacks. They were interconnected, wired up, re-stacked, ready and reeking with efficiency—the lab, the library, six chambers full of mixed cargo, then—then the noise Teague made was as near to a shout of glee as Tod had ever heard from the man. The door he had just opened showed their instruments inside, all the reference tapes and tools and manuals. There was even a dome in the roof, and the refractor was mounted and waiting.

"April?" Tod looked, looked again. She was gone. "April!"

She emerged from the library, three doors back. "Teague!"

Teague pulled himself away from the array of instruments and went to her. "Teague," she said, "every one of the reels has been read."

"How do you know?"

"None of them are rewound."

Teague looked up and down the row of doors. "That doesn't sound like the way they—" The unfinished sentence was enough. Whoever had built this from their ship's substance worked according to function and with a fine efficiency.

Teague entered the library and picked a tape-reel from its rack. He inserted the free end of film into a slot and pressed a button. The reel spun and the film disappeared inside the cabinet.

Teague looked up and back. Every single reel was inside out on the clips. "They could have rewound them," said Teague, irritated.

"Maybe they wanted us to know that they'd read them," said Moira.

"Maybe they did," Teague murmured. He picked up a reel, looked at it, picked up another and another. "Music. A play. And here's our personal stuff—behavior film, training records, everything."

Carl said, "Whoever read through all this knows a lot about us."

Teague frowned. "Just us?"

"Who else?"

"Earth," said Teague. "All of it."

"You mean we were captured and analyzed so that whoever they are could get a line on Earth? You think they're going to attack Earth?"

"'You mean . . . You think . . .'" Teague mimicked coldly. "I mean nothing and I think nothing! Tod, would you be good enough to explain to this impulsive young man what you learned from me earlier? That we need concern ourselves only with evidence?"

Tod shuffled his feet, wishing not to be made an example for anyone, especially Carl, to follow. Carl flushed and tried to smile. Moira took his hand secretly and squeezed it. Tod heard a slight exhalation beside him and looked quickly at April. She was angry. There were times when he wished she would not be angry.

She pointed. "Would you call *that* evidence, Teague?"

They followed her gesture. One of the tape-readers stood open. On its reelshelf stood the counterpart of the strange object they had seen twice before—once, in miniature, found in Alma's Coffin; once again, huge in the sky. This was another of the miniatures.

Teague stared at it, then put out his hand. As his fingers touched it, the pilot-jewel on the tape-reader flashed on, and a soft, clear voice filled the room.

Tod's eyes stung. He had thought he would never hear that voice again. As he listened, he held to the lifeline of April's presence, and felt his lifeline tremble.

Alma's voice said:

133

"They made some adjustments yesterday with the needle-clusters in my Coffin, so I think they will put me back into it . . . Teague, oh, Teague, I'm going to die!

"They brought me the recorder just now. I don't know whether it's for their records or for you. If it's for you, then I must tell you . . . how can I tell you?

"I've watched them all this time . . . how long? Months . . . I don't know. I conceived when I awoke, and the babies are coming very soon now; it's been long enough for that; and yet—how can I tell you?

"They boarded us, I don't know how. I don't know why, nor where . . . outside, space is strange, wrong. It's all misty, without stars, crawling with blurs and patches of light.

"They understand me; I'm sure of that—what I say, what I think. I can't understand them at all. They radiate feelings—sorrow, curiosity, confidence, respect. When I began to realize I would die, they gave me a kind of regret. When I broke and cried and said I wanted to be with you, Teague, they reassured me; they said I would. I'm sure that's what they said. But how could that be?

"They are completely dedicated in what they are doing. Their work is a religion to them, and we are part of it. They . . . value us, Teague. They didn't just find us. They chose us. It's as if we were the best part of something even they consider great.

"The best . . . ! Among them I feel like an amoeba. They're beautiful, Teague. Important. Very sure of what they are doing. It's that certainty that makes me believe what I have to believe; I am going to die, and you will live, and you and I will be together. How can that be? How can that be?

"Yet it is true, so believe it with me, Teague. But—find out how!

"Teague, every day they have put a machine on me, radiating. It has to do with the babies. It isn't done to harm them, I'm sure of that. I'm their mother and I'm sure of it. They won't die.

"I will. I can feel their sorrow.

"And I will be with you, and they are joyous about that. . . .

"Teague—find out how!"

Tod closed his eyes so that he would not look at Teague, and wished with all his heart that Teague had been alone to hear that ghostly voice. As to what it had said, the words stood as a frame for a picture he could not see, showing him only where it was, not what it meant. Alma's voice had been tremulous and unsure, but he knew it well enough to know that joy and certitude had lived with her as she spoke. There was wonderment, but no fear.

Knowing that it might be her only message to them, should she not have told them more—facts, figures, measurements?

Then an old, old tale flashed into his mind, an early thing from the ancient Amerenglish, by Hynlen (Henlyne, was it?—no matter) about a man who tried to convey to humanity a description of the super-beings who had captured him, with only his body as a tablet and his nails as a stylus. Perhaps he was mad by the time he finished, but his message was clear at least to him: *"Creation took eight days."* How would he, Tod, describe an association with the ones he had seen in the sky outside, if he had been with them for nearly three hundred days?

April tugged gently at his arm. He turned toward her, still avoiding the sight of Teague. April inclined her shining white head to the door. Moira and Carl already stood outside. They joined them, and waited wordlessly until Teague came out.

When he did, he was grateful, and he need not say so. He came out, a great calm in his face and voice, passed them and let them follow him to his methodical examination of the other compartments, to finish his inventory.

Food stores, cable and conduit, metal and parametal rod and sheet stock, tools and tool-making matrices and dies. A hangar, in which lay their lifeboat, fully equipped.

But there was no long-range communication device, and no parts for one.

And there was no heavy space-drive mechanism, nor tools to make one, nor fuel if they should make the tools.

Back in the instrument room, Carl grunted. "Somebody means for us to stick around."

"The boat—"

Teague said, "I don't think they'd have left us the boat if Earth was in range."

"We'll build a beacon," Tod said suddenly. "We'll get a rescue ship out to us."

"Out where?" asked Teague drily.

They followed his gaze. Bland and silent, merciless, the decay chronometer stared back at them. Built around a standard radioactive, it had two dials—one which mea-

135

sured the amount of energy radiated by the material, and one which measured the loss mass. When they checked, the reading was correct. They checked, and the reading was 64.

"Sixty-four years," said Teague. "Assuming we averaged as much as one-half light speed, which isn't likely, we must be thirty light-years away from Earth. Thirty years to get a light-beam there, sixty or more to get a ship back, plus time to make the beacon and time for Earth to understand the signal and prepare a ship. . . ." He shook his head.

"Plus the fact," Tod said in a strained voice, "that there is no habitable planet in a thirty-year radius from Sol. Except Prime."

Shocked, they gaped silently at this well-known fact. A thousand years of scrupulous search with the best instruments could not have missed a planet like this at such a distance.

"Then the chronometer's wrong!"

"I'm afraid not," said Teague. "It's sixty-four years since we left Earth, and that's that."

"And this planet doesn't exist," said Carl with a sour smile, "and I suppose that is also that."

"Yes, Teague," said Tod. "One of those two facts can't exist with the other."

"They can because they do," said Teague. "There's a missing factor. Can a man breathe under water, Tod?"

"If he has a diving-helmet."

Teague spread his hands. "It took sixty-four years to get to this planet *if*. We have to find the figurative diving-helmet." He paused. "The evidence in favor of the planet's existence is fairly impressive," he said wryly. "Let's check the other fact."

"How?"

"The observatory."

They ran to it. The sky glowed its shimmering green, but through it the stars had begun to twinkle. Carl got to the telescope first, put a big hand on the swing-controls, and said, "Where first?" He tugged at the instrument. "Hey!" He tugged again.

"Don't!" said Teague sharply. Carl let go and backed away. Teague switched on the lights and examined the instrument. "It's already connected to the compensators," he said. "Hmp! Our hosts are most helpful." He looked at the setting of the small motors which moved the instrument to cancel diurnal rotation effects. "Twenty-eight hours, thirteen minutes plus. Well, if that's correct for this

136

planet, it's proof that this isn't Earth or Prime—if we needed proof." He touched the controls lightly. "Carl, what's the matter here?"

Carl bent to look. There were dabs of dull silver on the threads of the adjusting screws. He touched them. "Parametal," he said. "Unflashed, but it has adhered enough to jam the threads. Take a couple of days to get it off without jarring it. Look here—they've done the same thing with the objective screws!"

"We look at what they want us to see, and like it," said Tod.

"Maybe it's something we want to see," said April gently.

Only half-teasing, Tod said, "Whose side are you on, anyway?"

Teague put his eye to the instrument. His hands, by habit, strayed to the focusing adjustment, but found it locked the same way as the others. "Is there a Galactic Atlas?"

"Not in the rack," said Moira a moment later.

"Here," said April from the chart table. Awed, she added, "Open."

Tensely they waited while Teague took his observation and referred to the atlas and to the catalog they found lying under it. When at last he lifted his face from the calculations, it bore the strangest expression Tod had ever seen there.

"Our diving-helmet," he said at last, very slowly, too evenly, "that is, the factor which rationalizes our two mutually exclusive facts, is simply that our captors have a faster-than-light drive."

"But according to theory—"

"According to our telescope," Teague interrupted, "through which I have just seen Sol, and these references so thoughtfully laid out for us . . ." Shockingly, his voice broke. He took two deep breaths, and said, "Sol is two-hundred and seventeen light-years away. That sun which set a few minutes ago is Beta Librae." He studied their shocked faces, one by one. "I don't know what we shall eventually call this place," he said with difficulty, "but we had better get used to calling it home."

They called the planet Viridis ("the greenest name I can think of," Moira said) because none among them had ever seen such a green. It was more than the green of growing, for the sunlight was green-tinged and at night

137

the whole sky glowed green, a green as bright as the
brightest silver of Earth's moon, as water molecules,
cracked by the star's intense ultraviolet, celebrated their
nocturnal reunion.

They called the moons Wynken, Blynken and Nod, and
the sun they called—the sun.

They worked like slaves, and then like scientists, which
is a change of occupation but not a change of pace. They
built a palisade of a cypress-like, straight-grained wood,
each piece needle-pointed, double-laced with parametal
wire. It had a barred gate and peepholes with periscopes
and permanent swivel-mounts for the needle guns they
were able to fabricate from tube-sock and spare sole-
noids. They roofed the enclosure with parametal mesh
which, at one point, could be rolled back to launch the
lifeboat.

They buried Alma.

They tested and analyzed, classified, processed, re-
searched everything in the compound and within easy
reach of it—soil, vegetation, fauna. They developed an
insect-repellent solution to coat the palisade and an in-
secticide with an automatic spray to keep the compound
clear of the creatures, for they were numerous, large,
and occasionally downright dangerous, like the "flying
caterpillar" which kept its pseudopods in its winged form
and enthusiastically broke them off in the flesh of whatever attacked them, leaving an angry rash and suppurating
sores. They discovered three kinds of edible seed and another which yielded a fine hydrocarbonic oil much like soy,
and a flower whose calyces, when dried and then soaked
and broiled, tasted precisely like crab-meat.

For a time they were two separate teams, virtually isolated from each other. Moira and Teague collected minerals
and put them through the mass spectroscope and the radio-
analyzers, and it fell to April to classify the life-forms,
with Carl and Tod competing mightily to bring in new ones.
Or at least photographs of new ones. Two-ton *Parametrodon*, familiarly known as Dopey—a massive herbivore with
just enough intelligence to move its jaws—was hardly the
kind of thing to be carried home under one's arm, and
Felodon, the scaly carnivore with the catlike tusks, though
barely as long as a man, was about as friendly as a half-
starved wolverine.

Tetrapodys (Tod called it 'Umbrellabird') turned out
to be a rewarding catch. They stumbled across a vine which

bore foul-smelling pods; these the clumsy amphibious bats found irresistible. Carl synthesized the evil stuff and improved upon it, and they smeared it on tree-boles by the river. *Tetrapodys* came there by the hundreds and laid eggs apparently in sheer frustration. These eggs were camouflaged by a frilly green membrane, for all the world like the ground-buds of the giant water-fern. The green shoots tasted like shallots and were fine for salad when raw and excellent as onion soup when stewed. The half-hatched *Tetrapodys* yielded ligaments which when dried made excellent self-baited fish-hooks. The wing-muscles of the adult tasted like veal cutlet with fish-sauce, and the inner, or main shell of the eggs afforded them an amazing shoe-sole—light, tough, and flexible which, for some unknown reason, *Felodon* would not track.

Pteronauchis, or "flapping frog," was the gliding newt they had seen on that first day. Largely nocturnal, it was phototropic; a man with a strong light could fill a bushel with the things in minutes. Each specimen yielded twice as many, twice as large, and twice as good frog-legs as a Terran frog.

There were no mammals.

There were flowers in profusion—white (a sticky green in that light) purple, brown, blue, and, of course, the ubiquitous green. No red—as a matter of fact, there was virtually no red anywhere on the planet. April's eyes became a feast for them all. It is impossible to describe the yearning one can feel for an absent color. And so it was that a legend began with them. Twice Tod had seen a bright red growth. The first time he thought it was a mushroom, the second it seemed more of a lichen. The first time it was surrounded by a sea of crusher ants on the move—a fearsome carpet which even *Parametrodon* respected. The second time he had seen it from twenty meters away and had just turned toward it when not one, but three *Felodons* came hurtling through the undergrowth at him.

He came back later, both times, and found nothing. And once Carl swore he saw a brilliant red plant move slowly into a rock crevice as he approached. The thing became their *edelweiss*—very nearly their Grail.

Rough diamonds lay in the streambeds and emeralds glinted in the night-glow, and for the Terran-oriented mind there was incalculable treasure to be scratched up just below the steaming humus: iridium, ruthenium, metallic neptunium 237. There was an unaccountable (at first) shift toward the heavier metals. The ruthenium-rhodium-palladium group was as plentiful on Viridis as the iron-nickel-cobalt series on Earth; cadmium was actually more plentiful here than its relative, zinc. Technetium was present, though rare, on the crust, while Earth's has long since decayed.

Vulcanism was common on Viridis, as could be expected in the presence of so many radioactives. From the lifeboat they had seen bald-spots where there were particularly high concentrations of "hot" material. In some of these there was life.

At the price of a bout of radiation sickness, Carl went into one such area briefly for specimens. What he found was extraordinary—a tree which was warm to the touch, which used minerals and water at a profligate pace, and which, when transplanted outside an environment which destroyed cells almost as fast as they developed, went cancerous, grew enormously, and killed itself with its own terrible viability. In the same lethal areas lived a primitive worm which constantly discarded segments to keep pace with its rapid growth, and which also grew visibly and died of living too fast when taken outside.

The inclination of the planet's axis was less than 2°, so that there were virtually no seasons, and very little variation in temperature from one latitude to another. There were two continents and an equatorial sea, no mountains, no plains, and few large lakes. Most of the planet was gently rolling hill-country and meandering rivers, clothed in thick jungle or grass. The spot where they had awakened was as good as any other, so there they stayed, wandering less and less as they amassed information. Nowhere was there an artifact of any kind, nor any slightest trace of previous habitation. Unless, of course, one considered the existence itself of life on this planet. For Permian life can hardly be expected to develop in less than a billion years; yet the irreproachable calendar inherent in the radioactive bones of Viridis insisted that the planet was no more than thirty-five million years old.

V

When Moira's time came, it went hard with her, and Carl forgot to swagger because he could not help. Teague and April took care of her, and Tod stayed with Carl, wishing for the right thing to say and not finding it, wanting to do something for this new strange man with Carl's face, and unsure hands which twisted each other, clawed the ground, wiped cruelly at the scalp, at the shins, restless, terrified. Through Carl, Tod learned a little more of what he never wanted to know—what it must have been like for Teague when he lost Alma.

Alma's six children were toddlers by then, bright and happy in the only world they had ever known. They had been named for moons—Wynken, Blynken and Nod, Rhea, Callisto and Titan. Nod and Titan were the boys, and they and Rhea had Alma's eyes and hair and sometimes Alma's odd, brave stillness—a sort of suspension of the body while the mind went out to grapple and conquer instead of fearing. If the turgid air and the radiant ground affected them, they did not show it, except perhaps in their rapid development.

They heard Moira cry out. It was like laughter, but it was pain. Carl sprang to his feet. Tod took his arm and Carl pulled it away. "Why can't I do something? Do I have to just *sit* here?"

"Shh. She doesn't feel it. That's a tropism. She'll be all right. Sit down, Carl. Tell you what you can do—you can name them. Think. Think of a nice set of names, all connected in some way. Teague used moons. What are you going to—"

"Time enough for that," Carl grunted. "Tod . . . do you know what I'll . . . I'd be if she—if something happened?"

"Nothing's going to happen."

"I'd just cancel out. I'm not Teague. I couldn't carry it. How does Teague do it . . . ?" Carl's voice lapsed to a mumble.

"Names," Tod reminded him. "Seven, eight of 'em. Come on, now."

"Think she'll have eight?"

"Why not? She's normal." He nudged Carl. "Think of names. I know! How many of the old signs of the zodiac would make good names?"

"Don't remember 'em."

"I do. Aries, that's good. Taurus. Gem—no; you wouldn't want to call a child 'Twins.' Leo—that's *fine!*"

"Libra," said Carl, "for a girl. Aquarius, Sagittarius—how many's that?"

Tod counted on his fingers. "Six. Then, Virgo and Capricorn. And you're all set!" But Carl wasn't listening. In

141

two long bounds he reached April, who was just stepping into the compound. She looked tired. She looked more than tired. In her beautiful eyes was a great pity, the color of a bleeding heart.

"Is she all right? Is she?" They were hardly words, those hoarse, rushed things.

April smiled with her lips, while her eyes poured pity. "Yes, yes, she'll be all right. It wasn't too bad."

Carl whooped and pushed past her. She caught his arm, and for all her frailty, swung him around.

"Not yet, Carl. Teague says to tell you first—"

"The babies? What about them? How many, April?"

April looked over Carl's shoulder at Tod. She said, "Three."

Carl's face relaxed, numb, and his eyes went round. "Th—what? Three so far, you mean. There'll surely be more. . . ."

She shook her head.

Tod felt the laughter explode within him, and he clamped his jaws on it. It surged at him, hammered in the back of his throat. And then he caught April's pleading eyes. He took strength from her, and bottled up a great bray of merriment.

Carl's voice was the last fraying thread of hope. "The others died, then."

She put a hand on his cheek. "There were only three. Carl . . . don't be mean to Moira."

"Oh, I won't," he said with difficulty. "She couldn't . . . I mean it wasn't her doing." He flashed a quick, defensive look at Tod, who was glad now he had controlled himself. What was in Carl's face meant murder for anyone who dared laugh.

April said, "Not your doing either, Carl. It's this planet. It must be."

"Thanks, April," Carl muttered. He went to the door, stopped, shook himself like a big dog. He said again, "Thanks," but this time his voice didn't work and it was only a whisper. He went inside.

Tod bolted for the corner of the building, whipped around it and sank to the ground, choking. He held both hands over his mouth and laughed until he hurt. When at last he came to a limp silence, he felt April's presence. She stood quietly watching him, waiting.

"I'm sorry," he said. "I'm sorry. But . . . it *is* funny."

She shook her head gravely. "We're not on Earth, Tod. A new world means new manners, too. That would apply even on Terra Prime if we'd gone there."

"I suppose," he said, and then repressed another giggle.

"I always thought it was a silly kind of joke anyway," she said primly. "Judging virility by the size of a brood. There isn't any scientific basis for it. Men are silly. They used to think that virility could be measured by the amount of hair on their chests, or how tall they were. There's nothing wrong with having only three."

"Carl?" grinned Tod. "The big ol' swashbuckler?" He let the grin fade. "All right, Ape. I won't let Carl see me laugh. Or you either. All right?" A peculiar expression crossed his face. "What was that you said? April! Men never had hair on their chests!"

"Yes they did. Ask Teague."

"I'll take your word for it." He shuddered. "I can't imagine it unless a man had a tail too. And bony ridges over his eyes."

"It wasn't so long ago that they had. The ridges, anyway. Well—I'm glad you didn't laugh in front of him. You're nice, Tod."

"You're nice too." He pulled her down beside him and hugged her gently. "Bet you'll have a dozen."

"I'll try." She kissed him.

When specimen-hunting had gone as far as it could, classification became the settlement's main enterprise. And gradually, the unique pattern of Viridian life began to emerge.

Viridis had its primitive fish and several of the mollusca, but the fauna was primarily arthropods, and reptiles. The interesting thing about each of the three branches was the close relationship between species. It was almost as if evolution took a major step with each generation, instead of bumbling along as on Earth, where certain stages of development are static for thousands, millions of years. *Pterodon*, for example, existed in three varieties, the simplest of which showed a clear similarity to *pteronauchis*, the gliding newt. A simple salamander could be shown to be the common ancestor of both the flapping frog and the massive *Parametrodon*, and there were strong similarities between this salamander and the worm which fathered the arthropods.

They lived close to the truth for a long time without being able to see it, for man is conditioned to think of evolution from simple to complex, from ooze to animalcule to mollusc to ganoid; amphibid to monotreme to primate to tinker . . . losing the significance of the fact that all these co-exist. Was the vertebrate eel of pre-history a *higher* form of life than his simpler descendant? The whale lost his legs; this men call recidivism, a sort of backsliding in evolution, and treat it as a kind of illegitimacy.

Men are oriented out of simplicity toward the complex, and make of the latter a goal. Nature treats complex matters as expediencies and so is never confused. It is hardly surprising, then, that the Viridis colony took so long to discover their error, for the weight of evidence was in error's favor. There was indeed an unbroken line from the lowest forms of life to the highest, and to assume that they had a common ancestor was a beautifully consistent hypothesis, of the order of accuracy an archer might display in hitting dead center, from a thousand paces, a bowstring with the nock of his arrow.

The work fell more and more on the younger ones. Teague isolated himself, not by edict, but by habit. It was assumed that he was working along his own lines; and then it became usual to proceed without him, until finally he was virtually a hermit in their midst. He was aging rapidly; perhaps it hurt something in him to be surrounded by so much youth. His six children thrived, and with Carl's three, ran naked in the jungle armed only with their sticks and their speed. They were apparently, practically immune to everything Viridis might bring against them, even *Crotalidus'* fangs, which gave them the equivalent of a severe bee-sting (as opposed to what had happened to Moira once, when they had had to reactivate one of the Coffins to keep her alive).

Tod would come and sit with him sometimes, and as long as there was no talk, the older man seemed to gain something from the visits. But he preferred to be alone, living as much as he could with memories for which not even a new world could afford a substitute.

Tod said to Carl, "Teague is going to wither up and blow away if we can't interest him in something."

"He's interested enough to spend a lot of time with whatever he's thinking about," Carl said bluntly.

"But I'd like it better if he was interested in something

144

here, now. I wish we could . . . I wish—" But he could think of nothing, and it was a constant trouble to him.

Little Titan was killed, crushed under a great clumsy *Parametrodon* which slid down a bank on him while the child was grubbing for the scarlet cap of the strange red mushroom they had glimpsed from time to time. It was in pursuit of one of these that Moira had been bitten by the *Crotalidus*. One of Carl's children was drowned—just how, no one knew. Aside from these tragedies, life was easy and interesting. The compound began to look more like a *kraal* as they acclimated, for although the adults never adapted as well as the children, they did become far less sensitive to insect bites and the poison weeds which first troubled them.

It was Teague's son Nod who found what was needed to bring Teague's interest back, at least for a while. The child came back to the compound one day, trailed by two slinking *Felodons* who did not catch him because they kept pausing and pausing to lap up gouts of blood which marked his path. Nod's ear was torn and he had a greenstick break in his left ulna, and a dislocated wrist. He came weeping, weeping tears of joy. He shouted as he wept, great proud noises. Once in the compound he collapsed, but he would not lose consciousness, nor his grip on his prize, until Teague came. Then he handed Teague the mushroom and fainted.

The mushroom was and was not like anything on Earth. Earth has a fungus called *schizophyllum*, not uncommon but most strange. Though not properly a fungus, the red "mushroom" of Viridis had many of the functions of *schizophyllum*.

Schizophyllum produces spores of four distinct types, each of which grows into a genetically distinct, completely dissimilar plant. Three of these are sterile. The fourth produces *schizophyllum*.

The red mushroom of Viridis also produced four distinct heterokaryons or genetically different types, and the spores of one of these produced the mushroom.

Teague spent an engrossing earth-year in investigating the other three.

VI

Sweating and miserable in his integument of flex-skin, Tod hunched in the crotch of a finger-tree. His knees were drawn up and his head was down; his arms clasped his shins and he rocked slightly back and forth. He knew he would be safe here for some time—the fleshy fingers of the tree were clumped at the slender, swaying ends of the branches and never turned back toward the trunk. He wondered what it would be like to be dead. Perhaps he would be dead soon, and then he'd know. He might as well be.

The names he'd chosen were perfect and all of a family: Sol, Mercury, Venus, Terra, Mars, Jupiter . . . eleven of them. And he could think of a twelfth if he had to.

For what?

He let himself sink down again into the blackness wherein nothing lived but the oily turning of *what's it like to be dead?*

Quiet, he thought. *No one would laugh.*

Something pale moved on the jungle floor below him. He thought instantly of April, and angrily put the thought out of his mind. April would be sleeping now, having completed the trifling task it had taken her so long to start. Down there, that would be Blynken, or maybe Rhea. They were very alike.

It didn't matter, anyway.

He closed his eyes and stopped rocking. He couldn't see anyone, no one could see him. That was the best way. So he sat, and let time pass, and when a hand lay on his shoulder, he nearly leaped out of the tree. "Damn it, Blynken—"

"It's me. Rhea." The child, like all of Alma's daughters, was large for her age and glowing with health. How long had it been? Six, eight . . . nine Earth years since they had landed.

"Go hunt mushrooms," Tod growled. "Leave me alone."

"Come back," said the girl.

Tod would not answer. Rhea knelt beside him, her arm around the primary branch, her back, with his, against the trunk. She bent her head and put her cheek against his. "Tod."

Something inside of him flamed. He bared his teeth and swung a heavy fist. The girl doubled up soundlessly and slipped out of the tree. He stared down at the lax body and at first could not see it for the haze of fury which blew and whirled around him. Then his vision cleared and he moaned, tossed his club down and dropped after it. He caught up the club and whacked off the tree-fingers which probed toward them. He swept up the child and leapt clear, and sank to his knees, gathering her close.

"Rhea, I'm sorry, I'm sorry . . . I wasn't . . . I'm not—*Rhea!* Don't be dead!"

She stirred and made a tearing sound with her throat. Her eyelids trembled and opened, uncovering pain-blinded eyes. "Rhea!"

"It's all right," she whispered, "I shouldn't've bothered you. Do you want me to go away?"

"No," he said. "No." He held her tight. *Why not let her go away?* a part of him wondered, and another part, frightened and puzzled, cried, *No! No!* He had an urgent, half-hysterical need to explain. *Why explain to her, a child? Say you're sorry, comfort her, heal her, but don't expect her to understand.* Yet he said, "I can't go back. There's nowhere else to go. So what can I do?"

Rhea was quiet, as if waiting. A terrible thing, a wonderful thing, to have someone you have hurt wait patiently like that while you find a way to explain. Even if you only explain it to yourself . . . "What could I do if I went back? They—they'll never—they'll laugh at me. They'll all laugh. They're laughing now." Angry again, plaintive no more, he blurted, "April! *Damn* April! She's made a eunuch out of me!"

"Because she had only one baby?"

"Like a savage."

"It's a beautiful baby. A boy."

"A man, a real man, fathers six or eight."

She met his eyes gravely. "That's silly."

"What's happening to us on this crazy planet?" he raged. "Are we evolving backward? What comes next—one of you kids hatching out some amphibids?"

She said only, "Come back, Tod."

"I can't," he whispered. "They'll think I'm . . . that I can't . . ." Helplessly, he shrugged. "They'll laugh."

"Not until you do, and then they'll laugh *with* you. Not at you, Tod."

Finally, he said it, "April won't love me; she'll never love a weakling."

147

She pondered, holding him with her clear gaze. "You really need to be loved a whole lot."

Perversely, he became angry again. "I can get along!" he snapped.

And she smiled and touched the nape of his neck. "You're loved," she assured him. "Gee, you don't have to be mad about that. I love you, don't I? April loves you. Maybe I love you even more than she does. She loves everything you are, Tod. I love everything you ever were and everything you ever will be."

He closed his eyes and a great music came to him. A long, long time ago he had attacked someone who came to comfort him, and she had let him cry, and at length she had said . . . not exactly these words, but—it was the same.

"Rhea."

He looked at her. "You said all that to me before."

A puzzled small crinkle appeared between her eyes and she put her fingers on it. "Did I?"

"Yes," said Tod, "but it was before you were even born."

He rose and took her hand, and they went back to the compound, and whether he was laughed at or not he never knew, for he could think of nothing but his full heart and of April. He went straight in to her and kissed her gently and admired his son, whose name was Sol, and who had been born with hair and two tiny incisors, and who had heavy bony ridges over his eyes. . . .

"A fantastic storage capacity," Teague remarked, touching the top of the scarlet mushroom. "The spores are almost microscopic. The thing doesn't seem to want them distributed, either. It positively hoards them, millions of them."

"Start over, please," April said. She shifted the baby in her arms. He was growing prodigiously. "Slowly. I used to know something about biology—or so I thought. But *this*—"

Teague almost smiled. It was good to see. The aging face had not had so much expression in it in five Earth-years. "I'll get as basic as I can, then, and start from there. First of all, we call this thing a mushroom, but it isn't. I don't think it's a plant, though you couldn't call it an animal, either."

"I don't think anybody ever told me the real difference between a plant and an animal," said Tod.

"Oh . . . well, the most convenient way to put it—it's not strictly accurate, but it will do—is that plants make

148

their own food and animals subsist on what others have made. This thing does both. It has roots, but—" he lifted an edge of the skirted stem of the mushroom—"it can move them. Not much, not fast; but if it wants to shift itself, it can."

April smiled, "Tod, I'll give you basic biology any time. Do go on, Teague."

"Good. Now, I explained about the heterokaryons—the ability this thing has to produce spores which grow up into four completely different plants. One is a mushroom just like this. Here are the other three."

Tod looked at the box of plants. "Are they really all from the mushroom spores?"

"Don't blame you," said Teague, and actually chuckled. "I didn't believe it myself at first. A sort of pitcher-plant, half full of liquid. A thing like a cactus. And this one. It's practically all underground, like a truffle, although it has these cilia. You wouldn't think it was anything but a few horsehairs stuck in the ground."

"And they're all sterile," Tod recalled.

"They're not," said Teague, "and that's what I called you in here to tell you. They'll yield if they are fertilized."

"Fertilized how?"

Instead of answering, Teague asked April, "Do you remember how far back we traced the evolution of Viridian life?"

"Of course. We got the arthropods all the way back to a simple segmented worm. The insects seemed to come from another worm, with pseudopods and a hard carapace."

"A caterpillar," Tod interpolated.

"Almost," said April, with a scientist's nicety. "And the most primitive reptile we could find was a little gymnoderm you could barely see without a glass."

"Where did we find it?"

"Swimming around in—oh! In those pitcher-plant things!"

"If you won't take my word for this," said Teague, a huge enjoyment glinting between his words, "you'll just have to breed these things yourself. It's a lot of work, but this is what you'll discover.

"An adult gymnoderm—a male—finds this pitcher and falls in. There's plenty of nutriment for him, you know, and he's a true amphibian. He fertilizes the pitcher. Nodules grow under the surface of the liquid inside there"— he pointed—"and bud off. The buds are mobile. They grow

149

into wrigglers, miniature tadpoles. Then into lizards. They climb out and go about the business of being—well, lizards."

"All males?" asked Tod.

"No," said Teague, "and that's an angle I haven't yet investigated. But apparently some males breed with females, which lay eggs, which hatch into lizards, and some find plants to fertilize. Anyway, it looks as if this plant is actually the progenitor of all the reptiles here; you know how clear the evolutionary lines are to all the species."

"What about the truffle with the horsehairs?" asked Tod.

"A pupa," said Teague, and to the incredulous expression on April's face, he insisted, "Really—a pupa. After nine weeks or so of dormance, it hatches out into what you almost called a caterpillar."

"And then into all the insects here," said April, and shook her head in wonderment. "And I suppose that cactus-thing hatches out the nematodes, the segmented ones that evolve into arthropods?"

Teague nodded. "You're welcome to experiment," he said again, "but believe me—you'll only find out I'm right: it really happens."

"Then this scarlet mushroom is the beginning of everything here."

"I can't find another theory," said Teague.

"I can," said Tod.

They looked at him questioningly, and he rose and laughed. "Not yet. I have to think it through." He scooped up the baby and then helped April to her feet. "How do you like our Sol, Teague?"

"Fine," said Teague. "A fine boy." Tod knew he was seeing the heavy occipital ridges, the early teeth, and saying nothing. Tod was aware of a faint inward surprise as the baby reached toward April and he handed him over. He should have resented what might be in Teague's mind, but he did not. The beginnings of an important insight welcomed criticism of the child, recognized its hairiness, its savagery, and found these things good. But as yet the thought was too nebulous to express, except by a smile. He smiled, took April's hand, and left.

"That was a funny thing you said to Teague," April told him as they walked toward their quarters.

"Remember, April, the day we landed? Remember—" he made a gesture that took in a quadrant of sky—"Remember how we all felt . . . good?"

150

"Yes," she murmured. "It was like a sort of compliment, and a reassurance. How could I forget?"

"Yes. Well . . ." He spoke with difficulty but his smile stayed. "I have a thought, and it makes me feel like that. But I can't get it into words." After a thoughtful pause, he added, "Yet."

She shifted the baby. "He's getting so heavy."

"I'll take him." He took the squirming bundle with the deep-set, almost humorous eyes. When he looked up from them, he caught an expression on April's face which he hadn't seen in years. "What is it, Ape?"

"You—*like* him."

"Well, sure."

"I was afraid. I was afraid for a long time that you . . . he's ours, but he isn't exactly a pretty baby."

"I'm not exactly a pretty father."

"You know how precious you are to me?" she whispered.

He knew, for this was an old intimacy between them. He laughed and followed the ritual: "How precious?"

She cupped her hands and brought them together, to make of them an ivory box. She raised the hands and peeped into them, between the thumbs, as if at a rare jewel, then clasped the magic tight and hugged it to her breast, raising tear-filled eyes to him. *"That* precious," she breathed.

He looked at the sky, seeing somewhere in it the many peak moments of their happiness when she had made that gesture, feeling how each one, meticulously chosen, brought all the others back. "I used to hate this place," he said. "I guess it's changed."

"You've changed."

Changed how? he wondered. He felt the same, even though he knew he looked older. . . .

The years passed, and the children grew. When Sol was fifteen Earth-years old, short, heavy-shouldered, powerful, he married Carl's daughter Libra. Teague, turning to parchment, had returned to his hermitage from the temporary stimulation of his researches on what they still called "the mushroom." More and more the colony lived off the land and out of the jungle, not because there was any less to be synthesized from their compact machines, but out of preference; it was easier to catch flapping frogs or umbrella-birds and cook them than to bother with machine settings

151

and check-analyses, and, somehow, a lot more fun to eat them, too.

It seemed to them, safer, year by year. *Felodon,* unquestionably the highest form of life on Viridis, was growing scarce, being replaced by a smaller, more timid carnivore April called *Vulpidus* (once, for it seemed not to matter much any more about keeping records) and everyone ultimately called "fox," for all the fact that it was a reptile. *Pterodon* was disappearing, too, as were all the larger forms. More and more they strayed after food, not famine-driven, but purely for variety; more and more they found themselves welcome and comfortable away from the compound. Once Carl and Moira drifted off for nearly a year. When they came back they had another child—a silent, laughing little thing with oddly long arms and heavy teeth.

The warm days and the glowing nights passed comfortably and the stars no longer called. Tod became a grandfather and was proud. The child, a girl, was albino like April, and had exactly April's deep red eyes. Sol and Libra named her Emerald, a green name and a ground-term rather than a sky-term, as if in open expression of the slow spell worked on them all by Viridis. She was mute—but so were almost all the new children, and it seemed not to matter. They were healthy and happy.

Tod went to tell Teague, thinking it might cheer the old one up a little. He found him lying in what had once been his laboratory, thin and placid and disinterested, absently staring down at one of the arthropodal flying creatures that had once startled them so by zooming into the Coffin chamber. This one had happened to land on Teague's hand, and Teague was laxly waiting for it to fly off again, out through the unscreened window, past the unused sprays, over the faint tumble of rotted spars which had once been a palisade.

"Teague, the baby's come!"

Teague sighed, his tired mind detaching itself from memory episode by episode. His eyes rolled toward Tod and finally he turned his head. "Which one would that be?"

Tod laughed. "My grandchild, a girl. Sol's baby."

Teague let his lids fall. He said nothing.

"Well, aren't you glad?"

Slowly a frown came to the papery brow. "Glad." Tod felt he was looking at the word as he had stared at the

152

arthropod, wondering limply when it might go away. "What's the matter with it?"

"What?"

Teague sighed again, a weary, impatient sound. "What does it look like?" he said slowly, emphasizing each one-syllabled word.

"Like April. Just like April."

Teague half sat up, and blinked at Tod. "You don't mean it."

"Yes, eyes red as—" The image of an Earth sunset flickered near his mind but vanished as too hard to visualize. Tod pointed at the four red-capped "mushrooms" that had stood for so many years in the testboxes in the laboratory. "Red as those."

"Silver hair," said Teague.

"Yes, beau—"

"All over," said Teague flatly.

"Well, yes."

Teague let himself fall back on the cot and gave a disgusted snort. "A monkey."

"*Teague!*"

"Ah-h-h . . . go 'way," growled the old man. "I long ago resigned myself to what was happening to us here. A human being just can't adapt to the kind of radioactive ruin this place is for us. Your monsters'll breed monsters, and their monsters'll do the same if they can, until pretty soon they just won't breed any more. And that will be the end of that, and good riddance. . . ." His voice faded away. His eyes opened, looking on distant things, and gradually found themselves focused on the man who stood over him in shocked silence. "But the one thing I can't stand is to have somebody come in here saying, 'Oh, joy, oh happy day!' "

"Teague . . ." Tod swallowed heavily.

"Viridis eats ambition; there was going to be a city here," said the old man indistinctly. "Viridis eats humanity; there were going to be people here." He chuckled gruesomely. "All right, all right, accept it if you have to—and you have to. But don't come around here celebrating."

Tod backed to the door, his eyes horror-round, then turned and fled.

VII

April held him as he crouched against the wall, rocked him slightly, made soft unspellable mother-noises to him.

"Shh, he's all decayed, all lonesome and mad," she murmured. "Shh. Shh."

Tod felt half-strangled. As a youth he had been easily moved, he recalled; he had that tightness of the throat for sympathy, for empathy, for injustices he felt the Universe was hurling at him out of its capacious store. But recently life had been placid, full of love and togetherness and a widening sense of membership with the earth and the air and all the familiar things which walked and flew and grew and bred in it. And his throat was shaped for laughter now; these feelings hurt him.

"But he's right," he whispered. "Don't you see? Right from the beginning it . . . it was . . . remember Alma had six children, April? And a little later, Carl and Moira had three? And you, only one . . . how long is it since the average human gave birth to only one?"

"They used to say it was humanity's last major mutation," she admitted, "Multiple births . . . these last two thousand years. But—"

"Eyebrow ridges," he interrupted. "Hair . . . that skull, Emerald's skull, slanting back like that; did you see the tusks on that little . . . *baboon* of Moira's?"

"Tod! *Don't!*"

He leaped to his feet, sprang across the room and snatched the golden helix from the shelf where it had gleamed its locked symbolism down on them ever since the landing. "Around and down!" he shouted. "Around and around and down!" He squatted beside her and pointed furiously. "Down and down into the blackest black there is; down into *nothing*." He shook his fist at the sky. "You see what they do? They find the highest form of life they can and plant it here and watch it slide down into the muck!" He hurled the artifact away from him.

"But it goes up too, round and up. Oh, Tod!" she cried. "Can you remember them, what they looked like, the way they flew, and say these things about them?"

"I can remember Alma," he gritted, "conceiving and gestating alone in space, while they turned their rays on her every day. You know *why?*" With the sudden thought, he stabbed a finger down at her. "To give her babies a

154

head-start on Viridis, otherwise they'd have been born normal here; it would've taken another couple of generations to start them downhill, and they wanted us all to go together."

"No, Tod, no!"

"Yes, April, yes. How much proof do you need?" He whirled on her. "Listen—remember that mushroom Teague analyzed? He had to *pry* spores out of it to see what it yielded. Remember the three different plants he got? Well, I was just there; I don't know how many times before I've seen it, but only now it makes sense. He's got four mushrooms now; do you see? Do you see? Even back as far as we can trace the bugs and newts on this green hell-pit, Viridis won't let anything climb; it must fall."

"I don't—"

"You'll give me basic biology any time," he quoted sarcastically. "Let me tell you some biology. That mushroom yields three plants, and the plants yield animal life. Well, when the animal life fertilized those hetero-whatever—"

"Heterokaryons."

"Yes. Well, you don't get animals that can evolve and improve. You get one pitiful generation of animals which breeds back into a mushroom, and there it sits hoarding its spores. Viridis wouldn't let one puny newt, one primitive pupa build! It snatches 'em back, locks 'em up. That mushroom isn't the beginning of everything here—*it's the end!*"

April got to her feet slowly, looking at Tod as if she had never seen him before, not in fear, but with a troubled curiosity. She crossed the room and picked up the artifact, stroked its gleaming golden coils. "You could be right," she said in a low voice. "But that can't be all there is to it." She set the helix back in its place. "They *wouldn't.*"

She spoke with such intensity that for a moment that metrical formation, mighty and golden, rose again in Tod's mind, up and up to the measureless cloud which must be a ship. He recalled the sudden shift, like a genuflection, directed at them, at *him*, and for that moment he could find no evil in it. Confused, he tossed his head, found himself looking out the door, seeing Moira's youngest ambling comfortably across the compound.

"They *wouldn't?*" he snarled. He took April's slender arm and whirled her to the door. "You know what I'd do before I'd father another one like *that?*" He told her spe-

155

cifically what he would do. "A lemur next, hm? A spider, an oyster, a jellyfish!"

April whimpered and ran out. "Know any lullabies to a tapeworm?" he roared after her. She disappeared into the jungle, and he fell back, gasping for breath. . . .

Having no stomach for careful thought nor careful choosing, having Teague for an example to follow, Tod too turned hermit. He could have survived the crisis easily, perhaps, with April to help, but she did not come back. Moira and Carl were off again, wandering; the children lived their own lives, and he had no wish to see Teague. Once or twice Sol and Libra came to see him, but he snarled at them and they left him alone. It was no sacrifice. Life on Viridis was very full for the contented ones.

He sulked in his room or poked about the compound by himself. He activated the protein converter once, but found its products tasteless, and never bothered with it again. Sometimes he would stand near the edge of the hilltop and watch the children playing in the long grass, and his lip would curl.

Damn Teague! He'd been happy enough with Sol all those years, for all the boy's bulging eyebrow ridges and hairy body. He had been about to accept the silent, silver Emerald, too, when the crotchety old man had dropped his bomb. Once or twice Tod wondered detachedly what it was in him that was so easily reached, so completely insecure, that the suggestion of abnormality should strike so deep.

Somebody once said, *"You really need to be loved, don't you, Tod?"*

No one would love this tainted thing, father of savages who spawned animals. He didn't deserve to be loved.

He had never felt so alone. *"I'm going to die. But I will be with you too."* That had been Alma. Huh! There was old Teague, tanning his brains in his own sour acids. Alma had believed something or other . . . and what had come of it? That wizened old crab lolling his life away in the lab.

Tod spent six months that way.

"Tod!" He came out of sleep reluctantly, because in sleep an inner self still lived with April where there was no doubt and no fury; no desertion, no loneliness.

He opened his eyes and stared dully at the slender figure silhouetted against Viridis' glowing sky. "April?"

"Moira," said the figure. The voice was cold.

"Moira!" he said, sitting up. "I haven't seen you for a year. More. Wh—"

"Come," she said. "Hurry."

"Come where?"

"Come by yourself or I'll get Carl and he'll carry you." She walked swiftly to the door.

He reeled after her. "You can't come in here and—"

"Come on." The voice was edged and slid out from between clenched teeth. A miserable part of him twitched in delight and told him that he was important enough to be hated. He despised himself for recognizing the twisted thought, and before he knew what he was doing he was following Moira at a steady trot.

"Where are—" he gasped, and she said over her shoulder, "If you don't talk you'll go faster."

At the jungle margin a shadow detached itself and spoke. "Got him?"

"Yes, Carl."

The shadow became Carl. He swung in behind Tod, who suddenly realized that if he did not follow the leader, the one behind would drive. He glanced back at Carl's implacable bulk, and then put down his head and jogged doggedly along as he was told.

They followed a small stream, crossed it on a fallen tree, and climbed a hill. Just as Tod was about to accept the worst these determined people might offer in exchange for a moment to ease his fiery lungs, Moira stopped. He stumbled into her. She caught his arm and kept him on his feet.

"In there," she said, pointing.

"A finger tree."

"You know how to get inside," Carl growled.

Moira said, "She begged me not to tell you, ever. I think she was wrong."

"Who? What is—"

"Inside," said Carl, and shoved him roughly down the slope.

His long conditioning was still with him, and reflexively he sidestepped the fanning fingers which swayed to meet him. He ducked under them, batted aside the inner phalanx, and found himself in the clear space underneath. He stopped there, gasping.

Something moaned.

He bent, fumbled cautiously in the blackness. He touched

157

something smooth and alive, recoiled, touched it again. A foot.

Someone began to cry harshly, hurtfully, the sound exploding as if through clenched hands.

"April!"

"I told them not to . . ." And she moaned.

"April, what is it, what's happened?"

"You needn't . . . be," she said, sobbed a while, and went on: ". . . angry. It didn't live."

"What didn't . . . you mean you . . . April, you—"

"It wouldn't've been a tapeworm," she whispered.

"Who—" He fell to his knees, found her face. "When did you—"

"I was going to tell you that day, that very same day, and when you came in so angry at what Teague told you, I specially wanted to, I thought you'd . . . be glad."

"April, why didn't you come back? If I'd known . . ."

"You *said* what you'd do if I ever . . . if you ever had another . . . you meant it, Tod."

"It's this place, this Viridis," he said sadly. "I went crazy."

He felt her wet hand on his cheek.

"It's all right. I just didn't want to make it worse for you," April said.

"I'll take you back."

"No, you can't. I've been . . . I've lost a lot of . . . just stay with me a little while."

"Moira should have—"

"She just found me," and April. "I've been alone all the— I guess I made a noise. I didn't mean to. Tod . . . don't quarrel. Don't go into a lot of . . . It's all right."

Against her throat he cried, *"All right!"*

"When you're by yourself," she said faintly, "you think; you think better. Did you ever think of—"

"April!" he cried in anguish, the very sound of her pale, pain-wracked voice making this whole horror real.

"Shh! Shh! Listen," she said rapidly. "There isn't time, you know, Tod. Tod, did you ever think of us all, Teague and Alma and Moira and Carl and us, what we are?"

"I know what I am."

"*Shh!* Altogether we're a leader and mother; a word and a shield; a doubter, a mystic . . ." Her voice trailed off. She coughed and he could feel the spastic jolt shoot through her body. She panted lightly for a moment and went on urgently, "Anger and prejudice and stupidity, courage, laughter, love, music . . . it was all aboard that ship and it's all here on Viridis. Our children, and theirs—no matter what they look like, Tod, no matter how they live or what they eat—they have that in them. Humanity isn't just a way of walking, merely a kind of skin. It's what we had together and what we gave Sol. It's what the golden ones found in us and wanted for Viridis. You'll see. You'll see."

"Why Viridis?"

"Because of what Teague said—what you said." Her breath puffed out in the ghost of a laugh. "Basic biology . . . ontogeny follows phylogeny. The human foetus is a cell, an animalcule, a gilled amphibian . . . all up the line. It's there in us; Viridis makes it go backward."

"To what?"

"The mushroom. The spores. We'll be spores, Tod. Together . . . Alma *said* she could be dead, and together with Teague! That's why I said . . . it's all right. This doesn't matter, what's happened. We live in Sol, we live in Emerald with Carl and Moira, you see? Closer, nearer than we've ever been."

Tod took a hard hold on his reason. "But back to spores —why? What then?"

She sighed. It was unquestionably a happy sound. "They'll be back for the reaping, and they'll have us, Tod, all we are and all they worship: goodness and generosity and the urge to build; mercy; kindness.

"They're needed too," she whispered. "And the spores make mushrooms, and the mushrooms make the heterokaryons; and from those, away from Viridis, come the lifeforms to breed us—*us*, Tod! into whichever form is dominant. And there we'll be, that flash of old understanding of a new idea . . . the special pressure on a painter's hand that makes him a Rembrandt, the sense of architecture that turns a piano-player into a Bach. Three billion extra years of evolution, ready to help wherever it can be used. On every Earth-type planet, Tod—millions of us, blowing about in the summer wind, waiting to give. . . ."

"Give! Give what Teague is now, rotten and angry?"

"That isn't Teague. That will die off. Teague lives with Alma in their children, and in theirs . . . she *said* she'd be with him!"

"Me . . . what about me?" he breathed. "What I did to you. . . ."

159

"Nothing, you did nothing. You live in Sol, in Emerald. Living, conscious, alive . . . with me. . . ."

He said, "You mean . . . you could talk to me from Sol?"

"I think I might." With his forehead, bent so close to her, he felt her smile. "But I don't think I would. Lying so close to you, why should I speak to an outsider?"

Her breathing changed and he was suddenly terrified. "April, don't die."

"I won't," she said. "Alma didn't." She kissed him gently and died.

It was a long darkness, with Tod hardly aware of roaming and raging through the jungle, of eating without tasting, of hungering without knowing of it. Then there was a twilight, many months long, soft and still, with restfulness here and a promise soon. Then there was the compound again, found like a dead memory, learned again just a little more readily than something new. Carl and Moira were kind, knowing the nature of justice and the limits of punishment, and at last Tod was alive again.

He found himself one day down near the river, watching it and thinking back without fear of his own thoughts, and a growing wonder came to him. His mind had for so long dwelt on his own evil that it was hard to break new paths. He wondered with an awesome effort what manner of creatures might worship humanity for itself, and what manner of creatures humans were to be so worshipped. It was a totally new concept to him, and he was completely immersed in it, so that when Emerald slid out of the grass and stood watching him, he was frightened and shouted.

She did not move. There was little to fear now on Viridis. All the large reptiles were gone, and there was room for the humans, the humanoids, the primates, the . . . children. In his shock the old reflexes played. He stared at her, her square stocky body, the silver hair which covered it all over except for the face, the palms, the soles of the feet. "A *monkey!*" he spat, in Teague's tones, and the shock turned to shame. He met her eyes, April's deep glowing rubies, and they looked back at him without fear.

He let a vision of April grow and fill the world. The child's rare red eyes helped (there was so little, so very little red on Viridis). He saw April at the spaceport, holding him in the dark shadows of the blockhouse while the sky flamed above them. *We'll go out like that soon, soon,*

Tod. Squeeze me, squeeze me. . . . Ah, he'd said, *who needs a ship?*

Another April, part of her in a dim light as she sat writing; her hair, a crescent of light loving her cheek, a band of it on her brow; then she had seen him and turned, rising, smothered his first word with her mouth. Another April wanting to smile, waiting; and April asleep, and once, April sobbing because she could not find a special word to tell him what she felt for him. . . . He brought his mind back from her in the past, from her as she was, alive in his mind, back to here, to the bright mute with the grave red eyes who stood before him, and he said, "How precious?"

The baby kept her eyes on his, and slowly raised her silken hands. She cupped them together to make a closed chamber, looked down at it, opened her hands slightly and swiftly to peer inside, rapt at what she pretended to see; closed her hands again to capture the treasure, whatever it was, and hugged it to her breast. She looked up at him slowly, and her eyes were full of tears, and she was smiling.

He took his grandchild carefully in his arms and held her gently and strongly. Monkey?

"April," he gasped. "Little Ape. Little Ape."

Viridis is a young planet which bears (at first glance) old life-forms. Come away and let the green planet roll around its sun; come back in a while—not long, as astronomical time goes.

The jungle is much the same, the sea, the rolling savannahs. But the life . . .

Viridis was full of primates. There were blunt-toothed herbivores and long-limbed tree-dwellers, gliders and burrowers. The fish-eaters were adapting the way all Viridis life must adapt, becoming more fit by becoming simpler, or go to the wall. Already the sea-apes had rudimentary gills and had lost their hair. Already tiny forms competed with the insects on their own terms.

On the banks of the wandering rivers, monotremes with opposed toes dredged and paddled, and sloths and lemurs crept at night. At first they had stayed together, but they were soon too numerous for that; and a half-dozen generations cost them the power of speech, which was, by then, hardly a necessity. Living was good for primates on Viridis, and became better each generation.

Eating and breeding, hunting and escaping filled the days and the cacophonous nights. It was hard in the beginning

161

to see a friend cut down, to watch a slender silver shape go spinning down a river and know that with it went some of your brother, some of your mate, some of yourself. But as the hundreds became thousands and the thousands millions, witnessing death became about as significant as watching your friend get his hair cut. The basic ids each spread through the changing, mutating population like a stain, crossed and recrossed by the strains of the others, co-existing, eating each other and being eaten and all the while passing down through the generations.

There was a cloud over the savannah, high over the ruins of the compound. It was a thing of many colors and of no particular shape, and it was bigger than one might imagine, not knowing how far away it was.

From it dropped a golden spot that became a thread, and down came a golden mass. It spread and swung, exploded into a myriad of individuals. Some descended on the compound, erasing and changing, lifting, breaking—always careful to kill nothing. Others blanketed the planet, streaking silently through the green aisles, flashing unimpeded through the tangled thickets. They combed the riverbanks and the half-light of hill waves, and everywhere they went they found and touched the mushroom and stripped it of its spores, the compaction and multiplication of what had once been the representatives of a very high reptile culture.

Primates climbed and leaped, crawled and crept to the jungle margins to watch. Eater lay by eaten; the hunted stood on the hunter's shoulder, and a platypoid laid an egg in the open which nobody touched.

Simian forms hung from the trees in loops and ropes, in swarms and beards, and more came all the time, brought by some ineffable magnetism to watch at the hill. It was a fast and a waiting, with no movement but jostling for position, a crowding forward from behind and a pressing back from the slightest chance of interfering with the golden visitors.

Down from the polychrome cloud drifted a mass of the golden beings, carrying with them a huge sleek ship. They held it above the ground, sliced it, lifted it apart, set down this piece and that until a shape began to grow. Into it went bales and bundles, stocks and stores, and then the open tops were covered. It was a much bigger installation than the one before.

Quickly, it was done, and the golden cloud hung waiting. The jungle was trembling with quiet.

In one curved panel of the new structure, something spun, fell outward, and out of the opening came a procession of stately creatures, long-headed, bright-eyed, three-toed, richly plumed and feathered. They tested their splendid wings, then stopped suddenly, crouched and looked upward.

They were given their obesiance by the golden ones, and after there appeared in the sky the exquisite symbol of a beauty that rides up and up, turns and spirals down again only to rise again: the symbol of that which has no beginning and no end, and the sign of those whose worship and whose work it is to bring to all the Universe that which has shown itself worthy in parts of it.

Then they were gone, and the jungle exploded into killing and flight, eating and screaming, so that the feathered ones dove back into their shelter and closed the door. . . .

And again to the green planet (when the time was right) came the cloud-ship, and found a world full of birds, and the birds watched in awe while they harvested their magic dust, and built a new shelter. In this they left four of their own for later harvesting, and this was to make of Viridis a most beautiful place.

From Viridis, the ship vaulted through the galaxies, searching for worlds worthy of what is human in humanity, whatever their manner of being alive. These they seeded, and of these, perhaps one would produce something new, something which could be reduced to the dust of Viridis, and from dust return.

1955

I MENTIONED THE confusion over what "previous year" meant in the early Hugo selections. The 1953 convention recognized a novel serialized in 1952. *The Demolished Man* had its first *book* publication in '53, which does introduce a note of ambiguity, but the DeVore and Franson *History of the Hugo, Nebula, and International Fantasy Awards* specifically recognizes the magazine version of *The Demolished Man*.

The following year's lapse in Hugos mooted the point.

The Cleveland convention in 1955 seemed to go over to a loose sort of "Hugo year" rather than using the calendar year. The winning novel had been serialized in the autumn of '54. The winning novelette had appeared in a January 1955 magazine—meaning actual publication late in 1954. The winning short story had been published in a May 1955 magazine.

The 1956 convention, held in New York, stayed with that split-year concept. The winning novel and novelette had both been published in 1956 issues of *Astounding*. The winning short story had been in the very first issue of a new magazine, *Infinity Science Fiction*, dated November 1955. *Infinity* was edited by still another member of the Futurian fan group, Larry T. Shaw.

And to repeat, I will try to keep things straight throughout this anthology by keeping each story to the year in which it was published. In case of a magazine issue dated January of one year but copyrighted December of the previous year, I'll go by the cover date.

Phew!

In a sense, there had been no Hugo-winning novel for 1955. The 1955 convention recognized a 1954 serial. The 1956 convention gave its award to *Double Star* by Robert A. Heinlein—the first of a shelf full of awards he was to win. The novel had run in *Astounding* from February through April 1956.

But there had been plenty of first-rate science fiction novels published in 1955! I suspect it was that loony business of nobody being quite certain what a year was, that robbed them—not of the prize *per se,* but of the very chance to compete for the prize!

Consider: *Astounding* alone ran four serials in '55. These were *Time Crime* by H. Beam Piper, *The Long Way Home* by Poul Anderson, *Call Him Dead* by Eric Frank Russell, and *Under Pressure* by Frank Herbert. (You may know *Under Pressure* by one of its other names, *Dragon in the Sea* or *21st Century Sub.*) *Galaxy* ran *Preferred Risk* by Edson McCann (Fred Pohl and Lester del Rey), and *Ties of Earth* by James H. Schmitz. *Fantasy and Science Fiction* had cut back on serials, but the magazine did run one, *The (Widget), the (Wadget), and Boff,* by Theodore Sturgeon.

And original novels published without magazine versions were now commonplace. There were *Re-Birth* by John Wyndham (Ballantine), *Earthlight* by Clarke (Ballantine), *Not This August* by Kornbluth (Doubleday), *The Fittest* by McIntosh (Doubleday), and *The End of Eternity* by Asimov (Doubleday). The Asimov was of particular interest. It had been written as a long novelette for *Galaxy,* rejected, and then expanded to novel length for Doubleday! And Dutton brought out a novel-length version of Fredric Brown's earlier *Astounding* novella, *Martians Go Home.*

The winner for novelette was "Exploration Team" by Murray Leinster; and that for short story, "The Star" by Clarke.

Good stories? Yes. Truly the best of the year? I'm not so sure. Consider these other stories of 1955: Poul Anderson's "Time Patrol *(F&SF),* Bryce Walton's almost criminally overlooked "Too Late for Eternity" *(Startling Stories),* Philip K. Dick's "Autofac" *(Galaxy),* Charles Beaumont's stunning "The Crooked Man" *(Playboy),* Sturgeon's "So Near the Darkness" *(Fantastic Universe),* Cordwainer Smith's "The Game of Rat and Dragon" *(Galaxy),* Avram Davidson's "The Golem" *(Fantasy and Science Fiction),* J. Francis McComas's "Criminal Negligence" *(Astounding)....*

Oh, it was quite a year!

But I think the most overlooked story of 1955 was a little piece in the January *Fantasy and Science Fiction*—

"One Ordinary Day, with Peanuts," by Shirley Jackson. I can only hope that the voting fans missed the story because of that confusing "year" business. More likely, I'm afraid, it wasn't that at all.

"One Ordinary Day, with Peanuts," *has* to be recognized as a classic yarn. But it isn't quite science fiction, as we usually think of science fiction. There's no *hardware* in it, there are no *aliens* in it (or are there?).... It isn't exactly fantasy, in a common sense. Again, there are no *faeries* in it, no *ghosts* or *witches* or ...

It's a totally unclassifiable story, with *implications* of— what? Fantasy? Science fiction? *Paranoia?* Hmm.

Maybe that's what cost it the prize.

Or maybe it's the fact that Shirley Jackson, although she wrote almost entirely in the fantastic mode, wasn't generally regarded as a science fiction or fantasy author. She wasn't one of the gang. She popped up in *F&SF* now and then—a total of four times. And she had one story in *Fantastic.* But for the most part she appeared in "mainstream," "literary" magazines. And her books were published as general trade books and sold to large general readerships.

She was resented as an outsider, an interloper. Gee, if only she'd published in the sci-fi mags under the name L. Sprague de Camp or C. L. Moore, she might have got that toy rocket!

One Ordinary Day, with Peanuts

SHIRLEY JACKSON

Mr. John Philip Johnson shut his front door behind him and came down his front steps into the bright morning with a feeling that all was well with the world on this best of all days, and wasn't the sun warm and good, and didn't his shoes feel comfortable after the resoling, and he knew that he had undoubtedly chosen the precise very tie which belonged with the day and the sun and his comfortable feet, and, after all, wasn't the world just a wonderful place? In spite of the fact that he was a small man, and the tie was perhaps a shade vivid, Mr. Johnson irradiated this feeling of well-being as he came down the steps and onto the dirty sidewalk, and he smiled at people who passed him, and some of them even smiled back. He stopped at the newsstand on the corner and bought his paper, saying *"Good* morning" with real conviction to the man who sold him the paper and the two or three other people who were lucky enough to be buying papers when Mr. Johnson skipped up. He remembered to fill his pockets with candy and peanuts, and then he set out to get himself uptown. He stopped in a flower shop and bought a carnation for his buttonhole, and stopped almost immediately afterward to give the carnation to a small child in a carriage, who looked at him dumbly, and then smiled, and Mr. Johnson smiled, and the child's mother looked at Mr. Johnson for a minute and then smiled too.

When he had gone several blocks uptown, Mr. Johnson cut across the avenue and went along a side street, chosen at random; he did not follow the same route every morning, but preferred to pursue his eventful way in wide detours, more like a puppy than a man intent upon business. It happened this morning that halfway down the block a moving van was parked, and the furniture from an upstairs apartment stood half on the sidewalk, half on the steps, while an amused group of people loitered, examining the scratches on the table and the worn spots on the chairs, and a harassed woman, trying to watch a young child and the movers and the furniture all at the same time, gave the clear impression of endeavoring to shelter her private life from the people staring at her belongings. Mr. Johnson stopped, and for a moment joined the crowd, and then he came forward and, touching his hat civilly, said, "Perhaps I can keep an eye on your little boy for you?"

The woman turned and glared at him distrustfully, and Mr. Johnson added hastily, "We'll sit right here on the steps." He beckoned to the little boy, who hesitated and then responded agreeably to Mr. Johnson's genial smile. Mr. Johnson brought out a handful of peanuts from his pocket and sat on the steps with the boy, who at first refused the peanuts on the grounds that his mother did not allow him to accept food from strangers; Mr. Johnson said that probably his mother had not intended peanuts to be included, since elephants at the circus ate them, and the boy considered, and then agreed solemnly. They sat on the steps cracking peanuts in a comradely fashion, and Mr. Johnson said, "So you're moving?"

"Yep," said the boy.

"Where you going?"

"Vermont."

"Nice place. Plenty of snow there. Maple sugar, too; you like maple sugar?"

"Sure."

"Plenty of maple sugar in Vermont. You going to live on a farm?"

"Going to live with Grandpa."

"Grandpa like peanuts?"

"Sure."

"Ought to take him some," said Mr. Johnson, reaching into his pocket. "Just you and Mommy going?"

"Yep."

168

"Tell you what," Mr. Johnson said. "You take some peanuts to eat on the train."

The boy's mother, after glancing at them frequently, had seemingly decided that Mr. Johnson was trustworthy, because she had devoted herself wholeheartedly to seeing that the movers did not—what movers rarely do, but every housewife believes they will—crack a leg from her good table, or set a kitchen chair down on a lamp. Most of the furniture was loaded by now, and she was deep in that nervous stage when she knew there was something she had forgotten to pack—hidden away in the back of a closet somewhere, or left at a neighbor's and forgotten, or on the clothesline—and was trying to remember under stress what it was.

"This all, lady?" the chief mover said, completing her dismay.

Uncertainly, she nodded.

"Want to go on the truck with the furniture, sonny?" the mover asked the boy, and laughed. The boy laughed too and said to Mr. Johnson, "I guess I'll have a good time at Vermont."

"Fine time," said Mr. Johnson, and stood up. "Have one more peanut before you go," he said to the boy.

The boy's mother said to Mr. Johnson, "Thank you so much; it was a great help to me."

"Nothing at all," said Mr. Johnson gallantly. "Where in Vermont are you going?"

The mother looked at the little boy accusingly, as though he had given away a secret of some importance, and said unwillingly, "Greenwich."

"Lovely town," said Mr. Johnson. He took out a card, and wrote a name on the back. "Very good friend of mine lives in Greenwich," he said. "Call on him for anything you need. His wife makes the best doughnuts in town," he added soberly to the little boy.

"Swell," said the little boy.

"Goodby," said Mr. Johnson.

He went on, stepping happily with his new-shod feet, feeling the warm sun on his back and on the top of his head. Halfway down the block he met a stray dog and fed him a peanut.

At the corner, where another wide avenue faced him, Mr. Johnson decided to go on uptown again. Moving with comparative laziness, he was passed on either side by people hurrying and frowning, and people brushed past him going the other way, clattering along to get somewhere quickly. Mr. Johnson stopped on every corner and waited patiently for the light to change, and he stepped out of the way of anyone who seemed to be in any particular hurry, but one young lady came too fast for him, and crashed wildly into him when he stooped to pat a kitten which had run out onto the sidewalk from an apartment house and was now unable to get back through the rushing feet.

"Excuse me," said the young lady, trying frantically to pick up Mr. Johnson and hurry on at the same time, "terribly sorry."

The kitten, regardless now of danger, raced back to its home. "Perfectly all right," said Mr. Johnson, adjusting himself carefully. "You seem to be in a hurry."

"Of course I'm in a hurry," said the young lady. "I'm late."

She was extremely cross and the frown between her eyes seemed well on its way to becoming permanent. She had obviously awakened late, because she had not spent any extra time in making herself look pretty, and her dress was plain and unadorned with collar or brooch, and her lipstick was noticeably crooked. She tried to brush past Mr. Johnson, but, risking her suspicious displeasure, he took her arm and said, "Please wait."

"Look," she said ominously. "I ran into you and your lawyer can see my lawyer and I will gladly pay all damages and all inconveniences suffered therefrom but please this minute let me go because *I am late.*"

"Late for what?" said Mr. Johnson; he tried his winning smile on her but it did no more than keep her, he suspected, from knocking him down again.

"Late for work," she said between her teeth. "Late for my employment. I have a job and if I am late I lose exactly so much an hour and I cannot really afford what your pleasant conversation is costing me, be it *ever* so pleasant."

"I'll pay for it," said Mr. Johnson. Now these were magic words, not necessarily because they were true, or because she seriously expected Mr. Johnson to pay for anything, but because Mr. Johnson's flat statement, obviously innocent of irony, could not be, coming from Mr. Johnson, anything but the statement of a responsible and truthful and respectable man.

"What *do* you mean?" she asked.

"I said that since I am obviously responsible for your being late I shall certainly pay for it."

"Don't be silly," she said, and for the first time the frown disappeared. *"I* wouldn't expect you to pay for anything—a few minutes ago I was offering to pay *you.* Anyway," she added, almost smiling, "it *was* my fault."

"What happens if you don't go to work?"

She stared. "I don't get paid."

"Precisely," said Mr. Johnson.

"What do you mean, precisely? If I don't show up at the office exactly twenty minutes ago I lose a dollar and twenty cents an hour, or two cents a minute or . . ." She thought. ". . . Almost a dime for the time I've spent talking to you."

Mr. Johnson laughed, and finally she laughed, too. "You're late already," he pointed out. "Will you give me another four cents worth?"

"I don't understand why."

"You'll see," Mr. Johnson promised. He led her over to the side of the walk, next to the buildings, and said, "Stand here," and went out into the rush of people going both ways. Selecting and considering, as one who must make a choice involving perhaps whole years of lives, he estimated the people going by. Once he almost moved, and then at the last minute thought better of it and drew back. Finally, from half a block away, he saw what he wanted, and moved out into the center of the traffic to intercept a young man, who was hurrying, and dressed as though he had awakened late, and frowning.

"Oof," said the young man, because Mr. Johnson had thought of no better way to intercept anyone than the one the young woman had unwittingly used upon him. "Where do you think you're going?" the young man demanded from the sidewalk.

"I want to speak to you," said Mr. Johnson ominously.

The young man got up nervously, dusting himself and eyeing Mr. Johnson. "What for?" he said. "What'd *I* do?"

"That's what bothers me most about people nowadays," Mr. Johnson complained broadly to the people passing. "No matter whether they've done anything or not, they always figure someone's after them. About what you're going to do," he told the young man.

"Listen," said the young man, trying to brush past him, "I'm late, and I don't have any time to listen. Here's a dime, now get going."

"Thank you," said Mr. Johnson, pocketing the dime. "Look," he said, "what happens if you stop running?"

"I'm late," said the young man, still trying to get past Mr. Johnson, who was unexpectedly clinging.

"How much do you make an hour?" Mr. Johnson demanded.

"A communist, are you?" said the young man. "Now will you please let me—"

"No," said Mr. Johnson insistently, "*how* much?"

"Dollar fifty," said the young man. "And *now* will you—"

"You like adventure?"

The young man stared, and, staring, found himself caught and held by Mr. Johnson's genial smile; he almost smiled back and then repressed it and made an effort to tear away. "I got to *hurry,*" he said.

"Like surprises? Mystery? Unusual and exciting events?"

"You selling something?"

"Sure," said Mr. Johnson. "You want to take a chance?"

The young man hesitated, looked longingly up the avenue toward what might have been his destination and then when Mr. Johnson said, "I'll pay for it," with his own peculiar and convincing emphasis, turned and said, "Well, okay. But I got to *see* it first, what I'm buying."

Mr. Johnson, breathing hard, led the young man over to the side where the girl was standing; she had been watching with interest Mr. Johnson's capture of the young man and now, smiling timidly, she looked at Mr. Johnson as though prepared to be surprised at nothing.

Mr. Johnson reached into his pocket and took out his wallet. "Here," he said, and handed a bill to the girl. "This about equals your day's pay."

"But no," she said, surprised in spite of herself. "I mean, I *couldn't.*"

"Please do not interrupt," Mr. Johnson told her. "And *here,*" he said to the young man, "this will take care of *you.*" The young man accepted the bill dazedly, but said, "Probably counterfeit" to the young woman out of the side of his mouth. "Now," Mr. Johnson went on, disregarding the young man, "what is your name, miss?"

"Kent," she said helplessly. "Mildred Kent."

"Fine," said Mr. Johnson. "And you, sir?"

"Arthur Adams," said the young man stiffly.

"Splendid," said Mr. Johnson. "Now, Miss Kent, I would like you to meet Mr. Adams. Mr. Adams, Miss Kent."

Miss Kent stared, wet her lips nervously, made a gesture as though she might run, and said, "How do you do?"

Mr. Adams straightened his shoulders, scowled at Mr. Johnson, made a gesture as though he might run, and said, "How do you do?"

"Now *this*," said Mr. Johnson, taking several bills from his wallet, "should be enough for the day for both of you. I would suggest, perhaps, Coney Island—although I personally am not fond of the place—or perhaps a nice lunch somewhere, and dancing, or a matinee, or even a movie, although take care to choose a really *good* one; there are *so* many bad movies these days. You might," he said, struck with an inspiration, "visit the Bronx Zoo, or the Planetarium. Anywhere, as a matter of fact," he concluded, "that you would like to go. Have a nice time."

As he started to move away Arthur Adams, breaking from his dumbfounded stare, said, "But see here, mister, you *can't* do this. Why—how do you know—I mean, *we* don't even know—I mean, how do you know we won't just take the money and not do what you said?"

"You've taken the money," Mr. Johnson said. "You don't have to follow any of my suggestions. You may know something you prefer to do—perhaps a museum, or something."

"But suppose I just run away with it and leave her here?"

"I know you won't," said Mr. Johnson gently, "because you remembered to ask *me* that. Goodby," he added, and went on.

As he stepped up the street, conscious of the sun on his head and his good shoes, he heard from somewhere behind him the young man saying, "Look, you know you don't *have* to if you don't want to," and the girl saying, "But unless *you* don't want to . . ." Mr. Johnson smiled to himself and then thought that he had better hurry along; when he wanted to he could move very quickly, and before the young woman had gotten around to saying, "Well, *I* will if *you* will," Mr. Johnson was several blocks away and had already stopped twice, once to help a lady lift several large packages into a taxi and once to hand a peanut to a seagull. By this time he was in an area of large stores and many more people and he was buffeted constantly from either side by people hurrying and cross and late and sullen. Once he offered a peanut to a man who asked him for a dime, and once he offered a peanut to a bus driver who had stopped his bus at an intersection and had opened the window next to his seat and put out his hand as though longing for fresh air and the comparative quiet of the traffic. The man wanting a dime took the peanut because Mr. Johnson had wrapped a dollar bill around it, but the bus driver took the peanut and asked ironically, "You want a transfer, Jack?"

On a busy corner Mr. Johnson encountered two young people—for one minute he thought they might be Mildred Kent and Arthur Adams—who were eagerly scanning a newspaper, their backs pressed against a storefront to avoid the people passing, their heads bent together. Mr. Johnson, whose curiosity was insatiable, leaned onto the storefront next to them and peeked over the man's shoulder; they were scanning the "Apartments Vacant" columns.

Mr. Johnson remembered the street where the woman and her little boy were going to Vermont and he tapped the man on the shoulder and said amiably, "Try down on West Seventeen. About the middle of the block, people moved out this morning."

"Say, what do you—" said the man, and then, seeing Mr. Johnson clearly, "Well, thanks. Where did you say?"

"West Seventeen," said Mr. Johnson. "About the middle of the block." He smiled again and said, "Good luck."

"Thanks," said the man.

"Thanks," said the girl, as they moved off.

"Goodby," said Mr. Johnson.

He lunched alone in a pleasant restaurant, where the food was rich, and only Mr. Johnson's excellent digestion could encompass two of their whipped-cream-and-chocolate-and-rum-cake pastries for dessert. He had three cups of coffee, tipped the waiter largely, and went out into the street again into the wonderful sunlight, his shoes still comfortable and fresh on his feet. Outside he found a beggar staring into the windows of the restaurant he had left and, carefully looking through the money in his pocket, Mr. Johnson approached the beggar and pressed some coins and a couple of bills into his hand. "It's the price of the veal cutlet lunch plus tip," said Mr. Johnson. "Goodby."

After his lunch he rested; he walked into the nearest park and fed peanuts to the pigeons. It was late afternoon by the time he was ready to start back downtown, and he had refereed two checker games and watched a small boy and girl whose mother had fallen asleep and awakened with surprise and fear which turned to amusement when

174

she saw Mr. Johnson. He had given away almost all of his candy, and had fed all the rest of his peanuts to the pigeons, and it was time to go home. Although the late afternoon sun was pleasant, and his shoes were still entirely comfortable, he decided to take a taxi downtown.

He had a difficult time catching a taxi, because he gave up the first three or four empty ones to people who seemed to need them more; finally, however, he stood alone on the corner and—almost like netting a frisky fish—he hailed desperately until he succeeded in catching a cab which had been proceeding with haste uptown and seemed to draw in towards Mr. Johnson against its own will.

"Mister," the cab driver said as Mr. Johnson climbed in, "I figured you was an omen, like. I wasn't going to pick you up at all."

"Kind of you," said Mr. Johnson ambiguously.

"If I'd of let you go it would of cost me ten bucks," said the driver.

"Really?" said Mr. Johnson.

"Yeah," said the driver. "Guy just got out of the cab, he turned around and gave me ten bucks, said take this and bet it in a hurry on a horse named Vulcan, right away."

"Vulcan?" said Mr. Johnson, horrified. "A fire sign on a Wednesday?"

"What?" said the driver. "Anyway, I said to myself if I got no fare between here and there I'd bet the ten, but if anyone looked like they needed the cab I'd take it as a omen and I'd take the ten home to the wife."

"You were very right," said Mr. Johnson heartily. "This is Wednesday, you would have lost your money. Monday, yes, or even Saturday. But never never never a fire sign on a Wednesday. Sunday would have been good, now."

"Vulcan don't run on Sunday," said the driver.

"You wait till another day," said Mr. Johnson. "Down this street, please, driver. I'll get off on the next corner."

"He *told* me Vulcan, though," said the driver.

"I'll tell you," said Mr. Johnson, hesitating with the door of the cab half-open. "You take that ten dollars and I'll give you another ten dollars to go with it, and you go right ahead and bet that money on any Thursday on any horse that has a name indicating . . . let me see, Thursday . . . well, grain. Or any growing food."

"Grain?" said the driver. "You mean a horse named, like, Wheat or something?"

175

"Certainly," said Mr. Johnson. "Or, as a matter of fact, to make it even easier, any horse whose name includes the letters C, R, L. Perfectly simple."

"Tall Corn?" said the driver, a light in his eye. "You mean a horse named, like, Tall Corn?"

"Absolutely," said Mr. Johnson. "Here's your money."

"Tall Corn," said the driver. "Thank *you*, mister."

"Goodby," said Mr. Johnson.

He was on his own corner and went straight up to his apartment. He let himself in and called "Hello?" and Mrs. Johnson answered from the kitchen, "Hello, dear, aren't you early?"

"Took a taxi home," Mr. Johnson said. "I remembered the cheesecake, too. What's for dinner?"

Mrs. Johnson came out of the kitchen and kissed him; she was a comfortable woman, and smiling as Mr. Johnson smiled. "Hard day?" she asked.

"Not very," said Mr. Johnson, hanging his coat in the closet. "How about you?"

"So-so," she said. She stood in the kitchen doorway while he settled into his easy chair and took off his good shoes and took out the paper he had bought that morning. "Here and there," she said.

"I didn't do so badly," Mr. Johnson said. "Couple young people."

"Fine," she said. "I had a little nap this afternoon, took it easy most of the day. Went into a department store this morning and accused the woman next to me of shoplifting, and had the store detective pick her up. Sent three dogs to the pound—*you* know, the usual thing. Oh, and listen," she added, remembering.

"What?" asked Mr. Johnson.

"Well," she said, "I got onto a bus and asked the driver for a transfer, and when he helped someone else first I said that he was impertinent, and quarreled with him. And then I said why wasn't he in the army, and I said it loud enough for everyone to hear, and I took his number and I turned in a complaint. Probably got him fired."

"Fine," said Mr. Johnson. "But you do look tired. Want to change over tomorrow?"

"I *would* like to," she said. "I could do with a change."

"Right," said Mr. Johnson. "What's for dinner?"

"Veal cutlet."

"Had it for lunch," said Mr. Johnson.

176

1956

WHICH BRINGS US to 1957, the most bizarre year in the history of the Hugo awards. The World Science Fiction Convention took place in London that year—the first time it had ever been held outside the North American continent. (It had taken place in Toronto in 1948, the only previous instance of its moving out of the United States.)

The chairman was E. J. Carnell. Carnell had been a fan for many years and had been editing science fiction anthologies since 1946, had been founding editor of *New Worlds* magazine, and was a member of the International Fantasy Awards jury. Perhaps it was this last that caused the London convention's odd treatment of the Hugos. The IFA's were on their last legs. The upstart Hugo awards were burgeoning. And Carnell's committee almost demolished them by deleting *all* categories for individual works, and offering awards in only three categories: best professional magazine (American), best professional magazine (British), and best fan magazine. The winners, let me mention in passing, were *Astounding, New Worlds* (surprise!), and *Science-Fiction Times*.

What works would have been eligible, had the London convention recognized individual efforts as well as collective ones? In the magazines, *Amazing* surprised with a first-rate, old-fashioned adventure serial, *The Scarlet Saint* by Manly Banister (later published as *Conquest of Earth*). *Astounding* had *The Naked Sun* by Asimov. *Future* had *Vulcan's Hammer* by Philip K. Dick. *Galaxy* ran *Slave Ship* by Frederik Pohl and *The Stars My Destination* by Alfred Bester. *Fantasy and Science Fiction* serialized Heinlein's *The Door into Summer*. *Science Fiction Stories* ran Blish's *Giants in the Earth*. And a new magazine, *Satellite,* began publication with a policy of running a lead novel in each issue. There were two issues in 1956, containing

The Man from Earth by Algis Budrys and *A Glass of Darkness* by Philip K. Dick.

There were a large number of novels appearing as books without magazine versions: *Star Ways* by Poul Anderson (Avalon), *Solomon's Stone* by de Camp (Avalon), *Nerves* by del Rey (Ballantine—expanded from a 1942 short story), *The Man Who Japed* by Philip K. Dick (Ace), *The Green Odyss*ey by Philip Jose Farmer (Ballantine), *The Shrinking Man* by Richard Matheson (Fawcett), *Agent of the Unknown* by Margaret St. Clair (Ace), and *To Live Forever* by Jack Vance (Ballantine).

Which would have won? In all likelihood, *The Door into Summer* by Heinlein. He'd just come off a win, was at the top of his form and popularity, and *The Door into Summer* had certainly been well received. Second place would have been a close contest between the Asimov novel and the Bester. *The Naked Sun* had the advantage of appearing in *Astounding*—and was a sequel to the popular *Caves of Steel*. But *The Stars My Destination* was probably a better novel, with even more of the pyrotechnics and the wallop of Bester's *Demolished Man*. All three have showed plenty of staying power; any of them would have made a worthy winner.

In the shorter lengths there were plenty of strong stories, too: Poul Anderson's amusing fantasy "Operation Afreet" in *F&SF;* Alan E. Nourse's "Brightside Crossing," de Camp's "A Gun for Dinosaur," and Pohl's "The Man Who Ate the World," all in *Galaxy;* Blish's "Tomb Tapper" and James H. Schmitz's "Some Notes on Playata," both in *Astounding;* William Tenn's "Wednesday's Child," Clifford Simak's "So Bright the Vision," and Isaac Asimov's "First Law," all in *Fantastic Universe;* Idris Seabright's "White Goddess," Zenna Henderson's "Anything Box," and Jane Roberts's "The Red Wagon," all in *Fantasy and Science Fiction.*

But of all the short science fiction published in 1956, I think the single finest story was Poul Anderson's "The Man Who Came Early," in the June *Fantasy and Science Fiction.*

What Anderson did in the story was stand one of science fiction's hoariest clichés on its head. We've all read endless times of modern man, traveling into the past and using his superior knowledge and his era's advanced technology to rise in the world, improve the state of civilization, and generally play hero, superman, or even God.

Mark Twain did it in *A Connecticut Yankee*.

Sprague de Camp did it in *Lest Darkness Fall*.

But Poul Anderson is a thinker. I've been reading his stories since "Un-man" appeared in 1953, and I've known him personally since sometime in the early '60s, and whatever other virtues (or, for that matter, shortcomings) he may have, I have been above all impressed by his thoroughness.

Intellectual thoroughness.

Poul Anderson is the embodiment of the old Campbell notion of looking beyond the obvious application of some new idea, principle, or discovery. Campbell wanted his writers to think out the full implications of whatever idea they happened to seize upon.

And in "The Man Who Came Early," Anderson gives a harrowing picture of the civilized man suddenly set down to make his way in a relatively primitive milieu.

The Man Who Came Early

POUL ANDERSON

YES, WHEN A man grows old he has heard so much that is strange there's little more can surprise him. They say the king in Miklagard has a beast of gold before his high seat which stands up and roars. I have it from Eilif Eiriksson, who served in the guard down yonder, and he is a steady fellow when not drunk. He has also seen the Greek fire used, it burns on water.

So, priest, I am not unwilling to believe what you say about the White Christ. I have been in England and France myself, and seen how the folk prosper. He must be a very powerful god, to ward so many realms . . . and did you say that everyone who is baptized will be given a white robe? I would like to have one. They mildew, of course, in this cursed wet Iceland weather, but a small sacrifice to the house-elves should— No sacrifices? Come now! I'll give up horseflesh if I must, my teeth not being what they were, but every sensible man knows how much trouble the elves make if they're not fed.

Well, let's have another cup and talk about it. How do you like the beer? It's my own brew, you know. The cups I got in England, many years back. I was a young man then . . . time goes, time goes. Afterward I came back and inherited this my father's farm, and have not left it since. Well enough to go in viking as a youth, but grown older you see where the real wealth lies: here, in the land and the cattle.

Stoke up the fires, Hjalti. It's getting cold. Sometimes I think the winters are colder than when I was a boy. Thorbrand of the Salmondale says so, but he believes the gods are angry because so many are turning from them. You'll have trouble winning Thorbrand over, priest. A stubborn man. Myself, I am open-minded, and willing to listen at least.

Now, then. There is one point on which I must set you right. The end of the world is not coming in two years. This I know.

And if you ask me how I know, that's a very long tale, and in some ways a terrible one. Glad I am to be old, and safe in the earth before that great tomorrow comes. It will be an eldritch time before the frost giants fare loose . . . oh, very well, before the angel blows his battle horn. One reason I hearken to your preaching is that I know the White Christ will conquer Thor. I know Iceland is going to be Christian erelong, and it seems best to range myself on the winning side.

No, I've had no visions. This is a happening of five years ago, which my own household and neighbors can swear to. They mostly did not believe what the stranger told; I do, more or less, if only because I don't think a liar could wreak so much harm. I loved my daughter, priest, and after the trouble was over I made a good marriage for her. She did not naysay it, but now she sits out on the ness-farm with her husband and never a word to me; and I hear he is ill pleased with her silence and moodiness, and spends his nights with an Irish leman. For this I cannot blame him, but it grieves me.

Well, I've drunk enough to tell the whole truth now, and whether you believe it or not makes no odds to me. Here . . . you, girls . . . ! Fill these cups again, for I'll have a dry throat before I finish the telling.

It begins, then, on a day in early summer, five years ago. At that time, my wife Ragnhild and I had only two unwed children still living with us: our youngest son Helgi, of seventeen winters, and our daughter Thorgunna, of eighteen. The girl, being fair, had already had suitors. But she refused them, and I am not one who would compel his daughter. As for Helgi, he was ever a lively one, good with his hands but a breakneck youth. He is now serving in the guard of King Olaf of Norway. Besides these, of course, we had about ten housefolk—two thralls, two girls to help with the women's work, and half a dozen hired carles. This is not a small stead.

You have seen how my land lies. About two miles to the west is the bay; the thorps of Reykjavik are some five miles south. The land rises toward the Long Jökull, so that my acres are hilly; but it's good hay land, and we often find driftwood on the beach. I've built a shed down there for it, as well as a boathouse.

We had had a storm the night before—a wild huge storm with lightning flashes across heaven, such as you seldom get in Iceland—so Helgi and I were going down to look for drift. You, coming from Norway, do not know how precious wood is to us here, who have only a few scrubby trees and must get our timber from abroad. Back there men have often been burned in their houses by their foes, but we count that the worst of deeds, though it's not unheard of.

As I was on good terms with my neighbors, we took only hand weapons. I bore my ax, Helgi a sword, and the two carles we had with us bore spears. It was a day washed clean by the night's fury, and the sun fell bright on long, wet grass. I saw my stead lying rich around its courtyard, sleek cows and sheep, smoke rising from the roofhole of the hall, and knew I'd not done so ill in my lifetime. My son Helgi's hair fluttered in the low west wind as we left the buildings behind a ridge and neared the water. Strange how well I remember all which happened that day; somehow it was a sharper day than most.

When we came down to the strand, the sea was beating heavy, white and gray out to the world's edge, smelling of salt and kelp. A few gulls mewed above us, frightened of a cod washed onto the shore. I saw a litter of no few sticks, even a baulk of timber . . . from some ship carrying it that broke up during the night, I suppose. That was a useful find, though as a careful man I would later sacrifice to be sure the owner's ghost wouldn't plague me.

We had fallen to and were dragging the baulk toward the shed when Helgi cried out. I ran for my ax as I looked the way he pointed. We had no feuds then, but there are always outlaws.

This newcomer seemed harmless, though. Indeed, as he stumbled nearer across the black sand I thought him quite unarmed and wondered what had happened. He was a big man and strangely clad—he wore coat and breeches and shoes like anyone else, but they were of odd cut, and he bound his trousers with leggings rather than straps. Nor had I ever seen a helmet like his: it was almost square, and came down toward his neck, but it had no nose guard. And this you may not believe, but it was not metal yet had been cast in one piece!

He broke into a staggering run as he drew close, flapped his arms and croaked something. The tongue was none I had heard, and I have heard many; it was like dogs barking. I saw that he was clean-shaven and his black hair cropped short, and thought he might be French. Otherwise he was a young man, and good-looking, with blue eyes and regular features. From his skin I judged that he spent much time indoors. However, he had a fine manly build.

"Could he have been shipwrecked?" asked Helgi.

"His clothes are dry and unstained," I said; "nor has he been wandering long, for no stubble is on his chin. Yet I've heard of no strangers guesting hereabouts."

We lowered our weapons, and he came up to us and stood gasping. I saw that his coat and the shirt underneath were fastened with bonelike buttons rather than laces, and were of heavy weave. About his neck he had fastened a strip of cloth tucked into his coat. These garments were all in brownish hues. His shoes were of a sort new to me, very well stitched. Here and there on his coat were bits of brass, and he had three broken stripes on each sleeve; also a black band with white letters, the same letters being on his helmet. Those were not runes, but Roman—thus: MP. He wore a broad belt, with a small clublike thing of metal in a sheath at the hip and also a real club.

"I think he must be a warlock," muttered my carle Sigurd. "Why else so many tokens?"

"They may only be ornament, or to ward against witchcraft," I soothed him. Then, to the stranger: "I hight Ospak Ulfsson of Hillstead. What is your errand?"

He stood with his chest heaving and a wildness in his eyes. He must have run a long way. At last he moaned and sat down and covered his face.

"If he's sick, best we get him to the house," said Helgi. I heard eagerness; we see few new faces here.

"No . . . no. . . ." The stranger looked up. "Let me rest a moment—"

He spoke the Norse tongue readily enough, though with

183

a thick accent not easy to follow and with many foreign words I did not understand.

The other carle, Grim, hefted his spear. "Have vikings landed?" he asked.

"When did vikings ever come to Iceland?" I snorted. "It's the other way around."

The newcomer shook his head as if it had been struck. He got shakily to his feet. "What happened?" he said. "What became of the town?"

"What town?" I asked reasonably.

"Reykjavik!" he cried. "Where is it?"

"Five miles south, the way you came—unless you mean the bay itself," I said.

"No! There was only a beach, and a few wretched huts, and—"

"Best not let Hjalmar Broadnose hear you call his thorp that," I counseled.

"But there was a town!" he gasped. "I was crossing the street in a storm, and heard a crash, and then I stood on the beach and the town was gone!"

"He's mad," said Sigurd, backing away. "Be careful. If he starts to foam at the mouth, it means he's going berserk."

"Who are you?" babbled the stranger. "What are you doing in those clothes? Why the spears?"

"Somehow," said Helgi, "he does not sound crazed, only frightened and bewildered. Something evil has beset him."

"I'm not staying near a man under a curse!" yelped Sigurd, and started to run away.

"Come back!" I bawled. "Stand where you are or I'll cleave your louse-bitten head."

That stopped him, for he had no kin who would avenge him; but he would not come closer. Meanwhile the stranger had calmed down to the point where he could talk somewhat evenly.

"Was it the *aitsjbom?*" he asked. "Has the war started?"

He used that word often, *aitsjbom,* so I know it now, though unsure of what it means. It seems to be a kind of Greek fire. As for the war, I knew not which war he meant, and told him so.

"We had a great thunderstorm last night," I added. "And you say you were out in one too. Maybe Thor's hammer knocked you from your place to here."

"But where is here?" he answered. His voice was more dulled than otherwise, now that the first terror had lifted.

"I told you. This is Hillstead, which is on Iceland."

"But that's where I was!" he said. "Reykjavik . . . what happened? Did the *aitsjbom* destroy everything while I lay witless?"

"Nothing has been destroyed," I said.

"Does he mean the fire at Olafsvik last month?" wondered Helgi.

"No, no, no!" Again he buried his face in his hands. After a while he looked up and said: "See here. I am *Sardjant* Gerald Robbins of the United States Army base on Iceland. I was in Reykjavik and got struck by lightning or something. Suddenly I was standing on the beach, and lost my head and ran. That's all. Now, can you tell me how to get back to the base?"

Those were more or less his words, priest. Of course, we did not grasp half of them, and made him repeat several times and explain. Even then we did not understand, save that he was from some country called the United States of America, which he said lies beyond Greenland to the west, and that he and some others were on Iceland to help our folk against their foes. This I did not consider a lie—more a mistake or imagining. Grim would have cut him down for thinking us stupid enough to swallow that tale, but I could see that he meant it.

Talking cooled him further. "Look here," he said, in too calm a tone for a feverish man, "maybe we can get at the truth from your side. Has there been no war you know of? Nothing which— Well, look here. My country's men first came to Iceland to guard it against the Germans. Now it is the Russians, but then it was the Germans. When was that?"

Helgi shook his head. "That never happened that I know of," he said. "Who are these Russians?" We found out later that the Gardariki folk were meant, "Unless," Helgi said, "the old warlocks—"

"He means the Irish monks," I explained. "A few dwelt here when the Norsemen came, but they were driven out. That was, hm, somewhat over a hundred years ago. Did your kingdom once help the monks?"

"I never heard of them!" he said. The breath sobbed in his throat. "You . . . didn't you Icelanders come from Norway?"

"Yes, about a hundred years ago," I answered patiently. "After King Harald Fairhair laid the Norse lands under him and—"

"A hundred years ago!" he whispered. I saw whiteness creep up beneath his skin. "What year is this?"

We gaped at him. "Well, it's the second year after the great salmon catch," I tried.

"What year after Christ, I mean," he prayed hoarsely.

"Oh, so you are a Christian? Hm, let me think. . . . I talked with a bishop in England once, we were holding him for ransom, and he said . . . let me see . . . I think he said this Christ man lived a thousand years ago, or maybe a little less."

"A thousand—" Something went out of him. He stood with glassy eyes—yes, I have seen glass, I told you I am a traveled man—he stood thus, and when we led him toward the garth he went like a small child.

You can see for yourself, priest, that my wife Ragnhild is still good to look upon even in eld, and Thorgunna took after her. She was—is tall and slim, with a dragon's hoard of golden hair. She being a maiden then, the locks flowed loose over her shoulders. She had great blue eyes and a heart-shaped face and very red lips. Withal she was a merry one, and kindhearted, so that she was widely loved. Sverri Snorrason went in viking when she refused him, and was slain, but no one had the wit to see that she was unlucky.

We led this Gerald Samsson—when I asked, he said his father was named Sam—we led him home, leaving Sigurd and Grim to finish gathering the driftwood. Some folks would not have a Christian in their house, for fear of witchcraft, but I am a broad-minded man, and Helgi, at his age, was wild for anything new. Our guest stumbled over the fields as if blind, but seemed to rouse when we entered the yard. His gaze went around the buildings that enclose it, from the stables and sheds to the smokehouse, the brewery, the kitchen, the bathhouse, the god shrine, and thence to the hall. And Thorgunna was standing in the doorway.

Their gazes locked for a little, and I saw her color but thought nothing of it then. Our shoes rang on the flagging as we crossed the yard and kicked the dogs aside. My two thralls halted in cleaning the stables to gawp, until I got them back to work with the remark that a man good for naught else was always a pleasing sacrifice. That's one useful practice you Christians lack; I've never made a human offering myself, but you know not how helpful is the fact that I could do so.

We entered the hall, and I told the folk Gerald's name

and how we had found him. Ragnhild set her maids hopping, to stoke up the fire in the middle trench and fetch beer, while I led Gerald to the high seat and sat down by him. Thorgunna brought us the filled horns. His standing was not like yours, for whom we use our outland cups.

Gerald tasted the brew and made a face. I felt somewhat offended, for my beer is reckoned good, and asked him if aught was wrong. He laughed with a harsh note and said no, but he was used to beer that foamed and was not sour.

"And where might they make such?" I wondered testily.

"Everywhere," he said. "Iceland, too—no. . . ." He stared before him in an empty wise. "Let's say . . . in Vinland."

"Where is Vinland?" I asked.

"The country to the west whence I came. I thought you knew. . . . Wait a bit." He frowned. "Maybe I can find out something. Have you heard of Leif Eiriksson?"

"No," I said. Since then it has struck me that this was one proof of his tale, for Leif Eiriksson is now a well-known chief; and I also take more seriously those yarns of land seen by Bjarni Herjulfsson.

"His father, Eirik the Red?" went on Gerald.

"Oh yes," I said. "If you mean the Norseman who came hither because of a manslaughter, and left Iceland in turn for the same reason, and has now settled with his friends in Greenland."

"Then this is . . . a little before Leif's voyage," he muttered. "The late tenth century."

"See here," broke in Helgi, "we've been forbearing with you, but now is no time for riddles. We save those for feasts and drinking bouts. Can you not say plainly whence you come and how you got here?"

Gerald looked down at the floor, shaking.

"Let the man alone, Helgi," said Thorgunna. "Can you not see he's troubled?"

He raised his head and gave her the look of a hurt dog that someone has patted. The hall was dim; enough light seeped in the loft windows that no candles were lit, but not enough to see well by. Nevertheless, I marked a reddening in both their faces.

Gerald drew a long breath and fumbled about. His clothes were made with pockets. He brought out a small parchment box and from it took a little white stick that he put in his mouth. Then he took out another box, and a wooden stick therefrom which burst into flame when

187

scratched. With the fire he kindled the stick in his mouth, and sucked in the smoke.

We stared. "Is that a Christian rite?" asked Helgi.

"No . . . not just so." A wry, disappointed smile twisted his lips. "I thought you'd be more surprised, even terrified."

"It's something new," I admitted, "but we're a sober folk on Iceland. Those fire sticks could be useful. Did you come to trade in them?"

"Hardly." He sighed. The smoke he breathed in seemed to steady him, which was odd, because the smoke in the hall had made him cough and water at the eyes. "The truth is, well, something you will not believe. I can hardly believe it myself."

We waited. Thorgunna stood leaning forward, her lips parted.

"That lightning bolt—" Gerald nodded wearily. "I was out in the storm, and somehow the lightning must have smitten me in just the right way, a way that happens only once in many thousands of times. It threw me back into the past."

Those were his words, priest. I did not understand, and told him so.

"It's hard to grasp," he agreed. "God give that I'm merely dreaming. But if this is a dream I must endure till I awaken. . . . Well, look. I was born one thousand, nine hundred, and thirty-three years after Christ, in a land to the west which you have not yet found. In the twenty-fourth year of my life, I was in Iceland with my country's war host. The lightning struck me, and now, now it is less than one thousand years after Christ, and yet I am here— almost a thousand years before I was born, I am here!"

We sat very still. I signed myself with the Hammer and took a long pull from my horn. One of the maids whimpered, and Ragnhild whispered so fiercely I could hear: "Be still. The poor fellow's out of his head. There's no harm in him."

I thought she was right, unless maybe in the last part. The gods can speak through a madman, and the gods are not always to be trusted. Or he could turn berserker, or he could be under a heavy curse that would also touch us.

He slumped, gazing before him. I caught a few fleas and cracked them while I pondered. Gerald noticed and asked with some horror if we had many fleas here.

"Why, of course," said Thorgunna. "Have you none?"

"No." He smiled crookedly. "Not yet."

"Ah," she sighed, "then you *must* be sick."

She was a level-headed girl. I saw her thought, and so did Ragnhild and Helgi. Clearly, a man so sick that he had no fleas could be expected to rave. We might still fret about whether we could catch the illness, but I deemed this unlikely; his woe was in the head, maybe from a blow he had taken. In any case, the matter was come down to earth now, something we could deal with.

I being a godi, a chief who holds sacrifices, it behooved me not to turn a stranger out. Moreover, if he could fetch in many of those fire-kindling sticks, a profitable trade might be built up. So I said Gerald should go to rest. He protested, but we manhandled him into the shut-bed, and there he lay tired and was soon asleep. Thorgunna said she would take care of him.

The next eventide I meant to sacrifice a horse, both because of the timber we had found and to take away any curse that might be on Gerald. Furthermore, the beast I picked was old and useless, and we were short of fresh meat. Gerald had spent the morning lounging moodily around the garth, but when I came in at noon to eat I found him and my daughter laughing.

"You seem to be on the road to health," I said.

"Oh yes. It . . . could be worse for me." He sat down at my side as the carles set up the trestle table and the maids brought in the food. "I was ever much taken with the age of the vikings, and I have some skills."

"Well," I said, "if you have no home, we can keep you here for a while."

"I can work," he said eagerly. "I'll be worth my pay."

Now I knew he was from afar, because what chief would work on any land but his own, and for hire at that? Yet he had the easy manner of the high-born, and had clearly eaten well throughout his life. I overlooked that he had made me no gifts; after all, he was shipwrecked.

"Maybe you can get passage back to your United States," said Helgi. "We could hire a ship. I'm fain to see that realm."

"No," said Gerald bleakly. "There is no such place. Not yet."

"So you still hold to that idea you came from tomorrow?" grunted Sigurd. "Crazy notion. Pass the pork."

"I do," said Gerald. Calm had come upon him. "And I can prove it."

189

"I don't see how you speak our tongue, if you hail from so far away," I said. I would not call a man a liar to his face, unless we were swapping friendly brags, but—

"They speak otherwise in my land and time," he said, "but it happens that in Iceland the tongue changed little since the old days, and because my work had me often talking with the folk, I learned it when I came here."

"If you are a Christian," I said, "you must bear with us while we sacrifice tonight."

"I've naught against that," he said. "I fear I never was a very good Christian. I'd like to watch. How is it done?"

I told him how I would smite the horse with a hammer before the god, and cut its throat, and sprinkle the blood about with willow twigs; thereafter we would butcher the carcass and feast. He said hastily:

"Here's my chance to prove what I am. I have a weapon that will kill the horse with, with a flash of lightning."

"What is it?" I wondered. We crowded around while he took the metal club out of its sheath and showed it to us. I had my doubts; it looked well enough for hitting a man, I reckoned, but had no edge, though a wondrously skillful smith had forged it. "Well, we can try," I said. You have seen how on Iceland we are less concerned to follow the rites exactly than they are in the older countries.

Gerald showed us what else he had in his pockets. There were some coins of remarkable roundness and sharpness, though neither gold nor true silver; a tiny key; a stick with lead in it for writing; a flat purse holding many bits of marked paper. When he told us gravely that some of this paper was money, Thorgunna herself had to laugh. Best was a knife whose blade folded into the handle. When he saw me admiring that, he gave it to me, which was well done for a shipwrecked man. I said I would give him clothes and a good ax, as well as lodging for as long as needful.

No, I don't have the knife now. You shall hear why. It's a pity, for that was a good knife, though rather small.

"What were you ere the war arrow went out in your land?" asked Helgi. "A merchant?"

"No," said Gerald. "I was an . . . *endjinur* . . . that is, I was learning how to be one. A man who builds things, bridges and roads and tools . . . more than just an artisan. So I think my knowledge could be of great value here."

190

I saw a fever in his eyes. "Yes, give me time and I'll be a king."

"We have no king on Iceland," I grunted. "Our forefathers came hither to get away from kings. Now we meet at the Things to try suits and pass new laws, but each man must get his own redress as best he can."

"But suppose the one in the wrong won't yield?" he asked.

"Then there can be a fine feud," said Helgi, and went on to relate some of the killings in past years. Gerald looked unhappy and fingered his *gun*. That is what he called his firespitting club. He tried to rally himself with a joke about now, at last, being free to call it a gun instead of something else. That disquieted me, smacked of witchcraft, so to change the talk I told Helgi to stop his chattering of manslaughter as if it were sport. With law shall the land be built.

"Your clothing is rich," said Thorgunna softly. "Your folk must own broad acres at home."

"No," he said, "our . . . our king gives each man in the host clothes like these. As for my family, we owned no farm, we rented our home in a building where many other families also dwelt."

I am not purse-proud, but it seemed to me he had not been honest, a landless man sharing my high seat like a chief. Thorgunna covered my huffiness by saying, "You will gain a farm later."

After sunset we went out to the shrine. The carles had built a fire before it, and as I opened the door the wooden Odin appeared to leap forth. My house has long invoked him above the others. Gerald muttered to my daughter that it was a clumsy bit of carving, and since my father had made it I was still more angry with him. Some folk have no understanding of the fine arts.

Nevertheless, I let him help me lead the horse forth to the altar stone. I took the blood bowl in my hands and said he could now slay the beast if he would. He drew his gun, put the end behind the horse's ear, and squeezed. We heard a crack, and the beast jerked and dropped with a hole blown through its skull, wasting the brains. A clumsy weapon. I caught a whiff, sharp and bitter like that around a volcano. We all jumped, one of the women screamed, and Gerald looked happy. I gathered my wits and finished the rest of the sacrifice as was right. Gerald did not like having blood sprinkled over him, but then he was a

Christian. Nor would he take more than a little of the soup and flesh.

Afterward Helgi questioned him about the gun, and he said it could kill a man at bowshot distance but had no witchcraft in it, only use of some tricks we did not know. Having heard of the Greek fire, I believed him. A gun could be useful in a fight, as indeed I was to learn, but it did not seem very practical—iron costing what it does, and months of forging needed for each one.

I fretted more about the man himself.

And the next morning I found him telling Thorgunna a great deal of foolishness about his home—buildings as tall as mountains, and wagons that flew, or went without horses. He said there were eight or nine thousand thousands of folk in his town, a burgh called New Jorvik or the like. I enjoy a good brag as well as the next man, but this was too much, and I told him gruffly to come along and help me get in some strayed cattle.

After a day scrambling around the hills I saw that Gerald could hardly tell a cow's bow from her stern. We almost had the strays once, but he ran stupidly across their path and turned them, so the whole work was to do again. I asked him with strained courtesy if he could milk, shear, wield scythe or flail, and he said no, he had never lived on a farm.

"That's a shame," I remarked, "for everyone on Iceland does, unless he be outlawed."

He flushed at my tone. "I can do enough else," he answered. "Give me some tools and I'll show you good metalwork."

That brightened me, for truth to tell, none of our household was a gifted smith. "That's an honorable trade," I said, "and you can be of great help. I have a broken sword and several bent spearheads to be mended, and it were no bad idea to shoe the horses." His admission that he did not know how to put on a shoe was not very dampening to me then.

We had returned home as we talked, and Thorgunna came angrily forward. "That's no way to treat a guest, Father," she said. "Making him work like a carle, indeed!"

Gerald smiled. "I'll be glad to work," he said. "I need a . . . a stake . . . something to start me afresh. Also, I want to repay a little of your kindness."

Those words made me mild toward him, and I said it

192

was not his fault they had different ways in the United States. On the morrow he could begin in the smithy, and I would pay him, yet he would be treated as an equal since craftsmen are valued. This earned him black looks from the housefolk.

That evening he entertained us well with stories of his home; true or not, they made good listening. However, he had no real polish, being unable to compose a line of verse. They must be a raw and backward lot in the United States. He said his task in the war host had been to keep order among the troops. Helgi said this was unheard of, and he must be bold who durst offend so many men, but Gerald said folk obeyed him out of fear of the king. When he added that the term of a levy in the United States was two years, and that men could be called to war even in harvest time, I said he was well out of a country with so ruthless and powerful a lord.

"No," he answered wistfully, "we are a free folk, who say what we please."

"But it seems you may not do as you please," said Helgi.

"Well," Gerald said, "we may not murder a man just because he aggrieves us."

"Not even if he has slain your own kin?" asked Helgi.

"No. It is for the . . . the king to take vengeance, on behalf of the whole folk whose peace has been broken."

I chuckled. "Your yarns are cunningly wrought," I said, "but there you've hit a snag. How could the king so much as keep count of the slaughters, let alone avenge them? Why, he'd not have time to beget an heir!"

Gerald could say no more for the laughter that followed.

The next day he went to the smithy, with a thrall to pump the bellows for him. I was gone that day and night, down to Reykjavik to dicker with Hjalmar Broadnose about some sheep. I invited him back for an overnight stay, and we rode into my steading with his son Ketill, a red-haired sulky youth of twenty winters who had been refused by Thorgunna.

I found Gerald sitting gloomily on a bench in the hall. He wore the clothes I had given him, his own having been spoilt by ash and sparks; what had he awaited, the fool? He talked in a low voice with my daughter.

"Well," I said as I trod in, "how went the tasks?"

My man Grim snickered. "He ruined two spearheads, but we put out the fire he started ere the whole smithy burned."

"How's this?" I cried. "You said you were a smith."

Gerald stood up, defiant. "I worked with different tools, and better ones, at home," he replied. "You do it otherwise here."

They told me he had built up the fire too hot; his hammer had struck everywhere but the place it should; he had wrecked the temper of the steel through not knowing when to quench it. Smithcraft takes years to learn, of course, but he might have owned to being not so much as an apprentice.

"Well," I snapped, "what can you do, then, to earn your bread?" It irked me to be made a ninny of before Hjalmar and Ketill, whom I had told about the stranger.

"Odin alone knows," and Grim. "I took him with me to ride after your goats, and never have I seen a worse horseman. I asked him if maybe he could spin or weave, and he said no."

"That was no question to ask a man!" flared Thorgunna. "He should have slain you for it."

"He should indeed," laughed Grim. "But let me carry on the tale. I thought we would also repair your bridge over the foss. Well, he *can* barely handle a saw, but he nigh took his own foot off with the adze."

"We don't use those tools, I tell you!" Gerald doubled his fists and looked close to tears.

I motioned my guests to sit down. "I don't suppose you can butcher or smoke a hog, either," I said, "or salt a fish or turf a roof."

"No." I could hardly hear him.

"Well, then, man, whatever can you do?"

"I—" He could get no words out.

"You were a warrior," said Thorgunna.

"Yes, that I was!" he said, his face kindling.

"Small use on Iceland when you have no other skills," I grumbled, "but maybe, if you can get passage to the eastlands, some king will take you in his guard." Myself I doubted it, for a guardsman needs manners that will do credit to his lord; but I had not the heart to say so.

Ketill Hjalmarsson had plainly not liked the way Thorgunna stood close to Gerald and spoke for him. Now he fleered and said: "I might also doubt your skill in fighting."

"That I have been trained for," said Gerald grimly.

"Will you wrestle with me?" asked Ketill.

"Gladly!" spat Gerald.

Priest, what is a man to think? As I grow older, I find life to be less and less the good-and-evil, black-and-white thing you call it; we are each of us some hue of gray. This useless fellow, this spiritless lout who could be asked if he did women's work and not lift ax, went out into the yard with Ketill Hjalmarsson and threw him three times running. He had a trick of grabbing the clothes as Ketill rushed on him. . . . I cried a stop when the youth was nearing murderous rage, praised them both, and filled the beer horns. But Ketill brooded sullen on the bench the whole evening.

Gerald said something about making a gun like his own, but bigger, a *cannon* he called it, which could sink ships and scatter hosts. He would need the help of smiths, and also various stuffs. Charcoal was easy, and sulfur could be found by the volcanoes, I suppose, but what is this saltpeter?

Too, being wary by now, I questioned him closely as to how he would make such a thing. Did he know just how to mix the powder? No, he admitted. What size must the gun be? When he told me—at least as long as a man— I laughed and asked him how a piece that size could be cast or bored, supposing we could scrape together so much iron. This he did not know either.

"You haven't the tools to make the tools to make the tools," he said. I don't understand what he meant by that. "God help me, I can't run through a thousand years of history by myself."

He took out the last of his little smoke sticks and lit it. Helgi had tried a puff earlier and gotten sick, though he remained a friend of Gerald's. Now my son proposed to take a boat in the morning and go with him and me to Ice Fjord, where I had some money outstanding I wanted to collect. Hjalmar and Ketill said they would come along for the trip, and Thorgunna pleaded so hard that I let her come too.

"An ill thing," mumbled Sigurd. "The land-trolls like not a woman aboard a vessel. It's unlucky."

"How did your fathers bring women to this island?" I grinned.

Now I wish I had listened to him. He was not a clever man, but he often knew whereof he spoke.

At this time I owned a half-share in a ship that went to Norway, bartering wadmal for timber. It was a profitable business until she ran afoul of vikings during the uproar while Olaf Tryggvason was overthrowing Jarl Haakon there. Some men will do anything to make a living—thieves, cutthroats, they ought to be hanged, the worthless robbers pouncing on honest merchantmen. Had they any courage or honor they would go to Ireland, which is full of plunder.

Well, anyhow, the ship was abroad, but we had three boats and took one of these. Grim went with us others: myself, Helgi, Hjalmar, Ketill, Gerald, and Thorgunna. I saw how the castaway winced at the cold water as we launched her, yet afterward took off his shoes and stockings to let his feet dry. He had been surprised to learn we had a bathhouse—did he think us savages?—but still, he was dainty as a girl and soon moved upwind of our feet.

We had a favoring breeze, so raised mast and sail. Gerald tried to help, but of course did not know one line from another and got them fouled. Grim snarled at him and Ketill laughed nastily. But erelong we were under weigh, and he came and sat by me where I had the steering oar.

He must have lain long awake thinking, for now he ventured shyly: "In my land they have . . . will have . . . a rig and rudder which are better than these. With them, you can sail so close to the wind that you can crisscross against it."

"Ah, our wise sailor offers us redes," sneered Ketill.

"Be still," said Thorgunna sharply. "Let Gerald speak."

Gerald gave her a look of humble thanks, and I was not unwilling to listen. "This is something which could easily be made," he said. "While not a seaman, I've been on such boats myself and know them well. First, then, the sail should not be square and hung from a yardarm, but three-cornered, with the two bottom corners lashed to a yard swiveling fore and aft from the mast; and there should be one or two smaller headsails of the same shape. Next, your steering oar is in the wrong place. You should have a rudder in the stern, guided by a bar." He grew eager and traced the plan with his fingernail on Thorgunna's cloak. "With these two things, and a deep keel, going down about three feet for a boat this size, a ship can move across the wind . . . thus."

Well, priest, I must say the idea has merits, and were it not for the fear of bad luck—for everything of his was

196

unlucky—I might yet play with it. But the drawbacks were clear, and I pointed them out in a reasonable way.

"First and worst," I said, "this rudder and deep keel would make it impossible to beach the ship or go up a shallow river. Maybe they have many harbors where you hail from, but here a craft must take what landings she can find, and must be speedily launched if there should be an attack."

"The keel can be built to draw up into the hull," he said, "with a box around so that water can't follow."

"How would you keep dry rot out of the box?" I answered. "No, your keel must be fixed, and must be heavy if the ship is not to capsize under so much sail as you have drawn. This means iron or lead, ruinously costly.

"Besides," I said, "this mast of yours would be hard to unstep when the wind dropped and oars came out. Furthermore, the sails are the wrong shape to stretch as an awning when one must sleep at sea."

"The ship could lie out, and you go to land in a small boat," he said. "Also, you could build cabins aboard for shelter."

"The cabins would get in the way of the oars," I said, "unless the ship were hopelessly broad-beamed or else the oarsmen sat below a deck; and while I hear that galley slaves do this in the southlands, free men would never row in such foulness."

"Must you have oars?" he asked like a very child.

Laughter barked along the hull. The gulls themselves, hovering to starboard where the shore rose dark, cried scorn.

"Do they have tame winds in the place whence you came?" snorted Hjalmar. "What happens if you're becalmed—for days, maybe, with provisions running out—"

"You could build a ship big enough to carry many weeks' provisions," said Gerald.

"If you had the wealth of a king, you might," said Helgi. "And such a king's ship, lying helpless on a flat sea, would be swarmed by every viking from here to Jomsborg. As for leaving her out on the water while you make camp, what would you have for shelter, or for defense if you should be trapped ashore?"

Gerald slumped. Thorgunna said to him gently: "Some folk have no heart to try anything new. I think it's a grand idea."

He smiled at her, a weary smile, and plucked up the

197

will to say something about a means for finding north in cloudy weather; he said a kind of stone always pointed north when hung from a string. I told him mildly that I would be most interested if he could find me some of this stone; or if he knew where it was to be had, I could ask a trader to fetch me a piece. But this he did not know, and fell silent. Ketill opened his mouth, but got such an edged look from Thorgunna that he shut it again. His face declared what a liar he thought Gerald to be.

The wind turned crank after a while, so we lowered the mast and took to the oars. Gerald was strong and willing, though awkward; however, his hands were so soft that erelong they bled. I offered to let him rest, but he kept doggedly at the work.

Watching him sway back and forth, under the dreary creak of the tholes, the shaft red and wet where he gripped it, I thought much about him. He had done everything wrong which a man could do—thus I imagined then, not knowing the future—and I did not like the way Thorgunna's eyes strayed to him and rested. He was no man for my daughter, landless and penniless and helpless. Yet I could not keep from liking him. Whether his tale was true or only madness, I felt he was honest about it; and surely whatever way by which he came hither was a strange one. I noticed the cuts on his chin from my razor; he had said he was not used to our kind of shaving and would grow a beard. He had tried hard. I wondered how well I would have done, landing alone in this witch country of his dreams, with a gap of forever between me and my home.

Maybe that same wretchedness was what had turned Thorgunna's heart. Women are a kittle breed, priest, and you who have forsworn them belike understand them as well as I who have slept with half a hundred in six different lands. I do not think they even understand themselves. Birth and life and death, those are the great mysteries, which none will ever fathom, and a woman is closer to them than a man.

The ill wind stiffened, the sea grew gray and choppy under low, leaden clouds, and our headway was poor. At sunset we could row no more, but must pull in to a small, unpeopled bay, and make camp as well as could be on the strand.

We had brought firewood and tinder along. Gerald, though staggering with weariness, made himself useful, his sulfury sticks kindling the blaze more easily than flint and steel. Thorgunna set herself to cook our supper. We were not much warded by the boat from a lean, whining wind; her cloak fluttered like wings and her hair blew wild above the streaming flames. It was the time of light nights, the sky a dim, dusky blue, the sea a wrinkled metal sheet, and the land like something risen out of dream mists. We men huddled in our own cloaks, holding numbed hands to the fire and saying little.

I felt some cheer was needed, and ordered a cask of my best and strongest ale broached. An evil Norn made me do that, but no man escapes his weird. Our bellies seemed the more empty now when our noses drank in the sputter of a spitted joint, and the ale went swiftly to our heads. I remember declaiming the death-song of Ragnar Hairybreeks for no other reason than that I felt like declaiming it.

Thorgunna came to stand over Gerald where he sat. I saw how her fingers brushed his hair, ever so lightly, and Ketill Hjalmarsson did too. "Have they no verses in your land?" she asked.

"Not like yours," he said, glancing up. Neither of them looked away again. "We sing rather than chant. I wish I had my *gittar* here—that's a kind of harp."

"Ah, an Irish bard," said Hjalmar Broadnose.

I remember strangely well how Gerald smiled, and what he said in his own tongue, though I know not the meaning: *"Only on me mither's side, begorra."* I suppose it was magic.

"Well, sing for us," laughed Thorgunna.

"Let me think," he said. "I shall have to put it in Norse words for you." After a little while, still staring at her through the windy gloaming, he began a song. It had a tune I liked, thus:

> *From this valley they tell me you're leaving.*
> *I will miss your bright eyes and sweet smile.*
> *You will carry the sunshine with you*
> *That has brightened my life all the while. . . .*

I don't remember the rest, save that it was not quite seemly.

When he finished, Hjalmar and Grim went over to see if the meat was done. I spied a glimmer of tears in my daughter's eyes. "That was a lovely thing," she said.

Ketill sat straight. The flames splashed his face with wild, running red. A rawness was in his tone: "Yes, we've

199

found what this fellow can do. Sit about and make pretty songs for the girls. Keep him for that, Ospak."

Thorgunna whitened, and Helgi clapped hand to sword. Gerald's face darkened and his voice grew thick: "That's no way to talk. Take it back."

Ketill rose. "No," he said. "I'll ask no pardon of an idler living off honest yeomen."

He was raging, but had kept sense enough to shift the insult from my family to Gerald alone. Otherwise he and his father would have had the four of us to deal with. As it was, Gerald stood too, fists knotted at his sides, and said: "Will you step away from here and settle this?"

"Gladly!" Ketill turned and walked a few yards down the beach, taking his shield from the boat. Gerald followed. Thorgunna stood stricken, then snatched his ax and ran after him.

"Are you going weaponless?" she shrieked.

Gerald stopped, looking dazed. "I don't want anything like that," he said. "Fists—"

Ketill puffed himself up and drew sword. "No doubt you're used to fighting like thralls in your land," he said. "So if you'll crave my pardon, I'll let this matter rest."

Gerald stood with drooped shoulders. He stared at Thorgunna as if he were blind, as if asking her what to do. She handed him the ax.

"So you want me to kill him?" he whispered.

"Yes," she answered.

Then I knew she loved him, for otherwise why should she have cared if he disgraced himself?

Helgi brought him his helmet. He put it on, took the ax, and went forward.

"Ill is this," said Hjalmar to me. "Do you stand by the stranger, Ospak?"

"No," I said. "He's no kin or oath-brother of mine. This is not my quarrel."

"That's good," said Hjalmar. "I'd not like to fight with you. You were ever a good neighbor."

We stepped forth together and staked out the ground. Thorgunna told me to lend Gerald my sword, so he could use a shield too, but the man looked oddly at me and said he would rather have the ax. They squared off before each other, he and Ketill, and began fighting.

This was no holmgang, with rules and a fixed order of blows and first blood meaning victory. There was death between those two. Drunk though the lot of us were, we saw that and so had not tried to make peace. Ketill stormed in with the sword whistling in his hand. Gerald sprang back, wielding the ax awkwardly. It bounced off Ketill's shield. The youth grinned and cut at Gerald's legs. Blood welled forth to stain the ripped breeches.

What followed was butchery. Gerald had never used a battle-ax before. So it turned in his grasp and he struck with the flat of the head. He would have been hewn down at once had Ketill's sword not been blunted on his helmet and had he not been quick on his feet. Even so, he was erelong lurching with a dozen wounds.

"Stop the fight!" Thorgunna cried, and sped toward them. Helgi caught her arms and forced her back, where she struggled and kicked till Grim must help. I saw grief on my son's face, but a wolfish glee on the carle's.

Ketill's blade came down and slashed Gerald's left hand. He dropped the ax. Ketill snarled and readied to finish him. Gerald drew his gun. It made a flash and a barking noise. Ketill fell. Blood gushed from him. His lower jaw was blown off and the back of his skull was gone.

A stillness came, where only the wind and the sea had voice.

Then Hjalmar trod forth, his mouth working but otherwise a cold steadiness over him. He knelt and closed his son's eyes, as a token that the right of vengeance was his. Rising, he said: "That was an evil deed. For that you shall be outlawed."

"It wasn't witchcraft," said Gerald in a stunned tone. "It was like a . . . a bow. I had no choice. I didn't want to fight with more than my fists."

I got between them and said the Thing must decide this matter, but that I hoped Hjalmar would take weregild for Ketill.

"But I killed him to save my own life!" protested Gerald.

"Nevertheless, weregild must be paid, if Ketill's kin will take it," I explained. "Because of the weapon, I think it will be doubled, but that is for the Thing to judge."

Hjalmar had many other sons, and it was not as if Gerald belonged to a family at odds with his own, so I felt he would agree. However, he laughed coldly and asked where a man lacking wealth would find the silver.

Thorgunna stepped up with a wintry calm and said we would pay. I opened my mouth, but when I saw her eyes I nodded. "Yes, we will," I said, "in order to keep the peace."

"So you make this quarrel your own?" asked Hjalmar.

"No," I answered. "This man is no blood of mine. But if I choose to make him a gift of money to use as he wishes, what of it?"

Hjalmar smiled. Sorrow stood in his gaze, but he looked on me with old comradeship.

"One day he may be your son-in-law," he said. "I know the signs, Ospak. Then indeed he will be of your folk. Even helping him now in his need will range you on his side."

"And so?" asked Helgi, most softly.

"And so, while I value your friendship, I have sons who will take the death of their brother ill. They'll want revenge on Gerald Samsson, if only for the sake of their good names, and thus our two houses will be sundered and one manslaying will lead to another. It has happened often enough ere now." Hjalmar sighed. "I myself wish peace with you, Ospak, but if you take this killer's side it must be otherwise."

I thought for a moment, thought of Helgi lying with his head cloven, of my other sons on their steads drawn to battle because of a man they had never seen, I thought of having to wear byrnies each time we went down for driftwood and never knowing when we went to bed if we would wake to find the house ringed in by spearmen.

"Yes," I said, "you are right. Hjalmar. I withdraw my offer. Let this be a matter between you and him alone."

We gripped hands on it.

Thorgunna uttered a small cry and flew into Gerald's arms. He held her close. "What does this mean?" he asked slowly.

"I cannot keep you any longer," I said, "but maybe some crofter will give you a roof. Hjalmar is a law-abiding man and will not harm you until the Thing has outlawed you. That will not be before they meet in fall. You can try to get passage out of Iceland ere then."

"A useless one like me?" he replied in bitterness.

Thorgunna whirled free and blazed that I was a coward and a perjurer and all else evil. I let her have it out before I laid my hands on her shoulders.

"I do this for the house," I said. "The house and the blood, which are holy. Men die and women weep, but while the kindred live our names are remembered. Can you ask a score of men to die for your hankerings?"

Long did she stand, and to this day I know not what her answer would have been. But Gerald spoke.

"No," he said. "I suppose you have right, Ospak . . . the right of your time, which is not mine." He took my hand, and Helgi's. His lips brushed Thorgunna's cheek. Then he turned and walked out into the darkness.

I heard, later, that he went to earth with Thorvald Halls-son, the crofter of Humpback Fell, and did not tell his host what had happened. He must have hoped to go unnoticed until he could somehow get berth on an east-bound ship. But of course word spread. I remember his brag that in the United States folk had ways to talk from one end of the land to another. So he must have scoffed at us, sitting in our lonely steads, and not known how fast news would get around. Thorvald's son Hrolf went to Brand Sealskin-Boots to talk about some matter, and mentioned the guest, and soon the whole western island had the tale.

Now, if Gerald had known he must give notice of a manslaying at the first garth he found, he would have been safe at least till the Thing met, for Hjalmar and his sons are sober men who would not needlessly kill a man still under the wing of the law. But as it was, his keeping the matter secret made him a murderer and therefore at once an outlaw. Hjalmar and his kin rode straight to Humpback Fell and haled him forth. He shot his way past them with the gun and fled into the hills. They followed him, having several hurts and one more death to avenge. I wonder if Gerald thought the strangeness of his weapon would unnerve us. He may not have understood that every man dies when his time comes, neither sooner nor later, so that fear of death is useless.

At the end, when they had him trapped, his weapon gave out on him. Then he took a dead man's sword and defended himself so valiantly that Ulf Hjalmarsson has limped ever since. That was well done, as even his foes admitted. They are an eldritch breed in the United States, but they do not lack manhood.

When he was slain, his body was brought back. For fear of the ghost, he having maybe been a warlock, it was burned, and everything he had owned was laid in the fire with him. Thus I lost the knife he gave me. The barrow stands out on the moor, north of here, and folk shun it, though the ghost has not walked. Today, with so much else happening, he is slowly being forgotten.

And that is the tale, priest, as I saw it and heard it. Most men think Gerald Samsson was crazy, but I myself now believe he did come from out of time, and that his doom was that no man may ripen a field before harvest season. Yet I look into the future, a thousand years hence, when they fly through the air and ride in horseless wagons and smash whole towns with one blow. I think of this Iceland then, and of the young United States men come to help defend us in a year when the end of the world hovers close. Maybe some of them, walking about on the heaths, will see that barrow and wonder what ancient warrior lies buried there, and they may well wish they had lived long ago in his time, when men were free.

1957

Now HERE'S AN oddity. There were no individual Hugos for works published in 1957 at the London convention of that year—since, as I've already explained, there were no Hugos given for *any* individual works that year. But because of the odd split-year system the fans were using, it worked out that there were no Hugos given for works of 1957 at the 1958 convention, either!

The convention was held in Los Angeles, and the fans voted the awards to two works from that same year. And, as we shall see in due course, the 1959 convention recognized works of 1958, also!

What a mess!

Just for the record, the winners in Los Angeles—no, come to think of it, let's save those for our next interlude. Unto each year are sufficient, and so on.

Not that there were no worthy works published in 1957. The magazines seemed to be backing away from serials, at the time, but *Astounding* did publish a couple of noteworthy ones. One was *The Dawning Light* by "Robert Randall"—Robert Silverberg and Randall Garrett writing in collaboration. The other was *Citizen of the Galaxy* by Heinlein, issued the same year by Scribner's in boards.

Galaxy serialized *Wolfbane* by Pohl and Kornbluth. And *Satellite* ran a couple of shortish novels worthy of recollection. One was *Planet for Plunder,* a very odd collaboration between Hal Clement and Sam Merwin in which the authors wrote essentially independent stories, interwoven chapter by chapter. The other was *The Languages of Pao* by Jack Vance, brought out the same year by Avalon.

And *Fantasy and Science Fiction* spun off a second magazine, *Venture Science Fiction,* edited by Robert P.

Mills. *Venture* ran Poul Anderson's double-entendre novel *Virgin Planet*.

Book publishers were busy, too. Ballantine brought out Blish's *The Frozen Year* (only marginally science fiction). Dutton issued Fredric Brown's *Rogue in Space*. Simon and Schuster published *No Blade of Grass* by John Christopher, based on material from the prestigious *Saturday Evening Post*. The success of the book with general readers —and its eventual successful screen adaptation—stimulated a long series of borderline-SF disaster novels, many of them by British writers.

In the vein of much "harder" science fiction, Harper & Row brought out *The Black Cloud,* the first and most successful of Fred Hoyle's science fiction novels. Harcourt Brace published Clarke's *The Deep Range;* Ballantine, Hal Clement's *Cycle of Fire;* and Shasta, a Chicago-based, fan-owned publishing enterprise, A. E. van Vogt's *Empire of the Atom.*

The shorter lengths were equally active, the leading stories of the year dividing into a group that proved to be springboards for highly successful series, and a group that were to stand alone in readers' fond recollections. The former class of stories included "Med Service" by Murray Leinster and "The Stainless Steel Rat" by Harry Harrison, both in *Astounding*. The latter group included Poul Anderson's superbly moving "Call Me Joe" in *Astounding* and Heinlein's ingenious "The Elephant Circuit" in a short-lived magazine called *Saturn*. Officially, *Saturn* was edited by Robert C. Sproul, but in actuality it was the product of veteran Donald Wollheim.

Larry Shaw's *Infinity* was doing well enough to add a second title, *Science Fiction Adventures;* the new magazine featured Thomas Scortia's ambitious "Alien Night" and Cyril Kornbluth's "The Slave."

In a lighter vein, Isaac Asimov contributed the well-remembered "I'm in Marsport Without Hilda" to *Venture;* Kornbluth, his comically and almost surrealistically paranoid "Ms. Found in a Chinese Fortune Cookie," to *Fantasy and Science Fiction. Galaxy* ran Avram Davidson's unforgettable "Help, I Am Dr. Morris Goldpepper," probably the first science fiction story about dentistry. The same magazine also featured "The Ifth of Oofth" by Walter Tevis. Certainly the title was too cutesy-poo to tolerate, but the story was excellent and Tevis went on to write *The Man Who Fell to Earth* and *The Hustler.*

None of these stories won.

None.

As Alfred Bester has commented, "The fans—the wonderful demented fans."

And of all the overlooked and neglected stories of that really rather excellent year, the one I have selected for *What If?* is "The Mile-Long Spaceship" by Kate Wilhelm.

Wilhelm made her debut with "The Pint-Size Genie" in the October 1956 *Fantastic*—the first issue edited by the brilliant Cele Goldsmith. A steady stream of stories (and, in later years, novels) followed. For a time, most of Wilhelm's output appeared in the *Orbit* series of anthologies and other volumes edited by her husband, Damon Knight, causing an unfortunate appearance of nepotism to shadow Wilhelm's works.

Actually, she had appeared in many other markets— *Future, Science Fiction, Amazing Stories, Fantastic Universe,* and *Astounding* among them. In later years her highly successful books, both novels and collections, won Wilhelm widespread recognition. Today, her popularity is growing with a general readership that quite transcends the usual science fiction audience.

Wilhelm published just twenty stories in the first five years of her career (1956–1960). As might be expected, they vary in quality. Not all have borne the years with equal grace. But "The Mile-Long Spaceship" has done so admirably. It is doubly readable today: as an outstanding short story in its own time, and as a portent of the sensitivity and skill that Wilhelm has honed and perfected in the 20-odd years since "The Mile-Long Spaceship" first appeared.

The Mile-Long Spaceship

KATE WILHELM

ALLAN NORBETT SHIVERED uncontrollably, huddling up under the spotless hospital sheet seeking warmth. He stirred fretfully as consciousness slowly returned and with it the blinding stab of pain through his head. A moan escaped his lips. Immediately a nurse was at his side, gently, firmly forcing him back on the bed.

"You must remain completely still, Mr. Norbett. You're in St. Agnes' Hospital. You suffered a fractured skull in the accident, and surgery was necessary. Your wife is outside waiting to see you. She is uninjured. Do you understand me?"

The words had been spoken slowly, very clearly, but he had grasped only fragments of them.

What accident? The ship couldn't have an accident. He'd be dead out there in space. And his wife hadn't even been there.

"What happened to the ship? How'd I get back on Earth?" The words came agonizingly, each effort cost much in pain and dizziness.

"Mr. Norbett, please calm yourself. I've rung for your doctor. He'll be here presently." The voice soothed him and a faint memory awakened. The wreck? His wife? HIS WIFE?

"Clair? Where's Clair?" Then the doctor was there and he also was soothing. Allan closed his eyes again in relief as they reassured him about Clair's safety. She would be here in a moment. The other memories receded and mingled with the anaesthetic dreams he'd had. The doctor felt his pulse and listened to his heart and studied his eyes, all the while talking.

"You are a lucky man, Mr. Norbett. That was quite a wreck you were in. Your wife was even luckier. She was thrown clear when the bi-wheel first hit you."

Allan remembered it all quite clearly now and momentarily wondered how he'd come out of it at all. The doctor finally finished his examination and smiled as he said, "Everything seems perfectly normal, considering the fact that you have been traipsing all over space for the last five days."

"Days?"

"Yes. The wreck was Saturday. This is Thursday. You've been under sedation quite a bit—to help you rest. There was extensive brain injury and absolute quiet was essential. Dr. Barnsdale performed a brilliant operation Saturday night."

Allan had the feeling the doctor was purposely being so loquacious to help him over the hump of the shock of awakening after almost six days. He was in no pain now while he kept his head still, but talking brought its own punishment and he was grateful to the doctor for answering unasked questions. The doctor waited by his side for a second or two, then in a professional tone he told the nurse to bring in Clair.

And again to Allan: "She can only stay a few minutes —less if you begin talking. I'll be in again this afternoon. You rest as much as possible. If the pain becomes severe, tell your nurse. She's instructed to administer a hypo only if you request it." Again he laughed jovially, "Don't let her talk you into it, though. She is really thrilled by that space yarn you've been telling and might want to put you to sleep just to hear more."

Clair's visit was very brief and very exhausting. Afterwards he rested comfortably for nearly an hour before the pain flooded his whole being.

"Nurse."

"Yes, Mr. Norbett?" Her fingers rested lightly on his wrist for a moment.

"The pain—"

"Just try to relax, sir. It will be gone soon." He didn't

209

feel the prick of the needle in his arm. But the pain left him in layers, gradually becoming a light enough load to permit sleep. And the coldness.

Space was so cold. No winds to blow in spurts and gusts, to relieve the cold by their absence, only the steady, numbing same black, empty cold. He turned his head to look over his shoulder and already Earth was indistinguishable among the countless stars and planets. Never had man, he told himself, seen all the stars like this. They were incredibly bright and even as he viewed them, he wondered at the movement of some of them. There was a visible pulsation, sometimes almost rhythmically, other times very erratic. A star would suddenly seem to expand enormously on one side, the protuberance around it glow even more brightly then die down only to repeat the performance over and over. Allan wished he knew more about astronomy. He had only the most rudimentary knowledge that everyone had since the first spaceship had reached Mars. He had been out of school when space travel had become possible and had never read past the newspaper for the information necessary to understand the universe and its inhabitants.

He shivered again and thought about the advantages of eyeless seeing. There was no pupil to dilate, no retina to burn or damage, no nerves to protest with pain at the brightness of the sight. It was, he decided smugly, much better to be here without his cumbersome body to hamper him. Then he suddenly remembered the ship—the mile-long spaceship. For an instant he sent his mental gaze deep into space all around him, but the ship was nowhere to be seen. He surmised it must still be millions of light-years from Earth. As he visualized it again he slowly became aware that once more he was aboard her and the stars he was seeing were on the giant wall screen.

He watched with interest as one planet after another turned a pale violet and became nearly invisible. He had grown accustomed to the crew of the ship, so paid little heed to them. Their voices were low, monotonous to his ear, never rising or speeding up or sounding indecisive. Completely expressionless, their words defied any attempt to interpret them.

"He's back," the telepath announced.

"Good. I was afraid that he might die." The navigator in charge went calmly about his duties of sighting and marking in a complex three-dimensional chart the course of the mighty ship as it ranged among the stars.

"He's recovering from his injury. He still can't receive any impulses from me." The telepath tried again and again to create a picture in the alien mind in their midst. "Futile," he said, "the differences are too great."

"Undisciplined," said the psychologist who had been waiting ever since that first visit by the alien. "A disciplined mind can be reached by telepathy."

"Can you see his world?" This from the astro navigator.

"Only the same intimate scenes of home-life, his work and his immediate surroundings. He is very primitive, or perhaps merely uneducated."

"If only he knew something about astronomy." The navigator shrugged and made a notation on his chart as two more distant planets registered violet.

"The names he associates with stars are these," the telepath probed deeper, "The Dipper, North Star, Mars . . . no, that is one of the planets they have colonized." A wave of incredulity emanated from him, felt by the others of the crew, but not expressed in his voice, "He doesn't know the difference between single stars, clusters, constellations, only that they appear as individual stars to him, and he thinks of them as such."

The navigator's calm voice belied the fury others felt well out from him. "Look at his sun, perhaps that will give us a hint." They all knew the inprobability of this. The telepath began droning what little Allan knew about the sun when the captain appeared through another wall screen.

He was accompanied by the ship's ethnologist, the expert who could reconstruct entire civilizations from the broken remains of a tool or an object of art, or less if necessary. The captain and his companions made themselves comfortable near the star screen and seemed immediately engrossed in the broken lines indicating the ship's flight in the three-dimensional reproduced outer spaces.

"Is he still here?"

"Yes, sir."

"Is he aware yet that we discovered his presence among us?"

"No, sir. We have made no effort to indicate our awareness to him."

"Very good." The captain then fell silent pondering his particular problem as the ethnologist began adding to the growing list of facts that were known to Allan about Earth.

211

They would have a complete picture of the present and the past. As complete as the alien's mind and memory could make it. But unless they could locate his planet they might just as well go home and view space-fiction films. This exploration trip had achieved very little real success. Only fourteen planets that could be rated good with some sub-intelligent life, several hundred fair with no intelligence and only one he could conscientiously rate excellent. This mind was of an intelligent, though as yet unadvanced humanoid race. The planet it inhabited met every requirement to be rated excellent. Of this the captain was certain.

Suddenly the telepath announced, "He's gone. He became bored watching the screen. He knows nothing about astronomy; therefore, the course loses its significance to him. He has the vague idea that we're going to a predetermined destination. The idea of an exploration, charting cruise hasn't occurred to him as yet."

"I wonder," mused the captain, "how he reconciles his conscious mind to his subconscious wandering."

The psychologist answered. "As he begins to awaken other dreams probably mingle with these memories causing them to dim at the edges, thus becoming to his mind at any rate merely another series of especially vivid well-remembered dreams. I believe much of what lies in his subconscious is dream memory rather than fact memory." The psychologist didn't smile, or indicate in any fashion the ridicule and sarcasm the others felt as he continued, "He has the memory of being always well fed. He has buried the memory of hunger so far down in his subconscious that it would take a skilled psychologist a long time to call it forth."

The telepath stirred and started to reply, then didn't. The alien's mind had been like a film, clear and easy to read. Some of the pictures had been disturbing and incomprehensible, but only through their strangeness, not because they were distorted by dream images. The psychologists never could accept anything at face value. Always probing and looking for hidden places and meanings. Just as he did when told of the world democracy existing on Earth.

"Most likely a benign dictatorship. A world couldn't be governed by a democratic government, a small area, perhaps, but not a world." Thus spoke the psychologist. But the telepath had been inside Allan's mind, and he knew it

212

could and did work. Not only the planet Earth, but also the colonies on Mars and Venus.

The captain was still pursuing his own line of questioning.

"Has he ever shown any feeling of fear or repulsion toward us?"

"None, he accepts us as different but not to be feared because of it."

"That's because he believes we are figments of his imagination; that he can control us by awakening."

The captain ignored this explanation advanced by the psychologist. A mind intelligent enough for dreams, could feel fear in the dreams—even a captain knew that. He was beginning to get the feeling that this Earth race might prove a formidable foe when and if found.

"Has he shown any interest in the drive?"

"He assumed we use an atomic drive. He has only the scantiest knowledge of atomics, however. His people use such a drive."

"The fact that the race has atomics is another reason we must find them." This would be the third planet using atomic energy. A young race, an unknown potential. They did not have interstellar travel now, but one hundred fifty years ago they didn't have atomic energy and already they had reached their neighbor planets. It had taken three times as long for the captain's people to achieve the same success. The captain remembered the one other race located in his time that had atomics. They were exploring space in ever widening circles. True, they hadn't made any startling advances yet in weapons, they had found decisive bombs and lethal rays and gases unnecessary. But they had learned fast. They had resisted the invaders with cunning and skill. Their bravery had never been questioned, but in the end the aggressors had won.

The captain felt no thrill of satisfaction in the thought. It was a fact, accomplished long ago. The conclusion had been delayed certainly, but it had also been inevitable. Only one race, one planet, one government could have the energy, and the right to the raw materials that made the space lanes thoroughfares. The slaves might ride on the masters' crafts, but might not own or operate their own. That was the law, and the captain was determined to uphold to the end that law.

And now this. One mind freed from its body and its

Earth roaming the universe, divulging its secrets, all but the only one that mattered. How many millions of stars lit the way through space? And how many of them had their families of planets supporting life? The captain knew there was no answer, but still he sought ways of following the alien's mind back to his body.

Allan stirred his coffee slowly, not moving his head. This was his first meal sitting up, now at its conclusion he felt too exhausted to lift his spoon from his cup. Clair gently did it for him and held the cup to his lips.

"Tired, darling?" Her voice was a caress.

"A little." A little! All he wanted was his bed under him and Clair's voice whispering him to sleep. "I don't believe I'd even need a hypo." He was startled that he had spoken the thought, but Clair nodded, understanding.

"The doctor thinks it best to put off having anything if you can. I'll read to you and see if you can sleep." They had rediscovered the joy of reading books. Real leather-bound books instead of watching the three-D set, or using the story films. Allan loved to lie quiescent, listening to the quiet voice of his wife rise and fall with the words. Often the words themselves were unimportant, but there was music in listening to Clair read them. They were beautifully articulated, falling into a pattern as rhythmic as if there were unheard drums beating the time.

He tried to remember what the sound of her voice reminded him of. Then he knew. By the very difference in tone and expression he was reminded of the crew of the mile-long spaceship in his dream. He grinned to himself at the improbability of the dream. Everyone speaking in the same metallic tone, the monotonous flight, never varying, never having any emergency to cope with.

The noises of the hospital dimmed and became obscure and then lost entirely. All was silent again as he sped toward the quiet lonesome planet he had last visited. There he had rested gazing at the stars hanging in expanding circles over him. He had first viewed the galaxy from aboard the spaceship. Interested in the spiral shape of it he had left the ship to seek it out at closer range. Here on this tiny planet the effect was startling. If he closed out all but the brightest and largest of the stars there was ring after ring of tiny glowing diamonds hanging directly above him. How many times had he come back? He couldn't remember, but suddenly he thought about the mile-long spaceship again.

"He's back." The telepath never moved from his position, before the sky screen, nor did the astro navigator. Abruptly, however, the panorama went blank and the two moved toward the screen on the opposite wall.

"Is he coming?"

"Yes. He's curious. He thinks something is wrong."

"Good." The two stepped from the screen into a large room where a group watched a film.

The navigator and the telepath seated themselves slightly behind the rest of the assemblage. The captain had been talking, he continued as before.

"Let me know what his reactions are."

"The film interests him. The dimensional effect doesn't bother him, he appears accustomed to a form of three-dimensional films."

"Very good. Tell me the instant something strikes a responsive chord."

The film was one of their educational astronomy courses for beginners. Various stars were shown singly and in their constellations and finally in their own galaxies. Novae and super novae, planets and satellites appeared. The telepath dug deep into the alien's memory, but found only an increasing interest, no memories of any one scene. Suddenly the telepath said,

"This one he thinks he has seen before. He has seen a similar galaxy from another position, one that shows the spiral directly overhead."

The captain asked, "Has this one been visible on the screen from such a position?"

"Not in detail. Only as part of the charted course." The navigator was making notes as he answered. "There are only three fixes for this particular effect. A minor white dwarf with six satellites and two main sequence stars, satellites unknown."

The captain thought deeply. Maybe only a similar galaxy, but again maybe he was familiar with this one.

The orders were given in the same tone he had used in carrying on the conversation. The alien had no way of knowing he was the helmsman guiding the huge ship through space.

The telepath followed the alien's mind as he gazed raptly at the ever changing film. Occasionally he reported the alien's thoughts, but nothing of importance was learned. As before, the departure of the alien was abrupt.

With the telepath's announcement, "He's gone," the film flicked off and normal activity was resumed.

Later the captain called a meeting of the psychologist, the telepath, the chief navigator and the ethnologist.

"We represent the finest minds in the universe, yet when it comes to coping with one inferior intellect, we stand helpless. He flits in and out at will, telling us nothing. We are now heading light-years out of our way on what might easily prove to be a fruitless venture, merely because you," he held the telepath in his merciless gaze, "think he recognized one of the formations." The captain's anger was a formidable thing to feel, and the rest stirred uneasily. His voice, however, was the same monotone it always was as he asked, "And did you manage to plant the seeds in his mind as suggested at our last meeting?"

"That is hard to say. I couldn't tell." The telepath turned to the psychologist for confirmation.

"He wouldn't know himself until he began feeling the desire for more education. Even then it might be in the wrong direction. We can only wait and hope we have hit on the way to find his home planet through making him want to learn astronavigation and astronomy." Soon afterward the meeting adjourned.

Allan was back at work again, with all traces of his accident relegated to the past. His life was well-ordered and full, with no time for schooling. He told himself this over and over, to no avail. For he was still telling himself this when he filled out the registration blank at the university.

"He's here again!" The telepath had almost given up expecting the alien ever again. He kept his mind locked in the other's as he recited as though from a book. "He's completely over his injury, working again, enrolled in night classes at the school in his town. He's studying atomic engineering. He's in the engine room now getting data for something they call a thesis."

Quietly the captain rolled off a list of expletives that would have done justice to one of the rawest space hands. And just as quietly, calmly, and perhaps, stoically, he pushed the red button that began the chain reaction that would completely vaporize the mile-long ship. His last breath was spent in hoping the alien would awaken with a violent headache. He did.

216

1958

WELL, ALFIE BESTER was right, of course. The fans—the wonderful demented fans. The 1958 World Science Fiction Convention in Los Angeles gave Hugos for the best works of 1958, and the 1959 World Science Fiction Convention in Detroit also gave Hugos for the best works of 1958. Their respective judgments of "best" weren't the same. In fact, even their designations of categories weren't the same.

Hoo!

But out of this chaos a certain amount of order was emerging. The toughest sticking point in determining eligibility was still that crazy *year* business. What the blankety-blank did "previous year" *mean?* The fans had struggled with that one from the very first set of Hugos, with the interpretation generally leaning toward some such definition as "a 12-month period directly preceding the World Science Fiction Convention"—i.e., September through August, a clumsy and difficult kind of "year" to have to deal with.

The Detroit committee—co-chaired by the colorful duo of Fred Prophet and Roger "Honey Bear" Sims, may blessings be upon them—finally decided that "the previous year" means *last year.* As of 1959, "the previous year" meant simply 1958, and if it made for an awkward moment in the history of the Hugos, it has clarified and simplified things ever since. To this day the simple principle of "last year" has been the basic law. There have been minor problems and exceptions. As I discussed in my general introduction to this book, one may question things like magazine issues cover-dated January of one year but copyrighted in December of the preceding year. One may wonder about serials split between two calendar years, or books that appear in several editions in several years.

But these are problems of detail, specific cases, fine points, and subtle, almost Talmudic, differentiations.

Prophet, Sims, & Company did set things basically to rights, and that's what really matters.

The problem of categories was still troublesome, however. And, in fact, it remained so until well into the 1960s, when the parallel (not to say competing) Nebula Awards provided the stimulus that finally brought stability to the Hugos, as well.

The Los Angeles convention gave a Hugo for best novel or novelette, and one for best short story. The winners were Fritz Leiber's *The Big Time* (serialized in *Galaxy*) and Avram Davidson's "Or All the Seas with Oysters," also from *Galaxy*.

The Detroit convention went back to the three-award system last used by the New York convention of 1956. Their winners were *A Case of Conscience* by James Blish (Ballantine Books), "The Big Front Yard" by Clifford Simak (*Astounding*), and "That Hell-Bound Train" by Robert Bloch (*Fantasy and Science Fiction*).

The awards themselves were remarkable. The first half of Blish's novel, you'll remember, had appeared in *If* magazine five years earlier. The Ballantine version was the first "full" edition of the novel, and no one squawked very much when the book won the award. Bloch's short story was a pure fantasy—the first ever to win a Science Fiction Achievement Award. In very recent years several series of competing fantasy awards have been instituted, and it is yet to be seen which will emerge with the prestige of a Hugo or Nebula (although the World Fantasy Award or "Howard" [for Howard Phillips Lovecraft] seems to be coming out ahead).

But fantasy and science fiction are of course closely allied fields, and Bloch's victory established the principle that fantasy works were not only eligible in theory to win Hugos, but could *actually* win them. (Still, I must concede that they have a rough time of it, and very few have actually brought home the toy spaceship.)

A final contribution of Detroit: up to this point in the history of the Hugos, only winners were recorded. Detroit published lists of nominees, and it has since become a point of auctorial prestige (and commercial value!) to receive even a Hugo nomination, no less the award itself.

The nominees for best novel were: *Have Spacesuit— Will Travel* by Heinlein, *Time Killer* by Sheckley, *We Have Fed Our Sea* by Anderson, and *Who?* by Budrys.

Nominated for best novelette or short story were works by Zenna Henderson, Fritz Leiber (two stories), Jack Vance, Rog Phillips, Cyril Kornbluth (three stories!),

Katherine MacLean and Charles V. DeVet, Pauline Ash-well, Algis Budrys, Alfred Bester, Manly Wade Wellman, Stanley Mullen, Anton Lee Baker, and J. F. Bone.

I direct your attention to the name of Pauline Ashwell. This byline appeared on only two stories, ever. Both were remarkable, both won Hugo nominations—and then the talented Ashwell disappeared. But hang around, we shall hear more of her before long!

It's hard to understand how the fans in 1958 and 1959 managed to overlook Cyril Kornbluth's stunning "Two Dooms." Perhaps it was the very fact that he had so many superb stories coming out at the time. Ironically, this final outpouring of sardonic wit, fierce social commentary, and altogether overwhelming narrative energy was posthumous.

In February of 1958 the popular writer Henry Kuttner had died suddenly in California at the tragically early age of 43. The following month a memorial symposium for Kuttner was held by an East Coast fan club. Kornbluth attended and participated, then traveled to his home on Long Island, and within a matter of hours, he also died.

He was 35 years of age.

As for "Two Dooms." Perhaps it was the fact that Kornbluth had no fewer than seven stories in the science fiction magazines in the year of his death that caused the fans' attention to be divided, and too much of it to be drawn away from "Two Dooms." Perhaps it was the fact that "Two Dooms" appeared in *Venture Science Fiction*.

Venture was never more than a second-line magazine in sales and popularity; it never managed to emerge from the shadow of its parent, *The Magazine of Fantasy and Science Fiction*. But, in fact, *Venture* featured a remarkable series of thoroughly memorable stories, "Two Dooms" standing high among them.

The editor of the magazine was Robert P. Mills; today, ironically, Mills is the literary agent for the estate of Cyril Kornbluth. When I contacted Mills to clear the rights for "Two Dooms" in the present anthology, Mills said that he'd been overwhelmed by the power of the story and baffled by its failure to achieve the fame it deserved in 1958.

Read it now if you've never done so before. If you have read it before, read it again. I guarantee, you will *never* be able to forget this story. But a word of warning: you may wish you could.

Two Dooms

CYRIL KORNBLUTH

IT WAS MAY, not yet summer by five weeks, but the after-noon heat under the corrugated roofs of Manhattan En-gineer District's Los Alamos Laboratory was daily less bearable. Young Dr. Edward Royland had lost fifteen pounds from an already meager frame during his nine-month hitch in the desert. He wondered every day while the thermometer crawled up to its 5:45 peak whether he had made a mistake he would regret the rest of his life in accepting work with the Laboratory rather than letting the local draft board have his carcass and do what they pleased with it. His University of Chicago classmates were glamor-ously collecting ribbons and wounds from Saipan to Brussels; one of them, a first-rate mathematician named Hatfield, would do no more first-rate mathematics. He had gone down, burning, in an Eighth Air Force Mitchell bomber ambushed over Lille.

"And what, Daddy, did you do in the war?"

"Well, kids, it's a little hard to explain. They had this stupid atomic bomb project that never came to anything, and they tied up a lot of us in a Godforsaken place in New Mexico. We figured and we calculated and we fooled with uranium and some of us got radiation burns and then the war was over and they sent us home."

Royland was not amused by this prospect. He had heat rash under his arms and he was waiting, not patiently, for the Computer Section to send him his figures on Phase 56c, which was the (god-damn childish) code designation for Element Assembly Time. Phase 56c was Royland's own particular baby. He was under Rotschmidt, supervisor of WEAPON DESIGN TRACK III, and Rotschmidt was under Oppenheimer, who bossed the works. Sometimes a General Groves came through, a fine figure of a man, and once from a window Royland had seen the venerable Henry L. Stimson, Secretary of War, walking slowly down their dusty street, leaning on a cane and surrounded by young staff officers. That's what Royland was seeing of the war.

Laboratory! It had sounded inviting, cool, bustling but quiet. So every morning these days he was blasted out of his cot in a barracks cubicle at seven by "Oppie's whistle," fought for a shower and shave with thirty-seven other bachelor scientists in eight languages, bolted a bad cafeteria breakfast, and went through the barbed-wired Restricted Line to his "office"—another matchboard-walled cubicle, smaller and hotter and noisier, with talking and typing and clack of adding machines all around him.

Under the circumstances he was doing good work, he supposed. He wasn't happy about being restricted to his one tiny problem, Phase 56c, but no doubt he was happier than Hatfield had been when his Mitchell got it.

Under the circumstances . . . they included a weird haywire arrangement for computing. Instead of a decent differential analyzer machine they had a human sea of office girls with Burroughs' desk calculators; the girls screamed "Banzai!" and charged on differential equations and swamped them by sheer volume; they clicked them to death with their little adding machines. Royland thought hungrily of Conant's huge, beautiful analog differentiator up at M.I.T.; it was probably tied up by whatever the mysterious "Radiation Laboratory" there was doing. Royland suspected that the "Radiation Laboratory" had as much to do with radiation as his own "Manhattan Engineer District" had to do with Manhattan engineering. And the world was supposed to be trembling on the edge these days of a New Dispensation of Computing that would obsolete even the M.I.T. machine—tubes, relays, and binary arithmetic at blinding speed instead of the suavely turning cams and the smoothly extruding rods and the elegant scribed curves of Conant's masterpiece. He decided that he wouldn't like that; he would like it even less than he liked the little office

221

girls clacking away, pushing lank hair from their dewed brows with undistracted hands.

He wiped his own brow with a sodden handkerchief and permitted himself a glance at his watch and the thermometer. Five-fifteen and 103 Fahrenheit.

He thought vaguely of getting out, of fouling up just enough to be released from the project and drafted. No; there was the post-war career to think of. But one of the big shots, Teller, had been irrepressible; he had rambled outside of his assigned mission again and again until Oppenheimer let him go; now Teller was working with Lawrence at Berkeley on something that had reputedly gone sour at a reputed quarter of a billion dollars—

A girl in khaki knocked and entered. "Your material from the Computer Section, Dr. Royland. Check them and sign here, please." He counted the dozen sheets, signed the clipboarded form she held out, and plunged into the material for thirty minutes.

When he sat back in his chair, the sweat dripped into his eyes unnoticed. His hands were shaking a little, though he did not know that either. Phase 56c of WEAPON DESIGN TRACK III was finished, over, done, successfully accomplished. The answer to the question "Can U_{235} slugs be assembled into a critical mass within a physically feasible time?" was in. The answer was "Yes."

Royland was a theory man, not a Wheatstone or a Kelvin; he liked the numbers for themselves and had no special passion to grab for wires, mica, and bits of graphite so that what the numbers said might immediately be given flesh in a wonderful new gadget. Nevertheless he could visualize at once a workable atomic bomb assembly within the framework of Phase 56c. You have so many microseconds to assemble your critical mass without it boiling away in vapor; you use them by blowing the subassemblies together with shaped charges; lots of microseconds to spare by that method; practically foolproof. Then comes the Big Bang.

Oppie's whistle blew; it was quitting time. Royland sat still in his cubicle. He should go, of course, to Rotschmidt and tell him; Rotschmidt would probably clap him on the back and pour him a jigger of Bols Geneva from the tall clay bottle he kept in his safe. Then Rotschmidt would go to Oppenheimer. Before sunset the project would be redesigned! TRACK I, TRACK II, TRACK IV, and TRACK V would be shut down and their people crammed into TRACK III, the one with the paydirt! New excitement would boil through the project; it had been torpid and souring for three months. Phase 56c was the first good news in at least that long; it had been one damned blind alley after another. General Groves had looked sour and dubious last time around.

Desk drawers were slamming throughout the corrugated, sun-baked building; doors were slamming shut on cubicles; down the corridor, somebody roared with laughter, strained laughter. Passing Royland's door somebody cried impatiently: *"—aber was kan Man tun?"*

Royland whispered to himself: "You damned fool, what are you thinking of?"

But he knew—he was thinking of the Big Bang, the Big Dirty Bang, and of torture. The judicial torture of the old days, incredibly cruel by today's lights, stretched the whole body, or crushed it, or burned it, or shattered the fingers and legs. But even that old judicial torture carefully avoided the most sensitive parts of the body, the generative organs, though damage to these, or a real threat of damage to these, would have produced quick and copious confessions. You have to be more or less crazy to torture somebody that way; the sane man does not think of it as a possibility.

An M.P. corporal tried Royland's door and looked in. "Quitting time, professor," he said.

"Okay," Royland said. Mechanically, he locked his desk drawers and his files, turned his window lock, and set out his waste-paper basket in the corridor. Click the door; another day, another dollar.

Maybe the project *was* breaking up. They did now and then. The huge boner as Berkeley proved that. And Royland's barracks was light two physicists now; their cubicles stood empty since they had been drafted to M.I.T. for some anti-submarine thing. Groves had *not* looked happy last time around; how did a general make up his mind anyway? Give them three months, then the ax? Maybe Stimson would run out of patience and cut the loss, close the District down. Maybe F.D.R. would say at a Cabinet meeting, "By the way, Henry, what ever became of—?" and that would be the end if old Henry could say only that the scientists appear to be optimistic of eventual success, Mr. President, but that as yet there seems to be nothing *concrete*—

He passed through the barbed wire of the Line under

223

scrutiny of an M.P. lieutenant and walked down the barracks-edged company street of the maintenance troops to their motor pool. He wanted a jeep and a trip ticket; he wanted a long desert drive in the twilight; he wanted a dinner of *frijoles* and eggplant with his old friend Charles Miller Nahataspe, the medicine man of the adjoining Hopi reservation. Royland's hobby was anthropology; he wanted to get a little drunk on it—he hoped it would clear his mind.

Nahataspe welcomed him cheerfully to his hut; his million wrinkles all smiled. "You want me to play informant for a while?" he grinned. He had been to Carlisle in the 1880's and had been laughing at the white man ever since; he admitted that physics was funny, but for a real joke give him cultural anthropology every time. "You want some nice unsavory stuff about our institutionalized homosexuality? Should I cook us a dog for dinner? Have a seat on the blanket, Edward."

"What happened to your chairs? And the funny picture of McKinley? And—and everything?" The hut was bare except for cooking pots that simmered on the stone-curbed central hearth.

"I gave the stuff away," Nahataspe said carelessly. "You get tired of things."

Royland thought he knew what that meant. Nahataspe believed he would die quite soon; these particular Indians did not believe in dying encumbered by possessions. Manners, of course, forbade discussing death.

The Indian watched his face and finally said: "Oh, it's all right for *you* to talk about it. Don't be embarrassed."

Royland asked nervously: "Don't you feel well?"

"I feel terrible. There's a snake eating my liver. Pitch in and eat. You feel pretty awful yourself, don't you?"

The hard-learned habit of security caused Royland to evade the question. "You don't mean that literally about the snake, do you Charles?"

"Of course I do," Miller insisted. He scooped a steaming gourd full of stew from the pot and blew on it. "What would an untutored child of nature know about bacteria, viruses, toxins, and neoplasms? What would I know about break-the-sky medicine?"

Royland looked up sharply; the Indian was blandly eating. "Do you hear any talk about break-the-sky medicine?" Royland asked.

224

"No talk, Edward. I've had a few dreams about it." He pointed with his chin toward the Laboratory. "You fellows over there shouldn't dream so hard; it leaks out."

Royland helped himself to stew without answering. The stew was good, far better than the cafeteria stuff, and he did not *have* to guess the source of the meat in it.

Miller said consolingly: "It's only kid stuff, Edward. Don't get so worked up about it. We have a long dull story about a horned toad who ate some loco-weed and thought he was the Sky God. He got angry and he tried to break the sky but he couldn't so he slunk into his hole ashamed to face all the other animals and died. But they never knew he tried to break the sky at all."

In spite of himself Royland demanded: "Do you have any stories about anybody who did break the sky?" His hands were shaking again and his voice almost hysterical. Oppie and the rest of them were going to break the sky, kick humanity right in the crotch, and unleash a prowling monster that would go up and down by night and day peering in all the windows of all the houses in the world, leaving no sane man ever unterrified for his life and the lives of his kin. Phase 56c, God-damn it to blackest hell, made sure of that! Well done, Royland; you earned your dollar today!

Decisively the old Indian set his gourd aside. He said: "We have a saying that the only good paleface is a dead paleface, but I'll make an exception for you, Edward. I've got some strong stuff from Mexico that will make you feel better. I don't like to see my friends hurting."

"Peyote? I've tried it. Seeing a few colored lights won't make me feel better, but thanks."

"Not peyote, this stuff. It's God Food. I wouldn't take it myself without a month of preparation; otherwise the Gods would scoop me up in a net. That's because my people see clearly, and your eyes are clouded." He was busily rummaging through a clay-chinked wicker box as he spoke; he came up with a covered dish. "You people have your sight cleared just a little by the God Food, so it's safe for you."

Royland thought he knew what the old man was talking about. It was one of Nahataspe's biggest jokes that Hopi children understood Einstein's relativity as soon as they could talk—and there was some truth to it. The Hopi language—and thought—had no tenses and therefore no concept of time-as-an-entity; it had nothing like the Indo-European speech's subjects and predicates, and therefore

225

no built-in metaphysics of cause and effect. In the Hopi language and mind all things were frozen together forever into one great relationship, a crystalline structure of space-time events that simply were because they were. So much for Nahataspe's people "seeing clearly." But Royland gave himself and any other physicist credit for seeing as clearly when they were working a four-dimensional problem in the X Y Z space variables and the T time variable.

He could have spoiled the old man's joke by pointing that out, but of course he did not. No, no, he'd get a jag and maybe a bellyache from Nahataspe's herb medicine and then go home to his cubicle with his problem unresolved: to kick or not to kick?

The old man began to mumble in Hopi, and drew a tattered cloth across the door frame of his hut; it shut out the last rays of the setting sun, long and slanting on the desert, pink-red against the adobe cubes of the Indian settlement. It took a minute for Royland's eyes to accommodate to the flickering light from the hearth and the indigo square of the ceiling smoke hole. Now Nahataspe was "dancing," doing a crouched shuffle around the hut holding the covered dish before him. Out of the corner of his mouth, without interrupting the rhythm, he said to Royland: "Drink some hot water now." Royland sipped from one of the pots on the hearth; so far it was much like peyote ritual, but he felt calmer.

Nahataspe uttered a loud scream, added apologetically: "Sorry, Edward," and crouched before him whipping the cover off the dish like a headwaiter. So God Food was dried black mushrooms, miserable, wrinkled little things. "You swallow them all and chase them with hot water," Nahataspe said.

Obediently Royland choked them down and gulped from the jug; the old man resumed his dance and chanting.

A little old self-hypnosis, Royland thought bitterly. Grab some imitation sleep and forget about old 56c, as if you could. He could see the big dirty one now, a hell of a fireball, maybe over Munich, or Cologne, or Tokyo, or Nara. Cooked people, fused cathedral stone, the bronze of the big Buddha running like water, perhaps lapping around the ankles of a priest and burning his feet off so he fell prone into the stuff. He couldn't see the gamma radiation, but it would be there, invisible sleet doing the dirty unthinkable thing, coldly burning away the sex of men and women, cutting short so many fans of life at their points of origin.

226

Phase 56c could snuff out a family of Bachs, or five generations of Bernoullis, or see to it that the great Huxley-Darwin cross did not occur.

The fireball loomed, purple and red and fringed with green—

The mushrooms were reaching him, he thought fuzzily. He could really see it. Nahataspe, crouched and treading, moved through the fireball just as he had the last time, and the time before that. Déjà vu, extraordinarily strong, stronger than ever before, gripped him. Royland knew all this had happened to him before, and remembered perfectly what would come next; it was on the very tip of his tongue, as they say—

The fireballs began to dance around him and he felt his strength drain suddenly out; he was lighter than a feather; the breeze would carry him away; he would be blown like a dust mote into the circle that the circling fireballs made. And he knew it was wrong. He croaked with the last of his energy, feeling himself slip out of the world: "Charlie! Help!"

Out of the corner of his mind as he slipped away he sensed that the old man was pulling him now under the arms, trying to tug him out of the hut, crying dimly into his ear: "You should have told me you did not see through smoke! You see clear; I never knew; I nev—"

And then he slipped through into blackness and silence.

Royland awoke sick and fuzzy; it was morning in the hut; there was no sign of Nahataspe. Well. Unless the old man had gotten to a phone and reported to the Laboratory, there were now jeeps scouring the desert in search of him and all hell was breaking loose in Security and Personnel. He would catch some of that hell on his return, and avert it with his news about assembly time.

Then he noticed that the hut had been cleaned of Nahataspe's few remaining possessions, even to the door cloth. A pang went through him; had the old man died in the night? He limped from the hut and looked around for a funeral pyre, a crowd of mourners. They were not there; the abode cubes stood untenanted in the sunlight, and more weeds grew in the single street than he remembered. And his jeep, parked last night against the hut, was missing.

There were no wheeltracks, and uncrushed weeds grew tall where the jeep had stood.

Nahataspe's God Food had been powerful stuff. Royland's hand crept uncertainly to his face. No; no beard.

He looked about him, looked hard. He made the effort necessary to see details. He did not glance at the hut and because it was approximately the same as it had always been, concluded that it was unchanged, eternal. He looked and saw changes everywhere. Once-sharp abode corners were rounded; protruding roof beams were bleached bone-white by how many years of desert sun? The wooden framing of the deep fortress-like windows had crumbled; the third building from him had wavering soot stains above its window boles and its beams were charred.

He went to it, numbly thinking: Phase 56c at least is settled. Not old Rip's baby now. They'll know me from fingerprints, I guess. One year? Ten? I *feel* the same.

The burned-out house was a shambles. In one corner were piled dry human bones. Royland leaned dizzily against the doorframe; its charcoal crumbled and streaked his hand. Those skulls were Indian—he was anthropologist enough to know that. Indian men, women and children, slain and piled in a heap. Who kills Indians? There should have been some sign of clothes, burned rags, but there were none. Who strips Indians naked and kills them?

Signs of a dreadful massacre were everywhere in the house. Bulletpocks in the walls, high and low. Savage nicks left by bayonets—and swords? Dark stains of blood; it had run two inches high and left its mark. Metal glinted in a ribcage across the room. Swaying, he walked to the bone-heap and thrust his hand into it. The thing bit him like a razor blade; he did not look at it as he plucked it out and carried it to the dusty street. With his back turned to the burned house he studied his find. It was a piece of sword-blade six inches long, hand-honed to a perfect edge with a couple of nicks in it. It had stiffening ribs and the usual blood gutters. It had a perceptible curve that would fit into only one shape: the Samurai sword of Japan.

However long it had taken, the war was obviously over.

He went to the village well and found it choked with dust. It was while he stared into the dry hole that he first became afraid. Suddenly it all was real; he was no more an onlooker but a frightened and very thirsty man. He ransacked the dozen houses of the settlement and found nothing to his purpose—a child's skeleton here, a couple of cartridge cases there.

There was only one thing left, and that was the road,

the same earth track it had always been, wide enough for one jeep or the rump-sprung station wagon of the Indian settlement that once had been. Panic invited him to run; he did not yield. He sat on the well curb, took off his shoes to meticulously smooth wrinkles out of his khaki G.I. socks, put the shoes on, and retied the laces loosely enough to allow for swelling, and hesitated a moment. Then he grinned, selected two pebbles carefully from the dust and popped them into his mouth. "Beaver Patrol, forward march," he said, and began to hike.

Yes, he was thirsty; soon he would be hungry and tired; what of it? The dirt road would meet state-maintained blacktop in three miles and then there would be traffic and he'd hitch a ride. Let them argue with his fingerprints if they felt like it. The Japanese had got as far as New Mexico, had they? Then God help their home islands when the counterblow had come. Americans were a ferocious people when trespassed on. Conceivably, there was not a Japanese left alive. . . .

He began to construct his story as he hiked. In large parts it was a repeated "I don't know." He would tell them: "I don't expect you to believe this, so my feelings won't be hurt when you don't. Just listen to what I say and hold everything until the F.B.I. has checked my fingerprints. My name is—" And so on.

It was midmorning then, and he would be on the highway soon. His nostrils, sharpened by hunger, picked up a dozen scents on the desert breeze: the spice of sage, a whiff of acetylene stink from a rattler dozing on the shaded side of a rock, the throat-tightening reek of tar suggested for a moment on the air. That would be the highway, perhaps a recent hotpatch on a chuckhole. Then a startling tang of sulfur dioxide drowned them out and passed on, leaving him stung and sniffling and groping for a handkerchief that was not there. What in God's name had that been, and where from? Without ceasing to trudge, he studied the horizon slowly and found a smoke pall to the far west dimly smudging the sky. It looked like a small city's, or a fair-sized factory's, pollution. A city or a factory where "in his time"—he formed the thought reluctantly—there had been none.

Then he was at the highway. It had been improved; it was a two-laner still, but it was nicely graded now, built up by perhaps three inches of gravel and tar beyond its old level, and lavishly ditched on either side.

If he had a coin he would have tossed it, but you went for weeks without spending a cent at Los Alamos Laboratory; Uncle took care of everything, from cigarettes to tombstones. He turned left and began to walk westward toward that sky smudge.

I am a reasonable animal, he was telling himself, and I will accept whatever comes in a spirit of reason. I will control what I can and try to understand the rest—

A faint siren scream began behind him and built up fast. The reasonable animal jumped for the ditch and hugged it for dear life. The siren howled closer, and motors roared. At the ear-splitting climax Royland put his head up for one glimpse, then fell back into the ditch as if a grenade had exploded in his middle.

The convoy roared on, down the *center* of the two-lane highway, straddling the white line. First the three little recon cars with the twin-mount machine guns, each filled brimful with three helmeted Japanese soldiers. Then the high-profiled, armored car of state, six-wheeled, with a probably ceremonial gun turret astern—nickel-plated gunbarrels are impractical—and the Japanese admiral in the fore-and-aft hat taking his lordly ease beside a rawboned, hatchet-faced SS officer in gleaming black. Then, diminuendo, two more little recon jobs. . . .

"We've lost," Royland said in his ditch meditatively. "Ceremonial tanks with glass windows—we lost a *long* time ago." Had there been a Rising Sun insignia or was he now imagining that?

He climbed out and continued to trudge westward on the improved blacktop. You couldn't say "I reject the universe," not when you were as thirsty as he was.

He didn't even turn when the put-putting of a westbound vehicle grew loud behind him and then very loud when it stopped at his side.

"Zeegail," a curious voice said. "What are you doing here?"

The vehicle was just as odd in its own way as the ceremonial tank. It was minimum motor transportation, a kid's sled on wheels, powered by a noisy little air-cooled outboard motor. The driver sat with no more comfort than a cleat to back his coccyx against, and behind him were two twenty-five-pound flour sacks that took up all the remaining room the little buckboard provided. The driver had the leathery Southwestern look; he wore a baggy blue outfit that was obviously a uniform and obviously unmilitary. He had a nametape on his breast above the incomprehensible row of dull ribbons: MARTFIELD, E., 1218824, P/7 NQOTD43. He saw Royland's eyes on the tape and said kindly: "My name is Martfield—Paymaster Seventh, but there's no need to use my rank here. Are you all right, my man?"

"Thirsty," Royland said. "What's the NQOTD43 for?"

"You can read!" Martfield said, astounded. "Those clothes—"

"Something to drink, please," Royland said. For the moment nothing else mattered in the world. He sat down on the buckboard like a puppet with cut strings.

"See here, fellow!" Martfield snapped in a curious, strangled way, forcing the words through his throat with a stagy, conventional effort of controlled anger. "You can stand until I invite you to sit!"

"Have you any water?" Royland asked dully.

With the same bark: "Who do you think you are?"

"I happen to be a theoretical physicist—" tiredly arguing with a dim seventh-carbon-copy imitation of a drill sergeant.

"Oh-*hoh!*" Martfield suddenly laughed. His stiffness vanished; he actually reached into his baggy tunic and brought out a pint canteen that gurgled. He then forgot all about the canteen in his hand, roguishly dug Royland in the ribs and said: "I should have suspected. You scientists! Somebody was supposed to pick you up—but he was another scientist, eh? Ah-hah-hah-hah!"

Royland took the canteen from his hand and sipped. So a scientist was supposed to be an idiot-savant, eh? Never mind now; drink. People said you were not supposed to fill your stomach with water after great thirst; it sounded to him like one of those puritanical rules people make up out of nothing because they sound reasonable. He finished the canteen while Martfield, Paymaster Seventh, looked alarmed, and wished only that there were three or four more of them.

"Got any food?" he demanded.

Martfield cringed briefly. "Doctor, I regret extremely that I have nothing with me. However if you would do me the honor of riding with me to my quarters—"

"Let's go," Royland said. He squatted on the flour sacks and away they chugged at a good thirty miles an hour; it was a fair little engine. The Paymaster Seventh continued deferential, apologizing over his shoulder because there

231

was no windscreen, later dropped his cringing entirely to explain that Royland was seated on flour—"*white* flour, understand?" An over-the-shoulder wink. He had a friend in the bakery at Los Alamos. Several buckboards passed the other way as they traveled. At each encounter there was a peering examination of insignia to decide who saluted. Once they met a sketchily enclosed vehicle that furnished its driver with a low seat instead of obliging him to sit with legs straight out, and Paymaster Seventh Martfield almost dislocated his shoulder saluting first. The driver of that one was a Japanese in a kimono. A long curved sword lay across his lap.

Mile after mile the smell of sulfur and sulfides increased; finally there rose before them the towers of a Frasch Process layout. It looked like an oilfield, but instead of ground-laid pipelines and bass-drum storage tanks there were foot-hills of yellow sulfur. They drove between them—more salutes from baggily uniformed workers with shovels and yard-long Stilson wrenches. Off to the right were things that might have been Solvay Process towers for sulfuric acid, and a glittering horror of a neo-Roman administration-and-labs building. The Rising Sun banner fluttered from its central flagstaff.

Music surged as they drove deeper into the area; first it was a welcome counterirritant to the pop-pop of the two cycle buckboard engine, and then a nuisance by itself. Royland looked, annoyed, for the loudspeakers, and saw them everywhere—on power poles, buildings, gateposts. Schmaltzy Strauss waltzes bathed them like smog, made thinking just a little harder, made communication just a little more blurry even after you had learned to live with the noise.

"I miss music in the wilderness," Martfield confided over his shoulder. He throttled down the buckboard until they were just rolling; they had passed some line unrecognized by Royland beyond which one did not salute everybody—just the occasional Japanese walking by in business suit with blueprint-roll and slide rule, or in kimono with sword. It was a German who nailed Royland, however: a classic jack-booted German in black broadcloth, black leather, and plenty of silver trim. He watched them roll for a moment after exchanging salutes with Martfield, made up his mind, and said: "Halt."

The Paymaster Seventh slapped on the brake, killed the engine, and popped to attention beside the buckboard. Royland more or less imitated him. The German said, stiffly but without accent: "Whom have you brought here, Paymaster?"

"A scientist, sir. I picked him up on the road returning from Los Alamos with personal supplies. He appears to be a minerals prospector who missed a rendezvous, but naturally I have not questioned the Doctor."

The German turned to Royland contemplatively. "So, Doctor. Your name and specialty."

"Dr. Edward Royland," he said. "I do nuclear power research." If there was no bomb he'd be damned if he'd invent it now for these people.

"So? That is very interesting, considering that there is no such thing as nuclear power research. Which camp are you from?" The German threw an aside to the Paymaster Seventh, who was literally shaking with fear at the turn things had taken. "You may go, Paymaster. Of course you will report yourself for harboring a fugitive."

"At once, sir," Martfield said in a sick voice. He moved slowly away pushing the little buckboard before him. The Strauss waltz oom-pah'd its last chord and instantly the loudspeakers struck up a hoppity-hoppity folk dance, heavy on the brass.

"Come with me," the German said, and walked off, not even looking behind to see whether Royland was obeying. This itself demonstrated how unlikely any disobedience was to succeed. Royland followed at his heels, which of course were garnished with silver spurs. Royland had not seen a horse so far that day.

A Japanese stopped them politely inside the administration building, a rimless-glasses, office-manager type in a gray suit. "How nice to see you again, Major Kappel! Is there anything I might do to help you?"

The German stiffened. "I didn't want to bother your people, Mr. Ito. This fellow appears to be a fugitive from one of our camps; I was going to turn him over to our liaison group for examination and return."

Mr. Ito looked at Royland and slapped his face hard. Royland, by the insanity of sheer reflex, cocked his fist as a red-blooded boy should, but the German's reflexes operated also. He had a pistol in his hand and pressed against Royland's ribs before he could throw the punch.

"All right," Royland said, and put down his hand.

Mr. Ito laughed. "You are at least partly right, Major Kappel; he certainly is not from one of *our* camps! But do not let me delay you further. May I hope for a report on the outcome of this?"

"Of course, Mr. Ito," said the German. He holstered his pistol and walked on, trailed by the scientist. Royland heard him grumble something that sounded like "Damned extraterritoriality!"

They descended to a basement level where all the door signs were in German, and in an office labeled Wissen-schaftslichesicherheitsliaison Royland finally told his story. His audience was the major, a fat officer deferentially addressed as Colonel Biederman, and a bearded old civilian, a Dr. Piqueron, called in from another office. Royland suppressed only the matter of bomb research, and did it easily with the old security habit. His improvised cover story made the Los Alamos Laboratory a research center only for the generation of electricity.

The three heard him out in silence. Finally, in an amused voice, the colonel asked: "Who was this Hitler you mentioned?"

For that Royland was not prepared. His jaw dropped.

Major Kappel said: "Oddly enough, he struck on a name which does figure, somewhat infamously, in the annals of the Third Reich. One Adolf Hitler was an early Party agitator, but as I recall it he intrigued against the Leader during the War of Triumph and was executed."

"An ingenious madman," the colonel said. "Sterilized, of course?"

"Why, I don't know. I suppose so. Doctor, would you—?"

Dr. Piqueron quickly examined Royland and found him all there, which astonished them. Then they thought of looking for his camp tattoo number on the left bicep, and found none. Then, thoroughly upset, they discovered that he had no birth number above his left nipple either.

"And," Dr. Piqueron stammered, "his shoes are odd, sir —I just noticed. Sir, how long since you've seen sewn shoes and braided laces?"

"You must be hungry," the colonel suddenly said. "Doctor, have my aide get something to eat for—for the doctor."

"Major," said Royland, "I hope no harm will come to the fellow who picked me up. You told him to report himself."

"Have no fear, er, doctor," said the major. "Such humanity! You are of German blood?"

"Not that I know of; it may be."

234

"It *must* be!" said the colonel.

A platter of hash and a glass of beer arrived on a tray. Royland postponed everything. At last he demanded: "Now. Do you believe me? There must be fingerprints to prove my story still in existence."

"I feel like a fool," the major said. "You still could be hoaxing us. Dr. Piqueron, did not a German scientist establish that nuclear power is a theoretical and practical impossibility, that one always must put more into it than one can take out?"

Piqueron nodded and said reverently: "Heisenberg. Nineteen fifty-three, during the War of Triumph. His group was then assigned to electrical weapons research and produced the blinding bomb. But this fact does not invalidate the doctor's story; he says only that his group was *attempting* to produce nuclear power."

"We've got to research this," said the colonel. "Dr. Piqueron, entertain this man, whatever he is, in your laboratory."

Piqueron's laboratory down the hall was a place of astounding simplicity, even crudeness. The sinks, reagents, and balance were capable only of simple qualitative and quantitative analysis; various works in progress testified that they were not even strained to their modest limits. Samples of sulfur and its compounds were analyzed here. It hardly seemed to call for a "doctor" of anything, and hardly even for a human being. Machinery should be continuously testing the products as they flowed out; variations should be scribed mechanically on a moving tape; automatic controls should at least stop the processes and signal an alarm when variation went beyond limits; at most it might correct whatever was going wrong. But here sat Piqueron every day, titrating, precipitating, and weighing, entering results by hand in a ledger and telephoning them to the works!

Piqueron looked about proudly. "As a physicist you wouldn't understand all this, of course," he said. "Shall I explain?"

"Perhaps later, doctor, if you'd be good enough. If you'd first help me orient myself—"

So Piqueron told him about the War of Triumph (1940–1955) and what came after.

In 1940 the realm of der Fuehrer (Herr Goebbels, of course—that strapping blond fellow with the heroic jaw and eagle's eye whom you can see in the picture there)

235

was simultaneously and treacherously invaded by the misguided French, the sub-human Slavs, and the perfidious British. The attack, for which the shocked Germans coined the name *blitzkrieg*, was timed to coincide with an internal eruption of sabotage, well-poisoning, with assassination by the *Zigeunerjuden*, or Jewspies, of whom little is now known; there seem to be none left.

By Nature's ineluctable law, the Germans had necessarily to be tested to the utmost so that they might fully respond. Therefore Germany was overrun from East and West, and Holy Berlin itself was taken; but Goebbels and his court withdrew like Barbarossa into the mountain fastness to await their day. It came unexpectedly soon. The deluded Americans launched a million-man amphibious attack on the homeland of the Japanese in 1945. The Japanese resisted with almost Teutonic courage. Not one American in twenty reached shore alive, and not one in a hundred got a mile inland. Particularly lethal were the women and children, who lay in camouflaged pits hugging artillery shells and aircraft bombs, which they detonated when enough invaders drew near to make it worthwhile.

The second invasion attempt, a month later, was made up of second-line troops scraped up from everywhere, including occupation duty in Germany.

"Literally," Piqueron said, "the Japanese did not know how to surrender, so they did not. They could not conquer, but they could and did continue suicidal resistance, consuming manpower of the allies and their own womanpower and childpower—a shrewd bargain for the Japanese! The Russians refused to become involved in the Japanese war; they watched with apish delight while two future enemies, as they supposed, were engaged in mutual destruction.

"A third assault wave broke on Kyushu and gained the island at last. What lay ahead? Only another assault on Honshu, the main island, home of the Emperor and the principal shrines. It was 1946; the volatile, childlike Americans were war-weary and mutinous; the best of them were gone by then. In desperation the Anglo-American leaders offered the Russians an economic sphere embracing the China coast and Japan as the price of participation."

The Russians grinned and assented; they would take that —at *least* that. They mounted a huge assault for the spring of 1947; they would take Korea and leap off from there for northern Honshu while the Anglo-American forces struck in the south. Surely this would provide at last a

236

symbol before which the Japanese might without shame bow down and admit defeat!

And then, from the mountain fastnesses, came the radio voice: "Germans! Your Leader calls upon you again!" Followed the Hundred Days of Glory during which the German Army reconstituted itself and expelled the occupation troops—by then, children without combat experience, and leavened by not-quite-disabled veterans. Followed the seizure of the airfields; the Luftwaffe in business again. Followed the drive, almost a dress parade, to the Channel Coast, gobbling up immense munition dumps awaiting shipment to the Pacific Theater, millions of warm uniforms, good boots, mountains of rations, piles of shells and explosives that lined the French roads for scores of miles, thousands of two-and-a-half-ton trucks, and lakes of gasoline to fuel them. The shipyards of Europe, from Hamburg to Toulon, had been turning out, furiously, invasion barges for the Pacific. In April of 1947 they sailed against England in their thousands.

Halfway around the world, the British Navy was pounding Tokyo, Nagasaki, Kobe, Hiroshima, Nara. Three quarters of the way across Asia the Russian Army marched stolidly on; let the decadent British pickle their own fish; the glorious motherland at last was gaining her long-sought, long-denied, warm-water seacoast. The British, tired women without their men, children fatherless these eight years, old folks deathly weary, worried about their sons, were brave but they were not insane. They accepted honorable peace terms; they capitulated.

With the Western front secure for the first time in history, the ancient Drive to the East was resumed; the immemorial struggle of Teuton against Slav went on.

His spectacles glittering with rapture, Dr. Piqueron said: "We were worthy in those days of the Teutonic Knights who seized Prussia from the sub-men! On the ever-glorious Twenty-first of May, Moscow was ours!"

Moscow and the monolithic state machinery it controlled, and all the roads and rail lines and communication wires which led only to—and from—Moscow. Detroit-built tanks and trucks sped along those roads in the fine, bracing spring weather; the Red Army turned one hundred and eighty degrees at last and counter-marched halfway across the Eurasian landmass, and at Kazan it broke exhausted against the Frederik Line.

Europe at last was One and German. Beyond Europe lay

the dark and swarming masses of Asia, mysterious and repulsive folk whom it would be better to handle through the non-German, but chivalrous, Japanese. The Japanese were reinforced with shipping from Birkenhead, artillery from the Putilov Works, jet fighters from Châteauroux, steel from the Ruhr, rice from the Po valley, herring from Norway, timber from Sweden, oil from Romania, laborers from India. The American forces were driven from Kyushu in the winter of 1948, and bloodily back across their chain of island stepping-stones that followed.

Surrender they would not; it was a monstrous affront that shield-shaped North America dared to lie there between the German Atlantic and the Japanese Pacific threatening both. The affront was wiped out in 1955.

For one hundred and fifty years now the Germans and the Japanese had uneasily eyed each other across the banks of the Mississippi. Their orators were fond of referring to that river as a vast frontier unblemished by a single fortification. There was even some interpenetration; a Japanese colony fished out of Nova Scotia on the very rim of German America; a sulfur mine which was part of the Farben system lay in New Mexico, the very heart of Japanese America—this was where Dr. Edward Royland found himself, being lectured to by Dr. Piqueron, Dr. Gaston Pierre Piqueron, true-blue German.

"Here, of course," Dr. Piqueron said gloomily, "we are so damned provincial. Little ceremony and less manners. Well, it would be too much to expect them to assign *German* Germans to this dreary outpost, so we French Germans must endure it somehow."

"You're all French?" Royland asked, startled.

"French *Germans*," Piqueron stiffly corrected him. "Colonel Biederman happens to be a French German also; Major Kappel is—hrrmph—an Italian German." He sniffed to show what he thought of that.

The Italian German entered at that point, not in time to shut off the question: "And you all come from Europe?"

They looked at him in bafflement. "My grandfather did," Dr. Piqueron said. Royland remembered; so Roman legions used to guard their empire—Romans born and raised in Britain, or on the Danube, Romans who would never in their lives see Italy or Rome.

Major Kappel said affably: "Well, this needn't concern us. I'm afraid, my dear fellow, that your little hoax has not succeeded." He clapped Royland merrily on the back. "I

238

admit you've tricked us all nicely; now may we have the facts?"

Piqueron said, surprised: "His story is false? The shoes? The missing *geburtsnummer?* And he appears to understand some chemistry!"

"Ah-h-h—but he said his specialty was *physics,* doctor! Suspicious in itself!"

"Quite so. A discrepancy. But the rest—?"

"As to his birth number, who knows? As to his shoes, who cares? I took some inconspicuous notes while he was entertaining us and have checked thoroughly. There *was* no Manhattan Engineering District. There *was* no Dr. Oppenheimer, or Fermi, or Bohr. There *is* no theory of relativity, or equivalence of mass and energy. Uranium has one use only—coloring glass a pretty orange. There is such a thing as an isotope but it has nothing to do with chemistry; it is the name used in Race Science for a permissible variation within a sub-race. And what have you to say to *that,* my dear fellow?"

Royland wondered first, such was the positiveness with which Major Kappel spoke, whether he had slipped into a universe of different physical properties and history entirely, one in which Julius Caesar discovered Peru and the oxygen molecule was lighter than the hydrogen atom. He managed to speak. "How did you find all that out, Major?"

"Oh, don't think I did a skimpy job," Kappel smiled. "I looked it all up in the *big* encyclopedia."

Dr. Piqueron, chemist, nodded grave approval of the major's diligence and thorough grasp of the scientific method.

"You still don't want to tell us?" Major Kappel asked coaxingly.

"I can only stand by what I said."

Kappel shrugged. "It's not my job to persuade you; I wouldn't know how to begin. But I can and will ship you off forthwith to a work camp."

"What—is a work camp?" Royland unsteadily asked.

"Good heavens, man, a camp where one works! You're obviously an *ungleichgeschaltling* and you've got to be *gleichgeschaltet.*" He did not speak these words as if they were foreign; they were obviously part of the everyday American working vocabulary. *Gleichgeschaltet* meant to Royland something like "coordinated, brought into tune with." So he would be brought into tune—with what, and how?

The Major went on: "You'll get your clothes and your bunk and your chow, and you'll work, and eventually your irregular vagabondish habits will disappear and you'll be turned loose on the labor market. And you'll be damned glad we took the trouble with you." His face fell. "By the way, I was too late with your friend the Paymaster. I'm sorry. I sent a messenger to Disciplinary Control with a stop order. After all, if you took us in for an hour, why should you not have fooled a Pay-Seventh?"

"Too late? He's *dead*? For picking up a *hitchhiker?*"

"I don't know what that last word means," said the Major. "If it's dialect for 'vagabond,' the answer is ordinarily 'yes.' The man, after all, was a Pay-Seventh; he could read. Either you're keeping up your hoax with remarkable fidelity or you've been living in isolation. Could that be it? Is there a tribe of you somewhere? Well, the interrogators will find out; that's their job."

"The Dogpatch legend!" Dr. Piqueron burst out, thunderstruck. "He may be an Abnerite!"

"By Heaven," Major Kappel said slowly, "that might be it. What a feather in my cap to find a living Abnerite."

"*Whose* cap?" demanded Dr. Piqueron coldly.

"I think I'll look the Dogpatch legend up," said Kappel, heading for the door and probably the big encyclopedia.

"So will I," Dr. Piqueron announced firmly. The last Royland saw of them they were racing down the corridor, neck and neck.

Very funny. And they had killed simple-minded Paymaster Martfield for picking up a hitchhiker. The Nazis always had been pretty funny—fat Hermann pretending he was young Seigfried. As blond as Hitler, as slim as Goering, and as tall as Goebbels. Immature guttersnipes who hadn't been able to hang a convincing frame on Dimitrov for the Reichstag fire; the world had roared at their bungling. Huge, corny party rallies with let's-play-detectives nonsense like touching the local flags to that hallowed banner on which the martyred Horst Wessel had had a nosebleed. And they had rolled over Europe, and they killed people. . . .

One thing was certain: life in the work camp would at least bore him to death. He was supposed to be an illiterate simpleton, so things were excused him which were not excused an exalted Pay-Seventh. He poked through a closet in the corner of the laboratory—he and Piqueron were the same size—

He found a natty change of uniform and what must be a civilian suit: somewhat baggy pants and a sort of tunic with the neat, sensible Russian collar. Obviously it would be all right to wear it because here it was: just as obviously, it was all wrong for him to be dressed in chinos and a flannel shirt. He did not know exactly what this made him, but Martfield had been done to death for picking up a man in chinos and a flannel shirt. Royland changed into the civilian suit, stuffed his own shirt and pants far back on the top shelf of the closet; this was probably concealment enough from those murderous clowns. He walked out, and up the stairs, and through the busy lobby, and into the industrial complex. Nobody saluted him and he saluted nobody. He knew where he was going—to a good, sound Japanese laboratory where there were no Germans.

Royland had known Japanese students at the University and admired them beyond words. Their brains, frugality, doggedness, and good humor made them, as far as he was concerned, the most sensible people he had ever known. Tojo and his warlords were not, as far as Royland was concerned, essentially Japanese but just more damnfool soldiers and politicians. The real Japanese would courteously listen to him, calmly check against available facts—

He rubbed his cheek and remembered Mr. Ito and his slap in the face. Well, presumably Mr. Ito was a damnfool soldier and politician--and demonstrating for the German's benefit in a touchy border area full of jurisdictional questions.

At any rate, he would *not* go to a labor camp and bust rocks or refinish furniture until those imbeciles decided he was *gleichgeschaltet;* he would go mad in a month.

Royland walked to the Solvay towers and followed the glass pipes containing their output of sulfuric acid along the ground until he came to a bottling shed where beetle-browed men worked silently filling great wicker-basketed carboys and heaving them outside. He followed other men who levered them up onto hand trucks and rolled them in one door of a storage shed. Out the door at the other end more men loaded them onto enclosed trucks which were driven up from time to time.

Royland settled himself in a corner of the storage shed behind a barricade of carboys and listened to the truck dispatcher swear at his drivers and the carboy handlers swear at their carboys.

"Get the god-damn Frisco shipment *loaded,* stupid! I don't *care* if you gotta go, we gotta get it out by *midnight!*"

So a few hours after dark Royland was riding west, without much air, and in the dangerous company of one thousand gallons of acid. He hoped he had a careful driver.

A night, a day, and another night on the road. The truck never stopped except to gas up; the drivers took turns and ate sandwiches at the wheel and dozed off shift. It rained the second night. Royland, craftily and perhaps a little crazily, licked the drops that ran down the tarpaulin flap covering the rear. At the first crack of dawn, hunched between two wicker carcasses, he saw they were rolling through irrigated vegetable fields, and the water in the ditches was too much for him. He heard the transmission shift down to slow for a curve, swarmed over the tailgate, and dropped to the road. He was weak and limp enough to hit like a sack.

He got up, ignoring his bruises, and hobbled to one of the brimming five-foot ditches; he drank, and drank, and drank. This time puritanical folklore proved right; he lost it all immediately, or what had not been greedily absorbed by his shriveled stomach. He did not mind; it was bliss enough to *stretch.*

The field crop was tomatoes, almost dead ripe. He was starved for them; as he saw the rosy beauties he knew that tomatoes were the only thing in the world he craved. He gobbled one so that the juice ran down his chin; he ate the next two delicately, letting his teeth break the crispness of their skin and the beautiful taste ravish his tongue. There were tomatoes as far as the eye could see, on either side of the road, the green of the vines and the red dots of the ripe fruit graphed by the checkerboard of silvery ditches that caught the first light. Nevertheless, he filled his pockets with them before he walked on.

Royland was happy.

Farewell to the Germans and their sordid hash and murderous ways. *Look* at these beautiful fields! The Japanese are an innately artistic people who bring beauty to every detail of daily life. And they make damn good physicists, too. Confined in their stony home, cramped as he had been in the truck, they grew twisted and painful; why should they not have reached out for more room to grow, and what other way is there to reach but to make war? He

242

could be very understanding about any people who had planted these beautiful tomatoes for him.

A dark blemish the size of a man attracted his attention. It lay on the margin of one of the swirling five-foot ditches out there to his right. And then it rolled slowly into the ditch with a splash, floundered a little, and proceeded to drown.

In a hobbling run Royland broke from the road and across the field. He did not know whether he was limber enough to swim. As he stood panting on the edge of the ditch, peering into the water, a head of hair surfaced near him. He flung himself down, stretched wildly, and grabbed the hair—and yet had detachment enough to feel a pang when the tomatoes in his tunic pocket smashed.

"Steady," he muttered to himself, yanked the head toward him, took hold with his other hand and lifted. A surprised face confronted him and then went blank and unconscious.

For half an hour Royland, weak as he was, struggled, cursed feebly, and sweated to get that body out of the water. At last he plunged in himself, found it only chest-deep, and shoved the carcass over the mudslick bank. He did not know by then whether the man was alive or dead or much care. He knew only that he couldn't walk away and leave the job half finished.

The body was that of a fat, middle-aged Oriental, surely Chinese rather than Japanese, though Royland could not say why he thought so. His clothes were soaked rags except for a leather wallet the size of a cigar box which he wore on a wide cloth belt. Its sole content was a handsome blue-glazed porcelain bottle. Royland sniffed at it and reeled. Some kind of super-gin? He sniffed again, and then took a conservative gulp of the stuff. While he was still coughing he felt the bottle being removed from his hand. When he looked he saw the Chinese, eyes still closed, accurately guiding the neck of the bottle to his mouth. The Chinese drank and drank and drank, then returned the bottle to the wallet and finally opened his eyes.

"Honorable sir," said the Chinese in flat, California American speech, "you have deigned to save my unworthy life. May I supplicate your honorable name?"

"Ah, Royland. Look, take it easy. Don't try to get up; you shouldn't even talk."

Somebody screamed behind Royland: "There has been thieving of tomatoes! There has been smasheeng and dee-

243

struction of thee vines! Chil-dren, you will bee weet-ness be-fore the Jappa-neese!"

Christ, now what?

Now a skinny black man, not a Negro, in a dirty loin-cloth, and beside him like a pan-pipes five skinny black loinclothed offspring in descending order. All were caper-ing, pointing, and threatening. The Chinese groaned, fished in his tattered robes with one hand, and pulled out a soggy wad of bills. He peeled one off, held it out, and said: "Begone, pestilential barbarians from beyond Tian-Shang. My master and I give you alms, not tribute."

The Dravidian, or whatever he was, grabbed the bill and keened: "Een-suffee-cient for the terrible dommage! The Jappa-neese—"

The Chinese waved them away boredly. He said: "If my master will condescend to help me arise?"

Royland uncertainly helped him up. The man was wob-bly, whether from the near-drowning or the terrific belt of alcohol he'd taken there was no knowing. They proceeded to the road, followed by shrieks to be careful about step-ping on the vines.

On the road, the Chinese said: "My unworthy name is Li Po. Will my master deign to indicate in which direction we are to travel?"

"What's this master business?" Royland demanded. "If you're grateful, swell, but I don't *own* you."

"My master is pleased to jest," said Li Po. Politely, face-saving and third-personing Royland until hell wouldn't have it, he explained that Royland, having meddled with the Celestial decree that Li Po should, while drunk, roll into the irrigation ditch and drown, now had Li Po on his hands, for the Celestial Ones had washed theirs of him. "As my master of course will recollect in a moment or two." Understandingly, he expressed his sympathy with Royland's misfortune in acquiring him as an obligation, especially since he had a hearty appetite, was known to be dishonest, and suffered from fainting fits and spasms when confronted with work.

"I don't *know* about all this," Royland said fretfully. "Wasn't there another Li Po? A poet?"

"Your servant prefers to venerate his namesake as one of the greatest drunkards the Flowery Kingdom has ever known," the Chinese observed. And a moment later he bent over, clipped Royland behind the knees so that he toppled forward and bumped his head, and performed the same

244

obeisance himself, more gracefully. A vehicle went sputtering and popping by on the road as they kowtowed.

Li Po said reproachfully: "I humbly observe that my master is unaware of the etiquette our noble overlords exact. Such negligence cost the head of my insignificant elder brother in his twelfth year. Would my master be pleased to explain how he can have reached his honorable years without learning what babes in their cradles are taught?"

Royland answered with the whole truth. Li Po politely begged clarification from time to time, and a sketch of his mental horizons emerged from his questioning. That "magic" had whisked Royland forward a century or more he did not doubt for an instant, but he found it difficult to understand why the proper *fung shui* precautions had not been taken to avert a disastrous outcome to the God Food experiment. He suspected, from a description of Nahataspe's hut, that a simple wall at right angles to the door would have kept all really important demons out. When Royland described his escape from German territory to Japanese, and why he had effected it, he was very bland and blank. Royland judged that Li Po privately thought him not very bright for having left *any* place to come here.

And Royland hoped he was not right. "Tell me what it's like," he said.

"This realm," said Li Po, "under our benevolent and noble overlords, is the haven of all whose skin is not the bleached-bone hue which indicates the undying curse of the Celestial Ones. Hither flock men of Han like my unworthy self, and the sons of Hind beyond the Tian-Shang that we may till new soil and raise up sons, and sons of sons to venerate us when we ascend."

"What was that bit," Royland demanded, "about the bleached bones? Do they shoot, ah, white men on sight here, or do they not?"

Li Po said evasively: "We are approaching the village where I unworthily serve as fortune teller, doctor of *fung shui,* occasional poet and storyteller. Let my master have no fear about his color. This humble one will roughen his master's skin, tell a circumstantial and artistic lie or two, and pass his master off as merely a leper."

After a week in Li Po's village Royland knew that life was good there. The place was a wattle-and-clay settlement of about two hundred souls on the bank of an irriga-

245

tion ditch large enough to be dignified by the name of "canal." It was situated nobody knew just where; Royland thought it must be the San Fernando Valley. The soil was thick and rich and bore furiously the year round. A huge kind of radish was the principal crop. It was too coarse to be eaten by man; the villagers understood that it was feed for chickens somewhere up north. At any rate they harvested the stuff, fed it through a great hand-powered shredder, and shade-cured the shreds. Every few days a Japanese of low caste would come by in a truck, they would load tons of the stuff onto it, and wave their giant radish goodbye forever. Presumably the chickens ate it, and the Japanese then ate the chickens.

The villagers ate chicken too, but only at weddings and funerals. The rest of the time they ate vegetables which they cultivated, a quarter-acre to a family, the way other craftsmen facet diamonds. A single cabbage might receive, during its ninety days from planting to maturity, one hundred work hours from grandmother, grandfather, son, daughter, eldest grandchild, and on down to the smallest toddler. Theoretically the entire family line should have starved to death, for there are not one hundred energy hours in a cabbage; somehow they did not. They merely stayed thin and cheerful and hard-working and fecund.

They spoke English by Imperial decree; the reasoning seemed to be that they were as unworthy to speak Japanese as to paint the Imperial Chrysanthemum Seal on their houses, and that to let them cling to their old languages and dialects would have been politically unwise.

They were a mixed lot of Chinese, Hindus, Dravidians, and, to Royland's surprise, low-caste and outcaste Japanese; he had not known there were such things. Village tradition had it that a *samurai* named Ugetsu long ago said, pointing at the drunk tank of a Hong Kong jail, "I'll have that lot," and "that lot" had been the ancestors of these villagers transported to America in a foul hold practically as ballast and settled here by the canal with orders to start making their radish quota. The place was at any rate called The Ugetsu Village, and if some of the descendants were teetotallers, others like Li Po gave color to the legend of their starting point.

After a week the cheerful pretense that he was a sufferer from Housen's disease evaporated and he could wash the mud off his face. He had merely to avoid the upper-caste Japanese and especially the *samurai*. This was not exactly a stigma; in general it was a good idea for *everybody* to avoid the *samurai*.

In the village Royland found his first love and his first religion both false.

He had settled down; he was getting used to the Oriental work rhythm of slow, repeated, incessant effort; it did not surprise him any longer that he could count his ribs. When he ate a bowl of artfully arranged vegetables, the red of pimiento played off against the yellow of parsnip, a slice of pickled beet adding visual and olfactory tang to the picture, he felt full enough; he *was* full enough for the next day's feeble work in the field. It was pleasant enough to play slowly with a wooden mattock in the rich soil; did not people once buy sand so their children might do exactly what he did, and envy their innocent absorption? Royland was innocently absorbed, then, and the radish truck had collected six times since his arrival, when he began to feel stirrings of lust. On the edge of starvation (but who knew this? For everybody was) his mind was dulled, but not his loins. They burned, and he looked about him in the fields, and the first girl he saw who was not repulsive he fell abysmally in love with.

Bewildered, he told Li Po, who was also Ugetsu Village's go-between. The storyteller was delighted; he waddled off to seek information and returned. "My master's choice is wise. The slave on whom his lordly eye deigned to rest is known as Vashti, daughter of Hari Bose, the distiller. She is his seventh child and so no great dowry can be expected [I shall ask for fifteen kegs toddy, but would settle for seven], but all this humble village knows that she is a skilled and willing worker in the hut as in the fields. I fear she has the customary lamentable Hindu talent for concocting curries, but a dozen good beatings at the most should cause her to reserve it to appropriate occasions, such as visits from her mother and sisters."

So, according to the sensible custom of Ugetsu, Vashti came that night to the hut which Royland shared with Li Po, and Li Po visited with cronies by his master's puzzling request. He begged humbly to point out that it would be dark in the hut, so this talk of lacking privacy was inexplicable to say the least. Royland made it an order, and Li Po did not really object, so he obeyed it.

It was a damnably strange night, during which Royland learned all about India's national sport and most highly developed art form. Vashti, if she found him weak on the theory side, made no complaints. On the contrary, when Royland woke she was doing something or other to his feet.

"More?" he thought incredulously. "With *feet?*" He asked what she was doing. Submissively she replied: "Worshipping my lord husband-to-be's big toe. I am a pious and old-fashioned woman."

So she painted his toe with red paint and prayed to it, and then she fixed breakfast—curry, and excellent. She watched him eat, and then modestly licked his leavings from the bowl. She handed him his clothes, which she had washed while he still slept, and helped him into them after she helped him wash. Royland thought incredulously: "It's not possible! It must be a show, to sell me on marrying her —as if I had to be sold!" His heart turned to custard as he saw her, without a moment's pause, turn from dressing him to polishing his wooden rake. He asked that day in the field, roundabout fashion, and learned that this was the kind of service he could look forward to for the rest of his life after marriage. If the woman got lazy he'd have to beat her, but this seldom happened more than every year or so. We have good girls here in Ugetsu Village.

So an Ugetsu Village peasant was in some ways better off than anybody from "his time" who was less than a millionaire!

His starved dullness was such that he did not realize this was true for only half the Ugetsu Village peasants.

Religion sneaked up on him in similar fashion. He went to the part-time Taoist priest because he was a little bored with Li Po's current after-dinner saga. He could have sat like all the others and listened passively to the interminable tale of the glorious Yellow Emperor, and the beautiful but wicked Princess Emerald, and the virtuous but plain Princess Moon Blossom; it just happened that he went to the priest of Tao and got hooked hard.

The kindly old man, a toolmaker by day, dropped a few pearls of wisdom which, in his foggy starvation-daze, Royland did not perceive to be pearls of undemonstrable nonsense, and showed Royland how to meditate. It worked the first time. Royland bunged right smack through into a two-hundred-proof state of *samadhi*—the Eastern version of self-hypnotized Enlightenment—that made him feel wonderful and all-knowing and left him without a hangover when it wore off. He had despised, in college, the type of people who took psychology courses and so had taken none himself; he did not know a thing about self-hypnosis except as just demonstrated by this very nice old gentleman. For several days he was offensively religious and kept trying to talk to Li Po about the Eightfold Way, and Li Po kept changing the subject.

It took murder to bring him out of love and religion.

At twilight they were all sitting and listening to the storyteller as usual. Royland had been there just one month and for all he knew would be there forever. He soon would have his bride officially; he knew he had discovered The Truth About the Universe by way of Tao meditation; why should he change? Changing demanded a furious outburst of energy, and he did not have energy on that scale. He metered out his energy day and night; one had to save so much for tonight's love play, and then one had to save so much for tomorrow's planting. He was a poor man; he could not afford to change.

Li Po had reached a rather interesting bit where the Yellow Emperor was declaiming hotly: "Then she shall die! Whoever dare transgress Our divine will—"

A flashlight began to play over their faces. They perceived that it was in the hand of a *samurai* with kimono and sword. Everybody hastily kowtowed, but the *samurai* shouted irritably (all *samurai* were irritable, all the time): "Sit up, you fools! I want to see your stupid faces. I hear there's a peculiar one in this flea-bitten dungheap you call a village."

Well, by now Royland knew his duty. He rose and with downcast eyes asked: "Is the noble protector in search of my unworthy self?"

"Ha!" the *samurai* roared. "It's true! A big nose!" He hurled the flashlight away (all *samurai* were nobly contemptuous of the merely material), held his scabbard in his left hand, and swept out the long curved sword with his right.

Li Po stepped forward and said in his most enchanting voice: "If the Heaven-born would only deign to heed a word from this humble—" What he must have known would happen happened. With a contemptuous backhand sweep of the blade the *samurai* beheaded him and Li Po's debt was paid.

The trunk of the storyteller stood for a moment and then fell stiffly forward. The *samurai* stooped to wipe his blade clean on Li Po's ragged robes.

Royland had forgotten much, but not everything. With

the villagers scattering before him he plunged forward and tackled the *samurai* low and hard. No doubt the *samurai* was a Brown Belt judo master; if so he had nobody but himself to blame for turning his back. Royland, not remembering that he was barefoot, tried to kick the *samurai's* face in. He broke his worshipful big toe, but its untrimmed horny nail removed the left eye of the warrior and after that it was no contest. He never let the *samurai* get up off the ground; he took out his other eye with the handle of a rake and then killed him an inch at a time with his hands, his feet, and the clownish rustic's traditional weapon, a flail. It took easily half an hour, and for the final twenty minutes the *samurai* was screaming for his mother. He died when the last light left the western sky, and in darkness Royland stood quite alone with the two corpses. The villagers were gone.

He assumed, or pretended, that they were within earshot and yelled at them brokenly: "I'm sorry, Vashti. I'm sorry, all of you. I'm going. Can I make you understand?

"Listen. You aren't living. This isn't life. You're not making anything but babies, you're not changing, you're not growing up. That's not enough! You've got to read and write. You can't pass on anything but baby stories like the Yellow Emperor by word of mouth. The village is growing. Soon your fields will touch the fields of Sukoshi Village to the west, and then what happens? You won't know what to do, so you'll fight with Sukoshi Village.

"Religion. No! It's just getting drunk the way you do it. You're set up for it by being half-starved and then you go into *samadhi* and you feel better so you think you understand everything. No! You've got to *do* things. If you don't grow up, you die. All of you.

"Women. *That's* wrong. It's good for the men, but it's wrong. Half of you are slaves, do you understand? Women are people too, but you use them like animals and you've convinced them it's right for them to be old at thirty and discarded for the next girl. For God's sake, can't you try to think of yourselves in their place?

"The breeding, the crazy breeding—it's got to stop. You frugal Orientals! But you aren't frugal; you're crazy drunken sailors. You're squandering the whole world. Every mouth you breed has got to be fed by the land, and the land isn't infinite.

"I hope some of you understood. Li Po would have, a little, but he's dead.

"I'm going away now. You've been kind to me and all I've done is make trouble. I'm sorry."

He fumbled on the ground and found the *samurai's* flashlight. With it he hunted the village's outskirts until he found the Japanese's buckboard car. He started the motor with its crank and noisily rolled down the dirt track from the village to the highway.

Royland drove all night, still westward. His knowledge of southern California's geography was inexact, but he hoped to hit Los Angeles. There might be a chance of losing himself in a great city. He had abandoned hope of finding present-day counterparts of his old classmates like Jimmy Ichimura; obviously they had lost out. Why shouldn't have they lost? The soldier-politicians had won the war by happenstance, so all power to the soldier-politicians! Reasoning under the great natural law *post hoc ergo propter hoc,* Tojo and his crowd had decided: fanatic feudalism won the war; therefore fanatic feudalism is a good thing, and it necessarily follows that the more fanatical and feudal it is, the better a thing it is. So you had Sukoshi Village, and Ugetsu Village; Ichi Village, Ni Village, San Village, Shi Village, dotting that part of Great Japan formerly known as North America, breeding with the good old fanatic feudalism and so feudally averse to new thought and innovations that it made you want to scream at them—which he had.

The single weak headlight of his buckboard passed few others on the road; a decent feudal village is self-contained.

Damn them and their suicidal cheerfulness! It was a pleasant trait; it was a fool in a canoe approaching the rapids saying: "Chin up! Everything's going to be all right if we just keep smiling."

The car ran out of gas when false dawn first began to pale the sky behind him. He pushed it into the roadside ditch and walked on; by full light he was in a tumble-down, planless, evil-smelling, paper-and-galvanized-iron city whose name he did not know. There was no likelihood of him being noticed as a "white" man by anyone not specifically looking for him. A month of outdoor labor had browned him, and a month of artistically composed vegetable plates had left him gaunt.

The city was carpeted with awakening humanity. Its narrow streets were paved with sprawled-out men, women, and children beginning to stir and hawk up phlegm and

251

rub their rheumy eyes. An open sewer-latrine running down the center of each street was casually used, ostrich-fashion—the users hid their own eyes while in action.

Every mangled variety of English rang in Royland's ears as he trod between bodies.

There had to be something more, he told himself. This was the shabby industrial outskirts, the lowest marginal-labor area. Somewhere in the city there was beauty, science, learning!

He walked aimlessly plodding until noon, and found nothing of the sort. These people in the cities were food-handlers, food-traders, food-transporters. They took in one another's washing and sold one another chop suey. They made automobiles (Yes! There were one-family automobile factories which probably made six buckboards a year, filing all metal parts by hand out of bar stock!) and orange crates and baskets and coffins; abacuses, nails, and boots.

The Mysterious East has done it again, he thought bitterly. The Indians-Chinese-Japanese won themselves a nice sparse area. They could have laid things out neatly and made it pleasant for everybody instead of for a minute speck of aristocracy which he was unable even to detect in this human soup . . . but they had done it again. They had bred irresponsibly just as fast as they could until the land was *full*. Only famines and pestilence could "help" them now.

He found exactly one building which owned some clear space around it and which would survive an earthquake or a flicked cigarette butt. It was the German Consulate.

I'll give them the Bomb, he said to himself. Why not? None of this is mine. And for the Bomb I'll exact a price of some comfort and dignity for as long as I live. *Let* them blow one another up! He climbed the consulate steps.

To the black-uniformed guard at the swastika-trimmed bronze doors he said: *"Wenn die Lichtstärke der von einer Fläche kommenden Strahlung dem Cosinus des Winkels zwischen Strahlrichtung und Flächennormalen proportional ist, so nennen wir die Fläche eine volkommen streunde Fläche."* Lambert's Law, Optics I. All the Goethe he remembered happened to rhyme, which might have made the guard suspicious.

Naturally the German came to attention and said apologetically: "I don't speak German. What is it, sir?"

252

"You may take me to the consul," Royland said, affecting boredom.

"Yes, sir. At once, sir. Er, you're an *agent* of course, sir?"

Royland said witheringly: *"Sicherheit, bitte!"*

"Yessir. This way, sir!"

The consul was a considerate, understanding gentleman. He was somewhat surprised by Royland's true tale, but said from time to time: "I see; I see. Not impossible. Please go on."

Royland concluded: "Those people at the sulfur mine were, I hope, unrepresentative. One of them at least complained that it was a dreary sort of backwoods assignment. I am simply gambling that there is intelligence in your Reich. I ask you to get me a real physicist for twenty minutes of conversation. You, Mr. Consul, will not regret it. I am in a position to turn over considerable information on—atomic power." So he had not been able to say it after all; the Bomb was still an obscene kick below the belt.

"This has been very interesting, Dr. Royland," said the consul gravely. "You referred to your enterprise as a gamble. I too shall gamble. What have I to lose by putting you *en rapport* with a scientist of ours if you prove to be a plausible lunatic?" He smiled to soften it. "Very little indeed. On the other hand, what have I to gain if your extraordinary story is quite true? A great deal. I will go along with you, doctor. Have you eaten?"

The relief was tremendous. He had lunch in a basement kitchen with the Consulate guards—a huge lunch, a rather nasty lunch of stewed *lungen* with a floured gravy, and cup after cup of coffee. Finally one of the guards lit up an ugly little spindle-shaped cigar, the kind Royland had only seen before in the caricatures of George Grosz, and as an afterthought offered one to him.

He drank in the rank smoke and managed not to cough. It stung his mouth and cut the greasy aftertaste of the stew satisfactorily. One of the blessings of the Third Reich, one of its gross pleasures. They were just people, after all—a certain censorious, busybody type of person with altogether too much power, but they were human. By which he meant, he supposed, members of Western Industrial Culture like him.

After lunch he was taken by truck from the city to an airfield by one of the guards. The plane was somewhat bigger than a B-29 he had once seen, and lacked propellers. He presumed it was one of the "jets" Dr. Piqueron had mentioned. His guard gave his dossier to a Luftwaffe sergeant at the foot of the ramp and said cheerfully: "Happy landings, fellow. It's all going to be all right."

"Thanks," he said. "I'll remember you, Corporal Collins. You've been very helpful." Collins turned away.

Royland climbed the ramp into the barrel of the plane. A bucket-seat job, and most of the seats were filled. He dropped into one on the very narrow aisle. His neighbor was in rags; his face showed signs of an old beating. When Royland addressed him he simply cringed away and began to sob.

The Luftwaffe sergeant came up, entered, and slammed the door. The "jets" began to wind up, making an unbelievable racket; further conversation was impossible. While the plane taxied, Royland peered through the windowless gloom at his fellow-passengers. They all looked poor and poorly.

God, were they so quickly and quietly airborne? They were. Even in the bucket seat, Royland fell asleep.

He was awakened, he did not know how much later, by the sergeant. The man was shaking his shoulder and asking him: "Any joolery hid away? Watches? Got some nice fresh water to sell to people that wanna buy it."

Royland had nothing, and would not take part in the miserable little racket if he had. He shook his head indignantly and the man moved on with a grin. He would not last long!—petty chiselers were leaks in the efficient dictatorship; they were rapidly detected and stopped up. Mussolini made the trains run on time, after all. (But naggingly Royland recalled mentioning this to a Northwestern University English professor, one Bevans. Bevans had coldly informed him that from 1931 to 1936 he had lived under Mussolini as a student and tourist guide, and therefore had extraordinary opportunities for observing whether the trains ran on time or not, and could definitely state that they did not; that railway timetables under Mussolini were best regarded as humorous fiction.)

And another thought nagged at him, a thought connected with a pale, scarred face named Bloom. Bloom was a young refugee physical chemist working on WEAPONS DEVELOPMENT TRACK I, and he was somewhat crazy, perhaps. Royland, on TRACK III, used to see little of him and could have done with even less. You couldn't say hello to

254

the man without it turning into a lecture on the horrors of Nazism. He had wild stories about "gas chambers" and crematoria which no reasonable man could believe, and was a blanket slanderer of the German medical profession. He claimed that trained doctors, certified men, used human beings in experiments which terminated fatally. Once, to try and bring Bloom to reason, he asked what sort of experiments these were, but the monomaniac had had that worked out: piffling nonsense about reviving mortally frozen men by putting naked women into bed with them! The man was probably sexually deranged to believe that; he naively added that one variable in the series of experiments was to use women immediately after sexual intercourse, one hour after sexual intercourse, et cetera. Royland had blushed for him and violently changed the subject.

But that was not what he was groping for. Neither was Bloom's crazy story about the woman who made lampshades from the tattooed skin of concentration camp prisoners; there were people capable of such things, of course, but under no regime whatever do they rise to positions of authority; they simply can't do the work required in positions of authority because their insanity gets in the way.

"Know your enemy," of course—but making up pointless lies? At least Bloom was not the conscious prevaricator. He got letters in Yiddish from friends and relations in Palestine, and these were laden with the latest wild rumors supposed to be based on the latest word from "escapees."

Now he remembered. In the cafeteria about three months ago Bloom had been sipping tea with somewhat shaking hand and rereading a letter. Royland tried to pass him with only a nod, but the skinny hand shot out and held him.

Bloom looked up with tears in his eyes: "It's cruel, I'm tellink you, Royland, it's cruel. They're not givink them the right to scream, to strike a futile blow, to sayink prayers *Kiddush ha Shem* like a Jew should when he is dyink for Consecration of the Name! They trick them, they say they go to farm settlements, to labor camps, so four-five of the stinkink bastards can handle a whole trainload Jews. They trick the clothes off of them at the camps, they sayink they delouse them. They trick them into room says showerbath over the door and then is too late to sayink prayers; *then goes on the gas*."

Bloom had let go of him and put his head on the table between his hands. Royland had mumbled something,

255

patted his shoulder, and walked on, shaken. For once the neurotic little man might have got some straight facts. That was a very circumstantial touch about expediting the handling of prisoners by systematic lies—always the carrot and the stick.

Yes, everybody had been so god-damn agreeable since he climbed the Consulate steps! The friendly door guard, the Consul who nodded and remarked that his story was not an impossible one, the men he'd eaten with—all that quiet optimism. "Thanks. I'll remember you, Corporal Collins. You've been very helpful." He had felt positively benign toward the corporal, and now remembered that the corporal had turned around *very* quickly after he spoke. *To hide a grin?*

The guard was working his way down the aisle again and noticed that Royland was awake. "Changed your mind by now?" he asked kindly. "Got a good watch, maybe I'll find a piece of bread for you. You won't need a watch where you're going, fella."

"What do you mean?" Royland demanded.

The guard said soothingly: "Why, they got clocks all over them work camps, fella. Everybody knows what time it is in them work camps. You don't need no watches there. Watches just get in the way at them work camps." He went on down the aisle, quickly.

Royland reached across the aisle and, like Bloom, gripped the man who sat opposite him. He could not see much of him; the huge windowless plane was lit only by half a dozen stingy bulbs overhead. "What are you here for?" he asked.

The man said shakily: "I'm a Laborer Two, see? A Two. Well, my father he taught me to read, see, but he waited until I was ten and knew the score? See? So I figured it was a family tradition, so I taught my own kid to read because he was a pretty smart kid, ya know? I figured he'd have some fun reading like I did, no harm done, who's to know, ya know? But I should of waited a couple years, I guess, because the kid was too young and got to bragging he could read, ya know how kids do? I'm from St. Louis, by the way. I should of said first I'm from St. Louis a track maintenance man, see, so I hopped a string of returning empties for San Diego because I was scared like you get."

He took a deep sigh. "Thirsty," he said. "Got in with some Chinks, nobody to trouble ya, ya stay outta the way,

256

but then one of them cops-like seen me and he took me to the Consul place like they do, ya know? Had me scared, they always tole me illegal reading they bump ya off, but they don't, ya know? Two years work camp, how about that?"

Yes, Royland wondered. How about it?

The plane decelerated sharply; he was thrown forward. Could they brake with those "jets" by reversing the stream or were the engines just throttling down? He heard gurgling and thudding; hydraulic fluid to the actuators letting down the landing gear. The wheels bumped a moment later and he braced himself; the plane was still and the motors cut off seconds later.

Their Luftwaffe sergeant unlocked the door and bawled through it: "Shove that goddam ramp, willya?" The sergeant's assurance had dropped from him; he looked like a very scared man. He must have been a very brave one, really, to have let himself be locked in with a hundred doomed men, protected only by an eight-shot pistol and a chain of systematic lies.

They were herded out of the plane onto a runway of what Royland immediately identified as the Chicago Municipal Airport. The same reek wafted from the stockyards; the row of airline buildings at the eastern edge of the field was ancient and patched but unchanged; the hangars, though, were now something that looked like inflated plastic bags. A good trick. Beyond the buildings surely lay the dreary red-brick and painted-siding wastes of Cicero, Illinois.

Luftwaffe men were yapping at them: "Form up, boys; make a line! Work means freedom! Look tall!" They shuffled and were shoved into columns of fours. A snappy majorette in shiny satin panties and white boots pranced out of an administration building twirling her baton; a noisy march blared from louvers in her tall fur hat. Another good trick.

"Forward march, boys," she shrilled at them. "Wouldn't y'all just like to follow me?" Seductive smile and a wiggle of the rump; a Judas ewe. She strutted off in time to the music; she must have been wearing ear-stopples. They shuffled after her. At the airport gate they dropped their blue-coated Luftwaffe boys and picked up a waiting escort of a dozen black-coats with skulls on their high-peaked caps.

They walked in time to the music, hypnotized by it, through Cicero. Cicero had been bombed to hell and not rebuilt. To his surprise Royland felt a pang for the vanished Poles and Slovaks of Al's old bailiwick. There were *German* Germans, French Germans, and even Italian Germans, but he knew in his bones that there were no Polish or Slovakian Germans . . . And Bloom had been right all along.

Deathly weary after two hours of marching (the majorette was indefatigable) Royland looked up from the broken pavement to see a cockeyed wonder before him. It was a Castle; it was a Nightmare; it was the Chicago Parteihof. The thing abutted Lake Michigan; it covered perhaps sixteen city blocks. It frowned down on the lake at the east and at the tumbled acres of bombed-out Chicago at the north, west, and south. It was made of steel-reinforced concrete grained and grooved to look like medieval masonry. It was walled, moated, portcullis-ed, towered, ramparted, crenellated. The death's-head guards looked at it reverently and the prisoners with fright. Royland wanted only to laugh wildly. It was a Disney production. It was as funny as Hermann Goering in full fig, and probably as deadly.

With a mumbo-jumbo of passwords, heils, and salutes they were admitted, and the majorette went away, no doubt to take off her boots and groan.

The most bedecked of the death's-heads lined them up and said affably: "Hot dinner and your beds presently, my boys; first a selection. Some of you, I'm afraid, aren't well and should be in sick bay. Who's sick? Raise your hands, please."

A few hands crept up. Stooped old men.

"That's right. Step forward, please." Then he went down the line tapping a man here and there—one fellow with glaucoma, another with terrible varicose sores visible through the tattered pants he wore. Mutely they stepped forward. Royland he looked thoughtfully over. "You're thin, my boy," he observed. "Stomach pains? Vomit blood? Tarry stools in the morning?"

"Nossir!" Royland barked. The man laughed and continued down the line. The "sick bay" detail was marched off. Most of them were weeping silently; they knew. Everybody knew; everybody pretended that the terrible thing would not, might not, happen. It was much more complex than Royland had realized.

258

"Now," said the death's-head affably, "we require some competent cement workers——"

The line of remaining men went mad. They surged forward almost touching the officer but never stepping over an invisible line surrounding him. "Me!" some yelled. "Me! Me!" Another cried: "I'm good with my hands, I can learn, I'm a machinist too, I'm strong and young, I can learn!" A heavy middle-aged one waved his hands in the air and boomed: "Grouting and tile-setting! Grouting and tile-setting!" Royland stood alone, horrified. They knew. They knew this was an offer of real work that would keep them alive for a while.

He knew suddenly how to live in a world of lies.

The officer lost his patience in a moment or two, and whips came out. Men with their faces bleeding struggled back into line. "Raise your hands, you cement people, and no lying, please. But you wouldn't lie, would you?" He picked half a dozen volunteers after questioning them briefly, and one of his men marched them off. Among them was the grouting-and-tile man, who looked pompously pleased with himself; such was the reward of diligence and virtue, he seemed to be proclaiming; pooh to those grasshoppers back there who neglected to Learn A Trade.

"Now," said the officer casually, "we require some laboratory assistants." The chill of death stole down the line of prisoners. Each one seemed to shrivel into himself, become poker-faced, imply that he wasn't really involved in all this.

Royland raised his hand. The officer looked at him in stupefaction and then covered up quickly. "Splendid," he said. "Step forward, my boy. You," he pointed at another man. "You have an intelligent forehead; you look as if you'd make a fine laboratory assistant. Step forward."

"Please, no!" the man begged. He fell to his knees and clasped his hands in supplication. "Please no!" The officer took out his whip meditatively; the man groaned, scrambled to his feet, and quickly stood beside Royland.

When there were four more chosen, they were marched off across the concrete yard into one of the absurd towers, and up a spiral staircase and down a corridor, and through the promenade at the back of an auditorium where a woman screamed German from the stage at an audience of women. And through a tunnel and down the corridor of an elementary school with empty classrooms full of small desks on either side. And into a hospital area where the fake-

259

masonry walls yielded to scrubbed white tile and the fake flagstones underfoot to composition flooring and the fake pinewood torches in bronze brackets that had lighted their way to fluorescent tubes.

At the door marked RASSENWISSENSCHAFT the guard rapped and a frosty-faced man in a laboratory coat opened up. "You requisitioned a demonstrator, Dr. Kalten," the guard said. "Pick any one of these."

Dr. Kalten looked them over. "Oh, this one, I suppose," he said. Royland. "Come in, fellow."

The Race Science Laboratory of Dr. Kalten proved to be a decent medical setup with an operating table, intricate charts of the races of men and their anatomical, mental, and moral makeups. There was also a phrenological head diagram and a horoscope on the wall, and an arrangement of glittering crystals on wire which Royland recognized. It was a model of one Hans Hoerbiger's crackpot theory of planetary formation, the *Welteislehre*.

"Sit there," the doctor said, pointing to a stool. "First I've got to take your pedigree. By the way, you might as well know that you're going to end up dissected for my demonstration in Race Science III for the Medical School, and your degree of cooperation will determine whether the dissection is performed under anaesthesia or not. Clear?"

"Clear, doctor."

"Curious—no panic. I'll wager we find you're a proto-Hamitoidal hemi-Nordic of at *least* degree five . . . but let's get on. Name?"

"Edward Royland."

"Birthdate?"

"July second, nineteen twenty-one."

The doctor threw down his pencil. "If my previous explanation was inadequate," he shouted, "let me add that if you continue to be difficult I may turn you over to my good friend Dr. Herzbrenner. Dr. Herzbrenner happens to teach interrogation technique at the Gestapo School. *Do—you—now—understand?*"

"Yes, doctor. I'm sorry I cannot withdraw my answer."

Dr. Kalten turned elaborately sarcastic. "How then do you account for your remarkable state of preservation at your age of approximately a hundred and eighty years?"

"Doctor, I am twenty-three years old. I have traveled through time."

"Indeed?" Kalten was amused. "And how was this accomplished?"

Royland said steadily: "A spell was put on me by a satanic Jewish magician. It involved the ritual murder and desanguination of seven beautiful Nordic virgins."

Dr. Kalten gaped for a moment. Then he picked up his pencil and said firmly: "You will understand that my doubts were logical under the circumstances. Why did you not give me the sound scientific basis for your surprising claim at once? Go ahead; tell me all about it."

He was Dr. Kalten's prize; he was Dr. Kalten's treasure. His peculiarities of speech, his otherwise inexplicable absence of a birth number over his left nipple, when they got around to it the gold filling in one of his teeth, his uncanny knowledge of Old America, all now had a simple scientific explanation. He was from 1944. What was so hard to grasp about that? Any sound specialist knew about the lost Jewish cabala magic, golems and such.

His story was that he had been a student Race Scientist under the pioneering master William D. Pully. (A noisy whack who used to barnstorm the chaw-and-gallus belt with the backing of Deutches Neues Buro; sure enough they found him in Volume VII of the standard *Introduction to a Historical Handbook of Race Science*.) The Jewish fiends had attempted to ambush his master on a lonely road; Royland persuaded him to switch hats and coats; in the darkness the substitution was not noticed. Later in their stronghold he was identified, but the Nordic virgins had already been ritually murdered and drained of their blood, and it wouldn't keep. The dire fate destined for the master had been visited upon the disciple.

Dr. Kalten loved that bit. It tickled him pink that the sub-men's "revenge" on their enemy had been to precipitate him into a world purged of the sub-men entirely, where a Nordic might breathe freely!

Kalten, except for discreet consultations with such people as Old America specialists, a dentist who was stupefied by the gold filling, and a dermatologist who established that there was not and never had been a *geburtsnummer* on the subject examined, was playing Royland close to his vest. After a week it became apparent that he was reserving Royland for a grand unveiling which would climax the reading of a paper. Royland did not want to be unveiled; there were too many holes in his story. He talked with animation about the beauties of Mexico in the spring, its fair mesas, cactus, and mushrooms. Could they make a short trip there? Dr. Kalten said they could not. Royland was becoming restless? Let him study, learn, profit by the matchless arsenal of the sciences available here in Chicago Parteihof. Dear old Chicago boasted distinguished exponents of the World Ice Theory, the Hollow World Theory, Dowsing, Homeopathic Medicine, Curative Folk Botany—

The last did sound interesting. Dr. Kalten was pleased to take his prize to the Medical School and introduce him as a protégé to Professor Albiani, of Folk Botany.

Albiani was a bearded gnome out of the Arthur Rackham illustrations for *Das Rheingold*. He loved his subject. "Mother Nature, the all-bounteous one! Wander the fields, young man, and with a seeing eye in an hour's stroll you will find the ergot that aborts, the dill that cools fever, the tansy that strengthens the old, the poppy that soothes the fretful teething babe!"

"Do you have any hallucinogenic Mexican mushrooms?" Royland demanded.

"We may," Albiani said, surprised. They browsed through the Folk Botany museum and pored over dried vegetation under glass. From Mexico there were peyote, the buttons and the root, and there was marihuana, root, stem, seed, and stalk. No mushrooms.

"They may be in the storeroom," Albiani muttered.

All the rest of the day Royland mucked through the storeroom where specimens were waiting for exhibit space on some rotation plan. He went to Albiani and said, a little wild-eyed: "They're not there."

Albiani had been interested enough to look up the mushrooms in question in the reference books. "See?" he said happily, pointing to a handsome color plate of the mushroom: growing, mature, sporing, and dried. He read: "'. . . superstitiously called *God Food*,'" and twinkled through his beard at the joke.

"They're not there," Royland said.

The professor, annoyed at last, said: "There might be some uncatalogued in the basement. Really, we don't have room for everything in our limited display space—just the *interesting* items."

Royland pulled himself together and charmed the location of the department's basement storage space out of him, together with permission to inspect it. And, left alone for a moment, ripped the color plate from the professor's book and stowed it away.

That night Royland and Dr. Kalten walked out on one of the innumerable tower-tops for a final cigar. The moon was high and full; its light turned the cratered terrain that had been Chicago into another moon. The sage and his disciple from another day leaned their elbows on a crenellated rampart two hundred feet above Lake Michigan.

"Edward," said Dr. Kalten, "I shall read my paper tomorrow before the Chicago Academy of Race Science." The words were a challenge; something was wrong. He went on: "I shall expect you to be in the wings of the auditorium, and to appear at my command to answer a few questions from me and, if time permits, from our audience."

"I wish it could be postponed," Royland said.

"No doubt."

"Would you explain your unfriendly tone of voice, doctor?" Royland demanded. "I think I've been completely cooperative and have opened the way for you to win undying fame in the annals of Race Science."

"Cooperative, yes. Candid—I wonder? You see, Edward, a dreadful thought struck me today. I have always thought it amusing that the Jewish attack on Reverend Pully should have been for the purpose of precipitating him into the future and that it should have misfired." He took something out of his pocket: a small pistol. He aimed it casually at Royland. "Today I began to wonder *why* they should have done so. Why did they not simply murder him, as they did thousands, and dispose of him in their secret crematoria, and permit no mention in their controlled newspapers and magazines of the disappearance?

"Now, the blood of seven Nordic virgins can have been no cheap commodity. One pictures with ease Nordic men patrolling their precious enclaves of humanity, eyes roving over every passing face, noting who bears the stigmata of the sub-men, and following those who do most carefully indeed lest race-defilement be committed with a look or an 'accidental' touch in a crowded street. Nevertheless the thing was done; your presence here is proof of it. It must have been done at enormous cost; hired Slavs and Negroes must have been employed to kidnap the virgins, and many of them must have fallen before Nordic rage.

"This merely to silence one small voice crying in the wilderness? I—*think—not*. I think, Edward Royland, or whatever your real name may be, that Jewish arrogance sent you, a Jew yourself, into the future as a greeting from the Jewry of that day to what it foolishly thought would be the triumphant Jewry of this. At any rate, the public questioning tomorrow will be conducted by my friend Dr. Herzbrenner, whom I have mentioned to you. If you have any little secrets, they will not remain secrets long. No, no! Do not move toward me. I shall shoot you disablingly in the knee if you do."

Royland moved toward him and the gun went off; there was an agonizing hammer blow high on his left shin. He picked up Kalten and hurled him, screaming, over the parapet two hundred feet into the water. And collapsed. The pain was horrible. His shinbone was badly cracked if not broken through. There was not much bleeding; maybe there would be later. He need not fear that the shot and scream would rouse the castle. Such sounds were not rare in the Medical Wing.

He dragged himself, injured leg trailing, to the doorway of Kalten's living quarters; he heaved himself into a chair by the signal bell and threw a rug over his legs. He rang for the diener and told him very quietly: "Go to the medical storeroom for a leg U-brace and whatever is necessary for a cast, please. Dr. Kalten has an interesting idea he wishes to work out."

He should have asked for a syringe of morphine—no he shouldn't. It might affect the time distortion.

When the man came back he thanked him and told him to turn in for the night.

He almost screamed getting his shoe off; his trouser leg he cut away. The gauze had arrived just in time; the wound was beginning to bleed more copiously. Pressure seemed to stop it. He constructed a sloppy walking cast on his leg. The directions on the several five-pound cans of plaster helped.

His leg was getting numb; good. His cast probably pinched some major nerve, and a week in it would cause permanent paralysis; who cared about *that*?

He tried it out and found he could get across the floor inefficiently. With a strong-enough bannister he could get downstairs but not, he thought, up them. That was all right. He was going to the basement.

God-damning the medieval Nazis and their cornball castle every inch of the way, he went to the basement; there he had a windfall. A dozen drunken SS men were living it up in a corner far from the censorious eyes of their company commander; they were playing a game which might have been called Spin the Corporal. They saw Royland limping and wept sentimental tears for poor ol'

264

doc with a bum leg; they carried him two winding miles to the storeroom he wanted, and shot the lock off for him. They departed, begging him to call on ol' Company K any time, "bes' fellas in Chicago, doc. Ol' Bruno here can tear the arm off a Latvik shirker with his bare hands, honest, doc! Jus' the way you twist a drumstick off a turkey. You wan' us to get a Latvik an' show you?"

He got rid of them at last, clicked on the light, and began his search. His leg was now ice cold, painfully so. He rummaged through the uncatalogued botanicals and found after what seemed like hours a crate shipped from Jalasca. Royland opened it by beating its corners against the concrete floor. It yielded and spilled plastic envelopes; through the clear material of one he saw the wrinkled black things. He did not even compare them with the color plate in his pocket. He tore the envelope open and crammed them into his mouth, and chewed and swallowed.

Maybe there had to be a Hopi dancing and chanting, maybe there didn't have to be. Maybe one had to be calm, if bitter, and fresh from a day of hard work at differential equations which approximated the Hopi mode of thought. Maybe you only had to fix your mind savagely on what you desired, as his was fixed now. Last time he had hated and shunned the Bomb; what he wanted was a world without the Bomb. He had got it, all right!

. . . his tongue was thick and the fireballs were beginning to dance around him, the circling circles . . .

Charles Miller Nahataspe whispered: "Close. Close. I was so frightened."

Royland lay on the floor of the hut, his leg unsplinted, unfractured, but aching horribly. Drowsily he felt his ribs; he was merely slender now, no longer gaunt. He mumbled: "You were working to pull me back from this side?"

"Yes. You, you were there?"

"I was there. God, let me sleep."

He rolled over heavily and collapsed into complete unconsciousness.

When he awakened it was still dark and his pains were gone. Nahataspe was crooning a healing song very softly. He stopped when he saw Royland's eyes open. "Now you know about break-the-sky medicine," he said.

"Better than anybody. What time is it?"

"Midnight."

"I'll be going then." They clasped hands and looked into each other's eyes.

The jeep started easily. Four hours earlier, or possibly two months earlier, he had been worried about the battery. He chugged down the settlement road and knew what would happen next. He wouldn't wait until morning; a meteorite might kill him, or a scorpion in his bed. He would go directly to Rotschmidt in his apartment, defy Vrouw Rotschmidt and wake her man up to tell him about 56c, tell him we have the Bomb.

We have a symbol to offer the Japanese now, something to which they can surrender, and will surrender.

Rotschmidt would be philosophical. He would probably sigh about the Bomb: "Ah, do we ever act responsibly? Do we ever know what the consequences of our decisions will be?"

And Royland would have to try to avoid answering him very sharply: "Yes. This once we damn well do."